RIDE FOR YOUR LIFE

The sun warmed Reddman's back and he seemed to flow through the turns like a skier in deep powder, anticipating the tight corners on down the road. He laid the bike over gently, cutting into the turn—

A truck blocked the inside lane. It sloped diagonally across the highway, its tailgate a foot from the hillside, its nose more than halfway across the road. Reddman gripped the brakes hard and jerked to his left as he steered for the opening in the oncoming lane. Beyond the truck, the road bent sharply to the right and he leaned hard in that direction, snapping the handlebars hard. I'm losing it, he thought, knowing that if he did, he would die. The truck started forward, crowding him toward the edge of the cliff . . .

A CLEAR CASE OF MURDER

WARWICK DOWNING

POCKET BOOKS

New York   London   Toronto   Sydney   Tokyo   Singapore

This book is a work of fiction. Names, characters, places and incidents are either the product of the author's imagination or are used fictitiously. Any resemblance to actual events or locales or persons, living or dead, is entirely coincidental.

An *Original* Publication of POCKET BOOKS

POCKET BOOKS, a division of Simon & Schuster Inc.
1230 Avenue of the Americas, New York, NY 10020

Hi, Puck.
Drive carefully, okay?
Call me the next time you're in town.

A CLEAR CASE OF MURDER

CHAPTER ONE

His leg hurt. Mostly lower thigh, pulses of pain reaching toward his hip and past his knee. Why can't you give me some peace? he begged it, gripping his leg with both hands. He was slouched behind the wheel of his pickup truck, waiting for the woman to appear. A trickle of sweat worked its way through the tangle of black curly hair under his Stetson, onto his neck, and down the back of his rayon rodeo shirt. It don't matter which way I move it, he thought. Stretch it out, let it hang, try to take the weight off by setting on the other cheek, the son of a bitch just keeps on screaming like a baby wants his mama. Wish I could die.

A thin hose, capped with a nipple, lay in his lap. It was connected to a quart of Jack Daniels, holstered in a cage that was screwed into the door panel. The man stuffed the nipple in his mouth and took a long drag. "Whew!" For a moment his face stiffened, then relaxed. He squinted down the street, gray eyes focusing on the sidewalk in front of the Sopris County Courthouse. The pure Colorado air shimmered in the unusual heat of the September day.

"The hell is keepin' that cunt?" he muttered. World is full of women like her, he thought, vaguely aware of his hatred and fear. Of all the damn libbers in this world—

dykey, dickless studs, the whole bunch—he believed she had to be the worst. "Hurry up, Miss Emm Ass O'Rourke," he spat, shifting his buttocks and grimacing. "Emm Ass," in his mind, stood for "Ms." He didn't like sitting there in his shined-up oversize Dodge 100 pickup truck, high-riding son of a bitch, waiting for anyone, much less some damn female stud.

'Course, she don't know I'm waitin' on her, he thought, letting the rage build, almost blotting out the pain. She will, though. Soon enough, and she'll know. The month he'd spent in that hot, stinking jail festered like an insult, as though someone had called him a coward. "You hear me, Emm Ass?" he said, his expression blank, but his brain vivid with memory. The smell of sweat and urine, the feel of Indians and Mexicans crawling all over him, animals fighting for a piece of air. All of us in one damn cattle car, he thought. Me, Johnny Blue, ex–rodeo star son of a bitch, settin' and sweatin' in a jail cell, courtesy of Emm Ass O'Rourke.

He took another drag. The hose had a one-way valve just below the mouthpiece, so he didn't have to suck the booze all the way to the top each time he wanted a hit. Who sir, me sir, no sirree sir, he thought, unconsciously massaging his thigh and showing his teeth as he swallowed. He remembered how her hand had felt on his arm, too, the night before the trial, asking him, more like begging him to flop her on her back and pour in the meat, then denying it when he grabbed her. She'd told him to fuck off, one more move and she'd call a cop herself!

Johnny Blue would not abide a woman talking to him like that. Even a woman lawyer, no different than any other cunt, they all want the same thing. Only difference, some will admit it, some won't. He wiped his mouth off with the back of his arm, watching the street below, his heart empty, feeling nothing except the excruciating throb in his leg. I don't get mad, just even, he thought, and she'll find out what that means real soon. You don't be America's Number One Cowboy and let some pretty little Emm Ass make you look like a fool.

He took another hit, then let the hose drop into his lap. That was me, he thought, the Big A's Number One Cowboy, where "A" stands for "America," not "asshole." Until that plow horse, couldn't step over a stool, got stung by a bee or something happened, the critter had to have some excitement, son of a bitch. Johnny smiled, remembering the sudden electric thrill of the unexpected. It had been at the rodeo in Salinas. That old stud must have jumped twenty feet straight up in the air, come down, and up he went again, back arched, leaning, tossing, sure caught me by surprise. Then out of the saddle I go, only my foot is caught in that stirrup, and Dog Meat leanin' this-a-way and me flyin' that-a-way, till I come to the end of the rope and then *down*.

And that was it for America's Number One Cowboy. When he hit the ground he went out; but old Dog Meat son of a bitch kept right on bucking, trying to shake little ole Johnny out of the stirrup. The bones in his leg twisted with Johnny spinning around on the ground until the femur exploded, the way the doctor explained it. Should have let them cut the son of a bitch off, he thought. Still oozes pus and, man, it just *hurts*.

"Here comes a cop. Bu-u-ullshit!" He'll recognize my truck; then he'll have to come take a look, catch me in the only thing I got left in this world, Blue thought. He slumped down in the cab of the high rider, its huge wheels and turbo oversized springs thrusting the gleaming cab upward so that it looked down on the earth below. Most of the time up there it felt real good, like ram it to 'em; but now he had to slump down, the brim of his hat over his nose. Leave me alone, asshole. Can't you see I'm asleep?

"Hi, Johnny. Mind stepping out of there?"

"What for, Brenfleck? I ain't done nothin'." The trouble with a small town, Johnny thought. Everybody knows everybody.

"You haven't, eh? How about driving after your license was revoked?"

"How do you know I was driving? You see me drive?"

The blond, blue-eyed officer reddened. "Well, that truck didn't get there by itself, I know that."

"My ex must've brought it down," Johnny said. "I just seen it here and got in it. Swear to God."

Officer Brenfleck knew he was on shaky ground. He stared venomously at Blue, then retreated to his patrol unit, which was parked directly behind the truck. He sat in his car doing a report.

Now what am I gonna do if Emm Ass Fancy Puss O'Rourke shows up? Johnny asked himself. Brenfleck, you bastard, mind your own damn business!

The radio in Brenfleck's patrol car crackled on. "Muldoon, Lobo Three."

Johnny watched through the rearview mirror as the officer reached for his transmitter. "This is Lobo Three."

"Got a ten-ten at Columbine and Railroad. Can you cover?"

"On my way!" The overheads went on and the Muldoon City Patrol Unit peeled around Johnny's pickup as though the fate of the world rested in the hands of the Muldoon City policeman. His vehicle swooped down the hill Johnny was parked on, past Citizens Bank on the west side of the street, leveled out in front of the courthouse, then jerked a hard right onto Sixth Street.

'At away, cowboy, Johnny thought, grinning at his luck. Citizens hereabouts can sure feel safe with a cop like you in charge, everything under control.

He looked at his watch, shifting his weight. Damn, he thought. Five-fifteen. They gonna hold court all fucking night? Then he saw her on the walk coming out of the courthouse and headed for her office across the street.

"Get ready, bitch."

He started the engine—smooth, low growl like a tensing dog—then let his high rider coast quietly down the hill. Got to time this right, he thought, momentarily not even aware of pain. She'll come through those cars parked diagonally there in front of the courthouse, then jaywalk across the street, got her nose buried in some papers, that's good. Always reading or talking lawyer talk, feet ten inches off the ground, wonder if she ever used that hairy little slot God give her to fuck with, probably not. His truck, in neutral, rolled quietly on.

The small, thin-boned woman popped into the street between a pickup and a Buick Skylark, glancing briefly both ways but not really paying attention. She walked past the center of the street and into the southbound lane with all the confidence of a small child absorbed in fitting an extension cord into a wall plug.

Johnny dropped the high rider into gear. "Fucking libber," he growled, teeth grinding with hate. Still she did not see him. "*Look* at me, bitch!" he shouted, standing on the horn, wanting her to see. Her head jerked up, her face a white blob, eyes wide open. "Pay!" he shouted, wanting her to hurt. "Pay, damn your hide! Pay!"

"Muldoon to all units. Emergency. Emergency." The dispatcher's voice, usually as soft and pleasant as a disk jockey's, crackled with tension. "Proceed immediately to Fifth and Beech. Hit-and-run, pedestrian down in front of courthouse. Repeat: Proceed—"

Byron "Rip" Judson, watching traffic on Canyon Drive, heard the call. Judson liked being a cop but hated emergencies. His stomach knotted up. He wished he could change reality by switching channels or something, but he'd called in his location and the dispatcher knew where he was. "Muldoon, this is Lobo Nine," he said, yanking the microphone off its hook and cradling it in his hand. "Broadway and Canyon. On my way."

"Ten-four, Lobo Nine. Seventeen twenty-five."

Sure hope I'm not first, he thought, his large, sun-hardened hands slipping the patrol unit into gear. But Brenfleck was the only other city unit on patrol, and he'd been called out on that fight. Maybe a sheriff's unit will beat me there, he hoped, or someone from the State Patrol—but he knew better.

Judson eased his squad car off Broadway and onto Fifth. He hadn't even activated the overheads, the way Brenfleck would have done. Brenfleck blazed his way through the streets of the small town like a comet, and Judson wished he could be like that. But at times like this, he'd rather be invisible. He could see a hundred people sitting in their kitchens, all of them with their scanners on. Dang scanners, Judson thought, feeling the clots in his stomach. Hard to work sometimes, knowing everybody in Muldoon is listening in.

A crowd had gathered on the street in front of the courthouse, and Judson blew enough air through his siren to let them know he was coming in. Dang it anyway, he thought. A cop in a small town was like a movie star in Hollywood, one of the celebrities; but sometimes Judson hated feeling like he was on television all the time.

The crowd parted, and a moment later the hair on Judson's neck prickled as he saw the horribly torn body of a woman on the pavement. "Muldoon, Lobo Nine."

"Go ahead, Lobo Nine."

"It's bad. Need EMT and ambulance right away."

Quickly Judson made his way to where the woman lay. She was face down on the pavement, in an odd cup-shaped position. A well-dressed man knelt beside her, touching her neck. "Everyone move back. Move back, please," Judson said.

"No carotid pulse, Rip," the man beside the woman's body said. He obviously did not think Judson's instruction applied to him. "She isn't breathing."

"You see it happen?" Judson asked, trying to think of the man's name as he knelt down next to the bloody form. As carefully as he could, he rolled her on her back, ready to give CPR.

"Hey! You know what you're doing? What if her back is broken?"

"Big thing right now is to keep her alive," Judson said.

6

The right side of the woman's face had been crushed, and blood gurgled weakly out of the tooth-filled gash that had been her mouth. "God." But the movement of the blood indicated life. Judson felt for her carotid artery and found a pulse. Bullshit there was no pulse, he thought. What the hell keeps her heart going? He bent down over the woman's chest, looking for some sign of breathing. Nothing. God, he didn't want to do CPR on that face!

"Judson, what the hell are you doing?" the man demanded as the officer reached inside the woman's mouth with his fingers and swept blood, gore, and teeth out of the way.

"Move back, please, sir," Judson told him. "Get names for me, will you?" he asked, giving the man something to do. "Witnesses?" He heard a siren as he pinched the woman's nose—and suddenly realized who it was. Ami O'Rourke, the public defender. Little blond-headed twitcher, he thought, bending over her mouth and covering it with his own. He forced air into her throat and lungs, tasting and smelling her blood.

It didn't revolt him, as he had expected. Instead, he felt softness, almost love. Don't die on me, Ami, he begged the lifeless form, rolling her toward him and pounding her back. Please don't die. As he eased her back to the pavement, following the CPR protocol, a feeling of tenderness washed through him. It was a tangible sensation, as though her heart—suddenly exposed—were in his hands. He pushed her stomach, just below the rib cage, with the heels of his hands. She gurgled blood.

"Shit," he heard the man above him say.

Judson remembered him now, a vice president at the bank across the street. You gonna faint? Judson wondered, working on—even though Ami's rib cage hadn't supported the pressure of his hands. He knew it was useless, but kept trying anyway. He wanted to cry. Maybe I should just hold her in my arms now and help her die, he thought, then wondered, What kind of freak am I, anyway? An ambulance pulled up, overheads sweeping colors across the pavement, as he bent over her mouth in another attempt to ventilate.

Brenfleck, siren blaring, pulled up just as the EMT unit prepared to load the mangled body into the ambulance. "Hey, hold it right there," Brenfleck demanded. "Is she dead? You get pictures?" he asked Judson.

"Let her go, Bren," Judson said. "Still a chance." He could feel wetness on his mouth and knew it was the woman's blood. He wiped it off with his hand. "You know who it is?"

"God, look at all these people. Who?"

"Ami O'Rourke."

"No shit?" Brenfleck asked grinning. "The P.D.?"

Judson also tried to grin, but found that he couldn't. "Reckon we better get after it before things really get stomped on," he said.

The two men worked the scene. The pavement was cleared of people; traffic was diverted off Beech; witnesses were encouraged to stay. Early on, a woman told Brenfleck that "It was one of those pickup trucks the kids drive, with those huge wheels big enough for a tractor."

Brenfleck's mind flashed to Johnny Blue. He radioed in an all-points bulletin to stop and arrest Blue for the hit-and-run of Ami O'Rourke and to impound the truck. He didn't bother to give a physical description of the truck or the driver, knowing every officer in Sopris County knew Johnny Blue and his high rider, because half of them had chased it.

When the investigators arrived, one of them told Brenfleck that Johnny Blue had been picked up. Brenfleck grinned his satisfaction. He'd been a year behind Blue in high school and remembered how the prettiest girls always fawned and fell all over the hot-shot athlete. But the guy had been a lush even then.

Nail his ass to the cross, Brenfleck thought happily.

"Why should we spin our wheels?" Bernie Lopes asked, angrily. "Brim won't give it to us anyway." Bernie Lopes, the city of Muldoon detective in charge of the case, flared out at Sergeant Jack Donovan of the State Patrol.

"Ain't the point, son," Donovan said. The older man, in his forties, looked like a tall, thin statue made of rock. "Don't worry about Brim; he's the only one can worry about bein' D.A. Besides, you don't ask the D.A. for what you think you can get. You ask him for what you think it is."

The two men were prowling around the squad room in the Justice Center, notes, diagrams, and photographs scattered on the table. It was three o'clock in the morning.

"Well, I don't see murder, Jack. Where do you get murder?" Lopes plopped his muscular frame into a chair and almost broke it. He weighed one-seventy, fifteen pounds more than he'd weighed five years ago when he graduated from the Colorado Law Enforcement Training Academy. Regular work and home cooking had done him in, he thought. The extra fifteen pounds was all in his ass. "You read his statement?"

"Nope," Donovan said, standing and stroking his chin. "But lemme see if I can't guess what he said. Prob'ly like, Well, I just looked up and there she was. Then after I hit her, well, you know, I'd been drinkin' some and they took away my license after that trial, and I knowed I was in deep shit, so I just run." He reached for his coffee mug. "That about it?"

"Pretty close," Lopes said, grinning and lighting a cigarette.

"So what we've got, if we buy his statement, is a hit-and-run, right?" Donovan suggested. "Traffic case, misdemeanor, six months in the county jail?"

"Hey, I don't like it either," Lopes said. "But we got the blood alcohol. A point-eighteen isn't too bad. That gives us drunk driving, driving without a license, and vehicular homicide, don't it? What's wrong with vehicular homicide?"

Donovan shrugged. "I've seen lots of vehicular homicides, Bernie. This one don't even come close. B.A. ain't high enough, one thing. High enough for you or me maybe, but everybody in the county knows Johnny'll have a point-eighteen for breakfast. Other is Ami O'Rourke was jaywalking, out there in the middle of the street, you know. A pedestrian is fair game if they ain't in a crosswalk." He couldn't articulate it very well, but he knew it. "But let's take and say we get vehicular homicide. What's that worth? One, two years is about all."

"Hold it, Sarge. You keep talking about what it's worth. That don't have anything to do with what it is either, does it? I mean, if that's all it is, that's all it is!"

"But what if it's murder?" Donovan asked. "Here's what I'm sayin'. Forget about his statement; the man's a liar. Take a look at what he done. We know he was settin' up on that hill above the courthouse, drinkin' whiskey in that high rider of his. We know what he could see from up there. We know of all the people in Muldoon, he hit the lawyer he accused of throwin' him over to the wolves. And we know he hit her hard enough to keep her on that tire about three turns."

"Hey, look. No question about it, Sarge, we got more than average gore here. But so what if she did get caught on that tire? What does that prove?"

"You know how hard it is to bump a truck over a boulder?" Donovan asked, staring harshly at the young detective. "Only way to do it is to punch it."

"So?"

"He punched it when he hit her, son. He was accelerating. That's deliberate action, like the book says." Donovan took off his cap and ran his hand through his hair. "Ain't you heard? Actions speak louder than words."

Walter Brim could remember when he was in control of his life. But those days had vanished when he became the Sopris County District Attorney. Two years ago the large, amiable man had moved his family out of the polluted urban rat race of Denver to the pristine mountains and valleys of southwestern Colorado, fulfilling a lifetime goal. Then he made the biggest mistake of his life: he allowed himself to become embroiled in small-town politics. He ran for district attorney, campaigning on the slogan "Fairness for Everyone"—a thinly veiled charge that justice, in Sopris County, had become a commodity that was available only to the privileged few. He won by the thinnest of margins.

Since that time he had felt like a canoeist spinning down a rapids with no paddle. The "privileged few" he had attacked in his campaign were the people who ran the county. They undercut him at every step. He found himself understaffed, underbudgeted, and at odds with the community leaders. Today, he noted ruefully, staring out the window into the beautiful clean air, was no exception. Upon reaching his office that morning, he had learned that a new charge had been pressed against Johnny Blue: first degree murder.

"Thanks for letting me know, guys," he said to himself.

The worst was yet to come. His only deputy was out of town, and Brim had spent the morning in county court. On his return, his secretary told him he had to be in district court in two hours. Johnny Blue wanted out of jail. His relatives had retained Saul Cole, Sopris County's leading defense lawyer, and Cole had called the judge. Cole and the judge were close friends. The bail hearing—to decide whether Blue should stay in jail—had been set for one o'clock that afternoon.

An important issue, Brim knew, because of how the community would read the result. The higher the bail, the better the case. But he couldn't even get a witness! When he tried to talk to Bernie Lopes, Dispatch refused to put the call through. Lopes had been up all night, the dispatcher told him, and the chief of police, who was out to lunch, had given the order that Lopes was not to be disturbed. Tears of frustration started to push their way into Brim's eyes when he finally reached Sergeant Donovan of the State Patrol. Ten minutes later, with no chance to prepare, they took their seats in Sopris County District Court.

As expected, the simple motion hearing turned into a

battle royal. Over the frequent objections of Cole, Donovan testified as to why Blue was guilty of murder. There was motive, in that the defendant was known to have blamed the deceased for losing a drunk driving case, resulting in Blue's incarceration.

"That's an opinion on top of hearsay, Judge!" Brim's fat, red-faced opponent screamed. "Sure, it's only a bail hearing, but you gonna let *that* in?"

"I am, Mr. Cole. Sit down."

There was also opportunity, in that Blue was seen in his truck minutes before the incident, on the Mears Street hill that rose over the courthouse. However, the judge would not allow any testimony regarding Blue's presumed familiarity with the habits of the victim—that she regularly jaywalked to her office across the street at the close of court, for example. The judge allowed Donovan, as an accident reconstruction expert, to testify that there were no skid marks at the scene to indicate evasive action by the defendant, but would not permit him to state that he thought it was deliberate.

Cole called two witnesses. He proved that Blue had often been in trouble with the law but had never failed to make a court appearance. He also proved that the former rodeo star had many substantial ties to the community. "This is a bail hearing, Judge," Cole argued. "The only real issue is whether or not my client will come to court when he's supposed to. You know, and I know, that he will."

"Do you have any rebuttal, Mr. Brim?"

"No, sir, I don't," Brim said. "Not at this time."

"I see. Well, do you have any further evidence, sir?" Judge Landry asked menacingly.

"Not at this time."

"Very well. I will say, for the record, that you have presented the thinnest, most speculative hogwash I've ever heard. This isn't a murder case at all! What is the bail for vehicular homicide?"

"Five thousand dollars, sir. But—"

"No buts about it. Sir, you are fortunate I don't authorize a personal recognizance bond in this case!" He banged his gavel down. "Bail is set in the amount of five thousand dollars. No. Make that *two* thousand dollars.

"Court is in recess."

Walter Brim was almost cheerful the following morning as he walked to work. He and his wife Patti had talked far into the night. They had even kissed, but Walter had been too tired to make love.

He knew she was right. "There is no way you can try the case against Johnny Blue and win it," Patti had said. "The police have no confidence in you. Someday they might, but they don't now. The judge and Cole will gang up on you—all of which will sound like sour grapes when you lose the case."

"But I've *got* to win," Brim told her for the umpteenth time. "I've got to show this town, this community, that they were *right* when they elected me to office. I simply *must* beat the tawdry legal machinery in Sopris County. I want so very much to make the law something people can honestly respect."

"Then get help," she said. "Admit it, Walter. You have to have help."

Brim knew what that would mean. The lawyers in town would gossip about him, see him as a coward who was afraid to try his own case. Other critics would call him a spendthrift, wasting taxpayer money.

"But if Johnny Blue gets convicted," Pattie told him, *"they* will be the ones making lame excuses."

"Mr. Trigge?" Brim said half an hour later into the telephone. At the other end, in Denver, was James R. Trigge. Trigge was the head of NASP—National Association of Special Prosecutors. "This is Walter Brim, district attorney down in Sopris County."

"How are you, Brim?" the cheerful voice replied. "What can I do for you?"

CHAPTER
TWO

The old Booker mansion, standing on the west slope of Capitol Hill, seemed to stare with bemusement over downtown Denver. Built in the 1880s out of massive brownstone blocks, it had somehow survived the modernizations that had leveled the neighborhood, which had filled up again with buildings of concrete and glass. The huge old residence seemed lonely now in their company, like an old tycoon in a roomful of young executives.

When James R. Trigge first saw it, he was intrigued. It struck him as a proper place for lawyers, with its nooks and crannies and gargoyles leering out, like a growth that wanted to conceal its true mission in life. He quickly acquired the property on behalf of the National Association of Special Prosecutors.

Trigge may have seen himself in the old building. The tough old advocate had dedicated his life to government service in spite of the fact that he was a true individualist. No one would have predicted his survival. Yet he had not only survived; he had advanced. A superb trial lawyer, he'd moved through the ranks of two United States attorneys' offices, becoming the chief trial deputy in each. Later he'd headed a team of Justice Department prosecutors in the fight against organized crime; and finally, he had answered the call to organize NASP.

NASP had been Trigge's brainchild from the beginning. At the request of a senator from Hawaii, Trigge had orchestrated the congressional hearings that resulted in its creation. The committee found that public confidence in the judicial system had eroded to dangerous levels. The reasons were many, but among them was the undeniable fact that too many well-publicized cases were lost. Among the recommendations: a new federal agency of special prosecutors, charged with the mission of helping local prosecutors on an as-needed basis.

And so NASP was born. Budgeted for ten lawyers, Trigge selected only seven: four men and three women. He still enjoyed clambering into the pit himself and slugging it out, and by keeping a small staff, he allowed himself that luxury. He also moved the agency to Denver, partly to distance it from the bureaucracies in Washington, but mainly because he wanted his troopers to "get wet" before going to the mat with the high-profile lawyers on the coasts. With NASP headquartered in Denver, he knew that most of the early cases would come out of the West.

That morning Trigge sniffed the air—the crispness of fall, a hint of frost in the shadows—then pushed through the wrought-iron gate that guarded the agency. A moment later he shuffled across the marble floor of the large foyer. "Good morning, Miss Gallegos," he said to his receptionist. The plumpish woman had a wide, radiant smile. She had been with Trigge for the last twelve years, and "receptionist" was only one of her many duties. Long streaks of white, like silver ribbons, attractively coiled in her Indian-black hair. Trigge didn't know how anyone could possibly grind out as much work as she did. "Frankie here yet?" he asked.

He often referred to Frankie Rommel as "the little general." Of the stable of lawyers he had amassed, she was the toughest. He picked up a stack of mail from the corner of the reception desk.

"Haven't seen her this morning, Mr. T.," Miss Gallegos said, smiling indulgently at her boss. Expensive shoes, unshined; tweed coat with leather patches over the elbows and unexpected bulges; trousers creased by too much sitting—she didn't know why she loved the frumpy old bastard, but she did. "The only person in so far is Reddman. Give him something to do, okay?" she asked. "He's driving me crazy."

"Reddman? That's the twirp Nolan unloaded on us, right?" Trigge had forgotten about his newest soldier, hired a week ago to fill NASP's first vacancy. Trigge had been in trial and hadn't had much of a chance to think about anything. "When Frankie gets here, tell her I want to see her," he said, searching through his mail and wandering away.

"You tell her, okay?" Miss Gallegos said warily. "I'll buzz you when she comes in."

"What? Oh."

Trigge's office was on the second floor. In the old days it had been the master bedroom of the mansion, the station from which the mistress commanded the household. It comprised a large living area with fireplace and mantel along one wall, a balcony overlooking the grounds, and huge sliding doors that closed off the alcove reserved for the bed. Now bookcases lined two of the interior walls, focusing attention on a massive hardwood executive desk. The desk stood near French doors that opened onto the balcony. A worktable behind the desk held dictating equipment and a computer terminal. Leather chairs, ornate coffee tables with large work surfaces, and a beautiful antique couch were spaced around the room, giving it the aspect of a private club.

Trigge pulled bifocals out of a pocket and put them on, then pulled a cigarette out of another and lit it. Settling behind his desk, he switched on the terminal and worked his way through the mail. He tossed half of it into the wastebasket, made a few rapid entries into the computer, then tossed in the rest. Then he punched up the daily calen-

dar—good. Nothing on that morning. Time to talk to
Frankie Rommel, his major strategist, and map out a plan
for *People v. Blue*. He reached for the intercom panel to
buzz her office when Miss Gallegos's voice issued out of
the speaker. "Mr. T.? Frankie on line one."

"Got it," Trigge said, punching a button and lifting the
telephone to his ear. "Frankie?" he demanded. "You
okay?" He knew she wouldn't call him if she was in the
building. Not her style. She would burst into his office if
she wanted to talk.

"Of course I'm okay. I feel wonderful."

"Where are you?"

"In bed."

He could hear the soft rustling sound that satin sheets
make when someone moves on them. "Well." He tried to
say something suggestive, but it caught in his throat. Trigge
could yell at the woman, but he couldn't flirt with her.
"What the hell are you doing in bed?"

"Having the time of my life," she told him. "I'm on
vacation."

Trigge would love to vacation with Frankie Rommel. She
was in her early forties and—except for her politics—made
him think of early Jane Fonda. But he couldn't possibly
broach the subject to anyone. His wife at the very least
would have serious misgivings, and Frankie might die of
laughter. "You can't go on vacation, damn it. We've got
too much to do!"

Rommel sneezed violently into the telephone. "I'm coming down with something, too. It's probably contagious."

"What the hell am I gonna do with *Blue*, Frankie? I've
got a D.A. down in Muldoon who—"

"Have you read that file?"

"Yes. It's a piece of shit!"

"Is that why you gave it to me?"

"Of course! You're the only one I've got who is subtle."
He snorted as he said it. "You can explain to Brim in your
own sweet, soft, feminine style that if this is a murder case,

the sky is yellow! You could go down there and lose the preliminary hearing and get him to thank you for it!"

"No."

"What do you mean *no*, God damn it? Be reasonable! The preliminary is tomorrow and you *know* it'll never go to trial."

"Wrong. Those are the cases that always go to trial."

Trigge mashed his cigarette into the ashtray. "Guess I'll have to go down there and be subtle myself," he said, thinking of his caseload.

"Give it to Reddman."

"Who?"

"Reddman, that young Turk you just bought from Terry Nolan."

"Hm." As Trigge thought about it, a malicious smile appeared on his face. "He's only been here a week."

"He's not a cherry, Trigge."

"Hm." His smile grew broader. "Gallegos wants me to give him something to do, you know that? Says he's driving her crazy."

"He's driving everybody crazy. You hear what Nolan said about him?"

"What."

" 'The kid is a law unto himself, but doesn't know it. He thinks he's normal.' " She laughed. "It fits, too. He dresses like a yuppie, but he just plain does not have a conventional head."

"You think we should send him out there without the usual bullshit indoctrination? While he's still on probation?"

"I can't think of a better way for him to get thoroughly drenched in the reality of his new situation."

The two lawyers knew one another so well that each knew what was going through the other's mind. An eager-beaver neophyte who wanted to strut his stuff, and a case that had "loser" written all over it—a perfect match. Especially considering that the trial would take place in a rural Colorado town, far enough away so that no one would hear about it.

"What a rotten thing to do to a fine young man," Trigge said.

"Gross."

"Take the day off."

"I already have."

Trigge arranged a couple of files on his desk. Then sent for Reddman. Minutes later the young man approached his desk.

He doesn't walk, Trigge noted. He stalks like a mountain panther approaching a meal. And he's way too pretty. Wavy jet-black hair, a bit unruly; a smooth, tanned face; pale blue eyes; and the economical body of an acrobat. He looked like Tarzan, Trigge decided, only smaller. "Have a chair," he said. "Pardon me for not standing. The social graces get less interesting as you get older."

Reddman found one and sat down.

"How long've you been here now? A week?"

"Yes, sir."

Trigge peered at him over his bifocals. "Should be long enough to know I don't like being called sir. Call me Trigge, all right? Call me sir and I'll want more money out of this chickenshit outfit."

Reddman fought to keep from blushing. He was tremendously impressed by his new employer. He had spent two days of his first week on the job watching the old man try a case, and he knew very well that Trigge would not want to be called sir. "Sorry."

"Shit. Don't be sorry," Trigge grunted. "You can't do anything right this morning, can you?"

"I guess not."

"Let's see. Your first name is David. A giant killer. Correct?"

Reddman shrugged.

"You were born in Colorado, but got your start in Arizona, then came back to Colorado, right?" Trigge fumbled for another cigarette. "Did two or three murders for Terry Nolan over in Steamboat Springs. He says you're a real fighter."

Reddman appeared embarrassed by the compliment. "Don't know if I'm a fighter or not," he said, perhaps too modestly. "I get—well, pissed at defense lawyers and all their games, and they tell me I'm fair at shutting them down. And I probably did forty felonies for Terry, five of them murders."

"You're Joe Reddman's son, aren't you?" Trigge said, grinning. "I know Joe. You look like him. *He's* a fighter."

"I hope he isn't the reason you hired me."

Trigge picked up the hostility in the lad's voice. He lit the cigarette he had finally located. "Being old Joe's son didn't hurt, Davey, but we hire lawyers, not their family baggage." The reaction annoyed him, however. Did this kid have problems? he wondered. "How come you joined up?" he asked. "You strike me more as the Steamboat Springs type. You know, ski, fish, hunt, chase after the ladies."

The burn in Reddman's face intensified. People didn't "join up" with the National Association of Special Prosecutors any more than they joined the Texas Rangers or the New York Mets. They were invited. But he didn't want to sound like an adoring schoolboy. "Well, you know how it is," he said, treating it lightly. "I wanted to be D.A. over there so I could run for governor some day, but Terry wouldn't resign."

Trigge nodded. He stared steadily at the boy, then flipped him the *People v. Blue* file. "Here's the perfect case for you to cut your teeth on," he said. "We don't get many as good as this one. Can't lose."

Reddman reached for it eagerly, then opened it. "Hey, great," he said. "Muldoon. Great little town!"

"You know it?"

"Sure do. They have a bicycle race over Memorial Day. I was in it last year."

"Bicycle! Good God. Sounds like exercise." Trigge blew smoke at him. Purposefully. "So you're a bicycle racer?" he asked, watching him avoid the cloud.

"I try."

"This thing is set for a preliminary tomorrow. Usually the local prosecutor puts on the preliminary and then we have to live with it, but the D.A. down there—Walter Brim—is scared. He wants us to do it all. Think you can handle it?"

"Yes, sir—ah, Trigge. I can handle it."

"Good." Trigge smothered his smile. He thought of giving Joe Reddman a call just to fill him in on the joke. But he wondered about Davey, too. A bicycle racer with a pretty face. Would he survive the probationary period? "Now get out of here. I've got work to do."

Reddman frowned at the file in the privacy of his office. Maybe I'm missing something, he thought. Once again he compared the five-count complaint to the police reports. Blue's blood alcohol level was .18, which was good enough for the drunk driving charge. The man admitted hitting the victim and running, which would prove the second count, hit-and-run. His license had been revoked less than two months before, so the charge of driving on a revoked license should also stick. And the woman, a deputy public defender, had died because of the accident, so the vehicular homicide charge was legitimate. It wasn't good, Reddman knew, because she'd been jaywalking when she got hit, but it was at least arguable.

That left count five. He remembered what Trigge had said: "We don't get many as good as this one. You can't lose."

Really? Reddman asked himself, thinking of the "Where's the beef" commercial. Where's the murder?

He sat for a moment, making faces at nothing and picking at his nose. Was this Trigge's idea of humor? he wondered. Toss the new guy onto the freeway and watch him dodge traffic?

It occurred to him that maybe James R. Trigge was fucking with his mind.

CHAPTER THREE

Sharon Sondenburg took a front row center seat and waited for the preliminary hearing to start. She knew her tight-fitting jeans and orange rayon shirt attracted drifting eyes and thoughts, but she was accustomed to that kind of attention. Johnny Blue and all his relatives sat near her, but she ignored them. The one-time rodeo queen wanted to kill the bastard, slowly, an inch at a time. Ami O'Rourke had been her closest friend.

The lawyer from Denver looked too beautiful and too young for the rough-and-tumble courts of Muldoon, she thought. Why did they send some rookie just out of law school? Adonis in a City Streets suit, she decided. He needed a roomful of mirrors so he could smile at his beautiful self. Not a courtroom.

"—waive the reading of the complaint," Saul Cole said, then plopped back into his chair next to Johnny Blue. Saul would tear huge chunks of flesh out of the "champion" Brim had hired to try this case, Sharon thought. She had known old Saul—a lard-protected bear—most of her life. Ten years ago he had been Sopris County's part-time district attorney. He had prosecuted her for a high school prank. Pissed off because of a parking ticket, she had taken her daddy's pickup truck and flattened a whole row of parking meters. Saul had the ethics of a timber wolf, she thought, which he hid behind an amiable exterior. If it moves, kill it and eat it. Then smile.

"Very well," the judge said, peering over the bench. The tiny woman judge had been brought in from another county for the preliminary hearing, and Sharon wondered if the small person would have to stand up to see over the edge. "Mr. Reddman, you may call your first witness."

Sharon felt helpless; bound up with ropes; a gag in her mouth. The proceedings were packaged and tasteless, like cold cuts in plastic wrappers from a supermarket, rather than butchered beef at a cow camp. What has this got to do with Ami? she wanted to shout. Not the statistic the lawyers were talking about: the person she could see in her mind.

Ami? Sharon asked the image. Why did you go and get yourself killed? You were so wired, so totally on, so wonderfully funny, caring, and—weird. You know what you were, little dumbshit? You were an offering. And now look at that son of a bitch, she thought, staring at one side of Johnny Blue's face. He took. He took you away.

Bernie Lopes climbed into the witness box, wearing a pin-striped suit and a thin tie. You're an asshole, Bernie, Sharon thought affectionately, smiling at him. The last time she'd seen him in a suit was at his grandmother's funeral. It was too tight for him then, and it looked tighter now. She remembered how skinny he had been in high school and how lean and muscular be became in college. It hadn't taken him long to thicken.

"I do," Lopes said, lowering his hand.

Adonis stood by the podium. "State your name and occupation, please, for the record."

"Bernie Lopes. I'm a detective for the city of Muldoon, Colorado."

"Earlier this year—September twenty-fourth to be exact—were you so employed?"

"Yes, sir."

"And on that date were you called upon to investigate an accident in front of the courthouse here in Muldoon?"

"Objection, if it please the court," Saul Cole said, from his half-crouch. It was as though he was testing the waters. "Leading."

"I'm going to allow the question, Mr. Cole," the judge said. "This is just a preliminary hearing, and the question—"

" 'Just' a preliminary, Judge? Don't my client have rights at preliminary hearings?"

"Mr. Cole, I'm allowing the question." Cole heaved a defeated sigh, glanced at his client, and sat down. "You may answer the question," the judge said to Lopes.

What was that all about? Sharon asked herself, wondering if anything important had happened. According to Ami, trials were mainly bullshit, but fun. Like most things in life, the two had decided—Ami from her perspective as a deputy public defender, caring for and bleeding for the losers of the world, and Sharon from her viewpoint as a tenured instructor of literature, with an emphasis in mythology, at Fort Sundown State College in Muldoon. "Like life," Ami had said, "a trial requires extensive posturing, a huge ego investment, an occasional drenching sweat when your self-image falls through the floor and leaves you naked—but like life, when you analyze it, it's pure bullshit."

The problem was that when you fucked up—and to Ami, "fuck up" meant "lose"—your client went to jail, and Ami couldn't stand the thought of people in cages. Even Johnny Blue, Sharon Sondenburg remembered, staring at the defendant as Lopes testified. The man had been guilty as sin; the evidence against him had been overwhelming; but Ami felt that she hadn't done enough. She said there were questions she could have asked, maneuvers she should have tried that might have won the case. She had blamed herself after losing Blue's drunk driving trial, and she had cried.

"Before you asked Mr. Blue any questions, did you give him the so-called Miranda warnings?" the prosecutor asked.

"Yes, sir, I did. I read them off a card we carry around that our district attorney gave us."

"After you warned him, did he still agree to talk?"

"Yes, sir. He seemed anxious to talk, in fact. Like he wanted to explain."

"Pardon me," Cole said, jumping up. "I didn't get that answer." He looked meaningfully at the judge. "You said he wanted to talk?"

"Yes, sir."

"Not like a man who wants to hide something?" Cole continued.

"Judge, I object," Reddman said quickly. "Mr. Cole will have his chance later."

"I agree, Mr. Reddman. Mr. Cole, save your questions for cross-examination."

"Just wanted to make sure I heard that right," Cole said.

Who did he think he was kidding? Sondenburg thought, angered by the interruption. The asshole was just trying to emphasize a favorable remark! Yet she had to admit, it was fascinating. She knew she could watch the process all day. There was something mythic about the courtroom, she decided: knights in shining armor on heroes' journeys, larger-than-life figures touching chords in a person's psyche. She just wished it didn't involve Ami.

Two hours later the judge asked the lawyers whether they could finish before noon. "If we can, let's keep going," she said, "but if not, I'll recess now."

"I'm almost done, Judge," Reddman said. "I just have a few more questions for Sergeant Donovan."

"Mr. Cole, are you going to put on any testimony?"

"No, Your Honor."

"All right, let's try to finish," the judge said.

"Sergeant Donovan," Reddman asked the tall, thin trooper in the witness box. "As an accident reconstruction expert, do you have an opinion as to whether or not this accident could have been avoided?"

"I do."

"And what is your opinion?" Reddman asked, watching Cole struggle to his feet.

"Wait a minute. Just a minute," Cole said, waving his hand. "There's something wrong with that question."

"Yes, Mr. Reddman," the judge said from her birdlike perch. "It strikes me that you're asking for speculation rather than an opinion."

"That's it," Cole said. "That's what's wrong with it."

"Let me rephrase the question then, if it please the court," Reddman said. "As an expert, do you have an opinion as to whether or not the striking of the victim in this case, when the defendant hit her with his truck"—he paused, as though to allow the image to linger—"do you have an opinion as to whether or not his act in hitting her with his truck was a deliberate act?"

"Just as bad, Your Honor. Same objection! Not even an expert can know something like that."

"I'm inclined to agree, Mr. Reddman," the judge said. "The mental state of the defendant isn't something which this witness can have an opinion on."

"Right! Right! Thank you, Judge," Cole said, obviously grateful. He sat down.

But Reddman apparently would not accept the ruling. "Your Honor, Sergeant Donovan has testified that there was nothing—no evidence of any kind—to indicate that the defendant took the slightest bit of evasive action here." His voice was tight, as though his whole case depended on this testimony. "Not only that, he's testified that the evidence clearly shows that the defendant stomped on the accelerator, so to speak. Sergeant Donovan has also told us he's been reconstructing accidents for years, has been thoroughly trained—"

"Mr. Reddman, I'm aware of what Sergeant Donovan has testified to, and of the inferences that can be drawn from his testimony—one of which is that the act was deliberate. You may argue the point, but I will not permit this witness to testify to it. Am I clear?"

"Yes, Judge," Reddman said, smiling. He folded his file. "No further questions."

"Cross-examination?"

Cole stood up, then looked at the clock on the wall. "Don't think so," he said. "He might accidentally say something that'd help the prosecution."

"All right. I'm prepared to rule now, but if either of you wish to argue, I suppose it's possible that I might change my mind." She smiled at the lawyers.

Say something! Sharon Sondenburg thought, glaring at the prosecutor. Don't you care what happened? "Submit it, Judge," Reddman said.

"Mr. Cole?"

"I'm ready for your ruling," the defense lawyer said.

"Very well. With respect to counts one through four, I find probable cause to believe that the defendant committed those offenses. However, the fifth count, the murder count, isn't that easy. You have real problems with that one, Mr. Reddman." She paused and fiddled with her pen. "However, the problems are yours, not mine. The law is quite clear as to the standard to be applied by the court at this stage of the proceedings. All inferences are to be drawn in favor of the prosecution; and I find, from the evidence—which includes some very shaky testimony regarding a possible motive, although there is more substantial physical evidence—that there is enough for me to infer that the defendant did in fact deliberately take the life of Ami O'Rourke.

"I therefore bind the defendant over to the district court on all counts."

The courtroom quickly emptied, except for those with a personal interest in the case. Blue's wife, mother, and father gathered around the defense table. Sharon knew they were good people, in spite of the fact they'd produced Blue. Then Johnny looked over at her and grinned.

Sharon snapped her head away. She leaned across the railing and punched the prosecutor on the shoulder. "Mr. Reddman?"

Reddman was laughing about something with Bernie Lopes. "Hi, Sharon," Lopes said pleasantly. "How'd you like that dazzling display of legal footwork?"

"About as much as I like green chile." She could feel Reddman's eyes on her face. "Can we talk?"

"Sure," Reddman said, trying not to stare. "What about lunch?"

"Have to be quick. I teach a class at one-thirty."

"That's okay. I catch a plane at two." Reddman moved his head, but his eyes were stuck on her face. He couldn't seem to help himself, and wondered if he should apologize. "What do you want to talk about?"

"Ami," Sharon said. "I think I can help." She grabbed Lopes by the arm. "Come on, Bernie. You're coming, too."

I'm in love, Reddman thought, as the fifteen-seat metroliner struggled to get off the ground. He leaned back and closed his eyes, allowing the image of Sharon Sondenburg to fill his mind. She had tried to talk about the victim in the case, but had given up. Reddman agreed with everything she said, but it was obvious he hadn't heard a word. He wondered how it would feel to touch her face.

The aircraft lurched to the left, and his eyes popped open.

"These planes are so *small*," the woman across the aisle from him said. Her knuckles were white from gripping the seat in front of her. "Whoever heard of a plane—a passenger plane—you can't even stand up in?"

"Where are you from?" Reddman asked, looking at her. Late thirties, great chest, nice skin—pouches for cheeks, though. She looked like a squirrel.

"Texas!" she cried, terrified. Her hand reached out, looking for something to hold on to.

"Take it easy, lady," Reddman said, extending his open palm across the aisle.

"Thanks," she said, grabbing his hand. "Just until we

get over the mountains. It scares me to death to fly over these mountains!''

The plane lifted off the ground and flew smoothly over the valley, skirting the mountains to the south. Large hay-fields stretched toward hillsides thick with conifers and aspens. Cattle and horses had been let into the hayfields to graze. "It's real pretty if you look out the window," Redd-man said, trying to give her something to do. He found the highway that stretched like a wire into the mountains north of Muldoon. "See that road over there?" He made her look out his window. "Goes to a little town called Fools Gold, about fifty miles away and straight up. They have a bicycle race on it over Memorial Day. The cyclists race a train.''

"Race a train? On bicycles?" she asked, letting go of his hand. "Tell you what. There is a lot of craziness in this world.''

"You okay?"

"I'm fine now," she said. "Just needed a little help there. Usually, you know, my husband is with me, but he had to get back to Fort Worth. We have family here in Muldoon—his brother. You might even know him." Uh-oh, Reddman thought. A nonstop talker. "Carlson? Tommy Carlson? Big ranch on out—"

"I'm not from Muldoon," Reddman said. "I'm from Denver.''

"What do you do?"

"I'm a special prosecutor. I was here on—"

"You *are*? Johnny Blue? Oh, honey, you're on the wrong side of that one!" She turned in her seat, facing him directly.

"What?"

"I heard all about it from Tommy and his wife, Julie? It's a big frame-up! Oh, I am so glad I can talk to you about it, so you can quit wasting all that taxpayer money! Do you know who Johnny Blue is?"

"A drunk, according to the cops.''

"Oh, I wish my husband was here," the woman pursued. "Johnny Blue was a rodeo star! My husband knows all about rodeo, you know, which is about the most de*mand*ing sport in the world!'' Her hands moved easily, emphasizing her words. ''I mean, talk about athletes and excitement, there is more in an afternoon of rodeo than a week of football! Can you imagine what it must take to ride a horse that's trying to throw you into the air, or wrestle with a bull?'' Her whole body asked the same question. ''Well, Johnny Blue was one of the greatest, like Roger Staubach or O. J. Simpson, you know? And he's from Muldoon! And the people love him, too, in spite of the fact he isn't a perfect human being.''

''Lady, what the hell are you talking about?'' a large, nattily dressed man asked. He turned to face her from his seat three rows in front of her. ''I know Johnny and I don't love him a damn bit. He don't work, he don't take care of his wife and kids, he drinks like a guppy, and he wants everybody to feel sorry for him.'' The man's frank gaze would not let the woman go. ''He's a damn piece of mistletoe! He's a wood tick! He sucks blood out of whatever he latches on to! Tommy's filled you up with a lot of bull.''

Reddman quietly pulled out a small spiral notepad and a ballpoint pen. ''Did you know him pretty well?'' he asked the man.

''Not too well. I know his pa. Hell, there's some others right here on this plane know Johnny a sight better'n me.'' He looked beyond Reddman at a man seated in the back. ''Tell him, Tish.''

Seven of the fifteen seats were occupied. The man called Tish sat in the rear seat next to a woman. ''You ain't gonna make me a witness or anything are you, mister?'' he asked Reddman.

''Not if you don't want to be,'' Reddman said.

''Well, I could tell you some stories about Johnny that'd curl your hair. But I agree with that lady from Texas. I think you're on the wrong side.''

''How so?''

''I think he was just at the wrong place at the wrong time. Take that woman he run over, that public defender?

30

Everybody in town knows she was sleeping with the D.A. and her boss and the judge, too, probably, except he might not—"

"Tish, what the hell are you talking about!" the large man said. It looked as though he wanted to go after Tish, except the plane wasn't large enough to stand up in.

Small towns, Reddman thought, folding his notebook and stuffing it in his shirt pocket. He had forgotten what they were like.

31

CHAPTER FOUR

Trigge stood in front of the French doors in his office, hands clasped behind his back, watching the late spring snow pile up on the balcony. Was it true that no two flakes were exactly alike? he wondered. Did that mean someone had looked at all of them?

Reddman's personnel file lay on Trigge's desk, and as he stared at the snow, he tried to make up his mind. Reddman had second-chaired three murder cases for NASP, and the evaluations of his performances were mixed. He was scheduled to try the *Blue* case in Sopris County, Colorado, in two weeks, but according to Walter Brim, the district attorney, he had done nothing. Trigge knew he could not simply pull Reddman off the case and plug in another lawyer. That would be too much of a slap in Reddman's face. Either fire him now, Trigge thought, or let him try *Blue* and see how he performs.

The worst evaluation had come from Stuart VanOchre who at forty-five was the oldest of Trigge's troops. VanOchre did not believe Reddman had what it took to be a NASP lawyer. "Too easily distracted," his confidential report stated. "Has a tendency to go off on tangents and a distinct inability to follow directions." Rachel Stone— who specialized in cases where insanity was the defense—

32

agreed with VanOchre. "Imaginative and articulate, but too combative and very undiplomatic," her report indicated. "Also, obvious to me there is some love-hate thing with his father he hasn't resolved." But Frankie Rommel thought otherwise. The woman drove Trigge crazy, which was perfectly all right with him, because in his day, that was what women were supposed to do to men. In any event, he trusted her judgment over his own. "Definitely of no value as a second chair," her report concluded. "But he has too much potential to toss away. Good instincts, great imagination. Just that he has to do it his own way." And what was it Terry Nolan had said? Something about Reddman being a law unto himself who thought he was normal?

There was a knock on the door. "Come in."

"Hi, boss," the tanned, fit-looking younger man said. "You rang?"

"Sit down," Trigge said, returning to his desk. Something in his tone sent a signal to Reddman, who crouched into a chair as though ready to spring into action. "How are you doing on *Blue?*"

"Great. Goes to trial in two weeks. Witnesses have been subpoenaed, discovery's been complied with. My plan is to go down next Monday, a week before the trial, and put it together."

"Will that give you enough time?"

"Should be plenty," Reddman said. "It's not a very complicated case."

Trigge grunted and butted his cigarette. He maintained a duplicate file in his office but had been too busy to monitor the case, even though Reddman was still on probation. "Have you been to Muldoon since the preliminary?"

"Once," Reddman said, blushing.

"Walter Brim called," Trigge said. "He's worried. I had the impression from him you hadn't been down at all."

"Well, I didn't see Mr. Brim," Reddman said. "Matter of fact, I took my skis. I met the cop in charge of the investigation, and we went over the case." He shrugged. "As I said, "it isn't very complicated.""

"Playtime, you mean?" Trigge asked, aware that his voice had gotten larger. "That bicycle race they have down there. Memorial Day, isn't it?"

"Yeah."

"Are you ready for the race?"

Reddman's eyes took on a few sparks. "I'm feeling pretty good," he said, leaning forward. "Hey. Is there a problem with my doing the race? When I asked you about it a month ago, you said as long as it didn't interfere—"

"Which is what I meant, Davey. As long as it doesn't interfere." The snow kept piling up on Trigge's balcony. "I have the impression you are more interested in that race than you are in *Blue*."

"I am," Reddman said emphatically. "I can win the race."

"What does that mean?"

"The case is a dog, Trigge. That murder count should never have been filed."

Trigge lit a cigarette and considered the exchange. He knew the case was a dog. He remembered that he and Rommel had thought it might be funny to throw the eager young timber wolf a rubber bone. But the fact that a case was weak didn't mean you could give up on it before you tried it.

"I've been going over your evaluations, Davey. They're not good."

"My what?" Reddman asked, surprised.

"Your evaluations. You knew you were on probation, didn't you?"

"Sure, but . . ." Reddman's legs bunched under him again as he leaned forward. It had not occurred to him that probation was anything more than a formality. "I'm really on the carpet here, aren't I? I mean, if there's something wrong with my performance, let me know about it. Okay?"

"That's what I'm doing." Trigge put both hands on top of his desk. "Let me say first of all that nobody's perfect."

Reddman glared angrily at his boss. "I don't like this,"

34

he said suddenly. "No one has ever questioned my ability before. You want me to quit?"

Twenty years ago Trigge would have tossed the kid out on his ear for a remark like that. Ten years ago he might have laughed, waited a week, and then dumped him. But prosecutors—good ones—were a special breed. They weren't that easy to develop. Trigge also had a feeling about the young man. He was Joe Reddman's son, so he was bound to be complicated. "No," he said, calmly. "But you can resign any time you want. Involuntary servitude went out with the Constitution."

"What do you want, then?" Reddman demanded.

"I want you to power down while I think." Trigge slowly inhaled a long drag. Reddman had pride, courage, and a short fuse. He liked the pride and the courage, but not the short fuse. And what of his judgment? "You haven't had any real responsibility yet, have you?"

"I've second-chaired three juries and done a few court trials, but nothing major."

Trigge nodded, trying to see behind the man's pale blue eyes. He still looked like a wolf. "So you haven't had a chance to prove yourself, have you?"

"No."

"I guess we'll find out, then. With *Blue*."

"That's a shitty case, Trigge. Have you looked at the file?"

"Of course it's shitty. None of them are easy. That's why we get them."

"If I win, I make it, but if I lose, I don't?"

"Give me a break. You know it isn't that simple."

"What's the problem, then?"

Trigge slowly shook his head, once again searching Reddman's eyes. Is anything back there? he wondered. Or is he like the rest of his generation, who think all it takes is looks? "I can't tell you. You'll have to figure it out yourself."

"The race?"

"Entirely up to you. I'm not a nursemaid."

Reddman laughed and started to stand. "So I'm on trial, too. Is that it?"

"I guess that's it," Trigge said. "Good luck."

The metroliner from Denver to Muldoon banked to the left, avoiding the edge of a thunderhead that piled high and white in the sky. Reddman stared at the head of the man in front of him as he played back the scene with Trigge earlier in the day. He had the uncomfortable feeling that the old man was right; he didn't deserve to be a NASP warrior. He'd spent more time in the saddle than at the office.

Reddman knew Trigge didn't hire clock punchers, and the fact that he'd trained hard for the bicycle race at the expense of office time wouldn't really matter to a person like Trigge. But as Reddman stared at the snow-filled bowls below, he knew there was more to it than that. He could have blown the whole case.

He had met with Bernie Lopes, the detective in charge of the file, on the ski slopes above Avalanche in January. Lopes had told him that the murder count sucked. "I talked to Johnny an hour after the hit," Lopes said. "I can spot a liar, and he didn't lie. I've known him all my life, too. He isn't that bad."

"What is he?"

"A wasted cowboy. Huge lush. Muldoon's All-American hero turned to shit. But he didn't murder her, pure and simple."

"What did he do?"

"The DUI, the hit-and-run, the driving without a license. Maybe even the vehicular homicide. But that's it."

"Why was the murder count filed if he didn't do it?"

"Politics is my guess," Lopes had explained. "That's why Brim brought you guys in. *He* knows it's a loser, but he can't afford to lose it because he wants to run for reelection. So he's dropped it off on you guys instead!"

And so Reddman had decided to lose the murder count—

which was really the whole case—as gracefully as possible. That way, he could concentrate totally on the bicycle race.

But as they flew over a lonely town in the Colorado mountains, the feeling of discomfort intensified. He hadn't even talked about the case to the man who had filed it: Walter Brim. He had been so eager to train for the race that he'd decided to lose on the basis of what one detective had told him.

The mountains grew closer as the small commuter jet began its descent. "Ladies and gentlemen, we've started our approach," the pilot announced. He had talked to the passengers often throughout the flight, like a tour guide, and had a nice fatherly air. "We should land in about eight minutes. Check your seat belt, okay? Nice and tight. Weather in Muldoon much warmer than what you saw in Denver. Sixty-four degrees Fahrenheit, just a few clouds. That's short-sleeve weather in these parts, folks. Thank you."

The craft banked to the right—Reddman's side—and he picked out the ribbon of highway that stretched from Muldoon to Fools Gold. He followed the road as far as he could, losing it when it twisted into the mountains, reappeared briefly near Avalanche, then was gone. That was the path the cyclists would take on Memorial Day. The year before, Reddman had done it in two hours, thirty-four minutes, twenty-seven seconds. Not good enough to win, but you have to be on a team to win. Still, he'd been the only rider to place in the top ten who hadn't belonged to a team. This year he'd trained harder than ever. Why?

Was it simply that it made him look good? He knew there was more to racing bicycles than that. There was the mystique, the strategy, the athletic skills involved, the heart. Each race was more than a simple challenge. Every time out was an ordeal. Furthermore, he had an intense urge to excel, to be really good at something. Racing bicycles was something he could do.

He wanted badly to do the race. All that time in the saddle, all that pain. Should he flush it down the tubes because of a job? It surprised him to realize that the question was serious! What were his priorities? he asked himself. The pit or the grind? But it was a serious question. I'm young and single, he told himself. I can always get another job. But another chance, at the age of thirty-three, to do the Iron Horse? His wheel—a handmade Pinarello, a fifteen hundred dollar frame—was in the plane's luggage compartment, and Reddman realized he really didn't know which meant more to him. He wanted to be one of NASP's warriors in the worst kind of way, and that meant giving the *Blue* case a real hard shot. But he could hardly wait to jump on his bike and do some serious spinning.

Ten minutes later the craft touched down, and Reddman got off. He hoped Sharon Sondenburg had gotten his message. When they had lunched together months ago, she had told him she wanted to help, and on an impulse Reddman had called her before leaving Denver. At lunch, all he'd done was lust after her with his eyes, and he hadn't listened. But he remembered the intensity of her belief that Ami O'Rourke had been murdered. He had to start somewhere. Probably she's just a beautiful bubblehead, he thought, who can't tell me anything I don't already know.

But she can still help, he told himself. She can hold my hand.

Sharon wasn't waiting at the airport. What did you expect? Reddman asked himself as he waited for his bags and his bike. That she would meet you in her Mercedes and whip you off to her boudoir?

"Message for Mr. Reddman. David Reddman. Please check at the Colorado Trails Airline reservation desk."

A moment later he ripped open a CTA envelope. A telephone message from Sharon Sondenburg: "Dinner at Ton Tin's at eight, okay? Call me, 555-3560, after seven."

Miss Gallegos had made reservations for Reddman at one of the two hotels in Muldoon, and half an hour later, after hitching a ride in a pickup truck, he thanked the cowboy who had driven him in to town and carried his bike and baggage inside. The old brick building—a renovated relic from the 1890s—was full of tourists in the summer but largely unoccupied in May. He uncrated his racing bike and stood it up against the television set in the sitting room, thinking about the race.

Two passes to climb, both over ten thousand feet. Fifty miles of mountain highway, complete with potholes and occasional stretches of gravel, as crews repaired the road after the ravages of winter. Three hundred riders, fighting the tourists for space on the road. And great descents! He remembered rounding that final corner where a huge throng of people had gathered, some taking pictures of the riders and others shooting pictures of Fools Gold, looking like a town made out of toy blocks, two thousand feet below. Right after the corner the road lost its bottom, and the final descent began. The cyclists—spread out over three or four miles by then, and either alone or in small groups—swerved around slow-moving RVs and lines of cars and one another, noses stuck to handlebars, leaning into curves and narrowly missing oncoming traffic.

He looked at his watch: 7:24 P.M. Sharon Sondenburg picked up the telephone on the fourth ring. "Hello?"

"Hi, Sharon," Reddman said. "Hey, sounds great. What kind of place, and where?"

"It's a Chinese place that just opened. Used to be the Westerner, and who knows what it'll be next year? I haven't been there."

"Is it near the New York Hotel?"

"Not too far," she said, her full voice sounding very, very nice. "About six blocks north, on Main. It has one of those neon dragons in front, you know? One of those huge red, white, and blue things?"

"Like, American-Chinese?"

"Something like that. See you there at eight?"

She's in a hurry, Reddman thought. "Okay."

The temperature had cooled to fifty degrees when Reddman went outside. He wore a light sport coat over a long-sleeve button-down shirt without a tie. The locals—mostly cowboys and college kids—wore everything from faded Levi's to blazing knee-length pants that flashed like strobe lights. He enjoyed the short walk through the busy mountain town, comparing it to others he had known: Telluride, Steamboat Springs, Aspen. Muldoon was like them, without the glitz. The streets were friendlier, full of couples on the sidewalk, window-shopping and greeting one another. Vehicles piloted by teenagers—low riders, high riders, and pickup trucks—dragged Main Street. He saw a lot of cyclists, mountain bikers for the most part, darting around and annoying everyone. A woman wearing a T-shirt that loudly proclaimed "Where the hell is Muldoon?" strolled by and grinned at him, then disappeared into a cowboy bar.

The neon dragon, flaming luridly like something from the Vegas Strip, was easy to find. Inside, the decor was ancient pagoda, like a Japanese tea garden, and Reddman was ushered to a table by a smiling Chinese. A few minutes later Sharon Sondenburg arrived.

Reddman had forgotten how beautiful she was. She seemed literally to glow with radiant health, and her smooth skin shone like that of someone who had just enjoyed good sex. Her eyes—hazel and clear—sparkled with good humor. Light crow's-feet, which she made no effort to hide, lined their outer corners. Nor did she make any effort to downplay her superb figure. With the naturalness of a person who had worn ranch clothes all her life, she walked to the table in boots, dress Levi's, and a short-sleeve yellow shirt molded to accommodate her breasts. "Hi," she said, sticking out a hand.

"Hi."

They talked for several minutes, sharing a carafe of wine, before ordering. Sondenburg had two passions, Reddman discovered: horses and mythology. She had been born and raised on a small ranch ten miles from Muldoon. Her parents still lived there, but she had moved into a trailer on a corner of the land and had built her own corral and stable. Occasionally she would have dinner with her folks or go dancing with her dad, but not often. She was too busy, and so were they.

"Mythology?"

"It's what I teach," she said, tamping an egg roll into a dish of mustard.

"Careful with that stuff," Reddman warned. "It's acid."

A moment later she was fanning her mouth and blinking. "Hot!" she gasped. "Hotter than Mexican hot! What do they do to it?"

"I tried to tell you," Reddman said, laughing.

"It's really okay. I'll be just fine in a couple of days." She drank some water. "This won't be your first case, will it?" she asked.

"What? No. Oh, God, no."

"How old are you?" She held the small teacup in her hands, staring frankly into his eyes.

"Hey, I'm the prosecutor. I should be asking the questions." Her expression didn't change. "Thirty-three."

"You don't look that old," she said critically. "I thought lawyers aged quick and drank scotch whisky. You don't drink scotch whisky, either."

Reddman looked at the woman's surprisingly muscular hands. Her nails were short and even. Like everything else about her, he thought: no pretensions. "Maybe you're looking for the myth," he said. "I exercise a lot. I'm a vegetarian. You don't—"

"Vegetarian! Really?" She laughed. "You better keep your voice down, honey. We lynch vegetarians in Muldoon."

"The economy's that bad?" he asked, trotting out a line he had used in other ranching communities.

"It's pretty bad." She smiled at him with interest. "Besides, everyone knows vegetarians compete with the cattle for graze. Have you really tried a lot of cases?"

"Hundreds," Reddman said. "I'm good."

"Hundreds? How long have you been at it?"

"Ever since I got out of law school, nine years ago."

"Your message said you wanted to talk about the case,"

she said, cutting up another egg roll with a fork. "You mean it, or will this be like last time?"

"I mean it," Reddman told her. "It's a tough case. You knew Ami, and you know the territory. I need a guide."

The waitress interrupted, spreading the meal in front of them. The steaming food, in bowls and trays, smelled exotic, like an east Indian bazaar. Sharon knew the waitress, a student at the college, and told her how nice it looked and how wonderful it smelled. "Of course my taste buds have been permanently damaged by that mustard."

"Do you always tell the truth?" Reddman asked when the waitress had gone, spreading white rice on his plate.

"You kidding?" she replied, heaping beef and pepper strips onto hers. "Shit, no. Not any more than you do."

"How did you know Ami?"

"She taught a course in constitutional law at the college. We got to talking. In spite of the difference in background, we found out we had a lot in common."

"Like what?"

"She was different. I'm different. She was intelligent. So am I." Sondenburg picked up a glistening piece of beef with her chopsticks. "She was committed, too, to what she did. Totally. A flake—you know, a bleeding heart who couldn't see bad in people—and I'd laugh at her about that, get her all stirred up." She put the meat in her mouth and chewed slowly, her eyes miles away. "A crazy person, really," she said, talking around the meat. "One of those people who just give themselves away, who let others use them up. I loved her a lot."

Reddman watched her chew, fascinated by the woman's natural grace. "A saint?"

"Possibly. Depends on how you define it. She had a boyfriend—lots of boyfriends—and she has a kid. Really a cute little guy."

"Where is he? Is it a he?"

"He's living with the public defender's family. Zack and Sonya Wolfman."

"Wolfman lives down here?" Reddman asked, recognizing the name. "The guy who was a linebacker for the Denver Broncos eight years ago?" He dipped a chestnut in reddish sauce and ate it.

"I think so. Do you know him?"

"No."

"Would you like to meet him?"

"I'll meet him soon enough," Reddman said. "The truth is, I don't like public defenders. Most of them are royal pains in the ass."

"How do you feel about the people who kill them?"

"I don't like them either," Reddman said cheerfully. "I'm a good prosecutor. I don't like anybody."

"This is a bit ironic, isn't it? Wouldn't you rather give good old Johnny Blue an award, like second place at the stock show?" Her eyes bit at him across the candlelit table. "After all, he killed a deputy P.D. Isn't that worth something?"

"What are you getting at?"

"I'm trying to decide whether or not you care about Ami. Or is this just a job to you, something you do because they pay you?"

"Hey. I've never gone into a trial—one that I believed in—where I didn't care. But this one . . ."

"You don't believe in it?"

"Parts of it, sure. I believe Johnny Blue was drunk. I believe he was driving without a license. I believe he hit her, than ran. I might even believe in the vehicular homicide, even though it sucks, so far—but murder?" Reddman shook his head. "What the hell makes this a murder case?"

"The people!"

"The people? How?" He held a clump of rice in his chopsticks. "A drunk cowboy and the woman who defended him and lost. So the drunk cowboy happened to run over the saint. What makes it murder?"

"That drunk cowboy happens to be an extraordinary athlete. Drunk or sober, he can shoot the eyes out of a snake. Johnny Blue would *never* run over something he didn't mean to run over."

"How do you know that?"

"I've known Johnny all my life. He's an outlaw stud, a whip-trained horse. Cowboy mean. Do you know what I'm talking about?"

"I've known a few cowboys," Reddman said. "Arizona is full of them, and that's where I got my start." He put the rice in his mouth.

"Johnny is killer mean," she said. "He's a psychopath. And Ami was the kind of person psychopaths find."

"What does that mean?"

"Personalities mesh, don't they? Isn't there—well, like a symbiosis to violence, like cogs that turn gears?" She asked the question haltingly, as though truly searching for the answer. "All I know is that Johnny would never try to kill me, because I'm not a gentle person."

"So you're telling me that gentle people ask to get killed?" Reddman asked, putting another clump of rice in his mouth.

"In a way. They are offerings, I suppose, to the cycle of life, which includes death. But that doesn't justify killing them, does it?" Her eyes deepened, taking on the colors in the darkening room.

"What is this?" Reddman asked, irritated. "Pop mythology? Pop psychology? Something out of a freshman course in American literature?"

"It's good old horse sense! It's what people around here know, even though they wouldn't say it the same way." Her eyes had locked on to his and wouldn't let go. She spoke with an intensity that was almost sexual. "Half these people were raised on ranches, and all of them hunt and fish. They *know*. They've seen the way a rabbit will offer itself to a hawk. They know a lot about predators and their prey."

"Well, how the hell can you blame a hawk for killing a rabbit?"

"You can't. Hawks don't know any better, but people do. That isn't the point anyway."

"What's the point?"

"The *people*. A hawk kills a rabbit for food. But when one person kills another, it's either a murder or an accident!"

"A bit simplistic," Reddman said, picking at a piece of cauliflower. "But I get your point."

Sondenburg leaned toward him as if to stab him with the intensity of her conviction. "Well, this was no accident. It wasn't even close to an accident. Can't you see that?"

"I can see it, maybe. But I'm having trouble believing it." Damn it anyway, he thought. Earlier that day his boss had chewed on his ass, and he'd spent most of the day wrestling with his conscience. Now this conversation had drifted off into outer space. "I'm tired," he said suddenly. "Want to go to bed?"

Sondenburg stared at him in disbelief. "Is that really what you want from me?"

"Hey. No big deal. Just thought I'd ask."

She patted her mouth with her napkin and stood up. "Fuck off."

CHAPTER FIVE

The next morning ahead of the sun Reddman clattered down the steps of the New York Hotel. He wore bicycle cleats and cycling shorts and carried his twenty-pound Pinarello under his arm. Ten minutes later he was alone on the highway miles from town.

He hated himself. "What is wrong with me?" he shouted into the air, feeling helpless and out of control. Sunlight from the east threw long shadows. He ground his teeth with effort as he hammered his way up a long, steep grade, sweat leaking into his mouth. He pushed through his own breath-clouds in the clean mountain air, sucking and blowing hard, punishing his body.

His muscular legs—clean-shaven and tanned—rippled with the motion of the pedals. The large veins in his arms and neck carried blood to oxygen-starved muscles as he pushed himself harder and harder, wanting to reach the limits of his endurance and keep going. He could feel the pounding of his pulse throughout his body and reveled in the sensation as he tried to blow himself apart. He remembered how Sharon Sondenburg had looked as she walked out on him the night before. Like a flame, a beautifully controlled torch, molded into the form of a woman. "Hurt, damn you!" he yelled at himself in a desperate effort to cleanse himself with pain. Not enough. "Fuck you, Trigge!"

He caught a huge tractor-trailer and tried to ride by, but the rig—wearing a Texas license plate—hugged the center of the road. "Move it over, Texas!" he yelled.

"Hey, you fuckin' scarecrow, don't tell me to move it over." The trucker's heavy face glared at Reddman from the rearview mirror. "You want me to squash your ass?"

You are exactly what I need, Reddman thought. Fate has provided me with a cause I can really believe in.

He knew better than to pass the rig on the passenger side where the trucker could crowd him off the pavement. He started around the diesel-pumping monster on the driver's side, riding in the oncoming lane and hoping nothing would come hurtling over the hill. The man's face in the mirror— fat, sallow, in need of a shave, no neck—grinned at him with no humor.

The grade increased, slowing down the rig. Reddman's lungs burned, and his thighs felt as though they would blow apart. He pulled against the drop-bars, his biceps ready to snap as he fought to maintain, even increase, his speed. Then he rose up out of the saddle and started to grind. "Sit on it!" he spat at the driver as he pulled past the cab.

The trucker was enraged. He made a motion with his hands on the wheel, as though swerving toward the rider. He swung his door open, trying to knock him down, but Reddman was too far away. "You wait, you little gnat on a elephant's laig," he snarled. "What goes up comes down, boy. We get on top of this hill, I'm comin' down on you!"

"Shit," Reddman sneered, managing a grunt.

Then he started cramping in the groin. Relax, he said to himself. Aren't I Joe Reddman's son? Isn't that part of my problem? And don't they call him the last wild Indian? Didn't I inherit this magnificent control over my body, the way of the savage, capable of enduring pain and torment without the flicker of an eye? "Then why am I cramping in the groin?" he heard himself shout. "Grit your teeth and relax!"

That made him laugh. And the cramp in his groin went away.

Reddman, showered and carefully dressed, walked past the Sopris County Courthouse and on to the district attorney's office, a block away. It had once been a brick house in a nice neighborhood. But in small town USA, houses are often converted into offices, Reddman thought, until the big spenders arrive with their new ideas. They will renovate the town, establishing memorials to themselves—and then go broke. But their buildings remain. It hadn't happened yet to Muldoon. Reddman straightened his tie and brushed back the hair over his temples. He took a deep breath, pushed the door open, and walked in.

The former living room had been divided by a counter into a reception area and secretarial space. A hallway off the reception area led to the offices. A large woman in her early thirties sat at a desk behind the counter, working on a legal document. She looked up quickly when Reddman entered, then went on with her typing.

"Pardon me—"

"Don't interrupt, please."

Reddman frowned, then sat down and picked up a magazine.

"Can I help you?" she asked, a few moments later.

"I'd like to see Mr. Brim."

"Your name?"

"Dave Reddman. NASP."

"Oh. We've been expecting you, Mr. Reddman." She rose briskly and pushed through the counter door. "Mr. Brim is on the telephone, but I'll let him know you're here." She walked down the hall to Brim's office.

The door across the hall from Brim's office cracked open and a blondish, freckled young man wearing thick glasses poked out his head. He reddened when he realized Reddman was watching him, then emerged, hand outstretched. "Hi, I'm Randy Turner. You're the special prosecutor, right?" he asked, walking into the reception area.

"That's me," Reddman said, standing and shaking hands. "You're new, aren't you? Last time I was here—"

"Tommy Snow. He quit, went to Grand Junction. More money."

Walter Brim's door jerked open and the large man filled the hallway as he trotted into the reception room. "Well, well, well, at last you're here, Reddman. We've been worried about you!" His large voice seemed to veil his true feelings. "I mean, of course it's different for you fellows who try cases every day, but this is an important case down here and—"

"I have almost two weeks to put the thing together, Mr. Brim. Should be plenty of time." Reddman tried to project confidence, even though he didn't feel like it.

"Of course. Please come in. I see you've met Randy." Brim propelled Reddman toward his office. "Nancy, would you hold my calls please, and bring us coffee?"

"I'll hold calls, Mr. Brim, but I don't do coffee."

"Oh. Right." Brim smiled harshly at the woman. "Well. Have a chair, Reddman." He shut the door to his office and sat behind his woefully cluttered desk. Reddman chose one of the two chairs facing the D.A. "She's new. An extraordinary worker, but a bit independent. No one else will put up with her, and frankly, I'm glad of it!"

Reddman laughed. "Hey, if you ordered a woman in Denver to get coffee, she'd break your arm. That's the way it is." He looked around the room, forming an impression of too much to do with no budget: steel desk, old furniture, secondhand bookcases, files piled on a worktable. A huge round clock on the wall stared down at the lawyer toiling below.

"Perhaps that's the way it is in Denver, but Muldoon is different," Brim said.

"How so?"

"A bit like stepping back in time," Brim said, sagging over his desk. "The values are those of the fifties and before. The cattlemen swagger around town like Gary Cooper and John Wayne." He managed a smile. "Rodeo is bigger than football. The businessmen are Babbitts. Several Fundamentalist churches, Mormons, an Indian reservation in the district—active prejudice against the Indians, I might add. *No* women in government. At all." He shook his head. "Rural America at its best, and worst."

"How did Ami O'Rourke fit in around here?"

"Ami was a very capable lawyer, but obviously she did not fit in comfortably."

"You know, I think I've been here," Reddman said. "I started in Holsteen, Arizona. Hotter, not as many mountains, but the same town. What about the case?"

"What do you mean?"

"I don't want to be critical, Mr. Brim—"

"Please. Call me Walter. May I call you Dave?"

"Fair enough. Whose idea was it to tack on that murder count?"

"The officers who investigated it made the initial charges, but I'm the one who filed the murder complaint." He stared at the wall. "I truly believe it was a deliberate killing, although you will have the devil's own time proving it."

Reddman tried not to sneer. "It isn't murder unless you can prove it," he said. "Where is my proof?"

"Well. Proof is a bit thin. But isn't that what you fellows are good at?"

"Hey. You can't make a butterfly out of a piece of cardboard. And I don't take guys down for things they didn't do just because they're assholes."

"No one expects you to do that, Dave," Brim said gently.

"Sorry. Why do you think it was murder?"

"I know a little bit about the people involved. It's the kind of thing Johnny Blue would do. He apparently blamed Ami for his stint in the jailhouse—which he richly deserved, incidentally."

"Blamed her enough to kill her?"

"The man has the conscience of a block of ice. Possibly that is why he was so good at what he did."

"How good was he?"

"Unbelievable, I am told. Can you imagine the coordination, the athletic ability, involved in staying on top of an enraged bull?" Brim shook his head, clearly indicating it was beyond him. "I understand bull riding was his best event, even though the bronc-riding contest is what ended his career."

"Do you know Sharon Sondenburg?" Reddman asked thoughtfully.

"Yes, of course. I mean, I don't know her. But I've seen her and lusted after her. Don't tell my wife! I expect Sharon knows who I am, too, although her thoughts regarding me are not apt to be lurid."

"I had dinner with her last night—"

"You dog!"

"—and she made the same points you make. Blue had too much balance, or something, to run over Ami by accident. Is that the general feeling of the town?"

"No. I would have to say it's a minority view. Most people think it was an accident." Brim stood up, rubbing his forehead tiredly. "Blue has told everyone, even Ami's parents, how bad he feels. He even had the effrontery to confront them when they came to get her body."

"Publicly?"

"Very publicly indeed. At a press conference, actually. Saul Cole, the lawyer you are up against, is very cagey. He tries cases the way politicians run for office."

"Tell me about the press conference."

"Ami's parents went to the funeral home to get her body, and Blue just happened to be there paying his respects. Saul was there, too, along with a newspaper reporter, who took a photograph of the lot of them." Brim smiled. "Of course the picture appeared on the front page the next day."

"What about a plea bargain? Vehicular homicide isn't murder, but it's a felony. Would he go for that?"

"Cole refuses even to consider it. He believes that is the worst that can happen to his client, so what has he got to lose by trying it?"

"In other words, he wants a misdemeanor?"

"Yes. He'd like a murder case reduced to hit-and-run!"

Reddman refrained from telling Brim what he thought. "Pretty gutsy. I guess Cole doesn't think the state has a chance."

"That's what I hear," Brim said, trying to smile. "He thinks he can prove Ami was a complete scatterbrain who wandered into the street without paying the least bit of attention. Blue just happened along at the wrong time."

Reddman looked at his watch: 9:30. "Will I have an investigator?"

"*I* don't even have an investigator, Dave." Brim laughed— more of a groan—waving his hand at the pile of files on his desk. "All this to do—everything from murder to disturbing the peace—and you have met my entire staff. We rely entirely on the police."

"Okay." Reddman stood up. "What about a car and an office?"

"Nancy has keys to both. I'm afraid they're not very nice, but I hope they'll do."

"What about the judge? I'd like to meet him."

"Excellent idea. In fact, let's do it now. It would be nice if you met him before he finds out you're here." He reached for the telephone.

The door opened, and Nancy poked her head in. "Mr. Brim? I know you don't want to be disturbed, but Judge Landry is on the line."

Judge Gilbert Landry, carefully dressed in an expensive three-piece suit, focused his attention entirely on Dave Reddman. The large, bespectacled man looked like pictures Reddman had seen of Earl Warren: white hair, broad face, commanding presence. Landry bounded vigorously from behind his hardwood executive desk, hand extended, ignoring the presence of Walter Brim. "Indeed, a pleasure. To have a real prosecutor in our midst! Not to say we don't have one now, of course, ha-ha!—but to have someone from NASP, down to help us poor country folk with what promises to be a difficult case." Landry not only shook Reddman's hand but gripped him by the shoulder. "Quite an honor!"

"My pleasure, sir," Reddman said, smiling. He liked working for NASP, even if it made him a target for small-town judges and their friends. "I'll be glad to help, too. Just rule for the prosecution, you know."

"Ha-ha! Hear that, Saul?" Landry said to a man slouched in a chair in front of his desk. Reddman hadn't seen him sitting there. "I have the feeling you'll have your hands full with this young man!"

"Already had a taste of him at the preliminary," Cole said, turning in his chair and sticking out his hand. The overweight, graying man measured Reddman like an under-taker sizing him for a coffin.

"Please, everyone. Sit down," Landry said.

"Nice to see you again, Mr. Cole," Reddman said, taking a chair next to Cole. "I've heard a lot of good things about you from people in the office."

"That so? Even Jim Trigge?"

"He has a lot of respect for your ability," Reddman lied.

"I don't even know how he knows me. We've never tried a case together."

"I don't know either, Mr. Cole—"

"Saul."

"—but he's heard of you."

Cole nodded coldly, clearly suspicious of the flattery. "Been checking up on you too, David," he said. "You're related to that Joe Reddman, right? Fellow that gets in all that trouble?"

"He's my father," Reddman said, as pleasantly as he could.

"Joe Reddman? Who are you talking about, Saul?" Landry asked. He sat in the large high-back chair behind his desk with dignity, as though it were a throne.

"You know, Gil, that wild man in Denver, private eye type, does funny stuff, gets in the papers." Cole watched

Reddman closely, as though dowsing for water with a divining rod. "Character. Thin ice. Indian, I think."

"Indian!" Landry blurted. "Are you an Indian, young man?" He laughed. "Not that I have anything against Indians, but do we have another Wolfman on our hands?"

"My father isn't an Indian," Reddman said, doing his best to smile and be nice. "He was raised by an Indian woman, kind of a surrogate mother, but he doesn't have any Indian blood."

"Huh. Just acts a little crazy, that it?" Cole asked, probing.

"So I've heard," Reddman said. The grin on his face had worn thin. "But he's always been—well, tame around me." He could feel the heat in his face. "I may be his son—one of his sons—but I don't think any of us are like him. He and my mom divorced a long time ago."

"You're not gonna put on war paint, you mean?" Cole asked. "For the jury, you know, liven things up?"

"I have this feeling things will be lively enough without that," Reddman said, suddenly staring without smiling at the older man. He could feel himself losing it. "I think we'll both be able to stay awake in there."

"That so? You think so?" Cole dropped his eyes, but appeared pleased with what he'd found.

"Yes, but what about the jury?" Landry asked. He smiled, too.

"What was that all about?" Brim asked later as the two men walked back to his office. "Who is your father?"

Reddman smiled grimly, feeling ice in the pit of his stomach. It hadn't even taken Cole five minutes to find a button he could push. "He's a private investigator. He's been around Denver a long time and has a reputation as a wild man, which may be good business for him, but I have to live it down."

"Well. I'm sure you will," Brim said with admiration. "Those two aren't easy to stand up to. I think you let Cole know he's in for a fight."

"Sure, he's in for a fight. But what have I got to fight with?"

Brim continued as though he hadn't heard. "Let me say this, too. When I first saw you eight months ago, I thought you were way too pretty, way too young. But you'll do fine in there, I can feel it!" He put his hand on Reddman's shoulder, obviously feeling better himself. "What kind of trial experience do you have?"

"Nine years."

"Really! You don't look that old."

"I'm thirty-three. Johnny Blue and I are the same age."

"Well. Let's hope the likeness ends there." Brim opened the door to the D.A.'s office and held it until both men were inside.

A ranch family, judging by their clothing, sat in the reception area. As Brim entered, the father jumped to his feet and took off his hat, revealing the line across his forehead that separated milk white skin from red leather. "Hello, how are you?" Brim said, beaming at them as though the election were only a few days away. He shook the man's hand. "I'll be with you folks in a minute. Nancy, hold calls and—well, hold calls. We won't be long."

Nancy, on her feet, was worried. "You couldn't . . . ?"

Brim looked more carefully at the family group. Two of the three children had been crying, and there was some discoloration under the mother's left eye. "What seems to be the problem?"

"She's a-tryin' to leave me, Mr. Brim," the rancher said, pointing to his wife. "Ain't there a law?"

"I see. Now I want you—all of you—to stay right where you are. I need to talk with this man here, but it won't take long, and I want all of you here when I get back. Do you understand?"

The father stuck his hat back on his head and sat down. "Yes, sir."

Reddman grinned as the two men entered Brim's office. Brim shut the door. "What are you going to tell him?" Reddman asked. "Smack her in the other eye?"

"I see so much of that," Brim said tiredly. "These people, many of them so poor it makes your heart ache, with no education, no hope. When they don't understand something, they just hit it."

"You really care, don't you?" Reddman said.

"Of course I care." Brim picked up the telephone. "There is precious little I can do about it, but I care." He dialed a number. "This is Walter Brim. Bernie Lopes, please."

It took less than ten minutes for Reddman to drive to the edge of town in the 1974 Chevrolet Impala that Brim had said was his to use. He parked in the spacious lot next to the Justice Center, a sprawling one-story building with mud-brick walls, and went inside.

Two uniformed cops seemed to measure him for signs of toughness as he was buzzed into the Authorized Personnel Only section. He found Lopes in a small basement office with three metal desks. The chunky thirty-year-old Mexican, sitting behind one of the desks and talking on the telephone, waved as he entered and motioned him to sit down.

For the most part, Reddman liked cops. He liked their world of right and wrong and their no bullshit manner, even though he hated the mistakes they always made. He thought of the differences between cops and lawyers as he waited for Lopes to get off the telephone. In his world, the lawyers did ego numbers on one another, but in the cops' world, it wasn't that way. The street, where the shit happened, was raw and real, but the courtroom, where it got proved, was an arena where games were played.

I should have been a cop, he thought, making faces at Lopes. Still, the game had its own kind of excitement. He liked the skill involved in putting the right spin on the facts.

"How've you been? Still a grazer?" Lopes asked, slapping Reddman's hand as he hung up. "You haven't gained any weight, I see."

"You have," Reddman told him. "Which one of you is the desk?"

"Quick. Very quick. A sure enough by God lawyer. All mouth. Ready to try this mother?"

"Not even close."

"What the hell's wrong?" Lopes asked, leaning back in his chair, hands laced behind his head. "I mean, shit. It's a clear case of murder."

Reddman laughed. "Yeah. Clear as mud."

"You know something? I still don't understand the charge."

"What do you mean?"

"How can one death be charged two ways? Isn't logical. I mean, here you've got it charged as a vehicular homicide in one count and as murder in another. Doesn't it have to be one or the other?"

"No, it can be both."

"How?"

Reddman patiently explained it to him again. "Murder is a deliberate killing, with intent to kill, right? Vehicular homicide is driving—either recklessly or drunk—where the driving is the proximate cause of the killing." He looked at Lopes for a sign of understanding. "As long as one doesn't *exclude* the other, it can be both at the same time."

"Shit," Lopes said helplessly.

"Look, take it slow. It's possible, isn't it, for a person to have the intent to kill and also to be drunk? So he deliberately uses a car as the weapon."

"That would be murder!"

"Right. Now look at it through a different camera. Say you have a drunk driver with or without the intent to kill— in other words, forget all about intent to kill—and the guy gets in a wreck he would have avoided if he hadn't been drunk. Then what?"

Lopes thought a moment. "Vehicular homicide?"

"Now add the intent to kill."

"Shit," Lopes said. "I like smoking guns. What's on the agenda?"

"I'm going to need help," Reddman said. "Lots of it. How much time can you give me?"

"As much as you want. How come? I mean, when we were in Avalanche last winter, you said—"

"I know. Things have changed." Reddman considered telling him what had happened, but decided against it. "I'd like to go over the crime scene as soon as possible with the cops who worked the case. Like this afternoon, early. Can you set it up?"

"Should be able to," Lopes said. "Brenfleck and Judson, anyway. I don't know about Sergeant Donovan. One-thirty?"

"Good. We also need to go over the witness list and make sure we've got everybody subpoenaed and all the exhibits lined up."

"Okay." Lopes had taken out a legal pad.

"Then we interview witnesses. Tomorrow, if possible. I'll do the talking, but you'll have to be there."

"Why do you need me?"

"So if a witness changes his mind on the stand, I can prove through you what he said when we talked to him."

"What about discovery? If I take notes—"

"Who said anything about you taking notes? *I* take notes. The law says lawyer's notes aren't discoverable, don't ask me why. But we can still go over them before trial."

Lopes frowned. "Is that fair? I mean, sounds awful close to the line. You don't want that poor old cowboy—"

"Hey, I'm the lawyer, you're the cop, all right? If we do it any other way you're right, it's discoverable and Cole would ask for a continuance."

Lopes shrugged. "Okay, man."

"I'll meet you at the scene at one-thirty, all right? With as many of the cops as you can round up." Reddman got to his feet. "You know Sharon Sondenburg, don't you?"

"Sure do. She's a good buddy. High school and college."

"Ami O'Rourke's best friend, too. Can she help?"

"Depends," Lopes said. "What do you need?"

"Something Brim told me, about how Ami would wander into the street without looking. Could Sharon rebut that?"

"Don't waste your time," Lopes said.

"What do you mean?"

"In the first place, it's true. A lot of rubber left on Mears Street, cars on their noses, barely missing Ami, from what I hear. The other thing is, you don't want to put Sharon on the stand. No one would believe her."

"Why?"

"She was married to Johnny Blue, and he divorced her. You know what they say about a woman scorned."

CHAPTER
SIX

Fort Sundown State College, where Sharon Sondenburg taught, got its start in 1854 as an Indian trading post. When the Indians realized what was happening to their land, they became hostile, and the post was converted into an army fort. After they were subdued, it was turned into a school for Indian boys, and finally was incorporated into the state college system. Originally built in a valley thirty miles from Muldoon, the small institution moved to its "new" campus—on top of a table mesa stretching along the city of Muldoon's eastern boundary—in the 1920s.

Because of its idyllic location, the college attracted a topnotch faculty. It also developed a reputation as a party school: skiing, mountaineering, hang-gliding, drugs-in-the-wilderness. Among students, it was known as Peyote State.

To the locals, the college was a mixed blessing. It infused money into the economy and provided an educational opportunity for those who could afford it; but the campus also attracted students from other states, and the homogeneity of attitude that characterized Muldoon and Sopris County started to crack. The cracks were attributed to the flakes at the college.

Sharon Sondenburg had no problem with the change in attitude. Her own personal world had been shattered shortly after high school. Her life had started out well enough. As Muldoon High School's prettiest girl, she had done the expected thing and married the greatest athlete the town of Muldoon had ever produced. Johnny Blue had graduated two years ahead of her.

But she and Johnny Blue did not live happily ever after. The brutality and violence she encountered were sudden and totally unexpected. As his sweetheart, she had found him wild and excitingly dangerous, but as his wife, she became the recipient of his secret rage. Once her parents' mountain cabin had been thoroughly trashed by vandals, and everyone in the family had felt violated. Blue abruptly made Sharon feel like that about herself—as though she'd been thoroughly trashed. But she was too proud to let anyone else see it. To the town, Blue was the quintessential cowboy, the reality that kept the myth alive, and Sharon also believed in the myth. He had already achieved national prominence as a rodeo star. Of course, he wasn't perfect— no one was perfect—but the young Mrs. Blue knew she should remain by his side.

But she could not stay with him, any more than she could show anyone—even her mother—the bruises on her breasts, thighs, and buttocks. Confused, torn, and friendless, she ran away. She couldn't stay away, however, for all the reasons that had been turned into clichés by country singers. The land she had been raised on was part of her blood. Seven months later—overweight, blotchy, tortured—she returned.

America's Number One Cowboy was revolted by the change in his wife's appearance. Reconciliation was out of the question, and he quickly got a divorce. Sondenburg found refuge with her parents, who didn't understand, but didn't need to. She enrolled at the college, driven by a fierce desire to make sense out of herself and her past.

The path took unexpected turns as she dug into her self, questioning all her inherited values. She reaffirmed many of them but painfully discarded many others. She took a degree in English literature with a minor in psychology at

Fort Sundown, and afterward wrote her doctoral thesis on comparative mythology at the University of Colorado. Then she came back to Muldoon and a job. Her confidence and health had been restored, but her personal journey toward self-understanding had just begun. She didn't know where the path would take her next.

Sondenburg pulled the key to her office out of her back pocket and juggled books as she opened the door. Three students waited in the hall to see her, as did Dave Reddman. She nodded carefully at Reddman and smiled at the others. "Hello, children," she said pleasantly to all of them. "Who's been here the longest?"

Reddman stepped forward. He wore a coat and tie, so he didn't look like a student, but he didn't look like a lawyer, either. "Me," he said. "I've been here an hour." He followed her into her office, shutting the door behind him.

Sondenburg took her time. This asshole was back, she thought, placing the books on a corner of her desk. She looked in the small mirror on her desk, smoothed her hair, and rubbed her lips together, then sat down, keeping the desk between them. "What do you want?"

"Look, I'm sorry about last night," Reddman said. "Can I sit down?"

She shrugged her shoulders. "Sure. Don't get comfortable, though. You aren't staying long."

"Why didn't you tell me you were married to Johnny Blue?" He squatted on the chair.

The poor boy sounded like some forlorn searcher on a daytime soap, Sharon thought. "I thought you knew. Besides, it's part of my life I try to forget."

"It's a part of your life I'd like to find out about."

"Why?" she demanded. "It doesn't have anything to do with him murdering Ami. And it's very private."

"You called him a psychopath last night. Is he?"

"Yes."

"How do you know? Do you know what a psychopath is?"

"Sure do, honey. It's a personality disorder. Antisocial, aggressive behavior. Johnny's as mean as a rabid dog."

Reddman leaned back in his chair, relaxing. "Maybe it's murder after all," he said. "Next question. Has he ever been diagnosed as a psychopath?"

"Yes."

"By whom?"

"Me."

"What are your qualifications?"

"I'm a woman. I minored in psychology. I lived with him for three months."

"Not good enough. You also hate him, don't you? Don't women hate men who leave them?"

"He didn't leave me, I left him. But I hate him all right. He beat me, raped me, and murdered Ami."

Reddman smiled. He felt better and better about the case. "Tell me about it."

"Why? You can't use it as evidence." She wondered suddenly if Reddman was a creep. "I mean, what do you want? The graphic details? Is this the kind of thing you get off on?"

"No! Damn it, I need to hate him, too. I need to know!" He leaned forward. "Look, can I see you again? Today? Tonight? I promise to be a perfect gentleman."

Damn you, she thought, staring at him with wide eyes. For a moment she felt a purely physical attraction, and it confused her until she realized what it was. She pushed it out of her mind, knowing she didn't have time for *that* kind of bullshit. "All right, if you'd like."

Reddman smiled at her. God, you are beautiful, he thought, making himself look away. "Thanks." He got up. "You name it, okay? When and where?"

"Why don't you come out to my place around six o'clock tonight?"

"How do I get there?"

She gave him directions, then smiled him toward the door. "Wear old clothes."

"Why?"

"You can help me train a horse."

Cops and robbers was a different game from the one you read about, Reddman thought, waiting in front of the Sopris County courthouse for the cops to show up. He glanced at his watch: twenty minutes to two. They should have met him at one-thirty.

He pulled a diagram marked Accident Scene out of his file. Why hadn't it been labeled Murder Scene? he wondered, knowing what Cole would do if given the chance: "See, ladies and gentlemen? *They* thought it was an accident, too!" Reddman walked between two cars parked diagonally in front of the courthouse.

He located himself on the diagram, then tried to put himself back to the day it happened. He stood where Ami O'Rourke might have stood before starting her final walk across the street. The same blue sky, the same sun, the same mountains reaching up in the distance. Had she seen them? He tried to feel and see what she had felt and seen. Yes. She might not have looked at them, but she'd have been aware of them. She'd have known they were there. A car went by, heading north toward the Mears Street hill. She'd have seen the car, too. He started jaywalking across Mears.

She'd have glanced both ways, Reddman thought, even with a stack of books in her arms. He cradled his arms as though carrying something in them. Then he walked toward the small brownish storefront on the other side of the street. The public defender's office was sandwiched between two larger buildings: an office building, and a savings and loan. He read the palms of his hands, as though they were an open book, but was still aware of traffic, and waited for another car to go by.

Small towns. Stop signs controlled the access to Mears Street from the side streets; there were no traffic lights. There weren't that many cars on the road. He glanced toward the Mears Street hill—but it felt all wrong. She should have seen Blue coming, he told himself, or at least have been aware of him. Especially in that pickup truck.

A car started downward from where Reddman supposed Blue had waited, and Reddman counted the seconds until it went by. Less than five. How could a person jaywalking across the street not be aware of a truck? And how could the driver of a truck fail to see someone in the road?

He considered conducting tests, to demonstrate the amount of time involved and, more importantly, to show the speed of Blue's truck at the moment of impact. He knew it could be demonstrated and knew, too, he should have done it long before now. The victim's body had been dragged through the tire well three times before finally falling away from the truck. It wouldn't be hard to calculate the amount of resistance and the amount of force needed to overcome it. "Shit," he said to himself, feeling that familiar twinge in his stomach over something he neglected to do in trial preparation. "Hey, Trigge, I told you already. You're right."

He waited five minutes longer, then walked to the D.A.'s office to find out what had happened to the cops.

"Message from Bernie Lopes, Mr. Reddman," Nancy said, looking up from her desk as Reddman entered. "He was called out on a robbery. He wants to know if nine o'clock tomorrow morning will work."

Great, Reddman thought. At this rate, I should have been here a month ago. "Tell him yes," he said, then asked her to pull all the files she could find on Johnny Blue. Psychopaths leave tracks, he reasoned. If the man is really psychopathic, he should have a history. Right here in Muldoon.

Nancy gave him four files, including the current one. Reddman sat down at a worktable and opened the first one, a juvenile delinquency petition, fifteen years old, charging Blue with assaulting an Indian. Judging by the mild disposition when contrasted with the severity of the victim's injuries—a broken jaw and two broken ribs—the incident occurred before assaulting Indians was considered a crime. He grabbed the second file. It was also an assault, characterized as a barroom brawl, involving the vicious beating of a hippie. The case had been plea-bargained to disorderly conduct because the victim couldn't be found.

So Blue had left tracks, Reddman thought. He knew that the record was often just the tip of an iceberg. He liked the feeling of anger that had started to glow in his stomach.

The third file was the drunk driving case that Ami O'Rourke had tried, and lost. That was the one and only time Blue had gone to jail. It was the thickest file, demonstrating how hard Ami had fought for her client. The deputy who prosecuted the case had filled the file with yellow sheets of paper covered with illegible notes.

Reddman turned to the murder file. He expected it to be a mere duplicate of his own, but it contained more. In addition to the pleadings and motions, there was a disorganized hodgepodge of notes by Walter Brim, copies of appellate court cases, and—stuffed in a manila envelope—newspaper clippings from the *Muldoon Journal*. There ought to be FBI and CBI rap sheets in here somewhere, Reddman thought.

Just then he saw a pleading he'd never seen before. It was a motion to suppress all evidence, based on lack of probable cause to arrest Johnny Blue. It claimed that all the evidence seized was tainted and couldn't be used because of the illegal arrest. Shit, Reddman thought to himself. If the judge granted this motion, there wouldn't be a case!

"Mr. Brim in?" he blurted to Nancy, jumping to his feet. He wanted to grab Brim by the throat and ask him how come NASP hadn't gotten a copy of the motion!

The woman looked startled.

"Never mind." Reddman scooped up the murder files and headed for the door. "I'll be at the courthouse if anybody's looking."

Frankie Rommel had warned him always to start at the beginning. Get the original file from the clerk of the court, she had told him, and make sure you have a copy of everything in it, because you can't depend on the local D.A. to forward all the pleadings, and you certainly can't depend on the defense lawyer. And when the fur starts to fly, you don't need surprises. Reddman trotted back to the courthouse and ran up the steps to the clerk's office, where he asked for the *People v. Blue* file.

He felt as though he was tripping over his stomach as he thumbed through the pleadings and compared them to the ones in his file. Everything checked out except for the motion to suppress all evidence. It was a good motion, too. Predictably, it enshrined the Constitution as it railed against the oppressive hand of authority and the arbitrary arrest of decent citizens. The only effective way to keep us safe from such conduct, the motion claimed, was to refuse to allow the fruits of such conduct to be used as evidence in courts of law. It had been filed three months ago, and a certificate of mailing showed a copy had been mailed to Brim but not to NASP. Games, Reddman wondered, or an honest mistake? The defense should have mailed a copy to NASP, although notice to the D.A. was enough. And Brim's office hadn't mailed a copy to NASP, either, probably because it assumed the defense had done so.

Either way, the motion had to be decided before the trial. And it hadn't even been set for a hearing! Reddman made a copy for his file, then asked the clerk if he could see the judge.

"Sure, honey," the elderly woman said, smiling. The skin around her eyes crinkled, a bit like worn leather. "He's in there where you was this morning, talking to Saul. Just go ahead and knock."

The door was open. Reddman could see Landry behind his executive desk talking to Cole, who lounged in a chair. Didn't Cole have anything to do except talk to the judge? Reddman wondered, knocking on the door.

Landry looked up. "Well! Come in, young man," he said heartily. "We were just talking about you."

The juices in Reddman's body warmed up, alerting him to danger. "Judge, do you suppose we could get the court reporter in here?" he asked, entering what had the sudden appearance of a lion's den. "I think it might be a good idea if we went on the record."

"Oh, ho! You do, do you?" Landry boomed. "We'll have to wait until Thursday, then, my good fellow. My reporter is in Utah, rafting down the Colorado River."

"Wish I was with him," Reddman said, trying to make the best of it. He sat down next to Cole. "I'm concerned about a pending motion, Judge," he continued. "It's one I just found out about. If you grant it, there won't be a trial on the homicide counts, because the people won't have any evidence."

"What motion is that?" Landry asked. "Do you have the file there? Let me look at it."

"He means my motion to suppress," Cole said. "Filed it three months ago."

"Why are you just now finding out about it, Mr. Reddman?" Landry asked, flipping through the file.

"I never got a copy, Judge."

"Yes. Well, whose fault is that? The certificate of mailing shows quite clearly that the district attorney's office received one. Didn't he send you a copy? Are you accusing Mr. Brim's office of something here?"

"No, sir." Reddman worked hard to keep his voice smooth and confident. "I'm not accusing anyone of anything, but NASP had entered the case by that time, and usually the defense sends us—"

"So," Cole said, glaring at the judge. "Reddman's not accusing anyone of anything, but it's my fault. Isn't bad enough the defendant has to deal with the state of Colorado. It now has to deal with *two* accusers!"

"Wait a minute," Reddman said, smiling and trying to touch Cole's arm. Cole jerked it out of the way. "Judge, I'm not saying the defense had a legal burden here," Reddman said. "I'm just telling you what happened. If it wasn't such a good motion, I wouldn't be worried about it. But it needs to be heard before the trial, and the trial is less than two weeks away. Can we set it for hearing sometime this week?"

"Confess it, if you like it so much," Cole snapped. "Save us all a lot of trouble. Then you can dismiss the case, lack of evidence, go back to Denver, everybody's happy." He grinned broadly at Landry.

"The motion isn't that good," Reddman said, doing his best to grin at Landry, too.

Landry read it over, shaking his head. "It wouldn't be possible to hear it this week," he said. "I have no reporter. But you needn't worry, young man. It's my practice to hear pending motions immediately before the commencement of the trial. It saves a lot of time. Then the whole case can be telescoped into one or two weeks, don't you see? Witnesses only have to be flown in once, that sort of thing. Unless you violently oppose the practice, that's what I propose to do here."

"What about the jury panel, Judge?" Reddman asked. "All of the prospective jurors would be in the courtroom and would hear the motion, wouldn't they? That could taint the whole panel."

"No, no, no," Landry gushed. "Don't you see, we pick the jury *before* the motion is heard. It rarely takes more than half a day to pick a jury in my court. I'm able to move things right along, don't you see? Then we excuse the jury and tell them to report back the following day. After they leave, I hear the motion. If need be, we have them come back the next day and the next, until I've made a ruling."

Landry and Cole looked at each other, and Reddman sensed a trap. "Once the jury has been sworn, jeopardy attaches, doesn't it?"

"Yes. Of course."

"Well, if you rule against me on the motion, leaving me without any evidence, what can I do? You'd dismiss the case for lack of evidence, wouldn't you, and discharge the jury?"

"I suppose so," Landry said slowly.

"I'd be in a box, Judge. It wouldn't do me any good to appeal your ruling, because the defendant can't be put in jeopardy a second time. So the people would lose."

Cole shoved his chair around to face Reddman. "Listen, the judge told you when we'll have the hearing," he growled. "I can't get ready this week anyway, what do you expect? You wanted things any different than the way we do them, you should have set the hearing right after I filed to suppress!" He sat back, plainly disgusted. "You come in here with two weeks to go and start throwing your weight around. That the way you do things in Denver?"

Reddman's face burned. He took a deep breath. "Judge—"

"Now, young man, don't get angry," Landry cautioned.

"Your Honor, all I said was 'Judge.' I know—"

Landry suddenly jumped to his feet. "That's quite enough, Mr. Reddman. It isn't always a question of *what* a person says, but his manner as he speaks. I find yours belligerent and offensive!"

"What?" Reddman asked incredulously. He didn't know what he'd done wrong. "Excuse me, Your Honor, but—"

"I suggest you apologize to both Mr. Cole and me."

"Apologize! For what?"

"You are suggesting that some devious kind of trickery has gone on here, are you not? Some complicity between Mr. Cole and me? You're saying that we would get a jury, then grant the defendant's motion to suppress, leaving you with no evidence, no case?"

"You betcha he is!" Cole glowered, lips drawn over his teeth. "Little snot."

Reddman jerked toward Cole, then tried to smile. He knew he had to get out of there. He stood up. "Excuse me, Judge. Later, Saul." He backed toward the door.

"What of your apology?" Landry demanded. "In my twelve years on the bench in this district, I have *never* been so insulted! I want an apology!"

Stuff it, you old bastard, Reddman thought angrily. "No," he said to the commanding figure. "Not at this time, sir." He shut the door behind him and ran for the D.A.'s office, not knowing where else to go. On the way, his mood

70

changed from anger to panic. What the hell had gone wrong?

Nancy lifted her head as he hurriedly entered, then continued typing. Reddman stood uncertainly in the reception area, needing to talk to someone! He could hear Brim in his office, patiently explaining to a merchant why he couldn't prosecute a bad check case. But Reddman didn't want to talk to the D.A. Brim should have sent NASP a copy of the motion, and Reddman was afraid if he saw him then, he might kill him. "Is Turner in?" he asked Nancy, knowing he was interrupting her, not caring.

"No."

"I'll be in his office."

He sat in the deputy's chair and tried to think. Should I call Trigge? he wondered, reaching for the phone. What if Landry had already called him, demanding an apology from NASP and a new lawyer? He thought of calling one of the other lawyers at NASP, but decided against it. One of them—he didn't know which one—was the reason he was still on probation. Besides, I didn't do anything wrong! he assured himself. I'm glad I didn't apologize to that old bastard!

Then he jumped to his feet. "I'll be at the public defender's office," he said to Nancy, hoping that Zack Wolfman—the subject of a host of war stories he had heard—would listen.

"Chrissake," Wolfman said to him fifteen minutes later. Reddman had been cooling his heels in a conference room by charging back and forth like a panther in a cage when the former Denver Broncos linebacker opened the door. "Take it easy, man!" the thick-set Sioux Indian continued, beads of sweat forming in his short-cropped blue-black hair. He held his hand high, thumb up, for a "brother" grip. "Zack Wolfman. You're Davey Reddman, right?"

"Yes."

"Power down, man. Never met a D.A. yet who didn't think everything was survival, like life and death."

Reddman glared at the man's amiable face, but took his

hand. "Hey, man, I don't need your bullshit philosophy," he said. "This place is a zoo!"

Wolfman laughed, then sat down. "Had a run-in with the judge, right?" he asked. "That's the only game in town, man. Better bend over and take it right in the ass. Heal up later. Then go home and kick the dog. That's what they're for. Hey. I hear you're Joe Reddman's kid." He waited expectantly for a reaction.

"Shit!"

"In fact, I hear you ain't even a real Indian," Wolfman taunted. "Cole says he's got you pegged. Says you'll be easy because you get steamed real fast and he's gonna dance circles around you!" He jumped up and began comically shuffling around in circles like a schoolboy pretending to be a warrior.

"What the hell is this?" Reddman demanded. "A test? Cole said that to you?"

"Yeah, I think, or else I heard it at lunch. You're news, man. Trial of the century in Sopris County. Like Clarence Darrow, come down to do Scopes. Concessionaires, T-shirts, people traveling fifty miles, all the way from Fools Gold!" He grinned, then sat down again, crushing the chair.

Reddman masked an urge to walk out. "She was your deputy, right? Ami?"

"Yeah."

"You want me to win this thing or lose it?"

"What the hell do you think?" Wolfman demanded. "I want you to grind that bastard into paste, man. Turn him into tortillas. Why do you ask?"

"You're a damn public defender, if you'll pardon the expression. The ones I've known all have their balls on crooked. They have a twisted sense of justice. They're legal perverts."

Wolfman's eyes had grown large. "You skinny little veggie!" he said. "You pedal-pumping weirdo! What the hell are you talking about, man? I played for the Broncos! Shit. I ain't no pervert!"

Reddman's mouth dropped open. Then he found himself trying to choke down laughter. "Three years was all you played. Big deal. If you'd been any good, you'd be on TV, wired for sound."

Wolfman's huge face broke into laughter. "Hey," he said. "I heard you was kind of an asshole, but maybe you're Joe's kid after all."

"You know my old man?"

"Yeah, I met him once. We got drunk." Wolfman squinted across the table. "How the hell did his kid turn into a D.A.?"

Reddman stiffened. He wondered why everyone liked old Joe except his sons. "I need help," he said. "Maybe you can explain what happened to me." He told Wolfman of his encounter with Cole and Landry. "Was I wrong? Do I apologize?"

"Fuck no, man, you wasn't wrong. You gotta stand up to those guys." His expression showed respect.

"How do I get the motion set for hearing?"

Wolfman shrugged. "Probably you don't. You're just gonna have to tough that one out."

"You mean beard him on the record, right?" Reddman asked, slumping against the table. "I really hate taking on judges."

"Hey, on my side of the street we do it for a living. But you're right. It isn't any fun."

Reddman got up. "Thanks. Sometime soon, could we have lunch? I need to know more about Ami."

"You want to know Ami, come over to my house for dinner. Meet Timmy, her son. How about tonight?"

"I'd love it, but not tonight. Tomorrow?"

Wolfman got up. With him on his feet, the room seemed smaller. "Tomorrow's good, too. I got lots of smoke."

"Come on man, I don't use the stuff."

"Even when nobody's looking?" Wolfman looked at his watch. "Shit. Never enough time. Goddam white man invention anyway. Who needs it?"

CHAPTER SEVEN

The directions to the Sondenburg ranch, a small for-ty-acre property off a county highway, had not mentioned a fork in the road. Reddman took the wrong turn and didn't find the place until six-thirty. The ranch house stood two hundred yards from the highway at the end of a tree-lined drive. He saw Sharon's mobile home in a corner of the property, protected from the sun by leafy maple trees. Reddman drove to the corral next to the trailer house. She was in the center of the corral, on the end of a longe line, working a horse.

"Hi," she said amiably. The line between trainer and horse looked like an umbilical connection. A thin whip in Sondenburg's left hand flicked toward the animal's flank as the horse stepped smartly in a circle. "This is Half Ton. Isn't he beautiful?"

Reddman, leaning against a rail, stared at her rather than the horse. She wore a brightly colored western shirt and tight denim pants. She glowed. "Yes," he said, clearing his throat. "Sorry I'm late. I got lost."

"Doesn't matter. This old pony is ready for a rest any-way." She tied him to a pole, brushed her hands against her thighs, and came over to Reddman. "Short pants?"

74

she asked, looking him over. "That's what you call old clothes?"

"It's all I've got."

"Couldn't stop off and get some Levi's?"

"You said old clothes, not new Levi's."

She climbed the rail fence and jumped down. Reddman was impressed. "Every time I try that with cowboy boots on, the heels catch on something and I do a face plant," he said.

"Poor baby. Come in. Have some coffee."

He followed her up the steps and into the trailer. The door opened into a surprisingly spacious living room, nicely furnished with rough-hewn but comfortable-looking wooden chairs and sofa. Blazing Navajo throw rugs were scattered over the burnished hardwood floor. A counter, made of pine, separated the living room from the kitchen. "Sit down. I'll pour you a cup," she said.

"This is really nice," Reddman said. "Like the lobby at the old Boulderado Hotel."

"Except you can play basketball there and you better not try that here." She put clay mugs with bright Navajo designs on the counter and poured. "Take anything?"

"No, thanks. Why a wheelchair?" Reddman asked, noticing a collapsible metal wheelchair, pushed under the counter and out of the way.

"It belongs to Jed Turner. He's a friend of mine."

"Good friend?"

"Very." Reddman waited for her to tell him more. "You don't have any hair on your legs," she said. "Are you a cyclist?"

"Yes." She obviously did not want to talk about Jed Turner. "Pretty serious, even."

"Are you going to race in the Iron Horse?" She sat easily on a stool on the kitchen side of the counter.

"I hope. It'll depend on the trial."

"Can't be too serious if that trial could get in your way." She smiled at him. "You have beautiful legs," she said with simple appreciation. "Is that why the cyclists shave them? So everyone can see and admire them?"

"No. When you crash and get a little road rash, you want to be able to keep the cuts clean. Hair gets in the way."

She frowned and shuddered, as though feeling the cuts. "That's no fun."

"Do you like training horses?"

"I love it," she told him. "Horses are such wonderful animals, so simple-hearted. It's hard to explain."

"What's so special about a simple heart? You could say the same thing about a cow, couldn't you? Or a pig? But nobody trains cows or pigs."

She laughed. "You're wrong, of course, but I get the point. Maybe there's more to a horse than a simple heart."

"For a teacher of literature, you have a decided twang. Did you know that?"

Sondenburg shrugged. "When I'm at the ranch, honey, I just let it all hang out." She looked at her watch. "I don't want to leave Half Ton too long. We'd better get started."

Reddman wanted to tell her how beautiful she was. Instead, he positioned his legal pad on the countertop. "I think if you know what I'm looking for, what I'm trying to do, it'll save time," he said.

"I hope what you're trying to do is convict that son of a bitch of murder," she said. "And I hope what you're looking for is ammunition."

"Well . . . more than ammunition. Understanding. I want to know what makes him tick."

"Why?"

"A lot of reasons. If I'm going to show that jury he murdered Ami, I need to know him. Inside and out. If he takes the witness stand—and he probably will—I want to know how to cross-examine him."

"Okay," Sondenburg said, "how's this for starters? His heart is made of ice. He can feel his own pain, but nobody else's."

Reddman frowned. Her anger pulsed out waves of heat. "Can he kill?"

"I don't think he'd bat an eye," she said. "Wouldn't surprise me if he's killed before."

"Hey, that's heavy stuff. How could he and get away with it?"

"For a D.A., you're awfully naive. More than a million girls run away from home every year. The bodies of young women are found alongside roads and in shallow graves all the time." She stood up angrily, then reached for the coffee pot as though needing to give her hands something to do.

"Thanks," Reddman said as she topped off his cup. "Do you really think he's killed others?"

"As I said, it wouldn't surprise me."

Maybe Lopes was right, Reddman thought, wondering if her hatred would taint everything she had to say. "Why wouldn't it surprise you?"

"Because there are so many girls out there who are easy to kill, and I think Johnny could be one of the animals doing it."

Reddman was tempted to ask her what television shows she'd been watching. "Anything's possible."

"You don't believe me," she said with exasperation. "Listen to me. Johnny Blue is thoroughly, totally, unredeemably bad."

"How do you know that? What did he do to you?"

"I told you before. He raped me. He beat up on me." She wrapped her hands around her mug, as though they were cold and needed the warmth.

It didn't seem to Reddman that he was getting anywhere. "I'm sorry," he said. "I don't feel it yet. Can I ask you questions about it?"

"Fire away."

"When were you married to him?"

"Right out of high school, almost thirteen years ago. I was eighteen and he was twenty."

"Was he in rodeo then?"

"Oh, yes. He was already a big star. He was beautiful—

just beautiful—to watch. I have never seen anyone before or since who could stick on a bull like Johnny."

"So you traveled to a lot of rodeos?"

"No. He'd busted some ribs two days before we were married, and by the time he was ready to go back, it was all over."

"How long were you together?"

"Three months. That was all I could handle." Her eyes slowly reddened as she protected herself from the memories. "I ran away."

"Where did you go?"

"Denver, where I stayed with a girlfriend—until he found out and came looking." Her manner changed. She seemed literally to shrink, like a turtle withdrawing into its shell. "So I moved to a fleabag hotel, which was all I could afford, and tried putting myself together. But it just got worse." She looked beyond him, unaware of the tears that slid down her cheeks. "I felt so—trashed. It was just such a shock."

"What?"

Her hand wiped at her face. "Do you really want to know?"

"Yes."

"All right." Her voice was distant, as though she were in a trance or chaneling some being from outer space. "Johnny taught me I wasn't a person. I was a cunt." Her mouth curved into an odd smile.

"What?"

"I found out I was a cunt. I discovered I wasn't this beautiful person my daddy and mommy loved. To one-half of the human race—the men—I was something else." She smiled. "Something they wanted and loathed at the same time. They'd buy me so they could beat me, and that's what I was."

Reddman stared at her. "What are you telling me?"

"You wanted to know what happened, and I'm trying to explain. I was raped by my husband, this big powerful man I thought I loved. It was awful."

Reddman found himself wondering about his own sensitivity, or lack of it. He did not know what to say. He would have liked to touch her, but hesitated to do so, "Look, I'm sorry. I guess those things happen," he said.

She came out of the trance. "That's right, honey, shit happens. It happened to me and it happens to millions of women every year, and I know how they feel about themselves." A spider started across the counter, and both of them watched. "When a woman starts in feeling that way, she's liable to do anything." She slid a piece of paper under the spider. "Do you know what I'm saying?"

"What did you do?"

"I ate, mainly. Guess I was lucky." She got up and went to the door. She opened it and blew the spider off the paper, then sat down again. "But I'll never forget all those women on the streets, with horrible ideas about themselves. Hundreds and thousands of them in big towns and little towns all over the place." She looked at him over her coffee. "They don't all make it home, Mr. Prosecutor. Nobody knows what happens to them, either—except the ones they find in ditches and shallow graves."

Reddman avoided her eyes. He remembered two brutal kidnap-rape-murders he'd prosecuted and the questions he'd had about the victims. A part of him had always blamed the women for putting themselves in places where they shouldn't have been. "Can you tell me what he did to you?" he asked.

"Why?"

"Maybe it's because I need to know in my own mind," Reddman said. "A lot of the time, well, it doesn't seem that way to a man."

"You don't know what you're asking me to do. You want me to bring those memories back and put them into words and then tell a virtual stranger about them." She looked away from him. "I don't know you that well. I don't know anybody that well."

"It won't go any further, Sharon. I promise."

"Mind if I smoke?"

"I don't mind," Reddman said.

She reached under the counter and pulled out a pouch. "Me and Grandma Moses. We smoke pipes," she said, tamping marijuana into the small bowl of a well-cured pipe. She lit it and inhaled deeply, holding the smoke in her lungs. "Want a hit?"

"No, thanks."

She took another drag, then smothered the smoke. "The first time it happened, I wasn't even sure myself whether it was rape. I was so young then." She shook her head. "We'd been to a barn dance about a month after we were married, and were coming home. I'd danced with some boys, and it made him mad. I didn't care—until he drove us out to Sullivan Lake and jerked me out of the car and said, 'Now you pay.'

"I didn't know what he was talking about. Pay for what? He said, 'You know.' And he slammed me up against the fender of the car"—her face started to break—"and he ripped my skirt up and tore my pants down. I hit him." She touched her forehead with the fingers of her right hand. "He grabbed my throat, slammed my head against the hood, like to broke my back. I couldn't breathe." She tried to laugh. "He said, real quiet, 'Don't do that.' And you know what I said?"

"No."

"I said, 'I'm sorry,' " Her shoulders began to shake. "Then he spun me around—he wasn't being gentle—mashing my face into the car metal, and said, 'Spread 'em.' " Her face had contorted into a terrible mask. "I was so scared."

"Okay," Reddman said, wanting her to stop.

"So he dropped his trousers and pushed in and said, 'You like that, don't you, baby?' and squeezed my neck so hard I finally said yes, and he said, 'Let's try it up here, then,' and—"

"Hey, I'm sorry," Reddman said, touching her arm. She recoiled, frozen. She walked woodenly to the sink, turned on the water, and dabbed at her face. "I'm sorry I put you through that," he said.

"Want to hear more?" she asked, facing him. The color slowly returned to her face. "There's lots more."

"Did you tell anyone?"

"I tried a couple of times. But I couldn't. This was almost thirteen years ago, and I was the prettiest, dumbest thing you ever saw, right out of high school. I just couldn't."

"Have you ever told anyone?"

"Not really. I tried to tell my girlfriend in Denver. And Ami. But all I could say was 'Be careful.' " She picked up the coffee pot. "More?"

He held his hand over his cup. "So then when you ran away, he came after you?"

Sharon nodded. "Cheryl—my girlfriend—said he called her, just as nice and polite as anything, wanted to know where I was and why I'd left, like he was all broken up over my leaving, you know." She spoke quickly, and laughed unpleasantly. "Cheryl said 'Don't you know?' and he said 'No, everything was goin' so good.' He almost broke her heart, she told me." Sondenburg laughed. "About then is when I ran out of money. I couldn't stay away anyhow, so I came back home."

"Did he try anything after you got back?"

"I was fat as a pig. That's why so many women overeat, so they can take themselves out of the meat market." She leaned against the stove, appraising him now. "He took one look at me, and it was all over. So I made sure I stayed fat until the divorce was final."

Reddman wondered what she was thinking. "You're not fat now," he said. "In fact, you're beautiful."

Sharon looked cooly at him. "Meaning?"

"Has he tried anything with you since—well, you got beautiful?"

She smiled at Reddman, knowing he meant it. "No, he won't either."

"Why not?"

"He knows I can shoot, too. Not as well as he can, but when a man is close enough, you don't have to be real accurate. I'd kill him."

Sharon also told Reddman that she had tried to warn Blue's second wife, Alicia, before they were married. She was certain the woman's life had been sheer hell. This was useful stuff, Reddman thought. If Cole decides to put Alicia on the stand—a defense lawyer ploy designed to generate sympathy—Reddman could take her on cross-examination and keep her talking as long as possible. From Reddman's point of view, it would be a no-lose situation. She would be expected to help Blue, so if she lived up to expectations, it wouldn't help him that much. But through her, some of the jurors might come to know the real Johnny Blue.

Twenty minutes later, Reddman drove toward the hotel in the cool, clean evening air. The sun dipped toward the mountains to the west, and the sky overhead—a deep high-altitude blue—looked alive. That's the price you pay when you move from the boonies into the city, he thought. The air. He wondered if he, like Sharon Sondenburg, would move back to the country someday.

He tried to sort out what she had told him. There was nothing he could use as evidence, but all of it helped: rape, shock, psychopathology, a murderous heart. As a prosecutor, he knew that not many people had the capacity to kill. But those who did—and who knew it—were a breed apart. He didn't doubt Sharon Sondenburg at all, in her assessment of either Johnny Blue or herself.

"Good," he said out loud. "I can hate the son of a bitch." He'd been in the business long enough to know it helped if you could hate the defendant.

Trials could get complicated, Reddman thought, relishing his craft. He wondered if he could map out a strategy that would compel the defense to put Alicia Blue on the stand.

Reddman still didn't have enough evidence. His prosecutorial burden was to prove murder beyond a reasonable doubt, and in spite of his interview with Sharon Sondenburg, he still realized that Ami's death could have been an accident. That's what half the town thinks, Reddman reminded himself. They still think it was an accident that's been blown out of proportion.

He wondered, too, who Jed Turner was. Where had he heard that name? What did Sharon mean by "very good friend"?

It was time to put all of it out of his mind, he thought, hurrying toward town while there was still light. He wanted to find a lightly traveled road with some good hills, where he could ride until his legs burned off and he could empty his body of everything but pain.

The face of his father blew across his mind. Why do I hate you so much, you old bastard? he asked himself. Is it because I know you can kill? What's the difference between you and Johnny Blue?

Am I the same way?"

CHAPTER EIGHT

On Wednesday morning, twelve days before trial, Reddman met with the officers in front of the courthouse. They were Sergeant Jack Donovan, built like a nail, State Patrol; Corporal David Brenfleck, who wore his cherubic, baby face like a mask, Muldoon City Police; Patrolman Byron "Rip" Judson, a large, farm-hardened country boy, Muldoon City Police; and Bernie Lopes. Donovan was the only person in uniform.

Reddman wanted to go over the scene a step at a time, looking for something—anything—he could use. As he explained to the officers, evidence in the form of testimony was different from evidence in the form of clues. They'd collected clues, but now he needed their help to turn them into persuasive, dramatic testimony.

The men trooped up the Mears Street hill and stood at the spot where Blue had been parked. When they looked back, it was apparent that Blue could easily have watched Ami leave the courthouse in time to roll down the hill and hit her.

"What about pictures?" Lopes suggested. "Should we shoot a couple posed shots and blow them up to eight-by-ten glossies?"

"They never work out," Reddman said. "I don't know

what it is about photographs, but you need a magnifying glass to identify people."

Donovan agreed. "Things look awful small in distance shots."

"So take a good look," Reddman told them. "I want all of you to be able to tell that jury what the scene looks like from up here."

"Hey, Sarge?" Judson asked. He spoke softly, as though hoping no one else would hear him ask a stupid question. "Something I don't get. How come she didn't see that big old truck?"

Donovan rubbed his jaw. "I don't know," he said. "Seems like she shoulda seen it in time to get out of the way, don't it?"

Reddman heard the exchange. The same question troubled him. "Any ideas?" he asked the others.

"Well, she was reading, I think," Brenfleck asked. "I mean, we found a lot of books and stuff. Files."

"That'd make it her fault, wouldn't it?" Judson pursued.

"Hey!" Reddman exclaimed. "Good point!"

"What?"

"This. If you're talking accident, the fact that she was reading might make it her fault. But not if you're talking murder." He scribbled in his pad. "Brenfleck," he said, looking up. "Let's go over what happened when you saw him up here."

"It's in the report," Brenfleck said, looking at his watch. He had better things to do than waste his time with this smooth-looking lawyer from Denver.

Reddman was aware of Brenfleck's attitude and rankled by it. However, he needed Brenfleck more than the small cop needed him. "I know," Reddman said, locating Brenfleck's report of his initial contact with Blue. "Here's what you say: 'Approximately seventeen-oh-six, while on routine patrol, Reporting Officer (RO) observed a Dodge pickup high rider parked on Mears Street hill between Fourth and Fifth southbound. The truck was known to RO to belong to Johnny Blue, who was known to RO to have lost his licence. The truck was occupied by Johnny Blue. Upon questioning, suspect denied driving his truck to that location.' ''

"See? It's all there," Brenfleck said.

"Well, but you know, case closed?" Reddman smiled carefully, trying to keep the sarcasm out of his voice. "Didn't you ask him how the truck got there?"

"Why would I do that?"

Reddman tried to keep his patience. "Just to satisfy your curiosity." He told himself to take it easy. "Hey, it could be important. How do you think he got there?"

"I think he said his wife left it there. What difference does it make?"

"Say that again?"

"He said his wife left it there, I think."

"Good!" Reddman wrote himself another note. "Anything else?"

"He told me how much fun he had in jail. You know what? I think he lied."

"Any of you guys talk to Mrs. Blue about the truck?" Reddman asked. "Her name's Alicia, isn't it?"

"Yeah," Lopes said.

"Did you talk to her?"

"No, her name's Alicia. What's going on? You're gettin' all excited, Davey. What's giving you a hard-on?"

"Tell you later." He went back to Brenfleck. "So—then when you got to the scene, you put out an all-points bulletin for Blue. How come?"

"That's in the report, isn't it?"

"Here," Reddman said, shoving his file at him. "I couldn't find it," he added, quietly.

Brenfleck glanced through it, blushing and grinning. "Guess I forgot," he said, glaring at Reddman. "Somebody told me."

"Told you what? Do you remember?"

"Not really."

"What about who then? Do you remember who told you?"

"Give me a sec." Brenfleck's attitude toward the special prosecutor hardened. He wanted to ask the weirdo if he ate vegetables for breakfast. "Some woman told me it was a truck with big wheels, like the kids drive."

"So you thought of Johnny Blue?"

"I sure did. What's wrong with that?"

"Nothing," Reddman said. "I'd say that's good police work. Did you get her name?"

"No. I mean, shit, me and Rip were workin' our butts off tryin' to get all those damn people outta there, get things secure, and you're raisin' hell with me—"

"Wait." Reddman put his hand on Brenfleck's shoulder. "I'm not hassling you, Bren. It was good police work. I mean it." Cops and their egos, he thought.

Brenfleck wouldn't be mollified. "How much longer will this take?"

As they walked back to the street in front of the courthouse, Reddman asked them to remember how it had looked the day of the killing. Brenfleck looked at Judson and rolled his eyes. Reddman started with Judson, who had been the first officer to arrive on the scene. The large man was painfully shy, and Brenfleck corrected much of what he said. When Judson stood on the pavement where Ami's body had lain, Brenfleck pointed out that Judson moved the body before he did CPR. Judson then described his efforts at CPR. He had followed the protocol to the letter: sweeping her mouth clean of debris, then covering her mouth with his own and forcing his breath into her lungs. "Sure hope she didn't have AIDS," he said, making light of the experience, although he remembered the tangible feeling of love that had washed through him as he worked to save her life.

"He looked like he'd been making it with a vampire," Brenfleck said, then added, in an effort to be funny, "It's all in the report."

As they worked through the morning, Reddman opened his senses and let his imagination work. He touched the pavement with his hands, trying to handle and feel the event, like a psychic. He waited for the magic that trial lawyers, hunters, and cops often experienced, that sense of having been there, having seen it happen. There was no word for it, although "déjà vu" was close.

Lopes had been the one to find the POI—the point of impact. He hadn't been sure because people had tramped over the crime scene like cattle before the two patrolmen secured the area. However, Donovan—an accident reconstruction expert—later verified Lopes's discovery. Measurements had been carefully taken so the exact spot could later be found. Reddman stared down at the smooth asphalt, a couple of stones embedded in the surface, and compared what he saw with the black-and-white photographs taken at the time. They didn't seem much alike. "Sergeant?" he asked.

"Wasn't much to go on, that's a fact," Donovan said. "See them lines of dirt?" He pointed at faint traces of dust shown in the photograph of the asphalt surface. They radiated away from a projected point, like sun rays through a cloud, or thin fingers of blood splattered against a wall. "Kind of a delta effect. Like to find some bits and pieces off the car, you know, broken headlight, maybe even some paint. Usually get a match that way."

"Did you?"

"Nope. Johnny loves that truck, keeps it clean as a whistle and tight as a tick. Nothing come off it."

Reddman looked at another set of photographs taken by Donovan; these were in color. *"This* is good testimony," he said with real admiration, examining the pictures of the front of Blue's truck and the undercarriage.

"Great gore," Lopes added.

"They show most of it," Donovan said. "Little dent there, blood kind of blown off." He pointed to a spot on the right fender. "Figure that's where her head smacked into it before she got rolled under. Not much left on the tires but still some strips of fabric caught in the springs and this crossbar, holds that shield." Reddman looked at another. "This one, taken with the tire off, shows the tire well," Donovan said. "Every time her body'd come around it'd punch about a cup of blood up in there, throw it under the fender, onto the axle housing, differential housing, clear back to the tank."

"And we got a blood match, right?" Reddman asked.

"Yep, her blood, all right."

"Shit," Lopes said. He looked a bit green. "Any skin?"

"Some, but the pictures don't show it," Donovan told him humorlessly. "When she came through, those metal creases on the inside of the fender ripped pretty hard, but her clothes slid over most of it. Some right here." Donovan spoke with a professional flatness, pointing to an edge of the fender. Reddman had to guess at the depth of the trooper's feelings. "Ain't pretty."

"It's beautiful," Reddman said, thinking of its impact on a jury. "How the hell did she stay on the tire that long?"

"Shows that here," Donovan explained. "She had a kind of scarf on. The thing got caught on the inside of the front axle, kept pulling her head through. See that piece of fabric there?" His jaws twitched angrily. "I ain't ever seen anything like it."

Reddman put the photographs away, then carefully went over the locations depicted on the diagram: the point of impact, the places on the pavement where blood had smeared and where her body had lain. He tried to see the whole event with omniscience, the way God had seen it, or as an artist might portray it: Blue watching his victim leave the courthouse, rolling down the hill in his high rider pickup truck, then the hit. He tried to imagine the woman's body caught on the tire and slamming into the ground, then dropping away—but it wouldn't come together. Why hadn't she seen him coming down the hill?

That afternoon, while working in the law library on jury instructions, he saw her spinning slowly on the tire of Blue's truck. The small woman had stayed in one piece. Reddman was awed by the life that had briefly survived the event.

*   *   *

Reddman arrived at Zack Wolfman's home with a six-pack of beer. The small two-story building stood on a two-acre plot of land three miles from Muldoon, beneath a layered sandstone cliff. Wolfman, sitting across from him on a worn sofa next to his wife, explained that one of his two acres was the face of the cliff, and he hadn't figured out how to use it yet. A small barn in a grove of aspen gave off the smell of horse, and Sonya asked Reddman if he'd like to buy the horse. She was an attractive blond, blue-eyed woman, seven months pregnant, with capable hands and a nice smile.

"How did you get into the public defender business?" Reddman asked his host, after they had exchanged a few good-natured barbs. "I mean, when you played for the Broncos, you weren't great, but everybody knew who you were. Couldn't you have made more money ripping the tops off beer cans in TV commercials?"

Wolfman smiled tolerantly at Reddman. "Yeah. But I always liked squashing quarterbacks, you know, breaking their legs and arms, and prosecutors remind me of quarterbacks. Kind of like you, that all-American look, lots of teeth, nice-looking hair, everything in place, until I get on top and kind of rearrange things." He swung an elbow back and forth as though working on a quarterback's face. "Seemed like a natural transition."

"I hear you were better as a linebacker."

"Hey, Sonya, is the pot big enough to put him in it?"

She laughed. "You guys gotta sound so tough." She got up and walked toward the kitchen. "Speaking of pots."

"So where's Sharon?" Wolfman asked his guest. "I was hopin' you'd bring her along."

"She sure is pretty," Reddman said. "Who's Jed Turner?"

"You mean you don't know who Jed Turner is?" Wolfman asked, feigning surprise. "Next to Johnny Blue and me, he's Muldoon's most famous resident, man."

"What does he do?"

"Writer. Arrogant son of a bitch." Wolfman took a pull

on his beer. "A Vietnam vet, took a shot in the ass during the war, severed his spine. Now he's numb from the waist down."

"What do you mean?"

"Paraplegic, man. I got to explain?"

Reddman thought of the wheelchair at Sharon Sondenburg's house. "What's the deal between him and Sharon?"

Wolfman shrugged his shoulders. "She pushes him around town when he's here, which isn't often. He's on some book tour now, I heard."

"Is that all?"

"What the hell else can there be? Like, he's got no dick!"

Sonya stuck her head out of the kitchen. "Zack, you are awful. It may surprise you to know there can be much more to a man than a penis!"

Wolfman's eyebrows went up. "Hey!" he demanded. "Woman! Me and my little buddy here havin' a private talk!"

"Dave, Jed Turner is not an arrogant son of a bitch," Sonya said. "My roommate has his head up his ass." She disappeared.

Reddman grinned over the good-natured flap. In spite of it, a feeling of affection ran between husband and wife, and it warmed the room. "I still don't know what the relationship is between Turner and Sharon," he said.

"You're not alone, man. Nobody does."

"Does she go out with other guys?"

"She's going out with you, isn't she? Count your blessings." Wolfman glanced at the kitchen door to make sure Sonya couldn't hear, then whispered, "What an ass!"

"I'm attracted to her mind," Reddman said.

"Sure. Anyway, you've got the whole town buzzin'. What I hear, she's finally figured out a way to get even with Johnny Blue."

"Small towns," Reddman said, annoyed. "You need a thick skin in a small town."

Wolfman shrugged. "Good people. They just like to stir

things up. Like on the reservation." He grinned. "I'm used to this bullshit. I was raised on the Sioux reservation, and man, white gossips don't know how. *Indian* gossips know how."

Sonya poked her head into the living room. "Dinner will be ready in fifteen minutes," she said, a can of beer in her hand. She winked at her husband, then disappeared.

"What're you grinning at, you little weirdo?" Wolfman asked.

"Must be nice," Reddman said.

"Yeah. It is."

Reddman felt very comfortable in Wolfman's living room. He knew they would get down to business later. "How would you put it on if you were prosecuting?" he asked idly.

"I'd do it like a personal injury case, I think." Wolfman's beer had been sitting on a magazine on the coffee table. He picked it up and drained the whole can. "Like she was still alive but busted all to hell, so bad she couldn't even remember what happened." He crushed the beer can like a piece of paper and tossed it toward a wastebasket. "I'd concentrate more on proving what happened to her, let that be the focus, show the jury what he did by proving what happened to her. Then at the last, I'd call her to the stand, man."

"Put her on the stand?"

"You know, pictures of her before and after, descriptions, autopsy reports, like a mangled mute. Let the jury see what that son of a bitch did to her."

"I thought you guys were supposed to be subtle." Reddman was drinking beer out of a bottle. He tipped it up.

"Never be subtle when you can do it with a sledgehammer," Wolfman told him. "Subtleties are lost on some people, but I never met a juror who didn't understand a sledge." He stretched his huge legs out in front of him. "We're subtle most of the time, though, you're right, because my side of the table, you gotta be. When you got

92

a thousand eyewitnesses who watched your client pull the trigger, you know, about all you have is innuendo."

Reddman stared at his own feet, thinking. "Like a personal injury case. Hmm." He watched his feet move. "Not a bad plan if I knew the jury was with me. But I've got to pin it on him first."

"Yeah, I know."

"I'm having trouble with it, Zack."

"You're having trouble?"

"In my own mind. I'm having trouble ruling out accident. What really happened?"

"Hey, man, it was murder. Real honest-to-God heavy-ass murder." Wolfman glared around the room. "The old kind. Lying in wait. Deliberation. He planned it, waited up on that hill till he saw her, waited for her to get out there where he could squash her." The man's whole body throbbed with intensity. He sat back, trying to shake it off.

"What makes you so sure?"

"I know him, man. The way he moves, the way he thinks. I've known other guys like him, played with guys like him." He got up, unable to sit still. "Guy's a psychopath. No conscience. That's why he was so great."

"I don't get you."

"Shit." Wolfman sat down again and turned his head away, blinking away tears. "I really loved Ami, man. Hard to talk about this."

"Why would that make him great? Great at what?"

"Rodeo. Athletics. He had no conscience, right? No father's voice or mother's voice or cultural voice inside his head yelling at him, keeping him under control, telling him 'Do it this way, you little peckerneck!' "

Reddman laughed. He enjoyed the man's company immensely, but felt, rather than understood, what he meant. "Look, Zack. As bad as the guy is, how do you know it wasn't an accident? All she did to him was lose the case. Would he kill her for that?"

"Hard to believe, isn't it? But it's true. Listen. Guys like that hate. That's the only emotion they feel. And they don't have accidents." He leaned forward and stared at Redd-man. "Guys like Blue are totally self-centered, totally aware. Everything is easy for them. You know why? Because their feelings don't get in the way. Nothing gets in the way of action, man, nothing!"

Reddman tipped up his beer and took another swallow. "I'm trying," he said.

"Yeah. A year from now it'll come to you. You'll think back and go, 'Hey! That handsome, charismatic Sioux I used to read about, and whose autograph I forgot to get, sure knew what he was talking about.' " Wolfman's huge head swung away. "Kind of an occupational hazard anyway."

"What?"

"For public defenders. Getting hammered by their clients. Ami never did like Johnny Blue, hard as she fought for him. He tried to put the make on her one time, you know? She told him to fuck off."

Reddman leaned forward, listening intently. "Can I prove that?"

"Why? Even if you can prove it, how can you use it? If I was defending, I'd scream like hell."

"Motive, man. The only motive so far is revenge against her for losing his case."

Wolfman frowned, then shrugged. "Okay, you might get it in. Prove it through him, man. He'll take the stand. Ask him."

"Sure," Reddman said. "Then what do I do when he lies? When he says, 'Yeah, we made love three times.' "

"That's when you shit."

The suddenness of the remark broke Reddman up. As Wolfman watched him laugh, he thought, I shoulda been a clown. But he also thought, Old Joe's kid is okay. Although I would not want to take him on. Cole will have his hands full.

"Come on, Zack. How do I prove it?"

"Shit, I don't know how to prove things. Just unprove."

"Well, Ami told you about it, didn't she? Isn't that how you found out?"

"You want to put *me* on the stand? Good! I'll crucify the bastard." He put his feet on the coffee table. "Except you can't. My testimony would be hearsay."

"Maybe not. What'd you do? Go to Blue about it? If you talked to him, I can put in what you talked about."

Wolfman shook his head. He hadn't done a damn thing, naturally. His deputies had to handle crap like that on their own. "Wait. Lance!" He jumped up. "The absolute nerd. A more perfect nerd than your average D.A. even. *He* might have." He charged into the hallway where a telephone hung on the wall. "Hello, Information? Denver. Lance Winchester the Third. I don't know his address." He held his hand over the mouthpiece and grinned at Reddman, who had followed him into the hall. "I fired his ass. Told him go be a D.A." His hand came off the mouthpiece, and he repeated the number the operator gave him, then disconnected and dialed. "Here," he said, handing the telephone to Reddman.

"Hello?" a male voice on the other end said.

"Wait!" Reddman called to Wolfman, who disappeared into the kitchen. "Ah, Mr. Winchester?"

"Yes, this is Lance Winchester."

"Dave Reddman, calling from Muldoon?" Reddman didn't know what to say. He hadn't figured out who the man was. "I'm with NASP—the National Association of Special Prosecutors?"

"Oh, yes, of course! You're calling about my application!"

"Actually, I'm calling about Ami O'Rourke." Reddman waited for a response, but none came. "Still there, Mr. Winchester?"

"Yes. Of course."

"It's my understanding you knew her," Reddman said, groping. "You were with the public defender's office in Muldoon when she was killed, weren't you?"

"Yes. Ami and I were deputies."

"What can you tell me about her?"

"Quite a lot, actually. But I'd rather not."

"Look, I'd really appreciate your help. I'm trying this case against Johnny Blue, and I need some ideas, you know."

The man sighed heavily. "Well, she and I were lovers, if that's what you mean, but I don't see how that can be of much help. As a matter of fact, I've already been subpoenaed by the defense."

"Lovers?" Reddman asked, thinking quickly. "And you're under subpoena?" Would Cole try to paint the victim a lurid red, hoping the small-town jury would figure tough shit? "Will this judge let that kind of garbage in?"

"If you are referring to Judge Gilbert Landry, I feel he's sufficiently knowledgeable of the rules of evidence to sustain an objection." Wolfman is right, Reddman thought. This guy's a nerd. "However, Saul isn't calling me as a witness for that purpose. I have his word he won't mention my relationship with Ami, except insofar as it goes to prove the point at issue."

"Which is?"

"He wants merely to show a character trait. And I'm afraid he's quite right. Ami *never*—simply *never*—paid the least bit of attention to traffic. She was always reading when she crossed the street. Or talking at the speed of sound, if she happened to be with someone. Or thinking at the speed of light. She was *completely* oblivious to danger. She wouldn't have lasted half a day in Denver. Of course, Muldoon is different. Much slower pace. Nevertheless, in my opinion, it was simply a question of time until someone ran over her."

"So you're going to testify she didn't pay attention to traffic?"

"Well, as you might expect, Saul is prepared to do a bit of sandbagging. If you object to the testimony on the basis of an insufficient foundation, he will dredge up our relationship, to prove that I did indeed know her well enough to be familiar with her habits."

"Half the town knows anyway, right?"

"I should say more like eighty percent."

"Well, what about Blue? Did she talk to you about him?"

"Of course. Often." Winchester pronounced the *t*. "She found him fascinating, a person quite beyond her experience."

"Did she like him?"

"Not in the least. She was repelled by him. He tried to seduce her, and she got very nasty with him."

"Did she tell you that?"

Winchester said nothing for a moment. Then: "I see. That's really what you're after, isn't it? You want me to testify . . . but that would be hearsay. Something Ami said to me, offered to prove the truth of the matter asserted. Certainly not a dying declaration."

"Sure, what she said to you would be hearsay. But I'm hoping you said something to Blue about it. That could go in. And if Blue made some kind of reply, that could go in, too."

"Yes. But—"

"You didn't just let it go, did you?" Reddman asked, doing his best to back the man into a corner. "Some creep insulting your lover?"

"Of course not. I was furious! But I only spoke to him on the telephone."

"What'd you say?"

"That I personally would smash in his face if he so much as touched her without her consent. Oh, I was furious!"

"What did Blue say?"

"He laughed, as I recall. Told me to come ahead. He talked, too, about the way she smelled. He said he could tell she was in heat, and I should keep her away from him when she was in heat."

"He said that?"

"Rather an awful man, actually. Can you imagine someone talking about whether or not a woman is in heat?"

Reddman liked it. "Ought to get the attention of the women on the jury, I'd think. Anything else?"

"No. I was quite disgusted with the fellow, but he didn't approach Ami again, and I let it drop."

"Winchester, I'd like to put you under subpoena, too. If I mail you one, will you accept it?"

"I assume you'll tender travel expenses and provide me with a place to stay?"

He wants to double-dip, Reddman thought. "Be glad to," he said, hoping the offer would make Winchester a better witness. "What's your address?"

Winchester rattled off an address in Denver.

"Thanks." Reddman scribbled it on a piece of paper he found on a table near the telephone. "I'll stay in touch."

Reddman could hear Zack and Sonya talking and laughing in the kitchen and was about to join them when he felt rather than saw someone in the living room. He stuck his head around the corner and got a good look at a boy sitting quietly, magazine in hand. "Hi," he said. "I'll bet you're Timmy."

"How did you know that?" the boy asked.

Blond, blue eyed, lightly tanned—Reddman was struck by his resemblance to pictures he'd seen of Ami O'Rourke. "You're the only nine-year-old boy around." If Ami had been a boy, this is what she would have looked like, he thought.

"Pretty shrewd," Timmy said. "Who are you? Did you know my mom?"

The small person had a hurt look. Reddman thought of a dog, in love with its master, who gets viciously kicked and doesn't know why. "Kind of," he said.

Wolfman charged into the living room, carrying a beer in each hand. "Timmeee!" he shouted. "It's the Timmee. The world's greatest kid!"

Timmy grinned at the huge figure. "Those beers for me?"

"Keep tellin' you to wait until you're ten!" He handed a beer to Reddman. "What'd Winchester say?"

Reddman sat in the overstuffed chair by the window. "He'll be at the trial. Cole has him under subpoena."

"To prove what?"

"A character trait. That Ami didn't pay attention when she walked across the street."

"The sleaze," Wolfman said, sitting down and hunching his shoulders. "Hey, Timmy, go help Sonya, okay?"

"It's all right. I won't hear anything."

"Yeah, but I'd feel better, okay? She's about to set the table; maybe you can help."

As Reddman watched him go, his stomach felt hollow. He remembered all the things he had heard, and not heard, at the same age. "Cole wants Winchester for more than that."

"Right. That's why I called him a sleaze." Wolfman's feet plopped heavily onto the coffee table.

"Ami was a complicated woman, I guess."

"What's complicated about getting laid?" Wolfman asked, thoughtfully sipping beer. "Although I never could put her with Winchester."

"Why?"

"Difference in age, partly. See I'm really a traditionalist, and Ami was ten years older than the fucker. But the guy looks like Superman. Body like a Greek god. I could understand Ami using him—you know, to scratch an itch—but getting involved with him? No way!"

"What was she like?"

"You'd have hated her, man. Tough, feisty, in your face, yappin' and snappin'. She took no shit from anybody, not even Landry. If he made a mistake, it didn't matter to her that he was on a throne and she was in the pit. She'd just surround him with words." The veins in Wolfman's eyes throbbed as he tried to blink away pain. "I don't know where she came from, how she happened. I mean Catholic family, middle America, righteous upbringing—how the fuck did she happen? We hated the same things, you know—stuffed shirts, D.A.'s, assholes, big cars, gates and fences to keep the riffraff out. We laughed at the same things, too, like nice juicy farts in church." A tear slid down the man's face. "You'd have hated her, but you'd have cried at her funeral, too."

"Hope you don't mind my asking, but was there anything . . . you know."

"Hell, yes, man, I loved her. Nothing physical, though. She had about as much sex appeal as a twelve-year-old boy, and they don't turn me on." He sipped beer. "She knew things, like all those drunk Indian women you see in the towns near Mesa Verde. She just knew things."

After dinner Reddman stayed longer than he should have. He met Heidi, the Wolfmans' four-year-old daughter, who was solidly filled with a sense of her own self. Heidi helped Sonya clear the table and later played with a toy tractor on the living room floor. Reddman also met Ami, not quite two, who crashed into everything as she roamed through the house like a small buffalo. Her name had been Sonya's idea, but Davey sensed a reserve on Sonya's part toward the child. Both of them were dark-skinned, like Zack.

After Timmy had gone to bed, Reddman examined a pile of photographs of Ami O'Rourke. They showed a small, blond, blue-eyed woman with a firm, strong face and delicate hands. He had the sudden sense that he knew her. Typical public defender attitude, he thought. You wouldn't kick a dog who's down, would you? he heard her asking. Then why are you doing this to my client? Where's your humanity? He knew she was someone he would have baited, a person he could have enjoyed hating.

Back at the hotel, Reddman couldn't sleep. He saw himself in Timmy's face. He even heard his mother cry the night old Joe left for good.

Reddman wondered if he would have cried at Ami's funeral.

CHAPTER
NINE

Friday morning. Sharon Sondenburg had to teach a class at nine and didn't know whether to let him sleep or wake him up. Reddman lay sprawled in her bed naked, on his stomach, pillow over his head.

How had it happened? she asked herself, crawling out of bed on the other side. She stared down at the sleeping figure. They had split a bottle of wine and found themselves gazing and smiling at each other like a couple of fools. . . .

Sondenburg smiled at the man and wondered why she felt no guilt, absolutely none. She could still smell him and feel him, his surprisingly gentle hands, his lean and muscular body covering her own. I never thought I'd sleep with a vegetarian, she thought. Quietly she stepped into the bathroom, shut the door, and looked at herself in the mirror. She felt wonderful, and it showed. It had been a long time since she'd made love to a man with a whole body, and her own firm, sensual body continued to vibrate with the sensations of their lovemaking. She turned on the shower and stepped in.

"Hi," she said later, coming out of the bathroom wrapped in a towel. "You're up."

Reddman sat on the edge of the bed, his pants on and his eyes half open, trying to jam his feet into his shoes.

"Yeah. I'm late." He looked at her and stopped breathing a moment, then tied his shoes. "You're beautiful."

Sondenburg liked the way he sounded, like a little boy. "Thank you. Do you have time for a cup of coffee?"

"No." He tucked his shirt in, then rapidly tied his tie. "Can I use your toothbrush?"

"Sure."

She could hear him flush the toilet and brush his teeth. What a nice man, she thought, stretching luxuriantly and letting the towel drop to the floor. She slipped into panties and a bra and was selecting a blouse when he came out.

"I can't believe the way I feel," Reddman said, putting on his coat. "Want to go to Denver with me this weekend?"

"I can't," she said, stepping into a skirt. "I've got plans."

"Sharon?"

"Yes?"

"I love you." The statement seemed to frighten him. "Kind of."

She laughed at him as he ran out the door.

Twenty minutes later Reddman walked into the district attorney's office to pick up the file. He ran into Walter Brim in the hallway.

"Well! How's it going?" the large man asked, smiling and blocking his way. "Heard you had some excitement in court yesterday. What happened?"

"I endorsed a new witness, Lance Winchester. You know him?"

"The former deputy public defender? Of course."

"Cole wanted a continuance. He said it was a late endorsement. You know, more than a week to go, a late endorsement?"

"And?"

"We spent three hours in court arguing about it. The law is entirely on my side, and I have to argue it! How can Cole complain about my endorsement of a witness *he* already has under subpoena!'' He glanced at his watch. "The judge finally allowed it, but now Cole acts as if I owe him one.''

Brim beamed at Reddman, as though to say, Now perhaps you understand. "What makes you think it matters what the law says?'' he asked.

Reddman grinned. "Well, you know, I'm a lawyer, and so I've got this set of expectations. The system doesn't seem to work that way around here, though.'' He moved around Brim. "Hey, I gotta go. Donovan lined up the eyewitnesses, and I need to talk to them.''

Sergeant Jack Donovan waited patiently in his small office at the Justice Center. The tall, thin trooper had been sitting there for twenty-five minutes. Nothing new about that, he thought. He'd spent a lot of time with his thumb up his ass, waiting for deputy D.A.'s to show up. "Morning, Counselor,'' he said when Dave Reddman blew into the room. Donovan noticed that he was wearing the same clothes he'd had on the day before, and he hadn't shaved.

"Sorry I'm late,'' Reddman said. "Are all of the witnesses here?''

"I don't know what you mean by 'all,' Mr. Reddman— ah, Dave. I got three people here who saw it happen. Two from the sidewalk, one a driver coming toward it.''

"That's Strickland, Goode, and Doppler, right? I've read their statements. Any others who saw it go down?''

"Not as we can find.''

"Okay, let's do it. Where are they?''

"In the squad room,'' Donovan said, "havin' coffee. Who do you want first?''

"How about we do them all at the same time?'' Reddman looked around the room. "We'll fit in here, won't we? Let's get some more chairs.''

"If they talk it over together, they ain't as apt to contradict each other when they testify. Is that the way we go?'' Donovan asked, smiling.

"Think of it as a permissible form of memory enhancement, where one mind jogs another.'' Reddman grinned back. "I guess it depends on which side of the lectern you're on."

Chairs were spaced around Donovan's small metal desk, and the three witnesses were herded into the room. Reddman looked them over as he shut the door. C. A. Goode, the banker, was the last one in but the easiest to see. Tall, distinguished-looking, well dressed, he'd been critical in his statement of Officer Rip Judson who had attempted CPR. "Let's see. You're Mrs. Doppler?" Reddman asked a matronly woman in her early fifties, who smiled at him as though she thought he was a nice young man.

"No, actually. I'm Cindy Strickland."

"Oh. Then I guess you're Mrs. Doppler?" Reddman asked the attractive young woman wearing faded jeans.

"That's right," she said, smiling.

"And you're Mr. Goode, Citizens Bank?"

"Yes, sir," the man said, thrusting out his hand. "You're the special prosecutor the town is buzzing about. My pleasure, sir."

"Thanks. I'd prefer it if you didn't call me sir, though," Reddman told the whole group. "I'm Dave Reddman. I'm from the National Association of Special Prosecutors, and I'm here to help Mr. Brim try this case." They nodded a greeting. "The three of you saw the incident happen?"

"We certainly did. *I* did, in any event. Saw it clearly," Goode said, sitting down. "I was just coming out of the bank, and I heard a horn, a honking horn, and looked toward the sound, this direction"—Goode pointed—"and I'll tell you, that truck of Blue's looked ten feet tall. As I remember, it seemed out of whack or something for a moment there. Then it sort of righted itself and took off. Then I heard someone screaming—"

"Me. That was me," Mrs. Doppler said. "I couldn't stop."

"Yes. Well, whoever it was, then I saw a body out there in the street. I ran over, of course, and tried to do what I could, but it was too late. I even tried to find a pulse—I've had first aid training—but she was gone, absolutely no question about it. Then Officer Judson arrived on the scene—"

"Thanks, Mr. Goode," Reddman said, interrupting. He hoped he could keep the man under control. "Before we go any further, let me get a couple of preliminary items out of the way. You're all under subpoena, right?" All of them nodded. "Have any of you testified in court before?"

"I have," Goode said importantly. "Several times. For the bank. We quite frequently—"

"Great. What about the others?"

Neither of them had.

"Some things I'd like to impress on you about testifying in court. One is that you'll probably be nervous, right?" Goode smiled at that, but the women nodded. "Well, don't let it bother you. I'll be nervous too. Usually everyone in the courtroom is pretty edgy, in spite of the fact they look so cool." Reddman was into a patter he'd used before in witness preparation. "The point is, don't make it harder on yourself than it is. Just accept your nervousness. Live with it."

Goode interrupted with a commanding laugh. "Possibly I'm the exception that proves the rule, but I've never been the least bit afraid."

Reddman and Donovan exchanged glances. "That's excellent, Mr. Goode," Reddman said, wishing the pompous ass would shut up. "But there are different kinds of trials. Most trials are just to the court, where there's a judge, but no jury. Are those the kind of trials you've done for the bank?"

"Yes."

"Have you ever testified at a jury trial?"

"No, but I don't see—"

"Court trials are much less formal, especially in situations where you know the judge and both lawyers and you're more or less going through the motions. This time you'll be testifying in front of the whole town. You probably won't be nervous, but if you are, just accept it. That's what I'm talking about. Okay?"

Goode stroked his chin and nodded, saying nothing.

"Another thing is this," Reddman droned on. "When you testify, be sure—and I cannot overemphasize this—be absolutely certain that you tell the truth. I am not going to ask you to slant the facts or to do anything other than tell the complete truth."

"Hmm," Mrs. Doppler said. "You really mean that?" She sounded disappointed.

"Yes."

"What if we're asked a question and we don't know the answer? I mean, lawyers can make a witness look pretty silly."

"Don't make up an answer just to keep from looking silly," Reddman said. "If you don't know the answer, say so. If you don't understand the question, say so. Just don't lie. This isn't idealism on my part, either," he said to all of them. "I've been around the judicial system long enough to know it really works if it's allowed to. Part of the reason is those twelve people sitting up there"—he motioned with his hand, as if indicating a jury box—"watching witnesses, watching you, concentrating on you. There is something about a lie they can spot. So please tell the truth."

Donovan, seated near the door, nodded approvingly.

"Mr. Reddman?" Cindy Strickland asked.

Reddman almost launched into his patter on the use of first names, but decided first names might be more awkward than formality, with Goode around. "Yes?"

"What about an accidental lie?"

"You mean a mistake? Where you mean one thing but say another, or where you get confused by a question?"

"I—well, both."

"Those aren't lies, Ms. Strickland. A lie is where a person intentionally misstates a fact. Jurors are human. They forgive mistakes."

"What if they don't know?"

"Don't know what?"

"Don't know I made a mistake."

The question was one Reddman had not heard before.

"You'll have to leave that to me," he said. "You'll have to hope I'm smart enough to catch it and clear it up."

"I need to know something," Muriel Doppler said. "Does it matter what I wear? I was in court just before this thing happened. That's why I was there that day. And the judge just chewed all over me because of the way I was dressed."

"What were you wearing?"

"What I have on now. Jeans. I mean, the judge thought I should wear hose or something."

"Can I ask why you were in court?"

"Shoot, that's no secret; they printed it in the paper and all. A DUI." She smirked, then looked toward Goode, as though for understanding. "They dropped it down to that other charge, after I got a lawyer and had to pay him a thousand dollars."

"What happened?" Reddman asked.

"I pleaded guilty."

"They dropped the charge to driving while impaired, instead of driving under the influence?"

"Yes."

"Your lawyer wasn't Saul Cole, was it?"

"Well, yes, it was. Does that matter?" Doppler fished around in her purse. "Anybody mind if I smoke? I mean, I can wait."

"Actually," Goode said, "I would prefer it if you didn't."

Doppler put her purse on the floor, then pushed it under her chair, out of sight. "He's supposed to be the best. I only saw him twice." She looked around the room, as though for approval. "Bastard charged me a thousand dollars."

"Do you have a dress, Mrs. Doppler?" Reddman asked.

"Sure I have a dress," she said angrily.

"Or a nice pants suit? Hey, I know it shouldn't be that important, but—"

"Goddam right it shouldn't be! I mean, I pay my taxes, and I work every bit as hard as my husband, and there were plenty of *men* in that courtroom wearing denim, and the judge didn't get upset over that! What the hell difference does it make how you dress anyway?"

"Well, the thing is—"

"I mean, only well-dressed people tell the truth? Shit!" They all laughed. "Mrs. Doppler—"

"I don't like you calling me Mrs. Doppler, either. I'm Muriel, she's Cindy, you're Dave, and he's . . . well, I guess he's Mr. Goode. He's a banker, so we better be polite."

"Ha-ha," Goode said, trying to be a good sport. "You may call me Charles."

"Gonna have to call me something, too," Donovan said from the corner. "Just so's you don't oink. Gets old when people oink."

"Smokey?" Cindy Strickland asked. Everyone laughed as she leaned over and she put her hand on his arm. "Sorry, Jack. Remember me? You pulled me out of a ditch once."

"Sure, sure, two winters ago, up near Avalanche."

"Are you the one who arrested me?" Muriel Doppler asked. "I know it was a trooper, but—"

"Lady, if you don't know who it was, then whoever busted you must have done the right thing."

She laughed along with everyone else.

"Jack, would you get that big diagram of the scene?" Reddman asked, deciding to take up the question of dress another time.

Donovan got up and walked to the corner of the room nearest his desk, where three or four large diagrams were rolled up and tied with rubber bands. He selected one of them, pulled off the band, and spread it out on his desk. "Got more. We can mark this up and it won't hurt. Let me get this set right." He turned the diagram so that the directions were the same as the scene. "That's right, ain't it? I always get switched around when I'm inside."

"You have it right," Goode told him.

"Okay, does everyone know where we are?" Reddman

asked, standing over the diagram. "This is Mears Street, between Fifth and Sixth. Fifth is the top of the chart, north, and Sixth at the bottom, south. The courthouse is on the east side of Mears, and the public defender's office is across the street, about the middle of the block."

"Was she that far into the street?" Goode asked critically, looking at a point labeled POI. "You've got it practically all the way across."

"Let's ask the man who drew the diagram," Reddman said. "Jack?"

"That's where Ami O'Rourke was when she got hit all right, Mr. Goode, eleven feet from the curb. Let's see, nine feet from the center line. Another three or four feet and she'd been into them cars parked along the street there."

"But she was jaywalking, wasn't she? And essentially in the middle of the street?"

"No question she was jaywalking. I do it, too, when I'm out of uniform. Don't know if she was in the middle, though. Depends on what you mean." Donovan bent over the diagram. "See, Mears is pretty wide there, forty-eight feet, not wide enough for two double lanes of traffic, though. Another thing, the center line ain't really in the center. That's because there's diagonal parking in front of the courthouse and parallel parking on the west side of the street. So that lane in front of the courthouse is wider than the southbound lane, see that? I got them distances marked on the chart, and it's to scale." He showed where the distances were marked. "The distance from the center of the roadway to the curb on the west side of the road is only twenty feet. Victim was nine feet from the center line and eleven feet from the curb, but there were cars parked along the curb, don't forget, so you've got to allow seven, eight feet. So it depends on what you mean by middle."

"Well, a car—a large pickup—couldn't have gotten around her without hitting her. That's what I mean by middle." Goode turned away from the diagram, as though his mind was made up.

Donovan glanced at Reddman, who nodded. "Blue could

have driven around her easy, Mr. Goode." Donovan turned the diagram around, gently compelling Goode to see. "Even a big pickup. Not many of 'em are more'n seven feet wide, and Blue's—from tire to tire—was slightly less than eight feet wide. If he'd swung less than a foot"—he held his hands apart—"that far is all, into the northbound lane, he wouldn't have touched her."

"My point exactly. He would have had to drive in the other lane of traffic to miss her! What about oncoming traffic?"

"Wasn't any, and even if there was, there's lots of room in that northbound lane to swerve a little. There's a good fourteen feet over there for traffic. It's easy for a northbound driver to move it over some, especially if they seen a woman about to get hit by a truck."

"This just isn't the way Saul Cole explained it to me," Goode said. "Here was this woman paying absolutely no attention to anything, wandering around in the middle of the street, reading. I remember, too, right after hearing the horn and looking up, seeing papers everywhere. Like feathers from a pillow. Why, she was asking for it!"

"It's possible the facts are somewhat different from Mr. Cole's explanation," Reddman said. He fumbled with his tie, but there was no mistaking the intensity of his voice. "Ami O'Rourke was in a hurry. She definitely was not the kind of person who would have been 'wandering around in the middle of the street,' if that's what Cole told you. I'm a prosecutor, but I have a lot of respect for public defenders like Ami O'Rourke. They have huge caseloads, and they work harder than it's possible to work."

"Well, I'll have to reserve my judgment," Goode said, rolling his arm over and looking at his watch. "I'm very sorry, but I have to leave. I've got an important meeting at ten that I can't afford to miss."

"You couldn't be a little late, could you?" Reddman asked.

"No. Perhaps if we'd started on time?" He opened the door.

"I apologize to all of you for being late," Reddman said. "Mr. Goode, can I get with you later?"

"Whenever it's convenient," the man said, shutting the door behind him.

"Dave?" Cindy Strickland asked. "I'm confused. I talked to Saul, too. In fact, he's been real nice to me lately, and the closer we get to trial, the nicer he is." She smiled. "Coffee, friendly waves, very solicitous when he sees me— and before this happened, he didn't even know me, even though I've waited on him plenty of times at the bank."

"The same with me," Muriel Doppler said. "Nice as pie even though he knows he blew it when he charged me a thousand dollars."

"What has he told you happened?" Reddman asked.

"About what he told Mr. Goode. He—well, he was very sympathetic, of course, talked about the poor woman, but he told me, too, she'd been having an affair with a much younger man."

"He said the same thing to me," Muriel said. "What's wrong with that? I mean, if you're not married."

"Right!" Cindy said. "I'm *looking* for a younger man!" They all laughed. "Back to my question. What are you doing with Muriel and me? I don't know whether you mean it when you say we should tell the truth, because it seems like you're really doing the same thing Saul did, trying to persuade us what the truth is." Both women watched him carefully. "I feel like the rope in a tug-of-war."

Reddman opened his face and looked at the two women, in the way an instructor had shown him at a school for prosecutors. According to the experts, it would make him look honest and likable at the same time. "It'll take me a minute to get there," he said, trotting out a routine he didn't have to use very often. "Most murder cases . . . See, when people think of murder, they think of some clever diabolical mind at work, and of the plodding detective or the brilliant supersleuth who works through all the clues and figures everything out. But the way it actually happens is a lot different. In most actual murder cases, there isn't any question who killed whom. The question, like here, is what was in the guy's heart when he did it. Was it even murder at all? Or was it an accident, just some dumb stupid woman out in the middle of the street who got creamed?

"So, as I just said, the problem is to prove what was in the guy's heart. No one can see what's inside, and also, a person's heart will change. A real mean son of a bitch might get it all out of his system in a killing, and this seems to be true. Statistics show that murderers don't repeat their crime. There's a lot less recidivism among murderers than there is among burglars and robbers.

"This gets complicated." He brushed back his hair. "See, to a lawyer, a fact isn't even what happened. Facts come later. A fact is something you prove in court. Until it gets proved, you can call the event that happened a fact if you want, but it's really just an event that has no legal significance until it becomes a proven fact.

"And when it comes to proving a fact, all kinds of things come to bear. Most facts—like what was in Johnny Blue's heart—are proved through witnesses. And like it or not, witnesses convey impressions that influence jurors. And jurors are the ones who have to decide what is 'fact' and what isn't. So—"

"Wait a minute. Just a darn minute!" Muriel Doppler said. She had lit a cigarette and obviously felt much better. "Knock off the bullshit, will you? Just tell us what happened, okay? Your version?"

"Deliberate cold-blooded murder."

Up to that moment, Reddman had not known. But now he was certain. What Sharon Sondenburg had told him; his day at the scene with the cops; meeting Ami's son Timmy and seeing the part of Timmy that had been Ami; the extraordinary athletic competence of Johnny Blue, and his awful hatred; measurements, statements, physical evidence, impressions, experience—all of it came together and transformed his doubts into certainty. "Funny things happen when you prepare a case for trial," he said. "You get to know the players. I never saw Ami O'Rourke in my life, but I know her as well as I know myself." Reddman realized that at last the complicated woman had become real to him. "I know a lot of little things about her. She wasn't absentminded at all when it came to crossing streets. Not at all. She'd have been a good cabdriver in Boston. She had the capacity to sense, to feel, danger and to react quickly. How else would she have lived as long as she did, charging back and forth across the street, reading, thinking, rehearsing as she walked?"

"Then how did Johnny manage to hit her?"

"He blindsided her. He ambushed her. He sneaked up on her when she wasn't looking."

Donovan, rubbing his jaw, felt good. That was the way he saw it, too. "In a truck, rolling toward her, big as a barn?" he asked, playing the devil's advocate.

"That's right. In a truck as big as a barn. Muriel, where were you when Blue hit her?" Reddman demanded, standing over the diagram. He felt like God looking down on earth.

She pointed to a spot toward the south end of Mears Street on the courthouse side of the road. "I was here, in a diagonal parking space," she said. "I was backing out. I mean, I had finished backing out and was putting the truck in drive, when—"

"Excuse me, wait a minute. You were driving a pickup?" Reddman asked.

"Yes." She returned to her chair and took a deep drag on the cigarette.

"The cab sits up high and gives you a wide view of the street, right?"

"Yes."

"So when you backed up, you turned around to see what was behind you?"

"Yes. Either that or I looked in the mirror."

"Do it now," Reddman told her. "Do it just the way you did it then."

"I don't know if I can."

"Sure you can. Role-play it. This is last summer and you just left court, and you're pissed off at the judge, and you're wearing what you're wearing now, and you're in your truck. What do you do?"

She stuck the cigarette in her mouth, put her hands in her lap, then with her right hand put the truck in gear. Her left hand reached for the top of the steering wheel, and she rolled her body to the right and lifted her right arm, as though putting it over the passenger seat. She looked behind her.

"Do you see anything?" Reddman asked.

"No. All clear."

"Now you're backing out?"

"Yes." She leaned back, as though the truck had started moving, then faced the front again. With her right hand, she started to change gears.

"Wait a minute," Reddman said. "You're all backed out now? And you're putting the truck in low gear?"

"Yes."

"And there isn't any traffic behind you?"

"Right."

"What about in front?"

"I haven't looked yet."

"But even without looking, you still see, don't you? I mean, you know it's okay to put the truck in gear?"

"Yes, but I still haven't really looked."

"Let me put it this way. Are you aware of any potential problem in front of you? Does anything attract your attention, such as a pedestrian or any sound or hint of traffic?"

"No, nothing."

"Is your window open or shut?"

"Open. It was a nice day."

"You know there's nothing behind you, and you're not aware of anything in front, right?"

"Right."

"Then what happened?"

"I hear it. A horn—a loud horn." Her head jerked up and she stared forward, hands gripping the wheel.

"What do you see?"

"Johnny's truck! That high rider, about to hit her! I can't be*lieve* it!"

"Then?"

She bunched her hands into fists and lifted them off the wheel, then raised them to her eyes like a boxer protecting his face. "Oh, no."

"Can you see?" Reddman asked. "Are your eyes open?"

"Yes, I can see." She sounded tired.

"What do you see?"

"He hit her. She's caught on the tire. It's awful."

"What are you doing?"

"What do you mean?" She continued to stare ahead through her hands in disbelief. "I'm watching and I'm screaming my fucking head off."

Donovan made a sound, then stared at the floor.

"Okay. In court, you don't have to be that explicit."

She nodded.

"Now. From the time you first looked up until the time he hit her . . . Are you with me?"

"Yes."

"A split second must have passed there. He honked, you looked up. What did he do in that split second?" No response. "Did he hit the brake, swerve, anything?"

"Yes." She stared at Reddman.

"What?"

"He sped up."

Reddman tried to contain his excitement. He turned his back on her and sat down. "Muriel, am I putting ideas in your mind? Are you telling the truth?"

"No."

"You're not telling the truth? You're lying?"

"No! I mean you are not putting ideas in my mind. I'm telling the truth!"

"Why haven't you said this before? None of this is in your statement."

"I don't know. I wasn't asked, exactly, and—I don't

know. Johnny's a good friend of my husband." She wiped some moisture off her cheek. "Maybe I didn't want to see it. But I see it now."

"Tell me again. What did you see? What happened in that flash of time between the moment you looked up and the instant he hit her?"

"The son of a bitch sped up."

Reddman turned to Donovan, pumped up and exultant. "That's how he blindsided her, Jack. Muriel didn't know he was there, either. You *can* sneak up on somebody in broad daylight in a truck as big as a barn."

CHAPTER TEN

It was Monday morning, a week before the trial. Reddman waited as patiently as he could at NASP headquarters in Denver for Trigge to arrive. He'd called the old man over the weekend and arranged for the meeting, but no one had predicted the spring snow. Trigge apparently had been held up by the storm.

Fifteen minutes later the two men were seated in Trigge's office. Trigge peered over his glasses at the younger man's deeply tanned face, noting the bright white gleam of his teeth. The kid is really handsome, he thought. With a mustache, he could be Errol Flynn in a swashbuckler. "What brings you to town, Davey?" he asked. "I thought you'd be spending all your spare time on that bicycle of yours."

"Not all of it," Reddman said defiantly, knowing the race was a bone of contention between them. "Most of it. I came to get my car and pick your brain."

Trigge frowned, although secretly he was flattered. He liked it when his confident young soldiers came to him for advice. His policy was to give them all the time they needed. "Shouldn't take long to pick my brain. There isn't that much left." He glanced out the French doors that opened onto the balcony and watched the snow pile up. Huge wet flakes were dropping like down fluff, bending the trees and covering the ground with white. "Still think it's a careless driving case?"

"No," Reddman said quietly. "He murdered her."

"You don't say." Trigge spoke with a trace of amusement. "I've read our duplicate file, Davey, and I have to admit the murder count doesn't jump out there and bite you in the ass. Is this something you feel or something you can prove?"

"I don't know if I can prove it. But it's murder."

Trigge grunted, letting his stomach feel the fire that still burned there in spite of the fact that everything had become a game. "Helps when you can prove it. What have you got?"

Reddman told him, starting with everything he felt he could safely prove: the complete lack of skid marks or swerve marks before or after the hit; the long distance between the point where the victim's body landed and the point of impact; and the periodic blood smears that blotched the pavement between the two. He detailed the inferences that could be drawn from such evidence. The victim was almost across the street when Blue hit her. If Blue had swerved slightly, the truck would have caught air. If he'd touched the brake, she'd have been out of the way. Also, her body was wrapped around the right front tire and would have acted like a brake, requiring Blue to accelerate in order to keep moving—which proved that Blue deliberately chose to accelerate.

Trigge nodded with approval. "So instead of braking or swerving, he appears to have tromped on the accelerator. So far so good."

Reddman then told of Officer Brenfleck's contact with Blue minutes before the incident. He set the scene: shortly after 5:00 P.M. on a summer day, two weeks after Blue's release from jail; Blue in his truck on Mears Street hill, as though waiting for something. Reddman described the view from the hill and how easily Blue could have seen and recognized Ami O'Rourke as she left the courthouse.

"So, the plot thickens," Trigge said. "A suggestion?"

"That's why I'm here."

"Start with Brenfleck and what he said, instead of the hit. Give your tale a nice dramatic beginning. You can lay the groundwork for it in your opening." He chopped out a laugh. "Try to get them hating the bastard fast."

Reddman nodded in agreement, then outlined the testimony of the eyewitnesses. Goode, the banker, from the sidewalk, heard the loud honk of a horn and looked up. He saw the back of the truck and a flurry of paper. He heard someone scream and described the action of the truck as "out of whack" until the victim's body worked its way free of the tire. Then the truck sped away. Cindy Strickland, on the sidewalk but closer to the scene, saw essentially the same thing. However, in addition to the horn, she heard loud shouting coming from the truck.

"Any words?" Trigge asked. "Something incriminating, like 'At last, I got you'?"

"No. She can't even characterize the shouts as angry. Just loud."

"That won't help you, then. It cuts two ways. Blue will say, 'Sure I yelled. I couldn't believe the dumb broad was in the road.' "

Reddman told him about the third witness, Muriel Doppler, seated in her pickup truck and facing the point of impact, who had the clearest view of all. He told of Doppler's certainty that Blue sped up between the time she heard the horn and the time of the hit.

"Well. You've been busy, haven't you?" Trigge said, smiling. "How will this Doppler woman come across? Will the jury believe her?"

"They will if I handle her right."

"What else have you got?"

"The athletic ability of the defendant."

"Relevant to what issue?" Trigge asked. "If I was defending I'd climb all over your ass if you tried anything very far out."

"Intent," Reddman said. "He didn't swerve, and he didn't brake, but he honked, shouted, and accelerated before he hit her. If he had time to do all that, didn't he also have time to swerve or brake—especially since he's a gifted athlete?" Reddman spoke with passionate vehemence. "It goes to prove he intended to hit her, not miss her."

Trigge liked what he saw in the lad. A kick in the ass may have been all he needed. "What bothers me about it is this: if you try to prove athletic ability, you could lose momentum."

"What do you mean?"

"You're trying to prove intent with a negative." Trigge paused to light a cigarette. "You're saying there's something asshole didn't do that he should have done. Asshole's lawyer will object because the inference is too tenuous, and the judge will probably sustain. Then you lose momentum." Through a haze of smoke, he watched his hardheaded soldier fight with the advice, but try to accept it. "You're going to have enough problems putting in evidence you're entitled to without fooling around with stuff that's questionable. Besides, you don't need to fight for this. Blue will take the stand, won't he?"

"I think so. But I have to survive the motion to dismiss."

"With what you have so far, you'll get by *that* little hurdle. Then you can prove he's a gifted athlete when he takes the stand. Should be easy to get him to brag about his triumphs." Trigge watched as Reddman struggled with the suggestion. "You'll still be able to argue intent when you make your summation."

"Assuming that's the best way to handle it, the problem is making him take the stand."

"You think he might not?"

"If I were Cole, I wouldn't put him on. Why should he? The jury will have Blue's statement, which is a self-serving piece of shit. If Cole is as smart as I think he is, he'll argue that statement just as if it was testimony."

"Do you have to put his statement in?"

"Yes. No one saw him driving. It's the only way I can prove he was the one driving the truck."

Trigge grunted. He understood the problem completely. Just as a hunter of pheasant needed to flush the bird to get a shot, so Reddman needed evidence that would force Blue to take the stand. Without it, there would be no cross-examination. "Have you got anything?"

"Motive, maybe, but it's pretty thin."

"Let's hear it."

Reddman told of the relationship between the defendant and the victim, how it started as attorney and client as they prepared for a drunk driving trial, but how Blue made a pass at Ami and she told him to fuck off. Motive: pride. Then how, after the trial, for the first time in his life, Blue went to jail and blamed the conviction on his lawyer. Motive: revenge.

"That's your motive?" Trigge asked. "You're right. It's thin."

Reddman then told of his certainty that the man was psychopathic. He had skated away from two vicious beatings, one an Indian, the other a hippie. He had raped and beaten his former wife, a professor of literature who minored in psychology, and through her Reddman had found and interviewed two other women Blue had raped and beaten.

"So that's how you know it's murder." Trigge leaned back in his chair and stared at the ceiling. So this is what the kid is really after, he thought. Reddman wanted to know how to use evidence to suggest that the defendant was psychopathic when he knew it was inadmissible. "What you want to do is prove character, that he is psychopathic, right?" he finally said. "You know as well as I do you can't do that. It's Blue's call. He'd have to put his character in issue first."

"What about character evidence as relevant to motive?"

"Hmm." Old Joe's kid might really have the stuff, Trigge thought, hiding his smile behind a puff of smoke. "You mean, use character to beef up motive? In other words, acknowledge that motive is thin, but if the man is a psychopath, just a little bit of motive is all he'd need. That it?"

"Yes."

"Not bad, Davey. Very imaginative." Trigge scratched a note on a legal pad. "I'll take a look. I can tell you this much right now, though. You'll be breaking new ground, laying groundwork for an appeal, and risking a reversal if you convict the bastard. You'll also need a whole set of curative instructions, making it plain to the jury that they are to consider the evidence only as it might relate to motive."

"I know," Reddman said. "I promise to use it only if I'm about to fall off a cliff."

"Have you endorsed these women as witnesses?"

"Not yet. I've filed the motion."

"Would they be worth a continuance?"

"Sure," Reddman said. "Aren't you going to wait until I lose the case before you fire me? A continuance could keep me on the payroll another month."

"Careful with your shots, my boy. I might not wait." Trigge butted his cigarette. "Have you thought about not calling the women as witnesses, but giving them front row seats during the trial? Does asshole have the kind of mind you can fuck with?"

"Hm." Reddman thought it over. "Do you think I should withdraw the motion to endorse? Give up on the issue?"

"No. You've already filed the motion, so fight for it. But win or lose, use the women as props, not as witnesses. If you win, Cole will get a continuance, won't he?"

"He shouldn't, but he will."

"That would be the time to give up on the issue. You don't want a continuance. The town is ready for the trial now." He watched Reddman frown, once again fighting with himself. "This is the big entertainment in Muldoon, a lot more exciting than a chickenshit bicycle race. More excitement than when Ma got her tit caught in the blender and Sister turned the dang thing on." Trigge gave Reddman a chance to laugh, but Reddman groaned instead. "Merchants and farmers and ranchers and filling station attendants and waitresses have been talking about it for eight months. Now it's coming to a head, and you can bet your ass the town is buzzing about you. That's built-in momentum, Davey. You don't want to lose it.''

"I don't know, Trigge. I'll have to weigh that one. Hope you trust me.''

"No question. You're closer to the scene than I am.'' He almost said something about trusting Joe Reddman's kid, but veered away from it. "Used to be 'wringer,' you know, the mechanical contraption that Ma got her tit caught in? Had to change it to blender, which is truly awful if you think about it, because nobody knows what a wringer is now. Most people think it's some kind of hot shot.''

"Pretty awful is right,'' Reddman said.

"What else have you got?''

"Standard stuff: identification of the victim; blood matches between her and the truck; great pictures of the truck showing her blood, even some skin and clothing, hanging from the undercarriage; cause of death et cetera. I'll talk to the pathologist Thursday.''

"In other words, good gory photographs, right?''

Reddman nodded. "Some real beauties. You should see the ones they took of her body at the hospital. The trouble is, I don't know what they prove. The pathologist took some more photographs after he opened her up. I can use those to prove cause of death.''

"The ones at the hospital, before the pathologist got to her?''

"Yes?''

"She was still dressed?''

"Yes.''

"What about tire marks on her clothing? Or abrasions on her body consistent with having been spun around on a tire? You'll think of something.'' Trigge watched Reddman scribble some notes. "I'd be careful about the ones the pathologist took, though. They might be so bad the jury will turn against you.'' He barfed conically. "Never let the jury know you're a ghoul.''

Reddman looked doubtful, but made a note.

"Now give me the bad news," Trigge asked, staring out the window at the snow. "What's old fat Saul got up his sleeve, besides the judge?"

"He'll have to stay consistent with Blue's statement. So Blue will admit he'd been drinking—he had a point-eighteen—and he'll say he found himself parked on the Mears Street hill without knowing how he got there."

"Blacked out, you mean?" Trigge asked. "A hard-drinking cowboy blacked out on an eighteen? That could ruin his reputation." Trigge lit another cigarette. "Think anyone will believe him?"

"I don't know."

"Put a couple of lushes on that jury. *They* won't believe him."

Reddman smiled at the veteran advocate. "Not a bad idea. Anyway, Blue will probably talk about the bad blood between himself and the cop who spotted him—Brenfleck—and how the cop even waited for him to drive off, knowing he could bust him for driving without a license." Reddman glanced at his notes. "Then Brenfleck drove off on an emergency, and Blue knew he had to leave, which he did. He'll say he didn't see Ami until just before he hit her because he was looking over his shoulder for the police. Then after he hit her he panicked and ran."

"So he'll try to walk away from the murder rap by admitting the misdemeanors. That would gut the vehicular homicide, too, wouldn't it?" Trigge flicked ashes off his cigarette. "Professionally speaking, it's not a bad defense. Anything else?"

"Cole will prove a character trait of Ami's, for walking across the street without paying attention."

"True?"

"No, but it might as well be, because he can prove it." Reddman twitched his mouth. "The victim was a city person. Small-town traffic was as easy for her as fast food. She could charge into a street, reading and talking to herself and seemingly oblivious to traffic. But she could sense it."

"How do you know that?"

"Come on, Trigge. I've been with this case a week now. I know her. I know Blue. I saw it happen."

Trigge grinned. He knew what Reddman meant, knew how the impressions a good trial lawyer accumulated could give him visions of the scene, enable him to watch it go down. Frankie Rommel was right in her evaluation of Reddman. Too bad he had to get along with other people. "Anything else we need to talk about?"

"Cole has changed his mind about a plea bargain. Now he'd be willing to take his man out on a manslaughter and two of the traffic counts. How do you think I should advise Brim?"

"Well! You've got him scared. Any agreement as to sentence?"

"No agreement, but he'd probably do less than a year. He'd pull county jail time on the misdemeanors and get probation on the felony. Brim says Cole wouldn't offer to plead him to a felony if he hadn't already talked the sentence over with the judge."

Trigge laughed. "That's the way they do it in those frontier towns. More blindsiding than at a duck hunt." He floated another cloud. "Will Brim follow your advice?"

"Yes. I've got good rapport with the officers, too, and they'd go along. The detective in charge of the case thinks I should take it."

"Realistically, what are your chances if you try it?"

"I should get the traffic counts, might even get the vehicular homicide. That first degree murder count is what I want, though. That'll be tough."

"Would you ask for a lesser included?" Trigge asked, referring to all the charges legally included within first degree murder: second degree murder, manslaughter, and criminally negligent homicide.

"I would if Cole didn't."

"And?"

"I might get lucky and nail him with second degree."

"You could lose the whole ball, too."

"Yeah." Reddman slumped into the palm of his hand.

"But if the whole town hears it, and I convict him of a felony, the judge will have one very hard time giving Blue probation."

"All right. Now tell me what you want to do."

"I want to try it. I want to tell Cole to stick it up his ass."

"Why? You know as well as I do a felony conviction out of that piece of shit would be a victory. You wouldn't take a chance on losing the whole case, either. You'd have time to train for that bicycle race, and I might even decide not to fire you." He grinned at the young man. "Don't give me a crock about sentence, either. That's a political problem in Muldoon. Not your problem. So tell me why."

"You don't know?" Reddman asked, locking eyes with the other man. "He murdered her. That's why."

Trigge's fist slammed down on the desk, surprising both of them. "Good for you, Davey. Good for you!"

But with Reddman gone, Trigge wondered if he would make it or not. Wait and see, he decided. Wait and see.

Reddman stared into the blizzard, looking for the snow-packed road. He was glad he had taken the time to see Trigge in spite of the weather. The old man knew what he was talking about, he thought.

Reddman also realized that Trigge had been right about him, too. He'd goofed off on the case. He'd become Lopes's buddy and taken the detective's view, rather than working the case himself. He only hoped it wasn't too late.

He looked at his watch. It was one o'clock and he was just beginning the climb over Kenosha Pass. He decided to call Sharon when he got to Fairplay and tell her he'd be late. Then he put on a Bob Jones tape and turned up the sound. He thoroughly enjoyed the excitement of the drive, slipping and sliding around stalled and slower-moving vehicles, keeping up his momentum, and hoping he was still on the highway. It was like cycling, riding in a peleton and fighting to avoid the crash in front, bicycles and squirming bodies all over the road.

"Whoa," he said, freezing his breath and slowing down. A large tractor-trailer blocked the oncoming lane. Reddman let it pass, then gently accelerated to pass a Chrysler sedan in front of him. "Flatlander," he scoffed at the Chrysler, listening to the chink-chink-chink of its chains. Carefully he maneuvered his front-wheel-drive Datsun sports car into the proper lane.

Then he gripped the wheel with sudden excitement. "What the fuck is wrong!" he shouted. The rear end of his car seemed to be catching up with the front end, leaving his stomach behind.

His car came gently to rest in a snowbank. Reddman breathed a sigh of relief and listened as the flatlander in the Chrysler chinked on by.

CHAPTER
ELEVEN

Some snow clung in white blotches to the north faces of the mountains, but most of it was gone and the roads were dry. Reddman wasn't sure where he was, but he knew he could get back. All he had to do was turn his bike around, press his nose to the handlebars, and hang on. "This is superb!" he grunted, exulting in his strength and climbing as well as he'd ever climbed.

He had found a paved road with virtually no traffic not even ten miles from Muldoon, twisting steeply up the mountain. Only two cars had passed him in the half-hour he'd been on the thin highway. Reddman glanced at his watch: 7:30 A.M. "It's rush hour!" he hollered happily, knowing that in Denver the highways would be bumper-to-bumper and even the bike paths would be wheel-to-wheel.

Since his return from Denver, Reddman had been riding twice a day—before breakfast and in the evening. The intensity with which he had been working demanded the release. They were short twenty-mile rides with a mix of sprints and hills, and a whole load of fun. They took the same amount of time he usually spent commuting to and from work, and they did more than get him ready for the race. In his mind, they cleaned him of impurities and prepared his body for the war to come.

In other words, they made him a bit crazy, and he loved the feeling. His legs felt as good as they'd ever felt, and his spirits soared high, way up there with the eagles. "Yodel-eh, hee-ho!" he howled for no good reason, lifting his butt off the saddle and standing on the pedals. He swung rhythmically back and forth, pulling on the handlebars, releasing the strength of his arms, his back, and his stomach. It was as though every muscle in his body had the same goal and worked together as a unit, blowing him up the hill. The grade he climbed was over five percent, and he was two gears above his lowest and picking up speed. "You and me, babe!" he shouted, envisioning himself in the French Alps, pulling for his good friend and idol, Greg LeMonde.

The road curved upward, bent around the mountain, and slid out of sight. He heard an engine and grudgingly moved into his own lane, giving up the middle. "Honk! Honk!" he shouted, his energy level huge, giving away air. A blue pickup truck burst around the corner, hugging the mountain side of the road as it wound down the hill. The driver—young, wearing a large Stetson, a rifle in the rack behind his seat—slowed quickly when he saw the cyclist. Then he grinned. "Hey, cowboy, go for it!" he shouted. Reddman lifted his hand in a salute and grinned back.

The grade lessened and Reddman dropped back in the saddle and shifted into a larger gear. He had heard stories of the confrontations between cowboys and cyclists in the boonies, how the cowboys seemed to enjoy bumping cyclists off the highways, abetted by arrogant cyclists who were stupid enough to demand the center of the road. Up to that point, however, Reddman hadn't had a problem. He'd met with annoyance from old-timers, but nothing homicidal, and often he encountered respect tinged with admiration. He thought he knew enough about the cowboy mentality to expect that. Once those country boys realized that bikers were athletes who competed in a demanding sport, they cut them some slack. The road flattened and curved slowly to the right. Reddman mopped the sweat from his eyes and focused ahead of him. Half a mile in front, the highway dropped out of sight, and he knew he'd climbed to the summit.

Quickly he went through the gears, jumping them and testing the grade, until he was in his highest gear, a 53-12. Reddman stood up and churned, then dropped back in the saddle when his legs were spinning at 90 rpm. He kept on churning. At 110 rpm, the road sloping gently downward, he went into a tuck and took full advantage of his 154 pounds. A feeling of pure joy filled him up; he felt like a kid let unexpectedly out of school. He wanted to fly. The Pinarello picked up speed as the road looped downward for a mile, then two miles—less than three minutes. Reddman prepared himself for the sharper corners ahead. His fingers reached over the brakes and he laid the bike over beautifully, into and out of the first corner. He braked slightly, then slowed some more, flying into a sharper turn to his right. "Candy ass!" he shouted at himself, letting go of the brakes and aiming fearlessly at the next bend. The pavement cut to the left and disappeared behind the mountain—and in front he saw an incredible amount of blue sky.

"Shit!" he screamed, blaring into the corner at more than forty miles an hour. He laid the bike down, slowing as much as he could without locking up. Even at the high end of the stroke, his left pedal almost scraped the asphalt surface and he stared in panic at the row of concrete-block abutments that lined the road's edge. They were there to prevent cars from spilling off the mountain, and they seemed to reach for him as he whirred by. The last one lunged at him as he skidded over a thin patch of sand, but he missed the concrete block by inches. Somehow the twenty-pound bike had held onto the surface of the road.

Reddman's hands and arms were shaking when he rolled to a stop. He looked over the edge. A valley floor stretched five hundred feet below, looking peaceful and serene. He couldn't possibly have articulated the terror he had felt, or the relief. He relaxed his shoulders, but his arms and legs continued to shake as he turned around and started slowly to pedal back toward the summit. The sky was a brilliant blue, accentuated by a huge lightning-white thunderhead that swam lazily through the air like a hot air balloon. Two or three imagined faces leered at him from the cloud's surface. "Thanks, God," he said, still feeling the chill. "Sure am glad you're up there." But Reddman warmed up as he worked his way to the top of the hill, and ten minutes later when he rolled over the flat summit, his strength had returned and he felt good.

But not stupid. Reddman glanced at his watch: almost eight o'clock. The hearing on his motion to endorse witnesses—the two rape victims Sharon had located—was scheduled for nine, and he had to be in Montrose in the afternoon to interview the forensic pathologist. Plenty of time, he thought, to shower and shave, eat a bagel, and scare the shit out of Cole with the new witnesses. He pushed on the pedals, dropping into 53-12 as he started the downward glide. He didn't push it to the max, but pedaled gently, increasing speed. He knew the roll to Muldoon would not be dangerous, because he would be on the inside lane, against the mountain. He also had seen the corners on the way up. Even so, he promised himself not to get crazy. One good scare was enough.

He dropped into a tuck, fingers over the brakes, bathing in the clean morning air. The sun warmed his back, and he seemed to flow through the lazy turns at the top like a skier in deep powder, anticipating the tight corners on down the road. He laid his bike over gently, cutting into the turn the cowboy had rolled around—

A truck blocked the inside lane. It sloped diagonally across the highway, its tailgate a foot from the hillside, its nose more than halfway across the road. Reddman gripped the brakes hard and jerked to his left as he steered for the opening in the oncoming lane, outside the truck. Beyond the truck, the road bent sharply to the right, and he leaned in that direction, snapping the handlebars hard, fighting for balance. I'm losing it, he thought, knowing that if he did, he would die. The bike was in a rolling skid, and Reddman struggled desperately to avoid blue sky. The truck started forward, crowding him toward the edge of the cliff.

Reddman knew if he hit the narrowing gap at that speed, he'd go over the edge. He deliberately put the bike down on the asphalt surface and skidded his body across the pavement. The front wheel caught something under the slowly moving truck and he arced around the corner, sliding into an abutment across the road. He stayed on the highway. The truck—a red late-model Dodge pickup—lunged forward; Reddman was sure he had seen it before. He tried to read the license plate as it backed abruptly, faced up the hill, and peeled up the mountain and out of sight.

There were no broken bones, but Reddman had lost a lot of skin and he couldn't work. Sharon recommended a doctor who specialized in sports medicine, who covered him with Neosporin and wrapped him in bandages. Then the next day—Friday—Sharon took him to the Inn at La Posada in Santa Fe.

Their suite was in one of the old adobe buildings that meandered in long lines away from the hotel. The windows looked onto the spacious and radiantly colorful courtyards. But the first thing Reddman had to do after their four hour drive from Muldoon was change the dressings.

Sharon watched. She sat on the closed bathroom seat, dressed in jogging shorts and a yellow blouse. Reddman was naked, his foot on the edge of the bathtub. "Doesn't it hurt?" she asked as he unwound the strip of gauze off his leg. "Where I'm from you kill the critter before you peel it."

"Critter?" Reddman said, mimicking her. "You're a professor of literature?" The muscles in his face knotted with pain. He had used petroleum jelly to keep the gauze from sticking to his leg, but it stuck anyway. He had to tug lightly on the blood-soaked bandage, easing it away from his skin.

"That's right, honey," she said, cheerfully. "It's just

that ah'm keerful to keep the twang out when ah teach." She smiled at him, knowing how badly the wound must hurt. "Want me to do anythang?"

"Yeah. Go watch TV."

"I declare," she said, lightly. "I can think of a lot of men who might just be flattered if I was to sit around on a toilet seat and watch them undress."

"Huh."

"I could cool your leg off with some wine."

"Don't even think about it."

Sondenburg took a sip of wine from the glass in her hand and watched him wad up the bandage and toss it into the trash. "Now what?"

"Now I get in the shower and scrub it with soap."

"Ugh." She shivered and stood up. "You don't need me for that." As he turned on the water in the bathtub and tested it with his hand, she looked him over. He had such a beautiful body, she thought, admiring his skin—what there was left of it. His left hand looked like a mitten, and scabs had formed through raw spots on his shoulder, back, and hip. He even had one on his right earlobe. "If you were a horse, I'd shoot you," she told him. "Put you out of your misery." She watched him step into the tub and close the curtain.

"Hey, Sharon?" Reddman asked when the shower was on. "Hand me a washcloth?"

"Okay."

Reddman opened the curtain suddenly and aimed the nozzle at her, drenching her with water. "Bastard!" she shouted, fleeing from the room.

"Old locker room trick," Reddman told her after he had toweled himself off and put on a pair of Jockey shorts. He sat gingerly on the couch in front of the TV, sipping a glass of wine. "You need to spend more time in locker rooms. You look great, you know that?"

Sondenburg had changed into slacks and a short-sleeve sweater. "You're just saying that so I won't squirt you with something." She sat down next to him. "Do you still think it was Johnny Blue?"

"I know damn good and well it was."

"He has lots of friends. Couldn't it have been one of them?"

Reddman shrugged. "Same difference. He's really scared now—thanks to you."

"But you won't be able to use them, will you?" Sharon asked, referring to Donna Lipton and Fran Kent, two of the women Johnny Blue had raped. "I thought you said you'd given up on the motion to call them as witnesses."

"I can still use them. They can sit in court and stare at the back of his head." Reddman lifted his buttocks into a more comfortable position. "I saw that truck before, earlier in the week, when I was on my bike."

"Are you going to report this?"

"No."

"Why not?"

Reddman shrugged. "Nothing I can prove beyond a reasonable doubt. What if it's really a case of prosecutorial paranoia?"

"What's that?"

"A mental disorder that afflicts us white hats."

"I thought you guys were perfect."

"We are." Reddman's mood lightened up, even as he touched a sore spot on his thigh with a bandaged hand. "Prosecutorial paranoia is not a defect. Great legs, right?" he asked, referring to his own.

"I'd like them better if they had some hair. Some skin, too. What is it?"

"The paranoia? Happens usually after you convict some loser and he gives you that cold fish stare when they send him away, and then he gets out. You start doing crazy things, like carrying a gun and looking over your shoulder."

"Don't they need to be convicted first?"

"I'm talking about the feeling." Reddman reached for the bottle and sloshed wine into both glasses.

"Want me to kill him for you?"

"Don't talk like that."

Men are such babies, Sondenburg thought. It isn't their fault, really. Society has taken away their rituals and myths. How can they grow up? "You're getting an erection," she said. "Don't try anything, though. You'll start to bleed."

Reddman looked at her with softness, then looked away. "Shit," he said, his eyes growing large with tears.

"What's wrong?"

"Trial starts in two days and I'll be in a big bicycle race the Monday after that, then I go back to Denver and you stay in Muldoon." Sondenburg looked at him, but said nothing. "Will you save me a weekend now and then?"

She touched his arm. Her eyes were also full. "Let's not talk about that now. Okay?"

It was Saturday, and Sondenburg and Reddman were driving back to Muldoon. They were traveling through the high desert country north of Santa Fe. The highway had climbed through a narrow sandstone canyon, over the rimrock, and onto a green shelf of desert bounded in the distance by layered cliffs. "Have you ever seen such rocks?" Sharon asked him, pointing at a thin line of spires near the walls. "They look like totem poles."

"They're like those Baby Rocks, near Kayenta in Arizona."

Sharon steered the car lightly with one hand, the other pushing at strands of hair. "You can see faces. Wouldn't it be fun to build narratives and histories around them?"

"You mean how come their heads are made out of rock?"

"You're such an asshole."

Reddman turned toward the window so she wouldn't see him smile. Something is seriously wrong here, he thought. I even like it when she calls me an asshole. "Hey, look." He put a hand on her thigh and pointed with the bandaged hand out his window. A scraggly juniper tree stood lonely in the desert except for a huge bird perched near the top.

Sharon slowed the car in an effort to see what he was pointing at. The bird flapped abruptly, disturbing the air, then rose gracefully into the sky. "Just a buzzard," she said. "Isn't he magnificent?"

They were caught for a moment by the scene. Sunlight coated the dry desert colors with radiance. The sage against the sand, the cliffs against the sky, the occasional lonely tree in the desert, struck them with startling clarity. "Really? Just an old buzzard?" Reddman inquired.

"Yes."

"He'd have to be an eagle to be magnificent."

"That's stupid," Sondenburg said. "Do you see with your eyes?"

"Sure."

"Then how does it matter what you call it?"

"Huh!" Reddman started to move his hand from her thigh.

"That's all right," she said. "It's not in the way."

"Okay."

She put her hand on top of his and loved the way it gave itself up to her. "Your trial starts Monday?"

Reddman nodded, then moved his hand away and stuck his thumb in his mouth. He assumed a comic fetal position. "Let's go back to Santa Fe." Sondenburg lifted her hand toward the steering wheel, but Reddman intercepted the motion and laced his fingers with her. "Sharon, I really appreciate—"

"You don't need to say anything."

Reddman laid his head back and put their hands on the leather car seat, pressing against his leg. "This is really nice."

"It doesn't get any better than this."

"Don't be such a cynic."

"Come on! I wanted to make up legends and myths, but you turned them into tales about people with rocks in their heads, but *I'm* the cynic?" Sondenburg tried—not very hard—to pull her hand away, but Reddman wouldn't let her. She liked the pressure of his flesh.

"I'm really scared," he said suddenly.

"You are?"

"I lost three days with that crash. Thursday, Friday, today. I'll have to put the pathologist on cold, with no chance to interview him."

"Are you sorry we went to Santa Fe?"

"Oh, no. I don't mean that at all. I couldn't have worked anyway."

"You'll be able to work tomorrow, won't you?"

"Yeah. Unbelievable how much there is to do yet. I still have to prepare instructions, rehearse arguments, get my trial notebook in shape." Reddman groaned and shook his head. "We still have to hear that motion to suppress evidence, too."

"Do you like what you do?"

"I don't like it a bit. I hate it. But I love it, too."

"Why do you do it?"

"For the victims, I guess. After a while you get to know them. Even the dead ones."

"Do you think you know Ami?"

"Yes."

"Tell me what you think she was like."

Reddman closed his eyes and let the murdered woman come into his mind. "A good lawyer. Had a chip on her shoulder—normal for a public defender. A lot of mouth—also typical—completely unable to understand why anyone should think her baby-raping client is a creep."

"Pretty good so far," Sondenburg said. "What did she look like?"

"Small, outdoorsy-looking, not very pretty, but not ugly, either."

"Do you know how old she was?"

"Thirty-six when it happened. She'd be thirty-seven now." Reddman frowned, opened his eyes, and sat up. "You know, the son of a bitch, he killed her. She didn't need that."

"Does seem a little extreme, doesn't it?"

Reddman was grinding his teeth, and his hand, still

in Sondenburg's, was closing into a fist. "It's really frustrating."

"What is?"

"The justice machine. Blue could walk away from this scot-free."

"You're hurting my hand." She watched him look down, then unlace his fingers and cup her hand. "You really care about this case, don't you?"

"Yeah."

"Why? Is it because of me?"

"Not really. You've helped me get to know the players, including myself, but I care for other reasons, too."

"What are they?" Sondenburg asked, genuinely curious. "You weren't here when it happened and you'll be gone when it's done. You can't bring her back." She glanced at him, trying to read his face. "Is it ego or what? Or do you even know?"

"Look out there," Reddman demanded, staring out the window. "It's more than just pretty out there. It's magnificent."

"So?"

"He took that away from her. Deliberately. For some asshole reason he probably doesn't understand himself. Some buried hate that bubbled up and spilled out, and he killed her." Reddman's breathing had deepened and his hand squeezed hers to the point of pain. "So he has problems. That isn't the way to solve problems. You know what I mean, don't you?" He waved his bandaged hand at the panoramic view. "He removed her from this."

"I'm sorry. You're hurting my hand." Reddman relaxed his grip. "Do you feel this deeply every time you have a trial?"

"I don't know. I don't keep a medical chart. But I usually get into them pretty far—especially when the son of a bitch I'm prosecuting pushes me off the road and relieves me of patches of skin."

Sondenburg took her hand out of his and put it on the steering wheel. "What if he didn't murder her at all? I mean, we could both be wrong about this. You don't know for an absolute certainty that he murdered her, do you? You're not God."

"Wrong. I *am* God and I *do* know for sure. I saw it happen."

"Uh-oh. More prosecutorial paranoia? Visions and omniscience?"

"Right!" Reddman said, cheerfully. "Not crazy at all. I won't be crazy in the courtroom, either," he leered, like a mad magician. "I'll be a sword in the courtroom"—he jabbed and slashed with the hand that was bandaged—"where I will peel away falsehood"—deftly peeling away—"and I slay terrible lies, seeking justice, seeking the truth! Aaagh!" He stabbed a piece of air, then held it on the tip of his sword where they could both see it.

"What have you got there?" Sharon asked, reaching out as though to touch.

"The truth! Don't you see it?" Reddman called out, like a street-corner prophet.

"But you've stabbed it with your sword." Sondenburg spoke theatrically and raised her eyebrows, as though high enough to be seen by an audience. "You didn't kill it, did you?"

139

CHAPTER TWELVE

The Sopris County District Courtroom is much larger than any of the courtrooms in Denver. The rows of bolted-down chairs behind the rail, with wooden armrest dividers and fold-up seats, give the courtroom the aspect of a high school auditorium. That Monday morning, the only matter on the docket was *People v. Blue,* set for 9:00 A.M. Except for the seats in the roped-off area reserved for prospective jurors, every chair had been claimed by eight o'clock. Forty minutes later, when the special prosecutor arrived, people were spilling into the hallway and gathering on the sidewalk in front of the building.

Dave Reddman walked slowly into the courtroom. People parted magically for him, as the Red Sea had for Moses, and he took his place in front of the rail at counsel table. Reddman wore light brown slacks and a dark brown gabardine jacket. According to the manual on jury selection, brown was the color that most jurors identified with sincerity, and according to the manual, the prosecutor should look sincere. Reddman wondered if the authors of the manual had thought about the irony of manipulating jurors into believing that cases were prosecuted by sincere people. He carried a briefcase with his good hand and a volume on procedure with the bandaged one. Light scabs had formed over his right earlobe and cheek, like a birthmark, as though God had known the perfectly formed face needed a blemish before anyone would believe it. He opened his briefcase, pulled out his trial notebook and three or four files, and arranged them neatly on the table in front of him.

A short heavy man wearing a solid green mail-order suit and a string tie marched up to Reddman from the judge's entrance behind the bench. A beautifully ornate gold, silver, and turquoise ring held the man's tie in place. "How're you doing, Roy?" Reddman asked, recognizing Roy Kellerman, former sheriff of Sopris County and now Judge Gilbert Landry's bailiff. He tried to sound casual, but his voice felt thin and tight. "Ready for the festivities?" As though he were E. F. Hutton, when he spoke, everyone listened.

"Reckon I am, Davey. Judge'd like to see you 'fore we get going, though."

Reddman followed the bailiff into the judge's chambers. "Sit down, young man," Landry said pleasantly. "Shut the door, will you, please, Roy? We don't need to involve all of Sopris County in this little discussion." He smiled engagingly, his manner very different from what it had been the last time Reddman saw him. "Now, then. We've called this meeting—"

"'We,' Your Honor?" Reddman asked, holding the challenging tone of his voice to a minimum. Saul Cole sat comfortably in one of the chairs in front of the large conference desk. Cole's suit was blue; according to the manual on jury selection, blue was the color of friendliness. Reddman thought Cole had probably read the same manual. "I assume you mean you and Mr. Cole here?" he asked, sitting down.

"Actually, I called the meeting, but Saul suggested that I do so. You see, Saul has appeared before me many times and knows how I operate, so to speak. He—we both—felt that in fairness to you, it might be helpful if I outlined some of my idiosyncrasies." He continued beaming at Reddman, who smiled back.

"Heard from Daddy?" Cole asked suddenly, his voice

amiable. "Maybe he'll come down, watch sonny boy perform?"

Reddman ignored the questions. He hadn't seen Cole since the day before his "accident," when the two men had met in Cole's office. Reddman had rejected Cole's plea offer, and Cole had called him a smart-ass, and a little punk. Reddman knew it was all part of the game, but didn't know how long he could take the crap. "I appreciate this, Judge," Reddman said, shutting Cole out. "I've been over the local rules, but the way they read and the way they are can be different, and I'd a lot rather be embarrassed in chambers than out there where everybody's watching."

"Will your father come down, young man?" Landry asked. "I've heard so much about him. I'd like to meet him."

"No, Judge, we don't stay in touch."

"What gets me is that we could avoid all this," Cole said. "Two, three weeks of trial—they must pay you special prosecutors by the hour. Tell you something, I've got better things to do with my time than try this case."

Landry looked at Reddman expectantly, as though he, too, was waiting for a reply. "Mr. Cole has informed me the defendant is willing to plead guilty to manslaughter and two of the misdemeanors, young man. Is this trial necessary?"

Reddman felt the heat rise in his face. The real purpose for the meeting had shown itself: pressure from the judge to accept a plea bargain. It confirmed what he had known all along: that Cole had been talking to Landry ex parte—without consulting the lawyer from the other side—and, what was worse, that the judge had been listening. "Absolutely."

"But have you gone over this matter with Mr. Brim? My recollection is that at one time Brim offered a similar disposition."

"That offer was withdrawn, Judge. I can assure you that I have gone over this carefully with Mr. Brim, and he agrees with me."

Landry's manner changed. The large man seemed to swell up slightly, and the expression in his eyes hardened.

"Young man, from my limited acquaintance with the facts in this case, it strikes me that a manslaughter conviction, which is a felony, would be a most advantageous disposition for the prosecution."

"I don't think so at all, Judge. It's the state position that this was a deliberate killing." Reddman tried to keep his words from shooting out of his mouth like bullets.

"Of course I recognize that the state's apparent position is first degree murder, inasmuch as that is what the information charges. But doesn't your obligation as an officer of this court go beyond that? Do you sincerely feel you can prove it?"

"Meaning no disrespect, sir, but you never know until you try."

"So *that's* it!" Landry suddenly boomed. "You intend to tie up my courtroom for two or three weeks in some vague expectation of a first degree murder conviction?"

Reddman knew it was never a good idea to tell a judge he was out of line; but he was ready to do it. "It won't take two or three weeks, Judge. It'll take one. And as far as—"

"In any event, I'm initiating some discussion here. I will inquire directly of counsel whether or not there is any possibility at this point of a plea bargain." He glared at Reddman.

"God knows I've tried, Gil," Cole said, turning angrily toward Reddman. "This your idea of sport, kid? Is that it?" His cheeks shook and his beautifully full and wavy head of silver hair sparkled, as though radiating energy. "I'm offering to plead my man to two out of three traffic, you pick, and to plead him to manslaughter! No agreement as to sentence, none! He could pull two years county jail and eight years in the pen, that's ten years jail, you think you're gonna get more'n that for *this* case out of a Sopris County jury, you're crazy!"

Reddman was grinning inside. An old mentor in Arizona had told him: "Davey, there's an imp in you. When that little fucker is ready to come out—when he wants to scream, holler, bite, scratch, and enjoy—then those other guys better look out." He smiled beatifically at the judge. He knew, at that moment, he was ready for trial. "If it please the court, I don't think there is any possibility of a plea bargain."

"Look at that, Gil! Little snot won't even look at me, I'm a leper with AIDS, he won't even *talk* to me!" Cole literally foamed at the mouth. "Not wet behind the ears but he's a by-god special prosecutor, one of them NASP nasties. Guess that's what makes him so smart!"

"Mr. Reddman, I will have to say your attitude appears to me to be most unreasonable," Landry said icily. "I suggest you explain to me why you have in such cavalier fashion rejected what appears to the court to be a most reasonable offer."

"I'd be glad to make a full and complete explanation, Judge. On the record."

"Why— Are you implying something here, young man?" Landry's face hardened into stone. "This isn't Denver, sir. We aren't—we can't afford to be—that formal! Don't you understand even that?"

"This may not be Denver, but we're still in the state of Colorado, aren't we?"

"Pardon me? What did you say?"

"I said that we're still in the state of Colorado and—"

"I see." Landry shot to his feet. "Very well. It is obvious to me this matter is a joke to you. Well, we shall see who has the last laugh." His nostrils flared like those of a frustrated bull. "That will be all."

Reddman and Cole filed into the courtroom and took their places at the counsel tables. An expectant hush filled the arena. Johnny Blue, wearing a brown western-style suit and smiling pleasantly at everyone, stood politely until both lawyers were seated, then painfully eased into his chair. He smiled sympathetically at Reddman, as though forgiving the man for doing what he had to do. Reddman took no notice. Walter Brim had unexpectedly been called out of the office, and Randy Turner, the deputy district attorney, sat importantly at the prosecution table. Reddman had wanted Brim there to help with jury selection. Turner wore a three-piece pin-striped suit. Bernie Lopes, resplendent in a dark blue summer suit, sat next to Turner. "How'd it go in there?" the deputy D.A. asked in a stage whisper, referring to the conference in chambers. "Saul sure is hot about something."

"The plot thickens," Reddman whispered back. "Later."

"All rise," the bailiff intoned as Judge Gilbert Landry swept majestically into the courtroom. "District court in and for the county of Sopris, state of Colorado, now in session." Landry seated himself behind the bench and impassively surveyed the room. "Resume your seats," the bailiff announced.

Landry opened the file in front of him. "Good morning, Counsel," he said to Cole and Reddman, who had remained standing. "It appears that everyone is here. For the sake of the record, we begin today the case of *People versus Johnny Blue,* which comes on at this time for trial to a jury. Are the people ready, Mr. Turner?"

"Pardon me?" Turner said, struggling quickly to his feet and looking at Reddman. He obviously had not expected to play an active role.

"Mr. Turner, I asked you whether or not the people are ready."

"If it please the court," Reddman said, speaking up quickly. He was amazed—as always, at the beginning of a trial—at the strength of his voice. "My name is David Reddman, my attorney registration number is one-six-seven-six, and I'll be appearing on behalf of the people."

"Mr. Reddman, is it?" Landry asked, as though they were meeting for the first time. "Who are you, sir?"

"I'm a special prosecutor, with the National Association of Special Prosecutors."

"Is that so? Well, I'm sorry, but I cannot allow your appearance at this late date. I know of my own knowledge that you are not on the district attorney's staff in Sopris

County, and the court has neither authorized nor approved the appointment of a special prosecutor." He turned to Turner. "Are the people ready, Mr. Turner?"

That's a new one, Reddman thought. "Excuse me, Judge Landry," he boomed confidently, searching quickly for the word "appointment" in the index of his trial notebook and opening it to the right page. "I've been specially appointed to prosecute this case by Walter Brim, the district attorney of Sopris County. He has acted pursuant to CRS 20-1-21(1)(c). I have that documentation here in my file, if the court wishes to examine it."

"Of course I wish to examine it!" Landry snapped, frowning and looking toward Cole. Reddman tore the special appointment out of his notebook and started toward the bench. "Has the law been changed?" Landry inquired, watching Reddman approach. "Isn't it my responsibility to make these designations?" He reached for a volume of the *Colorado Revised Statutes* and started turning it toward the section cited by Reddman. "Since when does the district attorney decide who will and who will not appear in my courtroom?"

"This is pursuant to a very recent statutory change, Your Honor," Reddman said. He handed Landry the paper. "I know how hard it is to keep up with the legislature."

Landry glanced imperiously over the document. "Wouldn't it have been much better, Mr. Reddman, to have clarified this matter in advance?" He snapped the *CRS* volume shut.

"Perhaps so, Judge," Reddman said, knowing he had taken the wind out of Landry's sails.

"I suggest that in the future you file the appointment with the clerk of the court. These matters should be taken care of well in advance of trial." He thrust the document at Reddman, dismissing him.

Reddman wondered how much interest the pointless flap had generated among the spectators in the courtroom. He returned to counsel table, fighting the urge to wink at Saul Cole. What have you guys cooked up for me next? he asked himself, smiling with friendliness at Cole, who scowled at the floor.

Landry cleared his throat. "We begin anew. Mr. Redd-man, is the prosecution ready to proceed?"

"There is a pending motion, Judge, that needs to be resolved before we can start the trial. Defendant Blue through his attorney has filed a motion to suppress evidence—"

"Mr. Reddman, we have previously discussed this matter, have we not?" Landry spat angrily into the mircrophone in front of him, his words bouncing off the walls throughout the room.

"Yes, Your Honor, we've discussed it in chambers, but not in open court or on the record, as we are now. The matter has not been resolved."

"Well, it *has* been resolved, Mr. Reddman. To everyone's satisfaction but yours! I believe my position is quite clear. Now are you or are you not ready to proceed to trial?"

The little imp in Reddman started to make a face at Judge Landry, but Reddman caught him in time. "I am not ready to proceed to trial, Judge, until there has been a resolution of that motion." He flipped easily to the pertinent page in his trial notebook. "I respectfully refer the court to rule forty-one, section *e* of the Rules of Criminal Procedure. May I quote—"

Cole lumbered to his feet. "If the prosecution isn't ready, Judge, I move to dismiss! What is this?" He stared around him, obviously wounded.

"Mr. Reddman, but for the seriousness of this charge, I would grant Mr. Cole's motion summarily! However, because of the significance of this case to the people in this county, I will afford you the courtesy of asking one more time: Are you or are you not ready to proceed?"

"All witnesses for the state are present, Judge Landry," Reddman said. "Everything that is necessary for trial has been prepared, and in that sense, I am ready to put the case on. But a motion was filed by the defendant some months ago—a motion to suppress all evidence—and the state has the right to have that motion determined prior to trial. It is the state's position that the court does not have the jurisdiction to proceed with a jury trial until after it has resolved that motion."

"What difference does it make, young man?" Landry exploded. "This jury panel has been summoned for *today*. All these people are here *today*. Is it your desire that all of these prospective jurors"—he waved his hand at the courtroom—"some seventy-odd citizens of this county, be inconvenienced and sent home? I have previously explained to you the practice of this court. We will hear that motion to suppress *after* we have selected the jury!"

"Meaning after the commencement of the trial?" Reddman asked.

"Yes! Of course! But the jurors will be excluded from the courtroom and won't be able to hear! Don't you see?"

"Judge, that would place the state in an untenable position." Reddman chose to label his side of the case "the state" rather than "the people" at that moment, to remind Landry that Sopris County was part of Colorado. "If you grant the defendant's motion after the trial has started, the state won't have any evidence. We would then be in a position where we could not go forward with the trial. We couldn't even appeal your ruling, because jeopardy would have attached, and the Constitution doesn't permit double jeopardy."

"These are matters you should have considered long ago! Furthermore, it is apparent you anticipate an incorrect ruling!"

"Not at all, Judge. I have every confidence in the court," Reddman said, lying through his teeth. "But I am charged with the responsibility of protecting the people's interest."

Landry was obviously at his wit's end. He banged the gavel against the marble plate on the bench. "Court will be in recess," he declared, rising angrily. "I apologize, ladies and gentlemen, for this unexpected delay, which—

Well, no matter. Let me see both attorneys in chambers immediately." He started to leave.

"I respectfully request the presence of the court reporter in chambers," Reddman declared, his skin literally prickling with excitement.

Landry whirled and glared at the young lawyer, who seemed to loom in front of him like a statue. "Very well."

Cole glanced sorrowfully at Reddman, shaking his head slowly, as the two men picked up their legal pads and followed the court reporter into chambers. Reddman glanced at the prospective jurors, wondering what they thought of all the posturing. He sensed encouragement. He picked up a few smiles and a couple of nods of approval. No one avoided his eyes.

"Well," Landry said a moment later. He smiled at Reddman from behind his desk with something like respect. "Nothing like a small scrap in public to get the blood going, is there?"

Reddman laughed. "The door, Judge?" he suggested.

"I'll get it, Gil," Cole said jovially, shutting it. His mood, too, had improved. "Better'n whiskey, you know?" The lawyers sat down in the chairs they had been in before, but leaned toward each other, waiting for the court reporter to set up his machine. "I'm higher'n a kite and so far we aren't even to where he asks me if I'm ready to proceed!"

A feeling of affection linked the lawyers and the judge. Reddman knew it would pass. Prizefighters exhibited the same syndrome, he thought, when they threw their arms around each other after a match.

"Remarkable, isn't it?" Landry continued amiably. "Out there, in front of all those people, half of whom have appeared before me in some capacity or other—young man, I wanted to wring your neck!" Everyone laughed.

"Ready, Judge," Carl, the court reporter, said. His eyes were half closed and his hands floated over the small box on the tripod like those of a fortune-teller conjuring images out of a crystal ball.

"Very well. We are conferring in chambers—Mr. Reddman, Mr. Cole, myself—regarding *People versus Blue,* and Mr. Reddman has requested that our discussion be reported." Landry's words seemed to flow through Carl's fingers and onto the thin roll of paper that ground slowly out of his machine. "The matter at issue has to do with whether we can select a jury at this stage, prior to hearing defendant's motion to suppress evidence. We previously discussed this matter off the record—"

"Judge, you want me to go off the record?" Carl asked, lifting his hands.

"No, no. Our previous discussion was off the record. Am I right so far, gentlemen?"

"Yes, sir," Cole said, and Reddman said, "Correct."

"Yes. And at that time, I indicated that the practice of this court has always been to select the jury, give them the rest of the day off, hear pending motions, and then bring the jury back. The practice appears to this court to be an efficient one, in that the remainder of the jury panel can be excused and those selected as jurors can have what is left of the day to get their affairs in order before beginning the serious business of the trial." He paused and thoughtfully examined the backs of his hands. "Further, in most instances, the witnesses called for the motions must also testify at the trial. Inasmuch as many of them are out of town, even out of state, it has always seemed cost-effective to proceed in the fashion outlined because then they have to make only one trip to Muldoon. Not, of course, that people don't enjoy coming to Muldoon!" He smiled benignly. "However, Mr. Reddman appears to object to that procedure. Mr. Reddman?"

Reddman's skin continued to prickle with excitement. He enjoyed knowing that his words were being transcribed, as though he was dictating a script for that Great TV Producer in the Sky. He chose his words carefully. "If it please the court, let me say initially that the practice you describe appears to be a very efficient one, a practice that in most situations would give all the advantages you speak of. But in this case—and perhaps this is an unusual one—there is pending a motion to suppress evidence. If the people lose that motion, we will not have enough evidence to go on."

"Specifically what evidence are you talking about?" Landry asked.

"Everything connecting Defendant Blue to the crime. His arrest, his statement admitting he was the driver, the examination of his vehicle, and—"

"Wait a minute, not everything," Cole said. "Mr. Reddman has made an overstatement, which needs to be corrected."

"You'll get your chance, Mr. Cole. Proceed, Mr. Reddman."

Reddman racked his brain, trying to understand what Cole was talking about. "The vehicle was examined after Blue's arrest, Judge, and the results of that examination—photographs showing what appears to be blood throughout the undercarriage, and expert testimony showing it is in fact the blood of Ami O'Rourke—those results would also be suppressed. And Mr. Cole is correct, Your Honor. The people would be able to show some minimal contact between the defendant and the crime. We could show that Blue was in the area just before the victim was struck, sitting in his pickup truck. He had a conversation with a police officer a few minutes before he ran over Ami O'Rourke. We could also show, through witnesses, that the victim was hit by a pickup truck. But the witnesses would not be able to identify the defendant's truck as the particular truck involved, or the defendant as the driver." Reddman suddenly realized he had forgotten to ask his witnesses that question.

Cole had been slouched in his chair with his chin on his chest. As Reddman watched in horror, the man lifted his leonine head and smiled. "You know for sure they can't identify Blue as the driver? You ever ask?"

Reddman smiled back, but his heart wasn't in it. Cole was better than he thought. Cole had caught him in an overstatement and quickly and deftly exposed him in front of the judge. "Didn't I say 'presumably'?"

"No, you didn't," Landry said, eyeing Reddman critically.

"My mistake, Judge. I should have said that presumably the witnesses would not be able to identify either the truck or the defendant. But even if they could, their identification would be suspect, because none of them could have seen the truck for more than a second."

"However, it's possible that they could name him as the driver?"

"Yes," Reddman conceded. "But my whole case is based on scientific evidence linking the truck to the crime, and on the defendant's admission that he was driving the truck."

"Let me make sure I understand," Landry said. "There is an abundance of evidence linking defendant Blue to the crime, which is the subject of a pending motion to suppress. That evidence appears principally to emanate from two sources: an examination of Mr. Blue's pickup truck, and Mr. Blue's admission that he was the driver of the truck when it struck the victim. I assume the evidence is challenged on the basis that it is the product of an unlawful search and seizure, am I correct so far?"

"You got it, Judge," Cole remarked laconically.

"Fine. And Mr. Reddman's problem is this: if the evidence is suppressed, then—although it would be possible for him to proceed—his case would be considerably weakened. Is that the situation?"

"Yes, sir," Reddman said.

"Fine. Now to the real question here. Should we proceed with jury selection in spite of Mr. Reddman's objection? Mr. Cole, let me hear from you first."

"You know my answer to that without asking, Judge. A jury panel has been summoned, more than seventy people, citizens Sopris County. We're talking administration of justice here. Mr. Reddman can't hide behind the fact he don't know the local rules. He's charged with that responsibility, same as any lawyer; it's his responsibility to find out. All he had to do was file a motion to set the motion to suppress for a hearing in advance of trial, what is this?" He glared angrily at his adversary. "I say the decision is discretionary with the court this point in time, the court should decide let's get on with this trial, let the chips fall where they may. And in spite of what Mr. Reddman says, the prosecution *does* have enough evidence to put on a case even if you grant my motion. Administration of justice is the real issue here, has to do with the way people in this community look at the criminal justice system, what they see. A man charged with a crime has a right to a trial, let's get on with it!"

"Suppose I do as Mr. Cole suggests, Mr. Reddman. What will you do?"

"I will refuse to go forward, Judge. I will force you to dismiss the case for failure to prosecute."

"Why?"

"Because I can appeal a dismissal as long as it happens before jeopardy attaches. But if you dismiss after we impanel a jury, then Blue walks. He's a free man."

"And if you are successful on the appeal, we'll have all this to do over again." Landry swiveled away from the lawyers and pressed the tips of his fingers into a steeple. "I can't tell you how much I dislike the idea of sending the panel home and directing them to come back tomorrow. I know these people; they look up to me; it looks bad." He frowned at Reddman. "However," he sighed, "I have examined the pertinent rule, and it appears that the prosecution is entitled to have the pending motion resolved before trial. It would be an abuse of my discretion to—"

"Wait a minute, Judge, we can have it both ways." Cole had been thumbing through the *Criminal Code* and sat up suddenly, placing the book on the desk.

"We can? How?"

"This statute says jeopardy doesn't attach until after the jury is sworn *in*. We can select the jury now. We just won't swear 'em in!" He grinned around the room. "Then the jurors leave, you tell the ones who've been selected to come back tomorrow, and as soon as they're gone we do the motion to suppress."

"Let me see if I understand you," Landry said. "You mean we select the jury but don't swear them in and thus avoid the double jeopardy problem. Then we go forward with the motion to suppress. And if the district attorney doesn't like my ruling he'll be able to appeal, because the jury will not have been sworn in." He brightened. "Or, we swear them in then and go ahead with the trial. Mr. Reddman?"

"Can we go off the record a minute, Judge, and look it up?"

"We're off the record, Carl," Landry said. The court reporter lifted his hands. "Let me see that book, Saul." Cole pushed the volume across the desk. "Well. It is helpful to go to the books on occasion," he said, showing the volume to Dave Reddman.

When the lawyers returned to their places in the courtroom, they were obviously in an improved state of mind. Reddman tried to keep a distance between himself and Cole, but the man followed him to his chair and—as though they were conspirators—stuck his face in Reddman's ear and whispered something amusing. Reddman tried not to smile at Cole's remark, remembering the advice of the chief trial deputy in Arizona before his first jury trial: "Never kiss the defense lawyer in public."

"What's keeping the judge?" Cole asked, obviously still Reddman's friend.

"He's talking to Conway, the ex-D.A.," Randy Turner said. He had joined the other two lawyers. Johnny Blue will come over next, Reddman thought, knowing the appearance of affection between the combatants at this early stage would blur the jury's vision.

"All rise," the bailiff suddenly announced.

Cole moved quickly back to the defense table, and Reddman, on his feet, watched Judge Landry stalk angrily into the courtroom and sit down. He was no longer the benign father figure he had been in chambers. He looked like a hand grenade ready to explode.

What happened? Reddman wondered, staring neutrally toward the bench. Was it something Conway told him? Suddenly the imp took over. Reddman felt a huge smile break out on his face. "Good morning, Judge Landry," he heard himself say.

CHAPTER
THIRTEEN

According to the manual on jury selection, one doesn't select a jury; one unselects. The opposing sides chisel away at the panel of jurors—the mass of people summoned to jury duty—like a sculptor at a block of wood, hoping a face will emerge that will favor their side. Judge Landry controlled the process with an icy formality, his barbs and interruptions favoring neither the prosecution nor the defense, and shortly before two o'clock that afternoon both sides declared that they were satisfied with the jury they had picked.

Reddman had practiced in rural jurisdictions before and was not surprised at the speed with which the jury was selected. Most of the members of the panel were known to the lawyers—in Reddman's case, through quick consultation with Bernie Lopes and Randy Turner—and the case had been the subject of speculation in the community for months. There weren't too many questions left to be asked. Nevertheless, the process was exhausting, and Reddman would have liked a break when they were done.

Before excusing the six men and eight women—twelve jurors and two alternates—who sat rather smugly in the jury box, Landry spoke to them like a stern parent. He told them they would be excused for the balance of the day and were to return the next morning at nine o'clock. He admonished them not to discuss the case with anyone and not to read any newspaper accounts. They were specifically ordered to leave the courtroom immediately, because of a hearing that would follow that afternoon. "Evidence may be presented that—for legal reasons—might be inadmissible at the trial," Landry explained. "You will be the triers of the fact, but your decision can be based only on the facts presented during the trial. You must trust the accumulated wisdom of centuries of jurisprudence in this regard." He lectured to them like a preacher from the pulpit, informing them that it would be illegal, prejudicial, and irresponsible—as well as the probable basis for a mistrial—if any of them were to taint themselves by finding out what that evidence was. "You are excused," he then said, and the fourteen citizens of Sopris County filed solemnly out of the courtroom. Landry ordered a short recess, and when court reconvened fifteen minutes later, many of the spectators had gone.

"We will now proceed with Defendant Blue's motion to suppress evidence," Landry said. "I will state for the record that I have read the motion and am familiar with the issues involved. Would either of you gentlemen care to make an opening statement?"

"Not me," Cole said. "Waste of time."

"Mr. Reddman?"

"No, sir."

"Very well. Even though it's the defendant's motion, the burden of proof is on the prosecution. If you are ready to proceed, Mr. Reddman, please call your first witness."

"Officer Dave Brenfleck, if it please the court."

The uniformed officer mounted the witness stand and was sworn in. Reddman stood behind the lectern, facing the witness box. During the recess, the imp in him had gone underground. At that moment, he was annoyed with himself for his inability to focus on the cherubic-looking cop. Reddman had that spacy, unreal feeling—like a puppet, with someone else pulling the strings—that he knew from experience meant he was trying too hard.

"Mr. Reddman?" Landry intoned, projecting an icy cordiality, like a hangman at a social event. "The witness has been sworn in, sir. Are you going to question him, or is he simply there for us to admire?"

"I beg your pardon, Judge." Reddman found what he had been looking for in his notebook. "Would you state your name, please, and spell it for the record?" Five of the eleven members of the Sopris County Bar Association were seated directly behind the rail, on the defense side of the bar. Reddman felt like a child at his first recital and wished he could make them disappear.

"David B. Brenfleck." He spelled his surname.

"You're called Bren, right?"

"Objection, Judge, leading," Cole said.

"I get called a lot—"

"One moment, Officer Brenfleck," Landry said. "Objection sustained."

"Officer Brenfleck and I have the same first name," Reddman said to the judge, as though to explain why he'd asked the question.

"I'm aware of that, Mr. Reddman. Please continue with your examination."

Reddman took a deep breath to fight off the jitters. Grit your teeth, old friend, he told himself. Good. Now relax. He pried his head from the notes on the lectern and smiled. "What is your occupation?"

"Police officer, city of Muldoon, Colorado."

"And how long have you been so employed?"

As the questioning continued, Reddman tried to loosen up. He stumbled his way through the witness's education, training, and experience, but somewhere along the line, he forgot himself. Then, like a downhill skier, he started watching the terrain twenty yards in front, as he flowed over where he'd just been. When he moved into the substance of the examination, he moved away from the lectern and asked questions without using his notes. He responded easily to the answers. The examination moved smoothly after that, back to that warm fall day the preceding September, when Ami O'Rourke had so suddenly been killed. Reddman started a line of questions about the conversation Brenfleck had had with Johnny Blue, on the Mears Street hill just minutes before the event.

Cole jumped to his feet. "Now, Your Honor, I'm going to object to this officer testifying as to what my client said to him. Rule Sixteen: prosecution has continuing duty to give defense all statements of defendant in advance of trial. Here we have a statement by the defendant to this officer, and this is the first I've heard about it."

"Mr. Reddman?"

As Reddman turned toward Cole, he saw Sharon Sondenburg sitting next to Zack Wolfman. It gave him a lift when she smiled at him. "Your Honor, this isn't the trial; it's a motion in advance of the trial," he said, locking in on the judge. "The jury has been excluded. They won't hear any of this testimony, and it can't have any bearing on their decision.

"This is an evidentiary hearing to the court," he went on. "The normal rules of evidence don't apply to such hearings and Rule Sixteen, which in part is a rule of evidence, also should not apply. Further, this is not the first time Mr. Cole has heard about statements made by the defendant to Officer Brenfleck. We discussed it this morning in chambers. And finally, if I may be permitted to continue, the statements made by the defendant will be fully developed. A little late, I admit, but there can at this time be full compliance with rule sixteen."

Landry didn't even take a deep breath. "I consider your last reason to be spurious in the extreme, Mr. Reddman. Rule sixteen was not intended to be complied with one day before the trial. And although the rules of evidence are not to be strictly applied at evidentiary hearings, this court feels strongly that the sanctions provided by the rule *should* be applied so as not to encourage sloppy prosecutorial practices, which frequently subvert the fairness of the trial machinery. One such sanction is to prohibit the introduction of the evidence. I am therefore going to invoke the sanction and sustain the objection.''

"Thank you, sir," Reddman said, smiling at the judge. He tried to make defeat look like victory.

"Why are you thanking me, young man? I just ruled against you."

Reddman felt the cool delight of Cole, as well as one or two of the lawyers behind the rail. "I'm thanking you because I appreciate the clarity of your ruling, and the fact it is well reasoned."

"You just don't happen to agree with the reasoning, is that it?" Landry allowed, softening a little.

"Well . . . from down here I don't, if it please the court, but from up there I might."

"Proceed, Mr. Reddman," Landry said, permitting himself the trace of a smile.

"Officer Brenfleck, please listen carefully to me. The court has ruled you cannot discuss any statements made to you by Defendant Blue on that Friday afternoon in September when you first saw him. You may mention the fact that a conversation took place, if that is a fact, but don't tell us what you said to him or what he said to you. Do you understand?"

"Yeah, I guess."

"Just a moment, Officer." Reddman was nettled by the cop's attitude and let it show. "There is to be no guesswork here. Do you or don't you understand?"

"I understand."

"Good. Now tell the court exactly where you were when you first saw Defendant Blue."

Brenfleck did. The examination was back on track, and Reddman had that lofty, omniscient feeling of an actor directing his own play. Through Brenfleck, he established that Blue was seen at 5:09 P.M., seated behind the wheel of his pickup truck; that the truck was parked within one block of what would later be established as the point of impact; that at that time, Blue's truck was facing south and, because of the hill on Mears Street, commanded a clear view of the courthouse and the roadway in front of it; but that, according to the dispatcher's log, Brenfleck responded to another incident at 5:15 P.M. Blue was still at that location when the policeman left. Also according to the dispatcher's log, the hit-and-run was reported at 5:24 P.M., not even ten minutes later.

Cole clambered slowly to his feet, anticipating the next line of questions, making himself ready to pounce. Here we go, Reddman thought, preparing for the next flap and knowing the outcome was crucial.

"Officer," Reddman said, "at that time, did you know the status of Defendant Blue's driver's license?"

"Objection! Hold it, don't answer that question!" Cole stormed.

The startled witness spun toward Cole, then settled back in his chair. "I won't."

"Your Honor, if it please the court, the status of my client's license is not in issue. No way does it have anything to do with anything, and it is totally irrelevant, immaterial, and prejudicial!"

"What is the purpose of the testimony, Mr. Reddman?"

"If permitted to do so, this witness will testify that he, along with virtually every other lawman in Sopris County, knew that Blue's driver's license had been revoked. In other words, all of them knew that if Blue drove, he'd be committing a crime." Reddman glanced at the defendant, who smiled back. Reddman did not like Blue's smile. "The status of the defendant's license is relevant to the issue of his arrest." Reddman tried to sound as though this was no big deal, even though he could feel every vein and every artery in his body.

"See what I mean?" Cole shouted belligerently, as though he had caught the prosecutor stealing files from the clerk's office. "Man wasn't arrested for that, Judge, vehicular homicide, trying to pull a fast one!"

"I'm afraid I don't understand your position, Mr. Cole. Try again, please."

"Judge. Probable cause to arrest my client—that's what we need to decide, and whether Mr. Blue's driver's license had been revoked doesn't have anything to do with that at all. Reason it doesn't is because he wasn't arrested for driving without a license. He was arrested for vehicular homicide! What the prosecutor needs to show is probable cause to arrest for vehicular homicide, in the minds of the officers who made the arrest—and there wasn't any probable cause!"

"Mr. Reddman?"

"Your Honor, I agree with Mr. Cole that the issue is whether or not there was probable cause to arrest the defendant. If Blue's arrest wasn't lawful, then evidence gathered as a result would be tainted and the people couldn't use it." Landry's eyes had drifted over Reddman's head, and focused on someone in the courtroom. Look at me, you old bastard, Reddman wanted to say. "Mr. Cole apparently believes that the defendant was arrested solely for vehicular homicide, and if that was true he might have a good argument. But count one of the information charges Blue with driving with a revoked license, and it's the people's position that Blue was arrested, among other things, for that crime as well as vehicular homicide."

"Baloney, if it please the court!" Cole shouted. "All you have to do is look at the booking slip to see why he was arrested. And the booking slip doesn't mention driving with a revoked license! Booking slip says hit-and-run and vehicular homicide! How can my client be arrested for something he wasn't even booked into jail for?"

"Your Honor, what—"

"Mr. Reddman, I am prepared to rule in your favor. Knowing that, do you wish to continue to argue the point?"

Reddman forced the air out of his lungs. One little mistake, he thought, and it's all over. He'd heard a dozen horror stories about lawyers who were ahead, but who kept talking long enough to bring up something the judge hadn't thought about, causing a complete reversal. Reddman didn't want to risk that. But what if Landry was sandbagging? "No, sir."

"Very well. What a person is booked into jail for is not necessarily what a person is arrested for, any more than the district attorney is bound to charge only what appears on the booking slip. There is a fluidity to events, which the law recognizes. Go ahead with your evidence, Mr. Reddman."

Reddman did. He felt great. Landry knew how to be a judge after all, he decided, as he crammed the testimony of his remaining witnesses down Cole's throat. He followed his evidence with argument, clear and concise, fitting the facts around the law and arriving at the only legitimate conclusion: that the arrest was lawful, that therefore all the evidence gathered as a result of the arrest should be allowed. The evidence, he argued, consisted of the statement made by Blue to the detectives and the physical evidence taken from Blue's truck.

However, Judge Landry didn't see it that way.

Landry ruled that Blue's statement to Detective Lopes would be allowed, because Blue's arrest had been lawful and the *Miranda* warnings had been given and understood. But he went on to rule that the photographs, blood smears, and scientific testimony tying it all together were inadmissible because they were produced by a search that was conducted without a warrant. Although the police had had time to obtain a warrant, they had not done so, Landry said. "We'll start tomorrow at nine o'clock sharp," he ordered. "As you know, Mr. Reddman, the jury has not yet been sworn. Consequently you are still in a position to appeal my ruling. I assume you'll know by that time whether or not you intend to do so?"

"Yes, sir."

"Do you know now?"

Reddman thought for a moment. "No, Judge, I don't."

Reddman waited until the courtroom had cleared, then walked to the D.A.'s office. He wanted to talk to Sharon, but she had gone. Walter Brim and Zack Wolfman greeted him in the reception room.

"Say, you're pretty terrific in there, guy!" Brim said, his mammoth hand slapping Reddman between the shoulder-blades.

Reddman had not seen Brim in the courtroom and didn't know how much Brim had heard. He did know, however, that there were scabs all over his back, and he winced in pain.

"How about this guy, Wolfie?" Brim went on. "Would you want to go up against this tiger?"

"He'd be easy," Zack Wolfman said. "All D.A.'s are easy." He grinned at Reddman with obvious respect. "Needs props, something to lean on, same as all you guys. Just figure out what the prop is and kick it. Know what I'd do?"

"Tell me," Brim said.

"I'd mix up the pages in the puppy's trial notebook."

The juices of combat still flowed through Reddman, and he wanted to hit something. "That shithead judge," he said evenly, slamming his briefcase into a chair. "He gave me what I don't want, but he's keeping out what I do."

"You don't want the confession?" Brim asked, surprised.

"Not if I can put Blue behind the wheel some other way. Besides, it isn't even a confession."

"What is it?"

"It's Blue's explanation. And the way he explains it, he's just a poor innocent victim of circumstances! Judges!" He loosened his tie with his good hand and yanked it off. "Now I have to make Blue's explanation a part of my case, and I won't be able to use all that gore under the truck. The jury won't even see it!"

"What happened to you?" Wolfman asked, referring to the scabs and bandages he could see. They had moved into Brim's office and Wolfman sat in the chair behind the desk, his feet propped up on the edge, barely away from the clutter. "You look like you should be in a body bag."

"I bit it on my bike. There goes the guts of my case.

Hasn't the judge heard about the automobile exception? The *Carroll* doctrine?"

"You gonna appeal?" Wolfman asked him.

Reddman looked at his watch. It was too late to call NASP. He decided to wait an hour, then call Trigge at home. "I don't know. What would you do?"

"You'd lose on the appeal," Wolfman told him. "Old judge is right."

"Bullshit I'd lose. You don't need a warrant to search a car!"

"Wrong," Wolfman said. "I'm telling you, man. Even an average public defender knows more about search and seizure than the smartest D.A. anywhere in the world, and I'm grade A material. You'd lose." He took his feet off Brim's desk and leaned forward. "Listen. Even to make an automobile bust, you need exigent circumstances. Which you don't have!"

"Come off it," Reddman said. "That guy's truck is a built-in exigent circumstance."

"Right," Wolfman said sarcastically. "It's towed to the yard behind the jail, and Blue is in jail, so the truck is liable to drive off someplace on its own? You had the damn truck in jail, too, for chrissake. Where was the pressing need to search without a warrant?"

"Inventory search. Not really a search at all, just going through it to make sure nothing was stolen."

"Yeah, but you're not talking about anything inside the truck. You want to put in all that shit from *under* it."

"The evidence was in plain view," Reddman said, trying hard.

"Sure, man. Put the truck on a lift in the garage so they can see all that gore and call that plain view? Ho-ho-ho. Merry Christmas."

Reddman glared at the man's round face, which at that moment looked like a basketball. He knew Wolfman was right; often the trial lawyer couldn't see the forest for the trees. "Pervert," he said. The pressure of trial was off him for the moment; the imp had returned; what he really wanted to do was go for a ride. "You're a pervert, Wolfman. Next you'll be telling me the judge did me a favor."

"Skinny little fucker," Wolfman declared. "About time you lightened up."

"Then you won't appeal?" Brim asked hopefully. "You'll go on with the trial?"

Reddman nodded. "Onward and upward, bearing the banner of righteousness."

"What?"

"Nothing. What happened to the judge? The old bastard changed. When Cole and I left chambers this morning I thought everything was cool, but he really savaged out. I'm telling you, picking that jury was really intense."

Brim and Wolfman glanced at each other. "You don't know?" Wolfman asked.

"Don't know what?"

"About that big black man from Judicial Qualifications? Andy something?"

Reddman had seen the fellow with a legal pad on his lap, seated behind the Sopris County Bar. He was the only black man in the courtroom. "I think I saw the guy. I thought he was a reporter."

"You really don't know who he is?" Brim asked incredulously.

"Why should I?" Suddenly Reddman saw the picture. "Landry thinks I made a complaint to JQ, right?"

"Yes. Of course he had some encouragement," Brim offered knowingly. "From Conway."

"Have you ever wondered about the splendiferous construct we are a part of?" Reddman announced. At that moment he ached to see Sharon Sondenburg, but words were pushing out of his mouth instead. "I mean, what the hell have we got here? Is Blue going to jam up the justice machine and ride off into the sunset—that good-old-boy sunset—because of an autocratic old son of a bitch judge who is pissed off at one of the jousting knights for the wrong reason?'' He had floated to his feet like an astronaut in space and it felt as if he were peering down on them from the ceiling. "Three rousing cheers for *justice!*"

"Uh-oh," Wolfman said, gazing somberly at the prosecutor. "Terminal."

CHAPTER FOURTEEN

The clerk will call the roll of the jury.''

Reddman tried to monitor the proceedings as he sat at counsel table, but the license number kept flashing in his mind. He had earlier watched the jurors file solemnly into the jury box, slightly above the courtroom floor but not as high as the judge's throne. In a moment they would be sworn in and the trial would begin. He knew he should be concentrating on what was going on. Instead, he was overwhelmed with rage.

He closed his eyes and watched it happen again. He was sliding on the pavement in front of the truck, crashing to a stop against the abutment. It was too soon to hurt. His mouth opened wide but no sounds came out when the truck lurched forward. It cranked a hard left, jammed to a stop barely an inch from another abutment, slammed into reverse, and backed toward him. Reddman saw himself staring at the word "Dodge," painted in off-white and embossed on the sparkling-clean red tailgate five feet from his nose. Colorado license plate number XL 370 hung from the heavy bumper. As he watched, the truck ground into a forward gear and, spewing gravel, was gone.

Reddman hadn't even remembered seeing the license plate until he saw it again, just before coming into the courthouse. The driver of the truck is probably in here right now, watching the trial, he thought. He might even be Johnny Blue, the photogenic Marlboro man with the sun- and whiskey-weathered face, sitting next to Saul Cole. Reddman wanted to kill him.

Bernie Lopes, sitting next to him at counsel table, looked more like the lawyer on the case than did Reddman. Lopes wore a gray-green suit with matching vest and a turquoise handkerchief stuffed like a flower in the breast pocket. Lopes tapped his pen softly on the legal pad in front of him. Reddman leaned toward him. "Can you run a license number for me?" Lopes nodded. Reddman scribbled the number on Lopes's pad. Now forget about it, he told himself. But the memory continued to eat at him.

The jury was sworn and seated. Landry gave a brief explanation of their duties as jurors, outlining the procedure to be followed. Then he read the five-count complaint, starting with driving under revocation and ending with first degree murder. When he finished he lifted his head from the document and looked down on the courtroom below him. "The prosecution will now give its opening statement," he said. "Mr. Reddman?"

Reddman jumped to his feet and approached the lectern, which had been positioned in the center of the courtroom. He faced the jury. No preliminary remarks, no fawning or flattery. He spoke without notes, as though he could hardly wait to get on with the trial.

"You all know Mears Street, right in front of where we are now. You probably drove on it, or across it, this morning." He fought to keep the intensity level of his voice down. "Citizens Bank on the corner, a couple of office buildings, including that of the public defender, across the street. On the west side of Mears there is parallel parking, but in front of the courthouse the parking is diagonal. Right?" He let his hands shape the scene. "And of course all of you know how Mears Street rises, slopes upward, as it goes north.

"You'll see Mears Street again, I hope, just the way it

looked eight months ago, on September twenty-third of last year. You'll see it through the evidence we bring to court. By the time this trial is over, you will have seen Ami O'Rourke, the deputy public defender, on that day. You'll have seen her—a small, blond woman wearing a gray suit, because she'd been in court all day. You'll have seen her leave the courthouse, this building, at ten or fifteen minutes after five, then start across Mears, hurrying toward her office.''

Saul Cole sorrowfully shook his head, silently and with seeming helplessness. He kept mouthing the word "tragic" over and over. Reddman couldn't believe it. He tried to position himself between Cole and the jury, like the earth eclipsing the moon. He gripped the jury with his eyes, allowing his voice to vibrate with intensity. "You'll see her start to cross in the middle of the block—jaywalking, which is not uncommon." Reddman's hands clung to the lectern, holding his rage in check. "You'll see, too, from our evidence, that she had almost reached the safety of the other side when she was struck by a high rider pickup truck." He paused long enough to sip water from the glass on the shelf beneath the lectern. He tried, once again, to make his voice conversational, easy to listen to. "She got wrapped around the truck's tire and dragged through the tire well. Seventy feet later her body fell off." Another sip. "You probably won't be able to see who was driving the truck— you might—but it won't matter. You'll find out from other evidence who the driver was. Johnny Blue.'' With a move of his head, he released the juror's eyes and let them look beyond him at the defendant. "Was it a tragic accident, as the defense will contend, or was it murder?''

"Objection, Judge, objection!" Cole demanded, lurching to his feet in anger. "He's arguing, this isn't argument, it's opening statement!''

"Mr. Reddman," the judge said, "you are right on the line between argument and statement, sir. I suggest you stay on the right side of that line.''

"Judge, in order to tell the jury what we expect the evidence will show, I need to let them know what the problem is," Reddman said. "I'm only trying to put the case in context."

"You have been warned, Mr. Reddman. Please proceed."

He nodded then faced the jury. "You will see Johnny Blue sitting in his truck—that high rider pickup truck of his—up there on Mears Street hill, just sitting there as though waiting, waiting for something. You'll see, through our evidence, what he was able to see on that day. A commanding view of the courthouse, including the sidewalk that leads from the main door to the street, the cars parked diagonally along the courthouse side, Mears Street itself, the double lane of traffic northbound, and the single wide lane that goes southbound. He could see the cars on the far side of the street parked parallel, against the curb. And you'll see the public defender's office in the middle of the block, right across from where we are now. You'll watch Ami leave the courthouse and head for her office. She was reading, probably. She worked hard—never had enough time—and might have been reading as she stepped into the street. She could not have known of the danger. She obviously did not see the defendant in his pickup—"

"Objection, Your Honor! Argument, prejudicial, way beyond the bounds of opening statement!"

"I most emphatically agree." Landry leaned forward, projecting disapproval. "Mr. Reddman. You will tone down your remarks, sir, or I will declare a mistrial. Am I clear?"

"Your Honor, I'm merely stating what the people's evidence will show."

The gavel cracked down. "Enough, sir! How is it possible for your evidence to show what the victim in this case did or did not see?"

Reddman took a deep breath and smiled. "I apologize, sir." He faced the jury. "Ladies and gentlemen, please bear in mind what Judge Landry said earlier. Opening statement is not evidence. That will come later. I pledge to you now, however, that I will not intentionally mislead you or misstate what the people's evidence will show. But if there is a discrepancy between what I say now and what the evidence actually shows when the witnesses get up on the stand, you have the obligation to base your decision on the evidence, not on this statement." He turned toward the judge, who nodded as though to accept his apology. Then he faced the jury, wondering about their perception of all the maneuvering.

"Our evidence will show that Ami O'Rourke crossed the northbound lane of Mears. She then crossed the center line that divides the lanes of traffic. She was eight feet past that center line—three or four feet from the cars parked along the curb—when she was hit by Johnny Blue in his high rider. Our evidence will show that there was no northbound traffic at that time. The only moving vehicles on the road were a pickup truck backing out of a space in front of the courthouse, and the defendant's high rider. The driver who was backing up had a clear and unobstructed view of the scene."

Cole lumbered slowly to his feet. Reddman watched him out of the corner of his eye.

"She will tell you what she saw—and what she saw will be corroborated by the physical evidence. No brakes were applied by the defendant. No skid marks of any kind were left on the paved surface of the road. There was no swerving to avoid the small person in front of the truck; nothing." Reddman turned toward Saul Cole and stared at him. "Your Honor, Mr. Cole is standing up for some reason," he said, after a moment of stillness.

"I am aware of that, Counsel," Landry said, as though to say, What does it matter?

"It's distracting, Judge."

"Mr. Cole? Do you have an objection to make?" Landry asked.

"I thought he was getting toward the edge there, Judge," Cole said, sitting down. "Just wanted to be ready."

Reddman recognized the tactic, which was designed to interrupt his rapport with the jury. He wondered if the defense attorney had accomplished his purpose. Reddman decided to make the incident look as much like a disruption as he could. "I forgot where I was, Judge. Would you ask the court reporter to read back my last sentence or two?"

"Yes. Of course."

Carl reached inside the box and pulled out a coil of green paper. He began to read. " 'Our evidence will also show that there—that there was no northbound traffic at that time. The only moving vehicles on the road were a pickup truck' "—he cleared his throat—" 'a pickup truck backing out of a space in front of the courthouse, and the defendant's high rider. The driver who was backing up,' let's see, 'backing up, had a clear and unobstructed view of the scene. She will tell you what she saw—and what she saw will be corroborated by the physical evidence. No brakes were applied by the defendant. No skid marks of any kind were left on the paved surface of the road. There was no swerving to avoid the small person in front of the truck; Nothing.' " Carl put the paper back in the box.

"Thank you," Reddman said to the reporter, aware of the flatness of Carl's voice compared to his own. Nevertheless, his remarks had been repeated, giving the jury another opportunity to hear them. Try me again, Cole, he thought to himself. "Our evidence will show that the defendant accelerated before he hit her. Please notice. I said *before*. The poor woman got caught on the tire, the right front tire, of his high rider. She was spun—dragged—through the tire well once, twice, perhaps three times, before her body dropped away from the truck." He felt like a flame and let himself burn for a moment in front of the jury. "Then the driver accelerated again, and was gone."

The jurors are with me, he thought to himself, feeling their eyes. Someone in the packed courtroom moved, the only sound in the building. "Our evidence will also show that the defendant had reasons to kill Ami O'Rourke," Reddman continued softly. "We will show that the victim had defended Mr. Blue on a drunk driving charge; that she lost the case and he was put in jail; and that he blamed her for it. Sort of like blaming the weatherman for the weather."

"Objection! Judge, objection!"

"Pardon me, Mr. Cole," Reddman said quickly, before Landry had an opportunity to lecture. "Your Honor, I withdraw the remark about the weather."

"You can't unring a bell, Mr. Reddman. Please be more careful," Landry said. Then to the jury: "You are directed not to consider Mr. Reddman's remark about the weather. Proceed, Mr. Reddman."

Reddman waited a moment for their attention. What a crock of shit, he thought. "Blue had another reason to kill Ami O'Rourke. Not long before the drunk driving trial, Blue had made a pass at her. He was rejected." As Reddman watched, a couple of the jurors lifted their shoulders, as though to say, So what? The eyes of other jurors fell away from him.

"Oh, boy," Cole muttered, as though distressed by the hopelessness and unfairness of it all. "Oh, my gosh."

Reddman turned toward him, glad this time for the distraction. If the jury felt discomfort over the last suggested motive, he hoped they would blame Cole. Quickly he moved on. "You'll also hear from the forensic pathologist who conducted the autopsy on Ami's body. He will tell you—"

"Judge, just a moment, Judge, he's calling her Ami, her name was Ms. O'Rourke, what's he trying to do here?" Cole's tone was accusatory, as though exposing a cheap lawyer trick.

"Her name *was* Ami," Reddman said.

"All the same, Mr. Reddman," Landry said, "I don't believe it's appropriate to call the victim by her first name."

"Very well, Your Honor." Reddman turned once again toward the jury. "The pathologist will describe the injuries that were suffered by the victim, Ms. O'Rourke, the woman who was run down by the defendant in his truck." Satisfied, Cole? he thought to himself. "Much of that testimony may seem unnecessary to you, but bear in mind that the state has the burden of proving beyond a reasonable doubt what caused her death. The pathologist will clearly indicate that the injuries Ms. O'Rourke received, as a consequence of having been struck down by the defendant's truck, resulted in her death."

He paused long enough to walk over to the counsel table, pour water into a glass, and drink it. When he returned to the lectern, he let himself and the jury relax. "Up to this point, ladies and gentlemen, the evidence I've talked about relates to the murder count, the vehicular homicide count, and the hit-and-run. There's a bit more to the case than that, however. The evidence we put on will also show you that when the defendant drove his truck on that day, his driver's license was under revocation. Not a serious crime compared to murder, but a crime, nevertheless. You'll see a document, a certified document, from a state agency that will prove to you that Johnny Blue had no right to drive on that day. We will also show you that the defendant was arrested within half an hour of the time he struck the victim. He voluntarily submitted to a blood test, and the amount of alcohol in his blood stream was measured. The results of that test will show you that he was legally under the influence of alcohol."

Cole lumbered to his feet, seemed to think better of it, and sat down.

"We will present evidence to support each element of the five counts the defendant has been charged with. And at the conclusion of the case, you will have the responsibility of weighing that evidence and deciding the defendant's innocence or guilt.

"Whatever the outcome"—and Reddman leaned forward, speaking with obvious sincerity—"I want you to know right now that the people will be satisfied that this jury has acted with care, with caution, and with concern." Then he sat down as though to the strains of "God Bless America," knowing he felt more righteous than he had any right to feel.

Cole did not give an opening statement, but reserved the

right to give one at the beginning of the defendant's case. Reddman plunged ahead with his first witness.

Officer Brenfleck was sworn in and took the stand. At the hearing the day before on the motion to suppress evidence, the lightly freckled, boyish-faced patrolman had been direct and responsive. Now, in front of the jury and the large audience in the courtroom, his answers were abrupt and tinged with distaste. Drawing him out was like pulling teeth.

"Approximately what time was it when you first saw the defendant, Mr. Blue?"

"Seventeen-ten."

"That's military time?"

"Yes."

"So that's about ten minutes after five in the afternoon?"

"Yes."

"And where was Mr. Blue when you first saw him?" Reddman smiled at the witness in an effort to soften him.

"In his truck."

That isn't what I mean, asshole, Reddman thought. He waited, hoping a silence might work some magic on Brenfleck. Nothing. "In his truck?"

"Yes."

Very well, we'll go down that path, then, Reddman thought. "Can you describe the defendant's truck for the jury?"

"No."

What the hell is wrong with you? Reddman wondered angrily, still smiling at the man. "You've never seen Johnny Blue's high rider before?"

"Sure I have."

"Then can't you describe it?"

"Not without guesswork." Brenfleck glared with satisfaction at Reddman.

So that's it, Reddman realized. He's pissed off at me because I jumped him at the suppression hearing about guesswork. "I see. And you don't want to engage in guesswork now, I take it, Officer?"

"Objection, Judge. Leading, irrelevant. Who cares?" Cole demanded, projecting disgust.

"Mr. Reddman?"

"Your Honor, the witness obviously is taking his responsibility very seriously," Reddman said, nodding with approval at the witness. "I think he should be complimented."

"What does that have to do with Mr. Cole's objection?"

Absolutely nothing, Reddman knew, hoping he'd eaten enough crow to satisfy the cop's ego. "I'll withdraw the question, Judge." Brenfleck's glare had lost its edge. "Can you describe the truck, Officer?"

"That's been asked and answered, Judge," Cole said. "How long this gonna take?"

"Sustained."

Reddman nodded at the bench and smiled as nicely as he could, as though in complete agreement. Nothing like getting off to a great start, he thought to himself. "May I have a moment?"

"You may."

He selected an eight-by-ten-inch glossy photograph of the truck, showed it to Cole, and placed it in front of the witness. "Officer, I've just handed you a photograph previously marked for identification as people's exhibit P-fourteen. I ask you if you can identify it."

"Yes, I can. It's a picture of Johnny Blue's truck."

He's back on my side, Reddman hoped. "Do you know where and when the picture was taken, and who took it?"

"Just a moment, Mr. Reddman," Landry angrily interjected. "Counsel, approach the bench."

Cole scurried quickly around his table and got there first. The judge put his hand over the microphone, shook his head no at the reporter, and stared coldly at Reddman. "What do you think you are pulling, young man?"

"Gil, it's all right," Cole whispered. "Picture was taken before. No problem."

"What? Before what? I specifically ruled that the search of the truck was illegal, and I consider photographs of the truck— Taken when? When was this picture taken?"

"It was taken right after his arrest on the drunk driving charge, Judge," Reddman told him.

"Oh. Well, very well. Saul, I take it, you have no objection?"

"No, not if he lays a foundation."

As Reddman walked back to the lectern, he searched the audience for the man from Judicial Qualifications. He found him toward the middle of the courtroom, legal pad in hand. They made eye contact. Hang in there, fellow, the man's eyes seemed to say, and Reddman wired back: When I lose this case, tell Trigge why, okay?

The timbre in his voice was still there. Reddman's courtroom voice was pleasantly resonant and musical. A woman deputy he had worked with had said it had a needy sound, like a mating call. However, the jitters had attacked him, and he couldn't feel his feet. "Officer Brenfleck, referring to the photograph before you," he said, listening to the vibrations in his voice but staring at his shoes. "Does that photograph fairly and accurately portray the defendant's truck, as you saw it, on September twenty-third of last year?"

"That isn't when the picture was taken," Brenfleck said.

"I realize that. But is that the truck you saw?"

The witness studied the picture carefully. "Yes. Same truck; he hadn't changed anything. It's just the same."

"Then you have before you a photograph of Defendant Blue's truck, the same truck the defendant was sitting in when you saw him on the twenty-third of September?"

"Yes."

"I move that the exhibit be received in evidence, Your Honor."

"Any objection, Mr. Cole?"

" 'Course not. I agree with him when he's fair."

"The photograph is admitted as people's P-fourteen."

"May I show it to the jury, Judge?" Reddman asked, handing it to the closest juror.

"One moment, Mr. Reddman!"

Almost in terror, Reddman snatched the photograph back. "What?"

"Let me see it first, please."

Reddman hurried to the bench and gave the glossy to the judge. Landry whispered to him in a half-snarl, "You don't just hand things to the jury in my court, young man." His mouth hardly moved as he pretended to look at the photograph. "In the future, get my permission first!" Then he smiled at Reddman as a father might smile at a son and gave him back the exhibit. "Mr. Reddman," he said in a loud, friendly voice. "Please pass this photograph to the jury."

The members of the Sopris County Bar Association watched the baptismal ceremony with obvious glee. However, many of the spectators behind the rail avoided looking at the prosecutor, as though to avoid contamination. The imp in Reddman chose that moment to surface. "It only hurts when you laugh," he said.

When Reddman resumed his seat after releasing Brenfleck to Cole, he felt good. Eating all that crow had paid off. Brenfleck had been positive that Blue had told him his wife had parked the truck on Mears Street hill. Cole attacked the point on cross-examination, but Brenfleck drove it in deeper. "Your report doesn't mention Blue's wife at all, Officer, does it?" Cole shouted, waving a piece of paper in his hand.

"No, sir."

"Then how can you be sure?" Cole's mistake.

"I don't know, Mr. Cole. But I am."

What is he driving at? Reddman wondered an hour later, trying to understand Cole's cross-examination of the pathologist. "Isn't it true, Doctor, that there were more broken bones on her left side—I'm talking about ribs and her left arm and left leg—more muscle damage and tissue damage to the poor woman's left side than her right side, wouldn't you say that is so?"

The doctor, an athletic-looking man exuding professional

179

competence, referred to the report in his lap. "I'm sorry, Mr. Cole, I can't say that. There were multiple fractures throughout her body, severe trauma to all internal organs, massive rupturing of veins and arteries—all of it, of course, consistent with and obviously caused by having been run over by a truck. But I can't in all honesty say there was more injury to one side than to the other other."

"You mean you didn't count the broken bones?"

"Of course not. That was not necessary to a determination of cause of death. It is also impossible to do without extensive X rays, and there was no need to take X rays in this case."

"You didn't take X rays? Why not?"

"I needed to examine her organs. And I did that by opening up her body and looking at them."

"Oh." Cole nodded and swallowed. "You did take pictures, though, didn't you?"

"Yes. You've been provided with copies, haven't you?"

"Judge, move the answer be stricken as not responsive and the witness ordered to answer questions, not ask them."

"Yes, Dr. Hardesty. Mr. Cole will ask the questions," Landry said.

Hardesty nodded and smiled.

"Do you have those pictures with you?" Cole asked. "In that big pile of stuff you have up there?"

Hardesty searched through his file and pulled out several three-by-five-inch color photographs. "Yes."

Cole, standing beside the witness, took them from his hand and shuffled through them. "If it please the court, I'd like these pictures marked for identification. Seven of them, defense exhibits one through seven."

The photographs displayed the nude and horribly mangled body of Ami O'Rourke, on an operating table at Dr. Hardesty's laboratory in Montrose. They had been taken during various stages of the autopsy. Reddman, following Trigge's advice, had decided not to offer them into evidence, because they were so awful they were offensive. Has Cole gone out of his mind? he asked himself.

"These pictures don't reverse things, do they?" Cole asked Hardesty. "I mean what looks like left is really left and what's right is right?"

"Correct. No reverse imagery."

"Fine." Cole took them with him, back to the lectern. "Now, Doctor, when you first got this case, what were your instructions?"

"To determine cause of death."

"And the police gave you certain basic information, didn't they? I mean, they told you she'd been hit by a truck?"

"Yes."

"So it wasn't hard for you to figure out what had happened, to decide cause of death, was it?"

"Actually, it would have been extremely difficult to narrow it down to one precise failure. The victim was crushed, and there was a simultaneous or near-simultaneous failure of her cardiovascular and respiratory systems."

"Then you didn't narrow it down to a precise failure, did you?"

"No, I did not."

"So your examination didn't take all that long, then, I guess, did it?"

"It took about an hour, which is standard."

"Nobody asked you to try to figure out where she got hit first, what part of her body—front, back, right side, left side?"

"No. No one asked."

"So I guess, Doctor, your examination was not as great as it could have been, was it? A lot of things you didn't do, right? No reason, weren't asked to find out?"

"If I may say this, Mr. Cole, I only did what was—"

"Yes or no, Doctor, just answer the question, please."

Reddman stood up. "Which question? That the examination was not great or that there were things he didn't do?"

"You objecting or what?" Cole asked. "Withdraw the

question. Before I forget, I offer into evidence these photographs, one through seven.''

"Any objection, Mr. Reddman?''

"Your Honor, those photographs are truly gruesome. I have no objection, but I wonder if Mr. Cole has considered whether it's really necessary to—well, to inflict them on the jury.''

"I assume Mr. Cole knows what he's doing, Counsel. Any objection?''

"No, sir.''

The afternoon wore on. Reddman watched Cole for a clue as to why he had put the pictures in. How could they help him?

The youthful pathologist, who had to testify the next day in Grand Junction, had been called out of order and was excused. Lon Twilley, an emergency medical technician, was on and off the stand in fifteen minutes, followed by Patrolman Byron "Rip" Judson, whose testimony took an hour. It wouldn't have taken so long, Reddman thought savagely, if the man had any brains. It took him five minutes to decide who he was. You aren't real quick, Reddman said silently as he questioned the shy, bumbling cop. As a matter of fact, you're close to dead.

"It's almost five, gentlemen," Landry said after Judson was excused. "We'll break for the evening." He admonished the jury not to discuss the case or hear or read anything about it. After ordering them to return at eight-thirty the next morning, he excused them. "I'd like to see the lawyers in my chambers," he said wearily, standing up. "Court is in recess."

As soon as he was seated in front of Landry's desk, Reddman knew he was back in the lion's den. The court reporter had gone home. Landry talked of the instructions to be given the jury at the end of the case, then pointed out how the murder count complicated that particular task. Because of it, all the lesser included offenses to murder would have to be dealt with. The jury would have to sort through all those charges as well as all the other offenses the defendant had been charged with. "You are inviting error, young man. You are extending a clear invitation to the court of appeals to reverse any conviction you might be lucky enough to obtain." Then, as a father to a head-strong son, he urged the wisdom of compromise.

A guilty plea carries with it certainty, Landry told him. You will have a known result, secure from error and appeal. Who knows what will happen in the heat of battle, what instruction might be forgotten, what remark might be made, that would result in error? And if the case is reversed, what have you gained?

As Reddman listened, he used the tip of his tongue to trace the words "Fuck you" on the roof of his mouth.

CHAPTER FIFTEEN

It was a slow night. A half-moon radiated pale white light over the Sopris Mountains east of Muldoon, illuminating the long ridge of peaks above timberline, covered with snow. On the horizon, beyond the reach of the moonlight, the Milky Way punctured the deep black sky with millions of dots, smaller than pinpricks, perhaps each one a universe.

Rip Judson sat alone in his patrol car on Mears Street, staring over the courthouse at the nighttime sky. Sure am glad it's over, he thought, feeling a measure of peace for the first time in a week. Lawyers sure can make a man feel small.

That's the trouble with you, Rip, the voice in his head said. Rip knew who it was: his old man. No problem. A cop psychologist had explained it in a class he had taken, something about conscience, how we internalize the voice of our father and it helps keep us on the straight and narrow.

Still, Rip wished the old bastard would leave him alone. He'd been dead for seven years. Rip patted himself down, searching for the pack of cigarettes he'd put someplace. He found them in the breast pocket of his coat, pulled one out, and lit it.

It wouldn't have been so bad except the whole town was

there, watching. Including his wife. On the way home, she'd said, "Duh, duh, my name, let's see, Judson, ain't it? Pretty sure it's Judson."

You dumb-shit overgrown prick, the voice sneered. Why, you didn't even sit up straight. Slouched all over like a broken tree. Next time sit up! And *look* at people. You can't even look a man in the eye!

Rip sighed as he thought about it, gripped the wheel with both hands, and sat up. That was his whole problem, he thought. Got to learn to sit up straight. If you sit up straight and look people in the eye, then they don't get ahead of you.

"Lobo Nine, this is Lobo Three. You out there?" Judson's radio blurted.

He recognized Brenfleck. "I'm out here, Lobo Three. Barkin' at the moon like a good hound dog."

"Meet you at the Ramada, okay? Nothing doing out here."

"Sure. Ten-four."

After squirming around in the witness box for an hour, Judson knew it would be easy to talk. Minutes later, he told dispatch where he'd be and eased his large, lanky frame out of the patrol car. "Hey, bro," he said to Brenfleck, squeezing into a booth at the all-night diner.

Brenfleck looked up at him from the huge plastic menu. "Hear you got yourself a new asshole."

"Got *two* new assholes," Judson told him. "Makes for three all together, counting the old one."

"Yeah? How'd you get so many?"

"Two lawyers, two assholes. Both of 'em put one in me."

Brenfleck nodded and put the menu down. "You know, that Reddman, he tried to punch one in me, too." He told about the "guesswork" exchange, and how he cured the prosecutor. "What'd he do to you?"

"Kind of like that. Kept tellin' me to speak louder, the jury had to hear, the court reporter had to hear, the defense lawyer had to hear. You know, hell, felt like I was shouting the way it was." Rip didn't tell him the worst part, though, how he'd forgotten his own name. Brenfleck grinned at him and Rip felt good, talking about it. "Damn microphone. Judge said 'Hit it with your finger, boy. See if it's on.' Shit, I'd pop it and the damn thing sounded like an explosion! So he turns it up!"

"You weren't scared."

"Scared!" Judson reared back as if insulted. "Hey, bro, that was easy as— Remember that damn Indian had that shotgun? Willie Coyote?"

"You shoulda smoked that asshole."

"Uh-uh, Willie's a friend of mine." Judson plopped his large bony elbows on the table. "Probably a good thing the witness chair has all night to air out, though."

The waitress brought coffee, took Brenfleck's order, and avoided his playful hand. Brenfleck couldn't figure Judson out. There was no better man in the world to work with. In a tight spot—like the incident with Willie Coyote—Judson would automatically be the one who stuck his neck out. And if anything went wrong—like a couple of things about that Johnny Blue crime scene—Rip would automatically take the blame. Brenfleck had seen him fight and collar three drunk cowboys and then freeze tighter than an engine with no oil when demonstrating to a class how he'd done it. "You really forgot your name?"

Judson spluttered foolishly into his coffee. "Yeah, not for long, though. Question caught me by surprise."

"Old Cole get after you about the crime scene?"

"Yeah."

"What's that all about, I wonder? He did the same thing to me. 'It's standard operating procedure to close off the whole street, isn't it, Officer? Evidence—valuable evidence—can get lost? And the crowd, and take pictures of the victim, and clear the scene as soon as possible, don't let people pick things up, when you got there a lot of commotion, right?' " Brenfleck grinned. "Ever notice how he'll ask about ten questions without breathing, then say, 'Just give me a yes or no'?"

Judson felt good, knowing it was over and he'd sleep. "Yeah, really. How the hell do I know squat about standard operating procedure? This was the first murder scene I ever worked!"

"Shhh!" Brenfleck said, halfway meaning it. "Somebody might hear you."

"Did he ask you whether you thought Ami O'Rourke was dead?"

"He tried but Reddman wouldn't let him. Said I wasn't competent to give an opinion."

"She wasn't," Judson said.

"What?"

"She was still alive. Damn me to death." Judson had thought about it a lot. The thing that happened when he'd given that bloody face CPR. Something had actually passed from her to him, a kind of gift. It meant a lot to him. "First time I ever kissed a public defender," he said, masking the glow.

"Goode's gonna say she was dead. He's gonna say she didn't have a pulse."

"That asshole," Judson said, lifting his arms like a scarecrow, then wilting. "He damn near fainted. I thought the medics were gonna have to haul him out, too."

"You didn't make a mistake, did you?" Brenfleck asked, lifting his cup. "You sure she was alive?"

"I'm sure." Judson couldn't tell him about it, but that was all right. Ami had given him a feeling of life, even of love, as though she'd known how hard he tried to save her. "Not on that. Made a mistake when I arrested old lady Shard for careless driving! 'Member that? She like to beat me to death!"

Brenfleck smiled and looked around the room. "Shoulda smoked her."

CHAPTER SIXTEEN

It was early morning. Sharon Sondenburg lay next to Reddman in his bedroom at the New York Hotel, and as she slept, he watched the room fill slowly with light.

"Sharon?"

A part of her heard him and she missed a breath. Then she rolled away.

He looked at his watch: 4:57 A.M. He could go for a ride without waking her, or wake her up and make love. What if she didn't want to? He looked at her face, at her incredible beauty. God, he thought to himself. I hope she wants to. "Sharon?"

"What."

"If I brush my teeth and warm up the oil and slay all the dragons in the world and rescue you from—"

"Shit, no."

He sighed. "No?"

"Go for a ride."

He sighed again and lifted a lock of her hair. "You're beautiful," he said with reverence. "I don't believe you're real."

She sat up suddenly. "God damn it. You tell me I'm helping by watching the trial and giving you feedback and keeping your bed warm while you work these ridiculous hours, but do you know what you did last night? You jumped in the sack with me, then fell asleep! You put your face right here"—she pounded her fist between her breasts—"and conked out!"

"No." He shook his head emphatically, denying it. "You're wrong."

"What do you mean I'm wrong?"

"That wasn't me. I wouldn't do that." As she awoke, the color and tone of her skin subtly changed. Reddman watched her body come to life, fill with a magnificent glow.

"Let me see if I understand this," she said, moving his hand off her arm. "Your position is that you didn't fall asleep on me last night because that's not the kind of thing you would do?"

"Right. I'm too nice a guy."

She bounded out of bed, heaving the covers off both of them. "So even though I felt your face, held you in my arms, heard you breathe those deep breaths, and finally moved you onto a pillow and covered you up—that I'm wrong about what happened?" She spoke the last words from the bathroom.

Reddman could hear her brushing her teeth. "Did you really hold me in your arms?"

"Yes." She spit. "You were so tired. You slept like a baby."

"That was nice of you, you know that?"

She stuck her head into the bedroom. "You fall asleep this time, Buster, and I'll kill you."

They made long, slow, silent, soft, savage, screaming love. For an hour they filled themselves with each other, then emptied the cup and filled it up again.

Still glowing, they sat in the kitchenette drinking coffee. Sharon had put on one of his shirts, and Reddman wore Jockey shorts. "Am I really helping you?" she asked. "Or is this that same old ploy?"

"Are you kidding? Blue is scared. Why do you think he tried to force me off the road?"

"I scared him for you?" she asked.

"Yes. That motion to endorse witnesses? Those women you found? He knows who they are, and they'll be staring at him all through the trial. He and Cole will wonder if there's some way I can put them on."

"Can you?"

"No, but Blue and Cole don't know that."

She looked at her watch. "You've got less than an hour. Better get dressed."

He groaned. "Think I can go like this?"

"No. People in Muldoon don't understand men who shave their legs." Then: "What's it like? In the pit. Isn't that what you call it?"

"Yes. Bull terriers, fighting in the pit." Reddman lifted his mug. "Sometimes, when you're on top, you feel like God. Yesterday, though, I felt like I was on a tightrope over the Royal Gorge. You know, one little mistake." He looked at her and smiled, setting the coffee mug down without drinking from it.

"You mean lawyers aren't heroic?" she asked, somewhat mockingly. "You know, like knights searching for the Holy Grail?"

"No. More like doing a balancing act on a live wire. You're concentrating on the judge, the defense lawyer, the jury, and hoping the guy at the switch doesn't turn on the juice. Your mind is going a zillion different directions, like a rat in a shooting gallery, dodging bullets and looking for the way out. Not very heroic." She cares about me, he thought, suddenly. He could see it in her eyes. "You wish there was time to think before diving ahead with the next question, and you're wondering all the time how you're scoring with the jury. You really know it, too—a hot flash, followed by a cold one—when you've screwed up."

"What about Ami? Do you think about her?"

"No," he said honestly, "I think about Blue. I keep thinking, What if the son of a bitch walks?"

"Everyone says you're such a nice person."

"That's part of the image they teach you how to project. I'm not."

"Yes, you are." She put a hand over his. "Arrogant. Insensitive. Self-centered. Macho. But really very sweeeet."

"Hmm."

"Will you finish your side today?"

"Probably. After I rest there'll be a bullshit motion to dismiss; then Cole will put on his witnesses, then more bullshit motions, then jury instructions, and then final argument. The jury could get the case tomorrow, but probably not until Friday." He started to move his hand but she wouldn't let him. "I hate watching the jury file out and remembering all the things I should have done that I didn't do."

"Who are your witnesses today?"

"I'll start with Bernie Lopes, then Jack Donovan. Then I'll try to establish motive with a prisoner Blue talked to, and then I'll call Lance Winchester."

"Lance is such a nerd!"

"Yeah. Wolfman says he'd make a perfect D.A."

"He's not *that* nerdy."

"Huh. I like to finish with motive when it's strong, but this time I'm trying to bury it between witnesses. Just get enough in there so I can argue it."

"Then you'll finish with the eyewitnesses?"

"Right. Goode, Strickland, and Doppler. I'm really counting on Muriel."

"Be careful with her," Sharon said, getting up. She took her cup to the sink. "Her husband's a good friend of Johnny's."

"Hey. There's something you can do. Very important."

"What?"

"Talk to her. Find out if she'll still make a good witness."

"And if she won't?"

"I don't know," Reddman said.

Bernie Lopes, sitting easily in the witness box, knew he had come across well on direct examination. Now for the real test, he thought: cross-examination by Saul Cole.

Cole ambled up to the lectern like a friendly bear. He had already dropped his notes, which drew a laugh from the jury and put everyone at ease. Reddman came as close as he ever came to sneering, but he didn't need to. Lopes grinned at Cole, but he hadn't been fooled. "Now, Officer, when you questioned Mr. Blue— By the way, Detective Lopes, whose idea was it to talk? Yours or his?" Cole's elbows were on the lectern, but his face was toward the jury, as though inviting them to join in on the fun.

Lopes let his hands relax. Tell the truth, Reddman had told him, but remember whose side you're on. "Sergeant Winder and me got a message from the jailer that Mr. Blue wanted to make a statement."

"It was *his* idea, then, right? Mr. Blue wanted to talk—volunteered to, in fact, right?"

"Yes, sir."

"Then you— That's when you and that other detective from the sheriff's office, Sergeant Winder, talked to him?" Cole tilted his head in a certain way, bringing the jury into the conversation.

"Yes, sir."

"The two of you got together with Mr. Blue in that interrogation room in the basement, and went over his rights with him, didn't you? Very carefully, because you wanted to be a hundred percent sure he knew what he was doing and that he really wanted to talk?"

Lopes thought to himself, Reddman was right on. Cole wants the jury to believe Blue's statement. "That's right, sir."

"Not like a guilty man, would you say? Him wanting to talk that way, with nothing to hide?"

"Objection, Your Honor," Reddman said, jumping to his feet. "The question is argu—"

"My apology, Mr. Reddman," Landry said, "but I missed it. Will the court reporter read it back to me, please?"

" 'Not like a guilty man, would you say? Him wanting to talk that way, with nothing to hide?' "

Reddman's face darkened slightly as he nodded in seeming approval. "The question—"

"Yes. Sustained."

"Thank you, Your Honor," Cole said, as though the judge had ruled in his favor. Then he turned to the witness. "This was about an hour after the accident, right? Everything still fresh in Mr. Blue's mind?"

"Well . . ." Give me some help, Lopes thought, looking at Reddman. How am I supposed to know what was in Johnny's mind? "Within an hour, yes, sir."

"So everything was still fresh in his mind. And even after you warned him, advised him all those rights, Miranda, he still wanted to talk, right? Wanted to tell you what happened?"

Reddman stood up again. "Judge, I object to the form of the question. Mr. Cole has asked two questions."

"It's essentially one, Mr. Reddman. Overruled."

"He still wanted to talk, yes, sir," Lopes said.

"To tell you what happened. Now, Mr. Blue had been drinking hadn't he, you could smell it on him?"

"Yes, sir."

"Was he drunk?"

"I didn't think so, sir."

"But you found out later you were wrong, didn't you? That in fact he *was* drunk, took a blood test, the results came back a point-eighteen?"

"Yes, sir."

"That's pretty high, isn't it? Surprised you, I'll bet, how high?"

"Your Honor," Reddman said, once again on his feet, "objection. He's doubling up the questions, and he's asking the witness for opinions and reactions, not facts."

"Very well, though it hardly seems that important. Sustained."

Cole looked at Reddman as though he couldn't believe the man's pettiness. "If you want to play games, okay, we'll play games," he said. "Ask the court to take judicial notice of the statutes of the state of Colorado, in particular where it says a person is presumed to be under the influence if the blood test shows point-one-zero."

"Yes. Ladies and gentlemen, the court hereby takes judicial notice of *Colorado Revised Statutes,* at—" Landry located the correct volume from the row of books on the bench. "At subsection—now, where . . . ? Oh, yes. In pertinent part, as follows: 'The amount of alcohol in a person's blood,' and then, skipping, 'as shown by chemical analysis of such person's blood, shall give rise to the presumption that if there was zero point one zero grams of alcohol per one hundred milliliters of blood or more in such person's blood, it shall be presumed that such person was under the influence of alcohol.' "

He closed the book and looked benignly at the jury. "What that means quite simply is that a person with a blood alcohol content in excess of point-ten is presumed to be under the influence of alcohol. I must instruct you that this is merely a presumption, which means that you may, but are not required to, find that Mr. Blue was under the influence of alcohol. Proceed, Mr. Cole."

"Thank you, Judge." Cole settled comfortably behind the podium. "Now, Officer, Mr. Blue's blood was analyzed, the results came back at point-one-*eight*, almost twice the legal limit, right?"

"Yes."

"So he was drunk, wouldn't you say? Withdraw that," he said quickly before taking a chance on what Lopes might say. "Facts speak for themselves," he muttered as though to himself, but loud enough to be clearly heard. "Now. Mr. Reddman asked you if Mr. Blue admitted driving the truck that day, you remember him asking that question?"

"Yes, sir."

"And my client admitted it—no question—but he said more'n that, didn't he? I mean it wasn't just Okay, you drove the truck. Yes, I did, Officer. Okay, good, that's all we need to know. Blam, end of interview. Right?"

"There was more to it than that, yes, sir."

"A whole lot more, wouldn't you say? He told you what happened, right?"

"Well . . . he gave us his version," Lopes said, straightening his tie.

"His version! The man *wanted* to talk, still fresh in his mind, drunk! And you believed him, didn't you?" Cole waved a copy of Lopes's report at the witness. "Well, didn't you?"

Lopes smiled at Cole, trying not to sweat. Never again will I put an opinion in a report, he promised himself. "At the time I did, yes, sir. It wasn't until—"

"Hold it. Now, just answer the question please, Officer Lopes. At the time when he told you what happened, you believed him, didn't you?"

"Yes, sir."

"And your belief was based in part on the fact that he was drunk or had been drinking, hard to lie when you're drunk, plus he wanted to talk, natural thing after a few drinks, you didn't have to twist his arm, plus still fresh in his mind, and probably on your years of experience as a police officer, your good judgment, right? All of those thing?"

"I guess that's right, sir."

"Meaning yes, that's what you mean, right?"

"Yes, sir."

"Getting somewhere," Cole declared. "Now tell us what he said."

Lopes glanced at Reddman, as though for help. Reddman smiled coolly back at him, projecting the attitude that nothing out of the ordinary was happening. "He said— Do you want me to read this? His statement?"

"Now, Officer you were there. You remember what he said, right?"

"That's right."

Cole shook his head at the jury, as though to say, See what I have to go through to get the truth out of this man? "So just tell us what he said!"

Lopes smiled at his tormentor. "He said he didn't know

how he got in the truck, for one thing. He told us he was sitting in it when Brenfleck—Officer David Brenfleck—saw him there and asked him what he was doing. He said he felt kind of trapped like, because they'd taken away his driver's license, and he knew he shouldn't be driving, and he'd known Brenfleck ever since high school and didn't think Brenfleck liked him very much.''

"He was scared, too, wasn't he? Used the word 'scared'?"

"Yes, sir. He didn't look scared, but he said he was."

"So he was scared," Cole said, repeating the word. "Keep going."

"Well, Brenfleck was parked right behind him, just waiting for him to drive so he could bust him. Then all of a sudden Brenfleck took off.''

"Why did Brenfleck take off, Mr. Lopes?"

"He responded to a call."

"What happened after that?"

"Mr. Blue said he thought it might be a trick, but he knew he had to get out of there—"

"So that's when Mr. Blue started driving, far as you know?"

Reddman stood up quickly. "Objection, Your Honor. Mr. Cole is misrepresenting the situation."

"He is?" Landry asked. "How so, Counselor?"

"He's trying to make it appear as if this is what actually happened, when all this is is the statement of the defendant."

"I'm afraid I don't see the difference," Landry said. "I think the jury is quite aware of any distinction here. Proceed, Mr. Cole."

"So," Cole said, smiling nicely at Lopes and the jury. "That's when Mr. Blue started driving, right? What happened next?"

The objection had not been lost on Lopes. "That's what the defendant *said*, Mr. Cole. What he said was that after Brenfleck kind of zoomed out of there, he took off, too. Said he eased out into the street and was driving by the

196

courthouse when all of a sudden she was right in front of him."

"Forgot something there, didn't you, Detective Lopes?" Cole said angrily, shaking his head at the jury. "He was looking in the mirror, not paying much attention to what was right in front of him?"

"Oh. That's right, he told us he was looking in the rear-view mirror for cops."

"So he was looking in the mirror for cops when this happened, right? Suddenly she's right in front of him?"

"That's what he said."

"And you believed him, didn't you!" Cole stormed. "You knew he was telling you the truth! You said so right in your report! Right?"

"At the time, yes, sir, I believed him."

"That's right, you believed him. Then what did he do?"

"He said he honked, but it was too late and he ran into her. He told us he was scared and knew he shouldn't have run, but he did."

"So he honked, probably hit the brakes, that right?"

"He didn't say anything about brakes. Just honking."

"So you don't know whether he put the brakes on or not, do you?"

"Yes, I know. He did not put on the brakes."

"Now, is that something you *know*, Officer Lopes, or something you've been told? Isn't something you *know*, is it?"

Lopes hesitated. "I—"

"Just yes or no."

"No."

"How many vehicular homicide cases have you investigated?"

Lopes grinned at the son of a bitch. "This is my first one."

"Your first one? How about murder?"

"Also my first."

"So maybe that's why the subject of brakes never came up? Inexperience?"

Lopes looked at Reddman. The prosecutor's ears had started to darken, but he didn't react. "Could be."

"But you've interviewed hundreds—maybe even thousands—of people? Lots of experience?"

"I think so."

"You can spot a liar, right?"

"Most of the time."

"What about this time, Officer? Tell us now." Cole leaned forward intently. "Johnny Blue. Your opinion. Did he lie?"

Once again, Lopes hesitated. "I—" Shit. Do I have to tell the truth? he asked himself.

Cole knew he had him. "Just answer the question yes or no. Your opinion. Did he lie?"

"No."

Cole let the word hang in the courtroom as long as he could. Johnny Blue looked at Lopes gratefully, and at that moment, Lopes knew he'd been had. "Officer Lopes, can you describe Johnny Blue for us? Physically? What I'm getting at is this: he limps, don't he?"

"Yes. He has a slight limp."

"Slight limp, you say. Which leg?"

Blue chose that moment to move his right leg with his hands, in obvious pain. "I don't know," Lopes said, looking at the defendant and wishing he hadn't. "I never really noticed."

Cole let his eyes follow the witness's gaze, turning the faces of most of the jury. "Is it his right leg?"

"I really don't know, Mr. Cole."

"So, could be his right leg, I guess? Do you know how it happened?"

"Your Honor—"

"Yes, Mr. Cole, one question at a time, if you please."

"Sorry, Judge." A sheepish grin. "How'd it happen, you know?"

"Well, I heard—"

"Excuse me," Reddman said quickly. "Objection, Judge. The knowledge of the witness is based on hearsay."

"Judge, how Johnny Blue got that bad leg is common knowledge in this community. I could ask the court to take judicial notice!"

"Nevertheless, Mr. Reddman is right. Sustained."

Cole shrugged his shoulders and smiled, first at Reddman and then at the jury. "Whatever. So this man with a bad leg, scared and looking in his mirror, not the road, suddenly saw the victim"—his face showed horror and surprise—"maybe tried to hit the brake with his bad leg." He pushed desperately with his foot. "We don't know that, but he honked his horn, then hit her!" Anguish registered on Cole's face as he looked around the courtroom for a moment as though utterly lost. Then he seemed to realize where he was. "That's what happened, right, Officer? What you believe happened, you and Winder, based on your experience, after talking to my client, Johnny Blue?"

"Judge, how can the witness answer that question?" Reddman demanded, on his feet. His voice was on the edge of rage.

Cole looked at him with radiant sweetness. "How 'bout a yes or no, sonny boy?"

Reddman called Sergeant Jack Donovan to the stand. The thin, rock-hard trooper, wearing summer blues, looked alert but at his ease in the witness chair. His answers were slow and concise. An honesty and professionalism permeated his whole manner, from the quiet and unhurried tone of his voice to the clear, clean way he could look the lawyers in the eye. Cole wanted to stipulate to Donovan's qualifications as an accident reconstruction expert, but Reddman refused. He paraded the man's credentials, as well as his obvious modesty, in front of the jury.

Donovan described his findings in detail: how he carefully measured the driving lanes of Mears Street in front of the courthouse, identified the point of impact, and tracked the trail of blood smears to the victim's body, seventy feet down the road. The large chart, drawn to scale, was received in evidence as people's exhibit 1.

Donovan also testified to the width of the defendant's truck, clearly implying how easy it would have been for Blue to have swerved and avoided the victim, and to the complete absence of any indication of braking action. He was even permitted, as an expert, to express the opinion that immediately following the impact, the truck had to have been under heavy acceleration. "The victim's body would have acted like a brake," he said. "Until she fell off the tire, driving that vehicle would have been like pushing it up a steep hill."

Reddman kept him on as long as he could, then turned him over to Cole, for cross.

"You've been working accidents for more'n twenty years, Jack? I mean, Sergeant Donovan?"

"Yes, sir, Mr. Cole." Donovan's smile was not as wide as Cole's.

"Bet you've seen a lot, know a lot, odd things people do sometimes, you wouldn't expect?"

Donovan gazed directly at Cole. "What is the question, please?"

"Well, people do strange things under pressure, right?" Cole smiled and nodded at the witness to encourage agreement.

"Some do, some don't."

"That's fine, you get my meaning. Now you've seen—"

"Pardon, Mr. Cole, but I don't get your meaning at all," Donovan said. "Hope you don't mind the interruption."

"How people react under pressure?" Cole asked, surprised. "What's to misunderstand?" His face lost a bit of color, as though he wished he hadn't asked the question.

Donovan glanced apologetically at the judge, then let his level, honest gaze come to rest on Cole. "The question isn't easy, Mr. Cole, because the way people react—well, it ain't the kind of thing you can generalize about. *Some* people will do foolish things under pressure—kind of act startled, might aim for the brake and hit the accelerator, for example—but most people do all right, and then there's others will actually relax under pressure, do better when the heat is on than when it's off. Athletes are like that.''

Cole shot Reddman a look that accused him of preparing the witness's answer, then caught himself and smiled at the witness. "So you agree with me it happens a lot, right? A person will aim for the brake and hit the accelerator."

"I don't agree with that at all, sir. It happens, but not a lot."

"What foot on the brake—wait, let me get this right now. When a person hits the brake, what foot, Officer? Right or left?"

"Most people use the right foot."

Cole looked significantly at the jury, as though to remind them of Blue's bad leg. "You ever made a mistake in an investigation, Sergeant?"

"Yes, sir. Lots of times."

"In your more than twenty years, how many mistakes? Care to guess?"

"No, sir."

"How many mistakes today, Sergeant? One, two, ten?"

Reddman thought about objecting, but knew Donovan didn't need any help. "I don't believe I've made any," Donovan replied.

"Don't *believe*. Meaning you don't know, can't be sure, right?"

"That's not what I mean, sir. See, this is a jury trial—"

"Hold it, just a yes or no."

Reddman spoke up. "Judge, in all fairness, shouldn't the witness be permitted to explain?"

Landry nodded his head. "Let him explain his answer, Mr. Cole."

"When you prepare for a jury trial, you go over your data, go back out to the scene, do everything over lots of times," Donovan said. "If there's a mistake, you catch it."

"So you're trying to tell this jury that you've never made a mistake at a jury trial. That it, Sergeant?"

"I don't believe I have, sir."

"So you've never been wrong. Trials always turn out just the way you testify, right?"

"No, sir."

"Well, how can that be, Sergeant? If you never make a mistake but trials don't always turn out the way you testify—what? You mean juries make mistakes?" He waved his hand at the panel of jurors, as though inviting Donovan to call them a name.

"Now and then," Donovan said, smiling at Cole. "It doesn't happen often, but now and then."

Reddman fought and clawed his way through the balance of the day. The motive evidence went down rough, like swallowed sand. Then Landry dismissed the count on driving under revocation. After that, C. A. Goode told the jury that giving Ami O'Rourke CPR was a waste of time. And Cindy Strickland didn't help very much. She became confused on cross-examination and contradicted most of what she'd said on direct. But Muriel Doppler, his last witness, came on strong. "There is no doubt at all in my mind," she said, with total conviction. "When I first looked up and saw him there, after he'd honked at her but before he hit her, he sped up."

Reddman rested the people's case at five-fifteen, and court was in recess. He was totally exhausted and craved a glass of beer. He looked for Sharon, but she wasn't in the courtroom. He had that sinking feeling that trial lawyers get when they know they are losing and need to talk to someone—anyone—who will tell them they are doing fine. He jammed his books and papers into his briefcase and trotted toward the D.A.'s office.

The red Dodge pickup he had seen the day before, bearing license plate number XL-370, was parked alongside the deserted sidewalk. As Reddman approached, two beefy cowboys climbed out.

"Say, it's that prosecutor man," one of them said.

"Is? Why sure enough. Is."

Reddman stopped and let them block the sidewalk. Both

wore duckbill caps and denim jackets. "You're Shorty Wilson, right?" Reddman asked the taller of the two. The man fit the physical description Lopes had given him of the truck's owner.

The men looked at each other, then back at Reddman. "Nope," Wilson said, his grin turning into a sneer.

"Shorty who?" the other man said.

"You're the owner of that truck, right? The guy who tried to kill me?"

"What the fuck're you talkin' about, little prosecutor man?"

"You're being investigated right now, even as we speak. Did you know that?" Reddman asked conversationally. He showed the man his wristwatch. "I'm wired for sound."

"Investigated! What the fuck for?"

"Attempted murder. Vehicular assault. If I were you, I'd get myself a lawyer."

"Yeah, well you ain't me." Shorty glanced at his friend. "Come on, Lonnie, let's get outta here."

"Say hello to Johnny for me, okay?" Reddman called at them cheerfully. "Good old Johnny boy. Tell him I'm gonna put his ass in prison!"

The truck roared away, spewing gravel.

The encounter left Reddman shaking with fear and rage. He opened the door to the D.A.'s office, hoping Sharon would be there, but she wasn't. No one was there but Walter Brim. "How does it look, Walter?" Reddman asked, flopping on the couch in Brim's office. He realized then that virtually all the energy had been drained from his body. "No nicey-nice bullshit either, okay? I need to know."

"From what I saw—a bit from yesterday and most of today—you're looking good."

"I don't want to know how I look, Walter. What about the case?"

Brim leaned against his desk and thought a moment. "That Doppler woman—fantastic! Great way to finish your case. She couldn't have been better, especially the way her testimony dovetailed so nicely with Donovan's. But I'm not sure you have much else. Your motive evidence is weak. No one will believe that prisoner's testimony, and Winchester hurt you more than he helped."

Reddman was grinding his teeth. He had tried to get Winchester to testify about Blue's sexual jump at Ami—especially Blue's remark that he could smell her and to keep her away when she was in heat—but it had gone badly. Through innuendo, Cole had created the impression of an older woman trying to make her young lover jealous. And even though Winchester had not been allowed to testify about O'Rourke's general carelessness in crossing the street, the jury heard the implication. Winchester would be back as Cole's witness, and Reddman knew the testimony would come in then. "What about the rest of it?" he asked.

"You don't need a crystal ball to anticipate Cole's defense, do you?" Brim asked laconically.

Reddman tried to relax his jaw, but it wouldn't let go. "In other words, Cole has already proved his case through my witnesses. Is that what you mean?"

"Yes. He doesn't even need to put Johnny on the stand because that fairy tale he told Lopes is in. He even has Bernie telling the jury that the man spoke the truth! He also has enough to argue that Blue thought he had his foot on the brake, but it just happened to be the accelerator!" Brim laughed cynically. "And I'll have to say you looked a bit foolish when you tried to prove the driving-under-revocation charge. Perhaps that was my fault. I should have told you we'd need a witness from DMV."

Reddman shrugged off the dismissal of the traffic charge. Landry, a member of the old school, had not allowed the certified copy of Blue's driving record to go into evidence without someone from the Department of Motor Vehicles going through the useless formality of authentication. "So we lose a traffic count," Reddman said, getting up with renewed determination. "The bastard killed her. I want him for murder."

*   *   *

"Reddman? That you, honey?"

Reddman had been crouched over Walter Brim's desk, which he had cleaned off, then filled with his own clutter. He cradled the phone on his shoulder so he could use both hands: one to dogear the legal journal he was working with and the other to write. "Yeah, Zack, it's me." He copied the rest of the sentence, then leaned back in the large office chair, sticking his wrist under the light: 10:30 P.M.

"I saw you on your bike just before dark, pumping up Shiloh Hill. Looked like you were grittin' your teeth. Anybody ever tell you you have a nice ass?"

"You want a piece of it, too?"

"All I want is a yes or a no, sonny boy!"

Reddman tried to laugh at the reference to Cole's courtroom salvo. He wanted Wolfman to get on with it. "So what's happening?"

"I had a talk with Saul after court. You want to know what we talked about?"

"Damn right."

"He wanted to know if I thought he should put Johnny on the stand."

Reddman could hear music in the background. "What'd you tell him?"

"Told him no. He's proved everything he needs from Johnny through your witnesses. Why take a chance on cross?"

Reddman had the urge to slam the phone into the cradle, but held it against his ear. "What the fuck did you do that for?"

"Because I'm a terrible liar, man. I ain't no D.A."

"Where are you?" Reddman asked, hearing ice cubes.

"New York Saloon. Wanna come down, get drunk? Toast the system?" Wolfman took a long drink. "Here's to the system!"

"No."

"I knew you wouldn't. It wouldn't look good. All you guys ever think about is looking good."

"Piss on you. What will Cole do? Follow your advice or consider the source?"

"Hee-hee. He's terrible clever, just like you, sonny boy. I think he'll put Blue up."

"Really? Why?"

"I told him not to is part of it and he doesn't really trust me on this case. But he's got a gimmick he wants to trot out, one of the clever-as-hell gimmicks, and the only way to do it is through Blue."

"This gimmick. Something he told you?" Reddman asked, wondering if Wolfman would divulge a confidence.

"No, man. Something I've been watching him set up. He probably thinks you're too dumb to see it."

"So tell me."

"You know those gory photographs Cole put in through your pathologist? Then all those questions he asked, about more damage to her left side than her right side?"

"Yes. What's he doing?"

"Maybe he's trying to prove that Ami was runnin' *back* to the courthouse after she'd already crossed the street. You know, like she forgot something, had to get back quick?"

It clicked. Cole could use it to explain why Blue hadn't seen her in the street. "So you think Blue will testify that Ami jumped into the street from the P.D. side?" Reddman asked.

"You got it, honey. Jumped right in front of Johnny's truck."

"Hey, Zack?" Reddman said a moment later. "You're okay."

"No I'm not. I'm a fink."

It was after one o'clock. Reddman was asleep in his room at the New York Hotel when the telephone rang. He knocked it off the bedside table, then found it on the floor. "Yes."

"Dave? I'm sorry. Did I wake you up?"

It was Sharon Sondenburg. "Well, yeah." He sat up.

"Where've you been? I really wanted to see you after court."

"I've been playing cops and robbers. An exercise for my students. Trying to tap into the modern American myth."

"Okay. I'm awake now. You can tell me."

"Remember what Brenfleck said about the truck? Johnny's explanation as to how it got up on Mears Street hill?"

"Yeah. Johnny said his wife left it there."

"She didn't."

"How do you know?"

"She was in Oklahoma. Her dad had died. She was at his funeral."

CHAPTER
SEVENTEEN

When Reddman arrived at the courthouse the following morning, he looked for Sharon's car, but it wasn't there. The courtroom was packed with people, some of whom tried to smile at him as he pushed his way toward counsel table. Johnny Blue sat alone at the defendant's table and watched him come in, but Reddman ignored him. Bernie Lopes handed him some papers. "What are these?"

"Some defense motions. Saul just filed them."

"Where is he?"

"In chambers, talking to the judge."

At that moment Cole came into the courtroom and scurried to his chair. Shortly afterward everyone stood up as Landry mounted his throne and the bailiff announced that court was in session.

"Mr. Kellerman," Landry said to the bailiff, "are all the jurors assembled in the jury room?"

"Yes, sir."

"Very well. Mr. Reddman, do you have anything further to present at this time, or do the people rest?"

"The people rest, Your Honor."

"All right. I've been informed by Mr. Cole that he has filed three motions that must be heard out of the presence of the jury. The first is a motion to dismiss for lack of evidence, the second a motion to dismiss based on the destruction of evidence, and finally a motion to compel the prosecution to elect theories. Have you had a chance to consider them, Mr. Reddman?"

"No, sir." Bullshit motions, Reddman thought tiredly. He wanted to get on with the trial.

"What is your pleasure? Can you argue them without preparation, or do you need some time?"

"If I can have a minute to read them?"

"Of course."

The words on the pages played through Reddman's head, but their meaning didn't seem to reach below his neck. Uh-oh, he thought, recognizing the symptoms. In the course of a trial, this always happened to him at least once. The pressure, the fear of losing, the tight control over the imp, the mounting frustration with the ponderous justice machine—he felt disembodied, like a balloon in the wind. "Ready, Your Honor," he said a moment later, his voice cracking.

Saul Cole positioned himself behind the lectern and launched into his argument. Reddman tried to look as if he was listening. But the floor had tilted. Cole was not really standing at the lectern, whacking away at the law. The slope of the floor was such that everything in the courtroom should slide off. Both the man and the podium jutted out from the floor like huge spikes.

What holds everything in place? Reddman asked himself, even though he knew the answer before asking himself the question. Magnets. Tiny invisible magnets, clamping everything in the room firmly to the floor. They kept him and Cole and the spectators and all that furniture from crashing down on the judge's bench twenty feet below.

He tuned in on Cole.

"—don't beat around the bush, waste the court's time with games. The plain and simple truth: there is not enough evidence here to go to the jury on that murder count. Now I concede enough evidence on the drunk driving, on the hit and run—that driving under revocation charge already out, prosecutor made a mess out of that one—and maybe even on vehicular homicide for a jury to consider it—but evidence as to murder? Where is the *evidence?*

"Here's what the evidence is, Judge. A man, drunk, sitting in his truck, knows he doesn't have an operator's license, sees a cop, tries to sneak away. When he drives off he's looking behind him." Cole acted it out, his hands on an imaginary steering wheel and his head turned to the left. "He's looking into the mirror, nothing back there, no cops—when a jaywalker steps in front of him!" Cole's voice escalated and his head snapped quickly forward as his hands and arms braced for the blow. "He hits her, a woman jaywalker, tragic accident is what you have, Judge. *Not* murder. No way!" He glared around the room, enraged, his face filled with color. "Force a man to defend against a *murder* charge on evidence like that? Is this America, or what?" Then suddenly: "Want me to do these motions one at a time, Judge, or all together?"

"I think one at a time, Saul." Landry smiled at Cole with obvious good humor. "Do you have anything further on your motion to dismiss?"

"No, Your Honor. If it please the court, only one count you should dismiss, that murder count. Shouldn't be there."

"Suppose we hear from Mr. Reddman."

Reddman rose slowly and walked to the lectern, keeping his hand on the table for balance. He knew in his mind that the magnets would hold, but he didn't trust them. "Thank you, Your Honor," he said, again surprised at the power of his voice. "So I have it straight: This is on the motion to dismiss for lack of evidence?"

"Yes."

"And the only count Mr. Cole is talking about is the murder count?"

"Correct again, Mr. Reddman."

"Thanks, Judge. I'd like to point out that Mr. Cole has chosen to focus on only one aspect of the proof in connection with that count. He's only considering the explanation offered by the defendant! However, the proof goes way beyond that." The floor began to level out. Instead of peering down at the judge, Reddman found himself looking up. "Mr. Cole has completely ignored the compelling circumstantial evidence that has been introduced, and the inferences that can be drawn from that evidence. The defendant was sitting in his truck on Mears Street hill, where he could easily view the courthouse and the people leaving the courthouse. Why? Why was he sitting up there, presumably watching? Was he waiting for his former lawyer? The evidence also shows he had reasons—motive—to hurt her."

"Humph!" Cole snorted.

"The hit—the point of impact—shows clearly the complete absence of any kind of evasive action. The physical evidence of heavy acceleration is strong enough—"

"Perfectly consistent—man tromped on the wrong pedal!"

Landry glared at Cole. "Saul, be still."

Cole stared out the window like a pouting child.

"As I was saying," Reddman continued, "the acceleration was strong enough to pin the victim on the wheel of his pickup truck and spin her on it." Reddman caught the smirk of Johnny Blue's face. He began to feel the rage that his body tried to keep him from feeling. It glowed like a coal, about where his stomach ought to be. You puke, he thought to himself, smiling at Blue. "As to whether or not the man tromped on the wrong pedal, there is absolutely no evidence at all to suggest that he did. Mr. Cole has supplied us with a lot of innuendo, but that isn't evidence.

"But the evidence from Mrs. Doppler isn't innuendo. She didn't want to testify because the defendant is an acquaintance of hers, but she knows what she saw. She was in her truck, about a hundred feet away, facing both the victim and the defendant." Landry tried to let his eyes fall away, but Reddman wouldn't let go of them. "She wasn't aware of either the victim or the defendant until she heard the honk of Johnny Blue's horn. And then she saw. There is no doubt in her mind as to what she saw. She saw the defendant step on the gas. She witnessed the start of that heavy acceleration."

"Your point, Mr. Reddman?"

"That is evidence, Your Honor. Mr. Cole's statement about tromping on the wrong pedal isn't evidence at all. There is more than enough real evidence before this jury for it to decide that Mr. Blue deliberately murdered Ami O'Rourke."

"Yes. I'm inclined to agree. Motion to dismiss count five for lack of evidence is denied. Your next motion, Mr. Cole?"

Reddman sat down and Cole resumed his place at the lectern. "Case should be dismissed because of the destruction of evidence, Judge," Cole said. "Prosecution's fault, how can I prove my case? The evidence I need to prove my case, destroyed!

"Now, Judge, you know me, know I understand the problems of the police, our boys in blue, always have to look over their shoulder, act on the spur of the moment, Supreme Court decisions looking down on them like Big Brother, after the fact, second-guessing, hindsight, like schoolteachers. But things happened this case, inexcusable. No need. Unnecessary." He paused for a drink of water.

"Accident happened, first officer on the scene, Patrolman Judson. Every minute counts, every second, people all over, evidence disappearing like water down a drain, what does he do?" Cole pointed at Reddman, as though Reddman had been the first officer on the scene. "Gives the victim CPR! This woman, caught on the tire of a truck, rolled *through* the tire well two, three times, no offense but how dead can you be? No sign of life! You remember C. A. Goode, fine man, banker, witness for the prosecution, what he said? There was no sign of life! Mr. Goode had CPR training, too, every bit as qualified as Judson, felt the poor woman's carotid, nothing!"

Landry frowned and rubbed his chin, obviously attentive to the argument. Cole swallowed another mouthful of water.

"Photographs, showing her exact location, exact attitude, should have been taken, weren't. Why not? Because Judson, pardon me for putting it so bluntly, tried to revive a corpse! Five minutes, testimony, precious minutes, no crowd control, wasted."

"Mr. Cole, what difference does it make?" Landry asked. "I agree evidence may have been needlessly lost, but I don't see that it matters. There isn't any question that it was the defendant's truck that ran into her, is there? Or that he was driving it?"

"No, sir. But prosecution's whole case based on a scenario like this: Poor woman had just left the courthouse, was on her way back to her office when this happened. Clear inference there, in the street, books in her arms, jaywalking, how come Johnny Blue didn't see her?

"I'll tell you why. Something I can tell you but can't prove, because all of the evidence is gone. She had *crossed* the street, gone between a couple of cars parked on the other side, maybe remembered something she'd forgot about. She was on her way *back* to the courthouse when she got hit! Blue didn't see her because she was coming into the street from over here." Cole marched over to the portable chalk board where the large diagram of the scene of the crime had been pinned. He showed Landry exactly what he meant. He pointed at the opposite side of Mears street, near the public defender's office, and with gestures, ushered Ami O'Rourke into the road from that direction. "Goes right to the heart of the case, this planned or accidental, avoidable or unavoidable? but we can't prove it! Take that *Morgan* case, Judge, Colorado Supreme Court, 1980 case, got the cite here somewhere if you want it. Prosecution lost the defendant's fingertip in that case, you remember, we talked about it one time? Identical situation. Prosecutor in that case said Morgan shot it off when he shot the victim, tip of his own finger, but Morgan said, nope, the victim bit it off, remember? Issue was murder or self-defense, somebody found the tip of his finger on the scene, experts could tell by examining, was his finger bit off or shot off, then the prosecution lost it!"

The judge, who had been watching the diagram as Cole pointed at it, leaned back in his chair. "It's your contention you might have been able to deduce the direction in which she was running, or moving, from physical evidence that was destroyed? An intriguing theory. What evidence, exactly, might have been preserved?"

"Pictures of her body—we've already talked about that— weren't taken. They might have shown something. The way she fell off the tire could very well show how she got on it. Damage to her left side, tire marks on her clothing, innumerable little indications, enough maybe for an expert to tell."

"Seventy feet from the point of impact?"

"Who knows, Judge, experts can work miracles, we've both seen it, anyway, all that gone. Also gone, the cars parked along the curb. She went between a couple of cars our theory, what if there were footprints there, or if she brushed against a car, left a trace? Fibers from her suit, article of clothing, scarf, we'll never know. See my point?"

"Yes. Anything further?"

"No, sir, not on this motion. One more to go."

"Mr. Reddman?"

Reddman discussed the *Morgan* case briefly, pointing out that it applied only where the police were at fault for the lost or destroyed evidence. But in the *Blue* case, the police were not at fault. The primary duty of the police is to preserve life, Reddman said, and Officer Judson had detected signs of life in Ami O'Rourke. Hence, any evidence lost in the first five minutes—

"Yes," Landry said, drumming his fingers and glaring at his watch. "I quite agree, Mr. Reddman. Defendant's motion to dismiss based on the loss of evidence is denied. Mr. Cole? I believe your next motion is to compel the prosecution to elect theories."

Cole resumed his place at the lectern. Something about his manner suggested that this time he meant it. "Judge, only one woman died here, but we've got *two* homicide counts based on widely different theories. How could it happen both ways? Inconsistent! One way, the prosecutor wants the jury to believe the defendant did it on purpose, deliberately pulled the trigger so to speak, but the other way caused by the consumption of alcohol, lack of reflexes, whatever. Point is it can't be both. One way Johnny's a cold-blooded murderer, wants to kill, and kills. Other way not a murderer, just stupid. Drinks and drives, messes up because of the *drinking,* not because he sets out to kill somebody.''

Landry was clearly attentive. Cole paused long enough to take a long drink of water. "Dry. Sorry.'' He put the glass down. "Judge, take a look at CRS 18-1-408, subsection three. Gives the court the discretion to make the prosecution *elect,* only fair, what are we talking about here? Murder or vehicular homicide?''

"But, Mr. Cole, the statute clearly states 'at the conclusion of *all* the evidence,' does it not? Why are you bringing the motion now? 'All the evidence' isn't in yet, and won't be until you've presented your side. I think you're premature with this motion.''

"No, Judge, because we got a constitutional issue here, fact is, we got two of 'em. The Constitution gives my defendant the right to the effective assistance of counsel. No question there, right, Sixth Amendment? The Constitution also prohibits self-incrimination, proving a case out of the mouth of the defendant. Well, I got to recommend to my client, should he take the stand or shouldn't he, and my recommendation is effective assistance of counsel, right? But how can I advise him to give up his right against self-incrimination until I know what he's been charged with! Until I know which way the prosecutor wants to go, is he a murderer or just a victim of his own stupidity, I can't tell him anything, because I don't even know *myself* what he's opening up to on cross if he takes the stand!''

Landry stared at the silver-haired archetypical country

lawyer. "A most ingenious argument, Mr. Cole. You never cease to amaze me. Mr. Reddman?"

Reddman got up slowly, trying to give himself time to think. He felt helpless, like an engineer watching the bridge he had just built crumble and fall into the canyon below. He couldn't think of anything to say. He filled his argument with buzzwords, in the hope that something would occur to him that would work. But the drumming of Landry's fingers grew loud with impatience until it sounded like hail on a tin roof. Suddenly Landry's voice broke through Reddman's words. "It appears to me you are stalling, Mr. Reddman."

"Judge, I didn't get the motion until I came into court this morning."

"The problem didn't come up until this morning," Landry snapped back. "Gentlemen, this is a difficult question. I think it merits more attention than off-the-cuff argument." He looked at his watch. "It is now nine-thirty. I don't want to keep that jury waiting any longer than is necessary, but perhaps a short recess is in order. Suppose we reconvene at eleven. That will give each of you an hour and a half to research this question. When we return at that time, I quite naturally expect both of you to be thoroughly prepared, erudite, and persuasive." He lifted his gavel. "One other thing. Mr. Reddman, in the event I rule against you, please be prepared to make your election." The gavel came down. "We are in recess until eleven."

Reddman was desperate. He called NASP from Brim's office. Trigge had been summoned to Washington, leaving Frankie Rommel in charge. As quickly as he could, he explained Cole's argument to her, and the issue.

"*That's* a new one," she said, obviously impressed. "What do you want me to do?"

"Can you research it for me?"

"No kidding. The new kid on the block wants help?"

"Yeah." Reddman swallowed, remembering his lackadaisical attitude when he had second-chaired the *Byrne* case for her. "I know you don't exactly owe it to me," he said.

"You're right, sonny boy. Why can't you do it yourself?"

"The library here doesn't have anything in it and no one has *Lexis*. I need the time, too. I've got to figure out what to do if he makes me elect." His voice crackled with intensity and pressure.

"Settle down, Davey," the woman said. "Go have a beer. Call me back in an hour."

Reddman sat on the couch in Brim's office. He was not hearing what he wanted to hear. Both Brim and Wolfman told him that if the judge forced him to elect, he should keep the vehicular homicide count and dump out the murder count. He could win the vehicular homicide charge, they told him. But he'd lose the murder.

"It's a murder case, damn it!" Reddman said, jumping up. His voice was louder than it needed to be.

"Listen, what difference does it make if it's a murder case?" Wolfman asked. "I mean, move out all the bullshit, talk serious, talk penalty, okay? What's the most you can get out of this case?"

"Twenty to life if I get him on first degree." Reddman dropped back in his chair.

"I said talk serious. It isn't first degree, no way. You got a solid-thinking small-town jury, right? You got a jaywalking pedestrian who was run over by a truck. No smoking gun, not drilled with an arrow, stabbed with a knife. No way possible that jury'll come back with first degree, you put on your best case and Cole puts up his worst. You agree with that?"

Brim nodded, but Reddman stared ahead, refusing to concede.

"Go with me for the sake of argument, okay?" Wolfman asked. "I'd say second degree is the most you can get. That's eight to twelve years in the slam."

"So?"

"He gets a day for a day, so in actual time you're talking

four to six. I've got to say—and I hate that son of a bitch more'n anybody in this room—that's acceptable. Put him in a cage four years and I'll be satisfied."

"Yeah. Well, you're a public defender," Reddman said. "I'm not. And if I dump out the murder and get him on vehicular homicide, the most he can pull is two to four. That could come down to one year. Is that acceptable?"

Wolfman leaned back on the edge of Brim's desk. "Maybe you're right. If you stay with the murder, you'll have all those lesser includeds, too. Maybe that's the way to go."

"Wait. Forget penalty for a moment," Brim said. "Consider only the case, the evidence. That murder count is far too dependent on inference."

Reddman wished suddenly that he had not asked for advice. But he forced himself to listen. "Go on."

"Those are problems you don't have with the vehicular homicide. You have the defendant in his truck," Brim said, looking at one hand, "running away from the cops." He moved his hands, suggesting one running away from the other. "Nothing circumstantial about any of that. In fact, Blue admits it. He also admits drinking. He was drunk and he runs her down." One hand ran into the other and he looked at Reddman. "That's something the jury can visualize quite easily. You shouldn't take a chance on murder."

"As the district attorney of Sopris County, are you telling me to do it that way?" Reddman asked. "Because if you are—"

"Oh, no," Brim said. "It's your decision. And win or lose, you'll have my support."

Reddman had heard that before. Brim might feel that way now, he thought. But he wondered how the man would feel if he came away with nothing.

"You won't have mine," Wolfman told him, jumping away from Brim's desk. "If you don't hang something on him, man, I'll be highly pissed."

"Now you think I should go with the murder count, right?"

"Nope. The homicide. Cole will kill you on that murder charge. You know what he'll argue? 'Course not as good as me, the sleaze." He started pacing in front of Reddman, as though facing the jury. His face took on one of Cole's characteristic expressions. " 'Ladies and gentlemen, if this case is anything, it's vehicular homicide. But the D.A.' "— he stuck his finger under Reddman's nose—" 'has taken that count away from you. You don't have that one anymore. Now, ours is a system of law, ladies and gentlemen. You must follow the law, plain and simple. That means you can't convict this dirty rotten pervert of what you probably wanted to convict him of all along, what the evidence shows he's quite possibly even guilty of! Because—' "

"Get your finger out of my face."

The clock on the wall said three minutes after eleven. Reddman tried to read the notes he had scribbled minutes before, when Frankie Rommel had called him back. The judge came in. "Court will be in order," Landry declared, sitting down quickly. "Mr. Reddman, I'd like to hear from you first."

As Reddman spoke, he tried to mask the awful rage that had been burning in him all morning. "The issue is this, Judge," he said. "Can the prosecution be compelled to elect theories at this stage of the proceeding, before all the evidence is in?" He tried to smile, to soften his voice. "In order for you to compel an election now, you would have to hold that our statute is unconstitutional."

"Can you explain that, young man?"

"Yes, sir. As you pointed out earlier, the statute says no election can be compelled until *all* the evidence is in. It doesn't say part of the evidence, or some evidence. It says all. And that won't happen until the defense rests."

"And it is your position, I take it, that I cannot force you to elect without first finding that the statute is unconstitutional?"

"Yes, sir. Our basic posture is this: we should never be required to elect, because—on the basis of the evidence so far—there is no contradiction between the theories. The defendant clearly could be guilty of both vehicular homicide and murder.'' He quickly ran through the elements of both charges, demonstrating convincingly, he believed, that there was no logical inconsistency. "But even if you find otherwise, Judge, the prosecution can't be made to elect now." Reddman tried to take the intensity out of his voice. "Not without finding the statute unconstitutional."

"As serious as all that, is it?" Landry asked ironically. He appeared fully capable of shouldering such awesome responsibility. "Do you have anything further?"

Reddman knew he should quit, but couldn't stop. He felt the volume of his voice go up. He admitted there were no decisions directly on point, even though several courts in other jurisdictions had considered similar constitutional questions, but always in a different context. He cited authorities and watched as Landry dutifully copied them down. "Statutes are presumed to be constitutional," he heard himself shout, and "In the absence of precedent, the court should rely on the plain language of the statute." Reddman cited a string of authorities for that statement, too, but Landry copied only two of them down. He started drumming his fingers.

Reddman could feel Blue's eyes on the back of his head, mocking him. "Your Honor, the cases are legion in distinguishing between 'close of the prosecution's case' and 'conclusion of all the evidence.' " he said, tacking on the citations. "Submitted it is very clear, especially at this point in the trial, that the people should not be compelled to elect."

It was Cole's turn. He agreed that there were no authorities directly on point and used that as a platform from which to launch into his plea. "How can I be expected to render effective assistance of counsel to this man unless I know how to advise? Can't be done. Cornerstone of our system *fairness*, Judge, got to ask yourself what is *fair*, when one man stood up like a firing squad against the wall of the law!"

Both lawyers were in their chairs when Landry announced his decision. "Gentlemen, during the recess, I did much soul-searching and a certain amount of research. I've heard nothing to dissuade me from the conclusion I reached as a consequence of that process.

"There isn't time to give to this matter the attention it deserves. We have a jury waiting; there is other court business that must be attended to; all we can do is forge ahead and hope that the decision, which at this point is not much better than an educated guess, is the correct one.

"Mr. Reddman, I am not persuaded that these counts are logically consistent. I believe in all fairness that at some point you should be required to elect. On the face of it, it strikes me that there is a great disparity between vehicular homicide and murder, and I do not see how this man can be guilty of both. Therefore the only question I need to resolve, it seems to me, is this: When am I going to compel your election of theories?"

Hot flashes, followed by cold fear. Reddman felt himself expand and then contract.

"Our Supreme Court has adopted the rule of lenity as a tool of statutory construction, and I refer specifically to *People versus Lowe,* a 1983 case, and one which both of you gentlemen are familiar with. In effect, that rule states that ambiguities—differences, if you will—are to be resolved in favor of the defendant. I find myself on the horns of a dilemma here. Whose constitutional rights do I protect, those of the defendant or those of the people? On the basis of the rule of lenity, I find I must resolve that dilemma in favor of the defendant.

"It is therefore my decision that the prosecution shall, at this time, make its election of theories." He frowned, directing all his attention at the prosecutor. "Which will it be, sir? Murder or vehicular homicide?"

Reddman's stomach burned so badly he wanted to throw up. Not because of the judge or Cole and, at that moment, not even because of Johnny Blue. Sharon had asked him if he ever thought about Ami, the live-wire pain-in-the-ass public defender he had come to know. What about her? he wondered, trying to blink away the pain in his eyes and wishing he could visualize the snapshot he had seen of her in life. Already she was becoming a fading memory. What about that? he wanted to shout. What of Ami O'Rourke's right to live?

"Murder," he said—or tried to say. His vocal chords had tightened and there was no sound.

"Try again, Mr. Reddman," Landry said.

"If it please the court," Reddman said loudly. "The people elect to proceed on the murder count."

CHAPTER EIGHTEEN

The defense called Dr. Randolph Wilkerson to the stand. A tall man, as he sat in the witness box he looked like Gary Cooper astride a horse.

Cole handled the witness as though he were the master of ceremonies and Wilkerson was the star of the show. "Well, sir, my father—he was trained as a medical doctor, but never had the chance to set up his own practice." Wilkerson was responding to the question: Are you from a medical family? "You see, he knew where he wanted to live," the witness continued in the slow, easy manner of a person with plenty of time. "But when he first come here—that was in 1910—Muldoon already had a doctor, and as a consequence my father couldn't get any business. So he took over old Doc Hinckley's practice, the veterinarian." He looked for a moment at the back of one of his weathered, somewhat gnarled hands. "In answer to your question, you could say I come from a medical family."

Cole allowed the jury the time to enjoy the performance. Then: "When and where did you go to med school?"

"Over at Boulder—that's the University of Colorado—after the war. I'd started just before."

"And that's World War Two you're talking about?"

"That's right."

"You were a pilot during the war? Navy?"

"Yes."

"Even picked up some medals along the way, got shot at—all that, too, right?"

"Well, yes. I did my share of ducking during the war."

Cole nodded matter-of-factly at the witness. Wilkerson's heroic exploits during World War II did not need elaboration because everyone in Sopris County knew of them. "Now, when you and I—or is it me? Don't matter. Anyway, the two of us were talking about your testimony a week or so ago in my office, you remember that?"

"Yes, I do."

"You told me something then, Doc, didn't sound right at the time. You said after you got your license, you came back to Muldoon and went into practice with your father?"

"That's right."

"But he was still a veterinarian, wasn't he?"

Wilkerson's eyes crinkled with good humor. "Now, I know that might seem peculiar, but we shared the same building and even the same reception area for a time, and we kind of worked things out together, yes, sir."

"Go on."

"You see, the situation was some looser then than it is now. Not that constant worry over malpractice, and my dad and I would swap remedies now and then. I guess I birthed more than one calf, and my father—well, he might take an occasional house call for me, but he never delivered anyone."

"Didn't you tell me what your specialties were?" Cole innocently asked.

"Yes, sir, seems to me I may have mentioned it. Of course we both did a little of everything, but he specialized in cows, and I in humans."

The whole line of questions was leading. Reddman could have objected, but he knew it would be useless. Cole would get what he wanted out of the witness, no matter what Reddman did. Rather than make himself look like an obstructionist, he did his best to laugh at the folksy, home-spun doctor, along with everyone else in the courtroom.

Under Cole's skillful handling, Wilkerson graphically described the rodeo injury to Johnny Blue's right leg: the literal explosion of the femur, with pieces of bone splintering into the heavy musculature that surrounded it; the concurrent fractures in his fibula and tibia; the severely torn ligaments holding the patella—the kneecap—in place, so resistant to healing in spite of extensive surgical repair. When Wilkerson was asked to describe Blue's present condition, his quiet explanation, delivered in his full-toned voice, capable of conveying the depth of his feeling, made it real. "Constant debilitating pain. A chronic condition caused largely by the severe trauma to the muscles of his thigh." The crow's-feet around the doctor's eyes tightened as he spoke. "A large share of the trauma occurred when he got bucked off that horse, the god-awful yanking and wrenching his leg went through at that time. He was thrown clear of the animal, but his right foot had gotten wedged into the stirrup, and that horse flung him and dragged him around the arena as it tried to shake free. Afterward more trauma occurred because of the ten or so operations through those same muscles, necessary intrusions to rebuild the femur."

"So he's in pain?"

"Yes. Constantly. There are also fragments of bone, most of them so small they can't be detected until they surface, sliver-size, about as large as the splinters you get in your fingers when you work with wood. Some of them are still working through that muscle, don't you see, and the result is chronic infliction of infection, irritation, and pain."

Cole was obviously affected by Wilkerson's testimony and needed a moment before continuing with the examination. His attitude and expression provided a perfect mirror to show the jury how they should feel. "What about physical limitations, Doctor? I mean, we all know he can't ride a horse anymore. Can he drive a car?"

"Oh, yes. From what I understand, he drives perhaps more than he should."

Blue's ice-blue eyes crinkled with good humor at the jab. Reddman could feel the jury extending its warmth toward the man.

"What about flexion, Doctor? Medical term, flexion. Is it normal in that leg?"

"No, sir. Although as I think of it, that will depend— lawyer phraseology—on what you mean. If given the opportunity to move slow, he has close to normal movement, or flexion. Not without experiencing discomfort, of course. But sudden movements are accompanied by acute pain. I don't guess they are impossible, but that flash of pain has got to act as an inhibitor."

"Right leg we're talking about, isn't it? Don't know whether that came out."

"Yes. His right leg."

"So for him to lift his foot off the accelerator, for example, and hit the brake—you know, quick reaction—wouldn't be easy?"

"I would expect, at the very least, that he would experience a flash of pain."

"Make him stop and think, wouldn't you say?"

Wilkerson shrugged. "I can't really say whether he would stop and think."

" 'Course not. Stupid question," Cole said, gathering up his notes. "Thank you, Doctor. Your witness, Mr. Reddman."

Reddman took his time getting up. The knot in his stomach alternated rapidly between hot and cold. He had ten seconds to decide what to do. If he left Wilkerson alone, at least the old charmer couldn't do any more damage than he'd already done; but on a hunch—Cole's smile was too broad, too much of a challenge—Reddman decided to take a chance. He angled his legal pad on the lectern. "Doctor, was there any trauma to Mr. Blue's ankle?"

"Yes. His whole leg was severely traumatized—stretched

and twisted, as though on a rack—including the muscles and tendons of his ankle and foot."

The witness said nothing about broken bones, Reddman noted. "What about the bones in his ankle and foot, Doctor? Any breaks?"

"No, sir."

"And the tendons holding his ankle to his lower leg. Were they torn or broken?"

Wilkerson thought for a moment. "No. Stretched to the breaking point, yes. Severely traumatized, yes. But the forces causing the most severe injury were absorbed, or you might say released, in the fracturing of the bones in his leg."

Reddman continued with more confidence. The witness really was a straight shooter. "You saw him regularly, didn't you, Doctor, after this happened?"

"Yes."

"And the injury occurred approximately three years ago?"

"At a rodeo in Salinas, California. It will be three years in June."

"So there were two years, approximately, between the injury to the defendant and the death of Ami O'Rourke?"

Cole got up and walked over to the bailiff's desk, as though nothing of importance was happening in the courtroom. "Yes," Wilkerson said. "Slightly more than two years."

"In that period of time, would normal healing have occurred in his ankle and foot?"

"Should have."

Out of the corner of his eye, Reddman watched as Cole and the bailiff carried on a brief whispered conversation. The eyes of a couple of jurors strayed in that direction, then came back. Cole was purposely trying to distract the attention of the jury, but Reddman decided to do nothing about it. He took a deep breath and jumped over a cliff with his next question, knowing full well that a cardinal rule on cross-examination is never ask if you don't know the answer. "When was the last time he complained of pain in his ankle or foot?"

"May I look at my records?"

"Yes. Please do."

Wilkerson searched through the papers in his thin file. "I don't think he ever did."

Cole noisily clomped back in his chair. Reddman smiled at him and waited until he was fully settled. "Now, if his ankle and foot had healed—and incidentally, Doctor, this man healed perhaps better than the average person? By that, I mean his health was very good?"

"Yes. He had and has the resilience and healing capacity of an athlete."

Reddman nodded. "Is it fair to say, Doctor—considering that his ankle and foot had healed, and that presumably there was no pain in his ankle or foot—that he has full flexion in his right ankle? That it is just as good as his left one?"

"Well, not quite. You see, whenever you move your foot or ankle, there is corresponding muscle activity throughout the leg." One of the jurors wiggled her ankle and felt her thigh, nodding in comprehension. "As a consequence, some discomfort will accompany even an ankle movement, resulting in minor limitation."

"But Mr. Blue's right foot is capable of working the accelerator pedal of a car or truck, isn't it?"

"Wait. Just a minute there," Cole said, lumbering to his feet. "Object to the question, Judge."

"Your reason?"

"Immaterial and irrelevant. Not gone into on direct. Not the kind of thing this doctor can have an opinion about."

"In other words, general principles?" Landry suggested, smiling. "Overruled."

"What about it, Doctor?" Reddman pursued. "In your opinion, would there be any significant limitation there?"

"No."

"His right foot can depress the accelerator when the situation calls for speed, and it can lift off the accelerator if he needs to slow down?"

"Oh, yes."

Reddman studied his notes. The jurors were looking thoughtfully at the witness. Some of them stole glances at Johnny Blue. "Doctor, it's normal isn't it, for a person with an injury to compensate for that injury? Especially an athlete?"

"Not sure I get your drift. Whenever a person gets shot in the right hand, I guess he'll tend to use his left hand more. Is that what you mean?"

"Yes, sir. Would you say, because of the injury to his right leg, that Mr. Blue might tend to use his left leg more?"

"Quite likely."

"Now, a lifting motion, where Mr. Blue has to lift his right leg, causes pain. Correct?"

"Yes."

"That is something he might well learn to avoid, right?"

"I would think so."

"Such as lifting his foot off the accelerator in order to depress the brake pedal?"

Wilkerson nodded. "I believe he would avoid that motion as much as possible."

"Yet he has to use the brake, right?"

Wilkerson shrugged his shoulders. "Yes. Of course."

"Wouldn't he learn to use his other foot?"

"Objection, if it please the court. That one is *clearly*—"

"Yes. Sustained."

But the question was out there. And the only person who could answer it was Johnny Blue.

Lance Winchester, this time as a witness for the defense, assumed a righteous air, as though he saw himself as one of the Knights of the Round Table. He answered Cole's questions with a thoroughness and completeness that went beyond his obligation to tell the truth. His dynamic first impression showed signs of wear, so Reddman let him talk without objection. Two or three of the jurors squirmed with embarrassment as the man revealed his pompousness to them. Cole obviously wanted him off as soon as possible.

He testified that Ami O'Rourke had been both his colleague and "dear friend," that on occasions too numerous to estimate he had walked with her across Mears Street between the courthouse and the public defender's office, that she was completely oblivious to danger and always had a thousand matters of import on her mind. She was not unlike Joan of Arc, he mused, in that she seemed to him to have been protected by a succession of miracles as she dashed in front of oncoming traffic. She was, he stated in a tragic voice, continuously engaged in a mad, frantic effort to crowd more time into each hour than there were minutes and seconds.

He had also seen Ami literally spin on her heels in the middle of the street and scurry back, either to her office or to the courthouse, because of some forgotten matter or article, alarming motorists bearing down on her from both directions. It seemed to him that the local drivers were accustomed to her antics, in that they appeared to drive with extreme caution whenever they saw her in the street. It would not surprise Winchester at all if she were to—but at that point, Reddman objected to speculation on the part of the witness, and after two or three short exchanges between Cole and Winchester, Reddman took the man on cross.

Reddman knew the man was exaggerating. His tactic on cross-examination was to encourage it to the point of absurdity. Under Reddman's prodding, Mears Street became a busy thoroughfare instead of a moderately quiet roadway; and Winchester's efforts to save O'Rourke's life achieved heroic proportions. On many occasions, he testified, he not only grabbed her arm to keep her from stepping in front of oncoming vehicles, but actually stepped in front of traffic himself, shielding her fragile body with his. When asked whether traffic lights should be installed at the corners, Winchester replied, "Indeed, yes. Absolutely." Two jurors rolled their eyes. Somewhat reluctantly, the witness agreed that jaywalking was common at that location. But even though the whole block was "an accident waiting to happen," he had not heard of any in that vicinity until the present case.

Reddman derived a cruel sense of satisfaction out of the performance. He ended his cross-examination by asking Winchester if any of his testimony had been overstated, even to a minor degree. The witness angrily denounced the suggestion and stoutly maintained he had "told it precisely the way it was." Some of the jurors appeared offended, others amused.

"Your next witness, Mr. Cole," Landry ordered.

Cole stood thoughtfully at his place in the pit. "Judge, I need a recess."

"For what purpose?" Landry asked. His tone of voice suggested he did not want any undue delay.

"I need to talk to my client. Won't take long."

Landry looked at the clock on the wall: 1:45 P.M. "We'll reconvene at two, then. Ladies and gentlemen, please go with the bailiff to the jury room, and bear in mind my previous admonishments not to discuss the case." He banged the gavel down. "Court is in recess."

Reddman stood alone in the hallway behind the clerk's office, aware of the perspiration under his arms. He thought of the deodorant commercial that warned, "Never let them see you sweat."

Wolfman found him. "Skinny little fucker," he finally decided. "Man, you need some meat on your bones."

Reddman grinned. He had a sudden feeling of physical strength. He knew he could slug it out for as long as it took. "Cole is trying to figure out what to do."

"Yeah," Wolfman said. "What are his options?"

"He has two character witnesses. I hope—"

"No way, he's not that stupid. What else?"

"He can call Blue. Or he can rest."

Wolfman nodded. "He shouldn't have put on anybody,

you know that? Not even Wilkerson. You zinged him pretty good with the old doc."

"What should he do now, Zack? What would you do?"

"I'd rest. But he won't. You got him scared."

Reddman's body tingled with excitement. "You think he'll call Johnny?"

"Yup. He'll think it over, decide he's got to answer a few questions the jury might have, and put him up there. You watch. Johnny's gonna remember how Ami jumped out in front of him."

"Maybe she did."

"Bullshit."

Reddman stared at the floor. He wished Sharon was there. He felt like a little boy who needed to hold his mother's hand before starting his first day at school. "Is that guy from Judicial Qualifications still here?"

"Haven't seen him today. No room for him anyway; the place is packed. Johnny's got all his relatives here."

"Like I told you, Zack. It's more challenging to work my side. I get to stare down all the defendant's babies and wives and mothers and girlfriends and wonder how many of the menfolk are packing iron. Public defenders don't get a chance to do those things."

"Huh! Ever go to church with a whole congregation full of Mothers Against Drunk Drivers?"

Reddman laughed. "How are you betting on this one?"

"I'm not, man," Wolfman said. "Never bet on a horse race unless it's fixed, my daddy said. This one's too close."

Reddman looked at his watch and pushed away from the wall. "I'd better get in there."

"Hey," Wolfman said, smiling at him. He held his hand high for a brother's grip.

Reddman took his hand. "What?"

"I like the way you hate, baby. You're okay."

As Reddman entered the courtroom, Cole grabbed him by the arm. "Where you been?" he demanded, pushing him toward the judge's chambers. "Landry wants to see us."

Reddman followed Cole back into the lion's den. Landry had his robe on, but sat down quickly as the attorneys entered. "Mr. Reddman, I propose a short discussion, off the record, not to exceed five minutes. Is that agreeable?"

Reddman shrugged his shoulders. "Sure."

"Fine. Now. I implore you, young man, to reconsider Mr. Cole's offer. It frankly does not seem possible to me, at this point, that the jury will convict Johnny Blue of murder. And even if they were to do so, I would probably reduce the verdict to manslaughter or even criminally negligent homicide—assuming an appropriate motion had been filed—because, quite frankly, the evidence is not sufficient to sustain either first or second degree murder.

"For your information," Landry went on, "I might also reconsider the motions to dismiss we heard this morning. Several attorneys have followed these proceedings closely, and two of them have suggested to me I have probably made a grave mistake in overruling Mr. Cole's motion with regard to the destruction of evidence."

"Judge—"

"Please allow me to finish. At the present time, there are only three counts left to this information: drunk driving, hit-and-run, and murder. If you accept Mr. Cole's offer, you will obtain a guilty verdict in connection with each of the three counts. Of course manslaughter isn't as severe as either first or second degree murder, but under the circumstances, what more can you possibly expect?"

"What would you give him, Judge?" Reddman asked. "I mean as long as we're off the record . . ."

Landry looked quickly at Cole, then frowned at Reddman. "That will depend, of course, on the probation officer's report. After all, Blue would be eligible for probation."

"If I knew he'd get the maximum sentence, I'd do it," Reddman said, feeling hollow inside.

"What're you talking about?" Cole demanded.

"Two years county jail plus eight years in the slam. Which means he'd do five."

"Young man, I couldn't agree to that," Landry said, "as

you very well know. I would have to honestly consider his application for probation.''

"I'm sorry, then, Judge,'' Reddman said, pushing away from Landry's desk. ''No deal.''

"Why?'' Landry asked. He truly sounded perplexed.

"Blue owes Ami O'Rourke more than that.''

Johnny Blue limped to the stand. As the judge administered the oath, he did his best to stand up straight. Masking his pain, he climbed into the witness box and sat down.

Cole appeared to be angry at his client when the questioning began. He held the lectern with both hands, as though grateful for the barrier between him and the miscreant in front of him. His manner with Blue was harsh and accusatory, and Blue responded contritely, like George Washington confessing to a lie.

Blue admitted to more than drinking. He said he was drunk on the day Ami O'Rourke was killed. He apologized for feeling sorry for himself. But he told the jury that he had no idea how or when he'd gotten into the truck. It was just there, he said, and he must have seen it and climbed in. When he saw Officer Dave Brenfleck, whom he'd known since high school—well, it was just like he'd woke up out of a dream.

He'd always liked Brenfleck, he said. Thought the boy—man now, of course—done his level best. But, well, back to high school again—the girls never did like Dave much, and there was a particular girl Dave had his eye on, and—well, Blue wouldn't go into details, but he told the jury that him and Brenfleck just never could get on a friendly basis after that. Left Johnny with a feeling, too—probably wrong, he'd been wrong-headed about so many things, he could see that now—that Brenfleck had it in for him. So when Johnny saw him that day when he was sitting in his truck, it woke him up in a hurry and scared him, too, because he knew he shouldn't be driving and he sure didn't want to go back to that old jail. When asked what jail, he said the one he'd just been in for drunk driving.

An older man and woman, sitting in the front row near the bailiff's desk, watched Blue critically. Blue glanced at them often, seeming to beg their understanding. They looked familiar to Reddman, who finally realized he'd seen their photographs at Wolfman's house. They were Ami O'Rourke's parents.

As the examination continued, Cole's attitude toward Johnny Blue changed. The hostility, by degrees, faded from his voice and from his questions. Reluctantly, Cole appeared to understand the man, even to sympathize with him; and such was the force of Cole's personality that many of the jurors mirrored his attitude. Johnny told how he just plain froze up that day, couldn't think or do nothing, with Brenfleck setting in his patrol car, watching him. Seemed like the longest time, and then all of a sudden Brenfleck peeled out of there like a bull out of the chute, and he was gone!

The witness needed some water. His throat felt like summer sand, he explained. His stricken eyes found Ami's folks, and he went on.

All he could think to do was get away. But—well, he knows now he wasn't thinking right. Brenfleck wouldn't set him up, but that day, he just plain wasn't thinking right. He thought it might be a trick. So he kind of eased out of there, paying a lot more mind to what was behind him than what was in front . . . and then he saw her. Smack dab on top of his right fender, looked like a foot away, just all of a sudden! Blue turned his head toward his left shoulder, as though looking into the sideview mirror on the driver's side of his truck. Then he lurched around as though in sudden awareness, and leaned back rigidly, hands tightly gripping the wheel. A moment later he broke his posture and put his large weathered hands over his face, as if blotting out what he didn't want to see.

"I feel so bad," he said when he could speak, his deep voice low and trembling. His hands dropped uselessly into his lap. "All the things I coulda done and didn't do. Had me a whole second there, or at least part of one, but I don't know. Just wasn't doin' things right that day. I don't know how she got there, is part of it. I swear to God, I hadn't seen her in the street."

Cole said he didn't understand. Wasn't Blue's face turned in the direction of the courthouse, as he looked through the sideview mirror? If she was in the street, how could he have missed seeing her?

"I been askin' myself that same question," Blue said. "But the way it was, just all of a sudden and I was on top of her. Like one time when I hit a deer, sure didn't mean to, but the critter just—like somebody'd dropped it there, right in front of me, on the road." He gazed at Ami O'Rourke's parents. "I'm so sorry it happened."

Cole let the moment grow. Then: "Did you know the victim, Ami O'Rourke?"

"Sure did. She was my lawyer, did everything she could for me." Blue looked as if he would kill anyone who sullied her memory. "Fought for me at that trial like a she-bear fighting for her cubs, and I ain't about to forget it. Or her." He sighed, then looked down at his hands, as though he knew it was useless to try to explain.

"The prosecutor put on evidence here, cellmate of yours, Link somebody, you remember that evidence?"

"Yes, sir. That was old Link Neskahi, about one-quarter Navajo, a good friend. He can stick on a horse, long as it don't have a saddle on it, like a licked postage stamp."

"Neskahi said you told him you didn't get mad, just even, and you intended to even the score with your lawyer. You remember that testimony?"

"They must've promised him a bottle or something. Old Link'll do most anything—"

"Objection." Reddman knew it was useless to object. The jury had heard the response, and they hadn't believed Neskahi anyway. "Not responsive," he said. "Move to strike the answer, Judge."

Cole offered no argument.

"Very well, your objection is sustained and motion granted. The jury is admonished not to consider the witness's remark concerning the promise of a bottle for any purpose whatsoever. Proceed, Mr. Cole."

"Just answer the question, Johnny. Do you remember that testimony?"

"Yes, sir."

"You ever say anything like that to Link Neskahi?"

"No, sir. Not to him or anybody else." Blue's clear, pale eyes bored through Cole like laser beams.

"What did you think of your lawyer, Johnny? What did you think of Ami O'Rourke?"

Blue sighed again, as though he wished he could cry, and looked with sadness at Ami's parents. Mr. O'Rourke dropped his gaze to the floor, but Ami's mother glared back at him, as though to tell him she wasn't taken in by him at all. "I never met anyone like her," he said. "Shoot, she knew I was guilty, but she told me I might get lucky and I didn't have anything to lose by going to trial. I—well, I reckon I had respect for the woman more'n anything else. Thought she was tough."

"What about now, Johnny? This time? Are you guilty?"

"Guilty of what?"

"I want you to look at these people here who are sitting in judgment, who have to decide. Tell them, not me. What are you guilty of?"

"I was drunk, don't deny that, and I drove, so I done that one all right, the drunk driving. I run into her, too, and kept on goin', so I done that one, too.

"But they're sayin' I done it on purpose, like I aimed a rifle at her and shot her down. And I didn't." His voice rang with sincerity and conviction. "I didn't do that. Hell, I never even saw her till it was too late."

"So?"

"So that part's a lie."

Cole waited, letting the jury study the man. "Thank you, Mr. Blue," he said, as though satisfied that the man had told the truth. "You may examine, Mr. Reddman. He's your witness."

CHAPTER
NINETEEN

Reddman took a deep breath and stood up. He was aware of the distractions in the courtroom: the stillness, broken by the lonely sound of a cough, the rustle of paper, a movement behind him. He watched the jurors follow him as he arranged his notebook on the slanted surface of the lectern, and he tried to read their minds. Then he faced Johnny Blue.

When their eyes locked they were suddenly alone. There were only two people in the room: Dave Reddman, the prosecutor, and Johnny Blue, the defendant. They stared at each other, as if from opposite ends of a tunnel that Blue had to get through in order to avoid the consequence of his crime. Reddman was the only thing in his way.

"You say you were drunk, Mr. Blue?"

"Yes."

"What were you drinking?"

"Whiskey. Probably."

"As a matter of fact, you had a bottle of Jim Beam in a specially built cage in your truck, didn't you? You were sipping it through a hose?"

Blue looked apologetically at the jury. "It's not there any more. I took all that stuff out."

"But on the day Ami O'Rourke was killed you were sipping whiskey as you sat in your truck, weren't you?"

"I do that for the pain now and again. 'Bout the only thing that works." He shifted his weight. His face tightened suddenly as though someone had stuck a pin in him, then relaxed.

"And you're telling us it made you drunk?"

"Sure did."

"Just how drunk were you, Mr. Blue?"

" 'Bout as drunk as you can get and still move."

"Compare it to that drunk driving charge you testified about. Were you drunker this time or not as drunk?"

Blue looked questioningly at Cole, as though for advice. "About the same, I guess."

"About the same. You took a blood test then, didn't you?"

"Yes, sir. Sure did."

"What was the result of that blood test?"

Blue squirmed uncomfortably and again looked toward Cole. "I don't know. It was a long time ago."

"It was point-two-seven, wasn't it?"

"Seems like— Was it that high?"

"I'm asking you. I have a transcript here of that trial, if you think it will help you."

Blue gave an aw-shucks grin and shrugged his shoulders. "Didn't think it was that high."

"Mr. Blue, you still haven't answered the question. It was point-two-seven, wasn't it?"

"Well, you got the papers there. Why you askin' me when you know the answer?"

Reddman felt like a cop, trying to put the cuffs on a contortionist. "Your Honor, request the witness be instructed to answer the question."

"He did, Mr. Reddman. He said he didn't think it was that high."

"Then I ask the court to take judicial notice of the following fact: that on March fourteenth—"

Cole interrupted. "Judge, wait." He experienced difficulty getting to his feet. "We need to do this out of the presence of the jury, Judge." The man was red-faced, having hot and cold flashes, Reddman hoped, although his voice was even enough.

The bailiff led the jury out of the courtroom. Cole, standing on his hind legs, leaned on the table like a bear. "Move for a mistrial, Judge. Prosecutor here is bringing in all this evidence of another crime, way beyond the scope of the direct. Sure, we opened the door, but just a crack. That doesn't give him the right to retry that case, bring up all the old evidence, and put it before this jury here. Clearly inflammatory, prejudicial, mistrial."

"Mr. Reddman?"

Reddman fought to take the savage intensity out of his voice. "Your Honor, Mr. Cole opened the door when he questioned Mr. Blue about the other crime. Once the door is open, it's open. The cases don't talk about opening the door just a crack."

"That may be so, Mr. Reddman, but how is this relevant? We're talking about a crime that was committed a year ago. What does it matter what his blood alcohol level was then?"

"He testified at that trial, Judge." Reddman locked eyes with Johnny Blue, who stared at him coolly from the witness stand. "He admitted he'd been drinking, but said he wasn't drunk. Now he comes to *this* trial—with a point-one-eight—and claims he was so drunk he could barely move!"

"No need to shout, young man. I'm not hard of hearing." Landry tapped the bench with his pen. "It appears to me you are taking inconsistent positions here. On the one hand, you want to prove Mr. Blue was drunk; yet on the other, you apparently want to show he was not. Now, which is it? You can't have it both ways."

Reddman poured himself a glass of water. The pitcher didn't shake; his hands were steady, and so were his legs; the only thing out of control was his voice. "Your Honor, we want to show he was intoxicated enough to be guilty of drunk driving, but not so far gone that he couldn't form the intent to commit murder.'' He took a mouthful of water, then smiled at Blue, as though they were the best of friends. ''He had a point-eighteen when he ran over Ms. O'Rourke, so as far as the drunk driving statute is concerned, he was presumptively under the influence. But he's testified he was blotted out so bad he couldn't even remember how he got in his truck.

''The People don't believe he was that drunk. This is offered to impeach him on that issue as well as to show he was sober enough to form the intent to commit murder.''

Landry frowned, obviously skeptical. ''Do you honestly believe this jury can draw those fine lines?''

''I have no doubt about that at all.''

Landry settled back in his chair. ''Mr. Cole?''

''Total surprise, Judge. I didn't expect him to dredge up that other case and go into detail. Prosecution has a duty to disclose all its evidence, but this is the first I knew they had all this garbarge.''

Reddman started to speak, but the judge held up his hand. ''Come, come, Mr. Cole. Certainly the prosecution has the right to anticipate your action in opening the door, and to prepare for it. On that basis, your motion for mistrial will be denied. As regards the request for judicial notice: Mr. Reddman, is your transcript certified?''

''Yes, sir.''

''May I see it please?''

Reddman showed it to him, opened to the pertinent page.

''Now, what is the fact you wish me to judicially notice?''

''That on March fourteenth of last year, this defendant was tried for driving under the influence of alcohol, and that the evidence presented at that trial showed—at the time of the offense for which he was convicted—he had a blood-to-alcohol ratio of point-two-seven.''

Landry copied it down, then read it back. ''Do you dispute that fact, Mr. Cole?''

Cole shrugged his shoulders. ''No.''

"Very well. Bailiff, please return the jury."

After the jury was seated, Landry told them of the judicially noticed fact. Reddman could feel the force of Blue's eyes, and their cold message. At that moment, he loved it. "Mr. Blue," he said, from his stance behind the lectern, "it's been established now that your blood alcohol at that drunk driving trial—the one where you told us in your testimony today, 'Shoot, she knew I was drunk,' or words to that effect—you remember saying that today?"

"Sure do."

"Fine. Now, at that other trial, your blood alcohol was point-twenty-seven. But we've heard testimony at this trial that on the day you ran into Ami O'Rourke your blood alcohol was only point-eighteen. Did you hear that testimony?"

"Seems to me I did."

Reddman scratched his ear, as though to say, what am I missing? "Yet just a few minutes ago, you testified that when you ran over Ami O'Rourke you were about as drunk as you could get and still move. Do you remember that?"

"Yep. Not hard at all to remember what I just said."

"And you also told this jury that your level of drunkenness was about the same on both days. Am I right?"

"Right on."

"Well, Mr. Blue, would you care to change your testimony? Or do you still want this jury to believe that your level of drunkenness with a twenty-seven was about the same as it was with an eighteen?"

Blue's attitude had changed. He no longer came across as the contrite penitent. He grinned at Reddman like a crapshooter rolling the dice. "Tell you the truth, all I know is I wasn't in any kind of pain either time."

Two of the men on the jury panel smiled. "Now, that other trial involved a high-speed car chase, didn't it?" Reddman asked.

"That's what they tell me."

Reddman let the answer stand. "As a matter of fact, the officers who chased you—I'll provide you with their names if you want them—testified that they were amazed at how well you handled your truck. Do you remember that?"

Blue grinned. "Like I was ridin' a bull before I done this." He touched his leg.

Reddman nodded. "They testified how you narrowly missed other cars, how you jumped your truck off the road and back on, how skillfully you cornered, how you went into controlled spins—isn't that true?"

"Yep. Haven't had fun like that since I was a kid."

"In fact, that was your argument at the trial, wasn't it? How could you have driven so well if you were as drunk as they said you were?"

Cole started to stand, then changed his mind.

"That's right," Blue said. "You can't trust them blood-alcohol tests anyhow. Everybody knows that."

"Not everybody, Mr. Blue. That jury convicted you, didn't it?"

Blue seemed to have stopped breathing. His expression had become a mask. The jury stared at him in fascination. "I reckon they did," he said in a low, controlled voice.

"But you *were* drunk then, weren't you?"

"You're twistin' things all around," Blue said. "You're twistin' things."

Reddman wanted the jury to see the man's hatred, his murderous rage. "Do you feel like someone is twisting you?"

"Objection!" Cole shouted, struggling to stand. "What kind of question is that?" In his effort to get to his feet he knocked a book off the table. "Totally reprehensible, Judge. Move for mistrial!"

"Your objection is sustained, Mr. Cole. However, your motion for mistrial is denied. Proceed, Mr. Reddman."

Reddman knew he had made a mistake, which Cole had jumped on, creating a commotion. He hoped the jury would remember Blue's face rather than the loud sound of books falling on the floor. He stared at his notes, calming himself. "Now, you were under oath when you testified at that earlier trial, weren't you? Just as you are under oath now?"

The color was back in Blue's face. "That's right."

"But at that trial, even though your blood alcohol was much higher than when you ran over Ami O'Rourke, you testified under oath that you weren't drunk. Right?"

Blue grinned. "Shoot, Mr. Reddman, that's what she told me to do. She said I didn't have anything to lose."

" 'She'? You mean your lawyer told you to lie?"

"They do it all the time!" Blue settled easily in his chair, reveling in the laughter. "You're a lawyer. Do I need to explain that to you?"

"No, Mr. Blue," Reddman said, noting the expressions on the faces of several jurors. "You don't need to explain that to me."

"Judge, how much longer is this gonna take?" Cole asked, getting up again. He arched his back, letting it pop. "This man's been on the stand a long time, got that bad leg, probably feels like a couple days to him." He smiled at the jury.

"Mr. Reddman? Would this be a good time to take a recess?"

Reddman wanted to keep the pressure on. But he needed time, too. Sharon Sondenburg was on a mission, and he needed to talk to her before he finished his cross-examination of Blue. "As good a time as any," he said.

There are times when trying a case is like playing a game of chess, Reddman thought. Your opponent will try to make you play his game. When Blue testified on direct, he made no mention of hitting the wrong pedal with his foot. An oversight? Reddman didn't think so. Neither had Blue explained why he tromped on the acclerator after hitting Ami O'Rourke.

Reddman sat at counsel table during the recess, reviewing his notes. He drew lines through those questions, deciding not to ask them. He had enough to argue what he wanted. Why take a chance on being sandbagged?

"Hi," Sharon Sondenburg said.

He hadn't seen her come up behind him. She put her

hand on his shoulder and her touch warmed him. When he looked at her, it was as if the two of them were alone in some kind of bubble. "Hi."

"You're as good as you said you were," she told him. She glowed at him from inside the bubble. "Almost."

"When did you get back?"

"During the last recess when you were talking to the judge."

"Did you find anyone?"

"Yes. Only he doesn't want to testify. He's afraid."

"Who did you find?"

"Manley Jude. He's the ticket agent at Trailways. He—"

Cole and Johnny Blue came through the gate in the rail. "Hey, baby, you look great," Blue said, grinning at Sharon. "Good enough to eat."

She did her best to ignore him.

"Say hello to your folks, hear?" Blue continued cheerfully. He climbed into the witness box.

"We're about to start up again," Reddman said. "Find Lopes, okay? Tell him what you've got and get the guy under subpoena."

She nodded. As she left, her hand slid down his arm and touched his fingers. "Good luck."

The judge returned to his throne, the bailiff brought in the jury, and Reddman took his place behind the lectern. It was obvious that during the recess Cole had worked his magic on Blue's manner. Once again the defendant was respectful, contrite, and apologetic, and his answers to Reddman's questions were measured and slow. Reddman decided to try a tactic of his own. "Whenever you can, show the jury how asshole looks with the gun in his hand," an old mentor had told him. "Chances are he'll look guilty as sin. It works especially well when asshole is coming across like an angel."

Reddman asked the defendant to describe his oversize pickup truck—the size of the engine, its length and width, the size of the tires, the height of the cab. Having Blue describe it was as close as he could get to putting a gun in the defendant's hand.

Then he started down the path that Sharon Sondenburg had prepared for him. If he did it right, he would have a chance. If he did it wrong—he chose not to think about that.

"You testified earlier that you can't even remember getting in your truck on the day Ami O'Rourke was killed?"

"No, sir, I don't. I was awful drunk."

"On a point-eighteen?"

"Yes, sir. The whiskey must've really got to me."

"You just woke up and found you were inside the truck?"

"That's right, sir. Officer Brenfleck, he saw me settin' there."

"You told him you hadn't driven there, right? That your wife had?"

"That's what I told him. Yes, sir."

"That was a lie, wasn't it? You drove the truck there yourself."

"Oh, no, sir. She done it. I asked her about it later."

Reddman appeared mildly annoyed. "That's what she told you?"

"Yes, sir."

"When did you talk to her about it?"

"The next day, I think it was. Soon as they let me out of jail."

"How many people have keys to your truck, Mr. Blue?"

"Just me and my wife. Actually only my wife now, but I still had a set of keys when this happened."

"You say you asked her about it. What did she tell you?"

"That's hearsay, ain't it? I don't think I'm supposed to answer a question like that."

"Hearsay is good evidence, Mr. Blue, as long as nobody objects to it." Reddman turned toward Cole. "Any objection."

"We got nothing to hide," Cole said. "No objection."

Blue shrugged. "Said she'd left it up there on the hill because the battery was low, and that way she wouldn't have to get a jump if it wouldn't start."

"Where was she?"

"At the movie."

"You live out in the country, don't you? Four or five miles out of town?"

"Yes, sir."

"Did your wife drive you in that day?"

"I don't know."

"Meaning you were so drunk that you don't even remember coming into town?"

"Mr. Reddman, I ain't even sure I went home the night before."

There was some laughter in the courtroom. Reddman smiled good-naturedly at the remark. "After Brenfleck left—you know where I am? I'm asking now about right after Brenfleck drove off, leaving you sitting in your truck. Did you have any trouble starting the truck?"

"I really don't remember, Mr. Reddman."

"You'd remember if you had trouble, wouldn't you?"

"Objection, Judge," Cole bellowed. "Calls for speculation."

"Sustained."

"All right," Reddman said. "Let me rephrase the question. Do you remember starting the truck?"

"No, sir."

"Was the truck running all the time Brenfleck was there?"

"No, sir, I'm sure it wasn't."

"Was anyone in the truck with you?"

"No, sir."

"Are you the one who started the truck?"

Blue grinned his lopsided grin. "I guess. Wasn't anybody else could have done it without me knowing."

"So you put the key in and started it, right?"

Blue stopped a moment, thinking. "Yes, sir. My key. I remember I put my key in, and started it."

"You didn't have to let it roll down the hill first?"

"No, sir. She started right up."

"But you knew about the bad battery, didn't you?" Reddman asked, vaguely accusatory.

"No, sir, I didn't. I didn't know about that at all."

"Then if you'd parked it somewhere, you wouldn't have picked a hill, right?"

"I guess not."

"That's just more evidence, I guess, to show your wife put it there, right?"

Blue was a bit more wary. "I guess."

"Why did you drive at all, Mr. Blue? Why didn't you get out of the truck and walk away?"

"I asked myself that question lots of times, Mr. Reddman," Blue said, staring with sincerity at Reddman's face. "I walked *to* it. Why didn't I walk *away* from it?"

"What did you decide, after asking yourself that question lots of times?"

"Nothin', really. That truck means a lot to me. I just wasn't thinking right."

"So you decided not to walk away, which would have allowed you to avoid Brenfleck altogether, right? You decided instead to take the chance and drive?"

"I didn't decide anything, Mr. Reddman. I just done it."

Reddman nodded. "Does your wife drink?"

"Does she what?"

"Drink whiskey, Mr. Blue. There was that bottle of Jim Beam in the cab, wasn't there? The one with the hose that ran between it and your mouth?"

"Yes, sir."

"Did she put it there?"

"No, sir, I done that."

"But she leaves the whiskey in place when she takes the truck?"

"She did that day, Mr. Reddman. She wouldn't now."

"Didn't you wife have a car then, Mr. Blue?"

"No, sir, she'd had to sell her car about that time. All we had was the truck."

"Why didn't you sell the truck?"

"Couldn't get enough for it."

"Okay." Reddman started gathering up his notes, as though to leave. "So she drove into town sometime that day. Do you know when?"

"No, sir, I don't."

"And you don't even know if you came in with her, right?"

"That's right."

"All you know is that she came in sometime that day and parked the truck on Mears Street hill. Right?"

"That's right, sir."

"Couldn't have been the day before?"

"No."

"How can you be sure?"

"I remember doing some work on the truck the day before."

"And there isn't anyone else who could have driven the truck in, is there? You and your wife were the only ones with keys?"

"We were the only ones."

"And you didn't lend the pickup to anyone, did you? Either of you?"

"No, I don't lend out my truck."

"Can I have a moment, Your Honor?" Reddman asked the judge.

"You may."

Lopes had returned to his place at the table. Reddman huddled with him. Lopes gave him a sheet of paper and briefly explained what it meant.

"This happened on September twenty-third of last year, right?" Reddman asked the witness, as he walked back to the lectern.

"Yes, sir."

"Mr. Blue, isn't it true that your wife was in Oklahoma then?"

Blue appeared startled for the barest part of a moment. "No, sir. She'd just come back."

"You're sure of that?"

"Sure as I am of sitting here. She'd just come back."

"She had taken the bus to Claremont, Oklahoma, hadn't she? Where her father lived?"

"Yeah, about a month before this happened." Blue scratched his ear and grinned. "I'm sure it was then."

"Mr. Blue, she left on September thirteenth, a Friday the thirteenth, didn't she? And she returned two weeks later, on the twenty-seventh?"

"That's not right," Blue maintained. "You ask her. She got back on the twenty-third."

"You know Manley Jude, don't you, Mr. Blue?"

"Yeah. I know Manley."

"Can you tell the jury who he is?"

"Your Honor," Cole said, standing, "this has gone on long enough. No showing of relevance, prosecution bringing up names of people I don't know anything about. What is this, trial by ambush?"

"I'll connect it up, Judge."

"Yes. Proceed, Mr. Reddman."

"Who is Manley Jude, Mr. Blue?"

Blue suddenly dropped his head. He covered his face with his large hands and took several deep breaths, as though in terrible anguish. Cole ran around his table and approached the witness. "Can we have a recess, Judge? Something going on I don't know about, and Mr. Blue needs some time!"

Blue removed his hands. His eyes were wet, his expression sorrowful, but firm. "I don't need a recess, Saul," he said. "I lied."

"Judge, I need to talk to my client! He needs counsel, Sixth Amendment says he's got a right to a lawyer, we need a recess right now!"

"No, I don't, Saul. I know what I'm doin'." Blue stared at Reddman like a defeated bull. "I been livin' with that lie too long."

"Johnny, don't say another word!"

"Shut up, Saul."

Landry glared at the defendant. "Mr. Blue. I don't know what is going on here, but I think you should talk to your lawyer before proceeding."

"Don't need to, Judge. I appreciate what you're tryin' to do, protectin' my rights and all, but I don't need to."

"I will leave that up to you, sir," Landry said. "If you want a short recess, you may have one."

"My mind's made up, Judge. That's all there is to it."

"Very well. Proceed, Mr. Reddman."

Reddman knew something had gone wrong. His cross-examination couldn't have gone better. Blue had bitten, hook, line, and sinker. But the man wasn't beaten. "Are you all right, Mr. Blue?" he asked solicitously.

"Couldn't be better."

"Who is Manley Jude?"

"He's the ticket agent at Trailways. He sold my wife the ticket to Claremont just like you said."

"And the dates?"

"She left on Friday the thirteenth and came back on the twenty-seventh, just like you said," Blue told him. "I lied."

Reddman knew better than to ask him why he'd lied. Sharon Sondenburg had said he could shoot the eyes out of a snake, and Reddman could feel him taking aim. "You wanted this jury to believe a lie, didn't you?" Reddman asked.

"Yes, sir."

"Just like you wanted that other jury to believe a lie."

"That was different, Mr. Reddman. That was more like a game."

"Different? You were under oath then, weren't you?"

"Yes, sir."

"And you're under oath now, aren't you?"

"Yes, I am."

"And you lied under oath both times. Am I right?"

"Mr. Reddman, I want to tell you why," Blue said, his voice ringing with sincerity. "I want you to understand."

This guy is really good, Reddman thought. Now I have to let him tell me why. "Go ahead."

"I was scared. I ain't used to bein' scared. I lied for the same reason that I ran." He rubbed his hands over his face, then dropped them in his lap. "I seen who it was, just before I hit her. It was Ami. I yelled at her, yelled something, don't know what, and then I hit her." His head slowly rolled, back and forth as if he was in agony. "I ran away. Me, a champion bull rider one time, pretty fair on buckin' horses too, and I'm a big coward. I ran away." Reddman watched the jury soaking it up. "It ain't easy for me to admit this. I felt so bad. But I knew I wasn't going to get away with it—me and my truck, you know, people know both of us. Somebody'd know. So when the cops picked me up, I told them the truth."

"Are you finished?" Reddman asked, hoping Blue had finished, but knowing he hadn't.

"No. You got to understand why I lied. I drove the truck up to Mears Street hill myself. I go up there a lot, Mr. Reddman, in the truck or out of it, look around. Used to go up there when I was a kid, watch the river sometimes or the sun comin' down. It's pretty from up there." Blue didn't even look at the jurors, as though they meant nothing to him. His trusting eyes were on Reddman, like those of a child unloading some heavy burden. "When Brenfleck seen me up there . . . well, shoot, I had to tell him somethin'. So I told him my wife had taken the truck up there. But after that murder charge got filed—well, I knowed how it looked. Me settin' up there waitin', waitin' for Ami to get out in the middle of the street, that's the way it looked. That's what Mr. Brim *said*. But that wasn't it at all! I wasn't waitin' for nothin', all I was doin' was settin' up there and lookin', like I used to do!"

"You expect this jury to believe that?" Reddman demanded. The man is awesome, he thought. Truly awesome. He even felt himself being drawn in.

"I don't care if they do or they don't," Blue said, his voice low. "All I know is this: I didn't mean to run over that woman. Not at all. But the way it looks now—me settin' up there and waitin'—that's the lie, Mr. Reddman. That's the lie."

CHAPTER TWENTY

The telephone woke him up. "Well, Davey my boy, are you ready?" a boisterous voice shouted.

"What?"

"This is Dave Reddman, isn't it?" the large voice asked. "Goddam hotel operator. What'd she do, put it in the wrong hole?"

Reddman realized it was James Trigge. He fumbled for his watch on the nightstand and knocked it to the floor. "What time is it?" he asked, giving it everything he had but knowing it sounded like slow motion.

"Good God. Did I wake you up?"

He found his watch. A quarter after eight. "Yeah, boss. Boy am I glad." His feet were on the floor and his whole body buzzed with interrupted comfort. "Slept through the alarm. Thanks." He started to hang up the telephone but caught himself. "We worked instructions last night until two. We argue it this morning."

"I know," Trigge said. "Brim tells me you're the greatest thing since sliced bread."

"Is sliced bread all that great?" By degrees, the world began to emerge. His stomach didn't feel right; Cole had sent out for hamburgers the night before, and Reddman had eaten one. He got his watch on.

"So tell me, my boy. How does the case look?"

"I don't know. Johnny is very, very tricky." Reddman quickly told him how Blue had turned a defeat into a possible victory.

"Well! That little battle down there has turned into a real war, hasn't it? Do you think the jury will see through his little deception?"

"Hard to say." Then it came to him: his theme. "They do it all the time. Hey! They do it all the time!"

"What?"

"Martin Luther King, remember? I've got a dream?"

"My boy, you sound a bit crazed in the head, which is perfectly normal, considering your line of work. You awake now? Ready to charge out there and bite, gouge, spit, and chew?"

"I'm ready!"

"Good! Call me when you get a verdict."

The lectern had been moved toward the center of the room and aimed at the jury box. Mechanically, Reddman followed the instructions as Landry read them to the jury. He felt a strange peace, instead of the tangle of emotions he usually felt before final argument. Earlier Sharon Sondenburg had put her arm around his waist and wished him luck. He could still feel her arm. "Part of the mythic ritual," she had explained, kissing him lightly on the lips. He knew if he turned around, she would be there.

"Mr. Reddman? You may proceed."

"Thank you, Your Honor." Reddman moved easily to center stage. "If it please the court, Mr. Cole, Mr. Blue, members of the jury." He placed his legal pad on the lectern, then launched into his opening patter. He modified it to fit the case of *People v. Blue*, but it was the same spiel he had used countless times before. He thanked the jury for their attention, which they had given in spite of the fact they were a captive audience and the pay was lousy. He told them he would have two opportunities to address them, but the defense would have only one, and explained the reason: the burden of the prosecution, that heavy burden of reasonable doubt. Having brought up reasonable doubt he went on to minimize it, by stressing the word "reasonable"—"Not just any doubt. We are talking about a doubt that is based on reason." Then he told them of their obligation to follow the law, and he referred to many of the instructions the judge had just read: presumption of innocence, that neither sympathy nor prejudice should influence their decision, and credibility of witnesses. "I'll come back to that one," he promised.

Then he turned to the charge. "We're down to three counts now: drunk driving, hit-and-run, and murder." With care, he went over the verdict forms with respect to each charge, showing the jurors that only one box on each form should be checked. The murder form especially should be approached with caution, he warned. "You have more boxes to choose from on his form, but the idea is the same. There are five possibilities, but you can check only one of them." He held a copy of the form high enough for all of them to see. "If you find the defendant not guilty, check this box at the top. If you find him guilty of murder in the first degree, check this one; second degree here; manslaughter here; criminally negligent homicide here." He pointed to each box. "The important thing to remember is this: you must agree unanimously on only one verdict. You can't find him guilty of both manslaughter and second degree murder; or not guilty but guilty of criminally negligent homicide."

As he reviewed the evidence, he maintained the same quiet academic tone. With the aid of the large diagram Sergeant Donovan had drawn, propped up on the portable blackboard stand in full view of the jury, he set the scene: the location, the time of year, the kind of weather, the time of day. Then he moved up Mears Street hill, focusing on the defendant, who was sitting—or waiting—in his high rider, with an overview of the street below. "And members of the jury, you know this now, too: *he* drove up there, not his wife. *He* is the one who parked his pickup on the hill."

Reddman felt himself warming up. He wanted to save his theme—"They do it all the time"—for rebuttal, and he glossed over the defendant's reasons for changing his testimony. Instead, he asked the question: What kind of man was Johnny Blue on that day?

"Maybe the evidence can't tell you the whole story, but it can tell you a lot," Reddman said. "You know he was an athlete, a rodeo star, whose career had been shortened by a savagely broken leg. You know, too, that he has a chronically painful condition, and that he blunts the pain with alcohol. But what was in his heart that day? Did he have a clean, generous heart or one of those mean ones?" He told them it might sound corny to talk in those terms, but added, "That's what this case is all about. Because if Johnny Blue had a clean heart on that September day of last year, he wasn't a murderer. However, if his heart was filled with hate and bitterness toward Ami O'Rourke—and it doesn't matter how or why it got that way—then you might well conclude he is a killer."

Reddman asked the jury to consider the evidence from both points of view. Assume his heart was clean, he suggested, and see how the evidence fits. Then try it on for size the other way.

This man—a former rodeo cowboy, a gifted athlete—had a blood-alcohol level of point-one-eight on that day. When it comes to driving a car, a person is presumed to be under the influence with a point-ten. But Johnny Blue had experience at drinking. "Remember the testimony about his earlier trial? He had a point-two-seven that time, and he drove with all the skill of a Mario Andretti. And remember how drunk he said he was with the point-one-eight? He told you he was really, really drunk, so drunk he had blacked out completely, only to find himself in his truck without even knowing how he got there. And members of the jury, he was convincing when he told you that. Totally convincing. So you know this much about the man, and about his heart:

he's a very good liar." He paused long enough to pour himself a glass of water and drink some of it.

"Then Brenfleck saw him. Blue knew right away he was in trouble, he told you, because he could have been busted for driving with no license. He was frightened, he said. Later he tried to tell you he was a coward, who wasn't thinking right. He told you he knew he had to get away.

"Get away? Get away from what? Brenfleck couldn't arrest him because he hadn't seen him drive, and you might ask yourself: If that was the extent of Johnny Blue's problem, why didn't he just open the door of his truck and walk off? And again: Remember how convincing Mr. Blue was when he said, under oath: 'I've asked myself that question many times? I walked *to* the truck, why didn't I walk away?' You have to give this man credit where credit is due: he is an extraordinarily talented liar."

In any event, he didn't walk away, Reddman told them. What he did, according to his testimony, was stay in his truck. Then after Brenfleck responded to a call, Blue tried to sneak off in the truck!

"And notice the direction he took in sneaking away. He didn't turn the truck around, or search for alleys or back roads. He drove right in front of the courthouse! This frightened, cowardly man—Johnny Blue, a frightened, cowardly man?—who wasn't thinking right and who thought the officer might have set him up, sneaked away in his truck by driving it right in front of the courthouse! What do we have here? you might ask yourself. The action of a man with a clean heart or the explanation of a killer?"

Reddman stopped long enough to look at his notes. They're listening to me, he thought. I've got a shot at it. He felt great. He paid absolutely no attention at all to his voice, his gestures, or his expressions, but knew—from the stillness in the courtroom, from the faces of the jurors—that all of it worked. He truly felt like a laser beam that could touch and burn. "Suddenly, Blue told you, Ami O'Rourke was in front of him. He swore to God he hadn't seen her, that it was as if someone had just dropped her there. And when he told you that, he was totally convincing." Reddman walked over to Donovan's diagram. "He had driven from here to here," Reddman showed them. "About one block and through an intersection. All that time, looking over his left shoulder and into the rearview mirror for Brenfleck.

"This man, this athlete—and in that rodeo accident, his eyes weren't hurt, his peripheral vision wasn't affected, and neither were those superb reflexes and quick reactions that had kept him on top of bulls and outlaw horses. Yet he was so surprised and astonished and stunned by the victim's sudden appearance, he told you, that he ran into her." Reddman wandered back to the lectern. "But he didn't just run into her. You know from other evidence that he had time—he had the time—to do two things first.

"He honked and yelled. That's the first thing. We have that testimony from two witnesses: Cindy Strickland, who was here"—he showed them on the diagram—"and Muriel Doppler, who was here. And the second thing he did was floor the accelerator.

"Can you doubt that he did that? Do you remember the vivid testimony of Muriel Doppler? She was in her truck, having just pulled out of a parking spot, getting ready to drive toward the defendant. Until he honked, she didn't know he was there. But when he honked, she turned her head—and saw. The scene has been burned in her mind forever. She saw his truck jump forward. She saw Johnny Blue tromp on the gas before he hit the victim."

Reddman looked toward the defendant. Several but not all of the jurors followed his glance. He wondered how far he should go. "You have that testimony from him, too, in a way. He took the stand and didn't deny it."

Then Reddman reminded them of Sergeant Donovan's testimony. Donovan had described the tremendous acceleration required to drive a motor vehicle with a human body wrapped around one of its tires. "He drove from here to here," he said, pointing at the diagram, "with Ami O'Rourke on the tire. And when she fell away, he took off."

Once again Reddman asked them, rhetorically, the question he had posed at the beginning: What kind of heart did this man have on that day? When you dress him up with the evidence, does it show him to have that clean, generous heart we all hope he had? Or when he wears all the evidence, doesn't it prove he had the malignant heart of a murderer? Reddman sat down.

Cole literally ran to the lectern in his eagerness to refute the prosecutor's remarks. "Funny, all the instructions the prosecutor talked about, several he didn't mention, I wonder why? I'll tell you why: he wants you to forget them!" Incensed, he ripped out his copy of an instruction and shouted, "It is an affirmative defense to the crime of murder that the defendant, by reason of intoxication, did not have the capacity to form the specific intent required by that offense! Forgot that one, didn't he? *Why!*" His hot eyes searched out and found some of the jurors.

"Look what else he's tryin' to do, ridiculous! He tells you the man was drunk on one hand and sober on the other, how can that be?" He elaborated his point with examples and gestures: apples aren't oranges, tangerines aren't either. Reasonable doubt! He says it's a doubt that's based on reason! "Our laws say you are drunk with a point-eighteen!" he said. "Is that based on reason?"

Cole calmed down and collected himself. "Put yourself here, in this man's chair," he said, pointing at Johnny Blue. "Charged with a crime, you'll understand why our law is the way it is. Don't smile, think it can't happen to you, happens all the time. He's entitled to the benefit! What the prosecutor says flies in the face of logic. Drunk for one charge, sober for the other, the prosecutor can't even make up his mind! If *he* can't, how can you be expected to say there isn't at least a *doubt?* And like the man said—he got this one right anyway—you must follow the law!" His anger at the prosecutor seemed to know no bounds.

"Then what do they use for evidence here, want you to convict of murder, I'll tell you the kind of evidence he wants you to use." He glared at Reddman, clearly accusing him of deliberate cheating. "The prosecutor says you should use for evidence things that my client, Mr. Blue, *wasn't asked!* Fair-minded prosecutor says *that* is evidence! Johnny Blue didn't deny a couple things, that is *evidence?"* Come on, Cole continued, making his point. Gonna convict this man of murder because of what I forgot to do or what the prosecutor could have done? He could have asked him the same *questions?* Can't reopen the case now, up to you now, put yourself in Johnny Blue's position when you're back there in the jury room deciding this man's fate. See how easy it is to answer all those questions I forgot to ask.

Cole let his breathing come back to normal, then drank some water. "What really happened here, folks?" he asked, searching for as many eyes as he could find. "Evidence isn't a suit of clothes—put them on, take them off, silly thing to say, facts are facts. And there are *some* facts our fair-minded prosecutor forgot to mention." He talked about the man poor Ami had worked with. Cole had forgotten his name—the other public defender, remember him? Poor Mrs. O'Rourke, always in a hurry, caseload like they have, crossed that street a thousand times, too many things on her mind. "Tragic, tragic." But probably bound to happen sooner or later. Remember he told you that, how she'd turn around in the middle of the street, not even looking?

"Here's what happened, ladies and gentlemen," Cole told them. "My very best guess. Been with this case eight months now, worrying and wondering about it, stay with a case that long, you get to where you can see it. Prosecutor has a point—peripheral vision. If she was crossing the street from the courthouse, why didn't Johnny Blue see her?" He held his hands on an imaginary wheel and turned his head as though looking out the window on the driver's side. "Here he is, driving, looking behind him, into the mirror mounted on the driver's side, sure as anything he'd have seen something in the street." He let go of the wheel and stared at the jury. "But what if she didn't come from that side? What if she jumped in front of him from *this* side"—he showed them with his hand—"like she forgot something, turned around without looking, had to get back to the courthouse?"

See what reasonable doubt is all about? he implored them. "I think that's what happened. Evidence shows it, too. Don't prove it beyond a reasonable doubt, but that's what it shows. And Mr. Blue doesn't have to prove his side to a reasonable doubt. If *any* of you think it happened that way, it isn't murder, because if you *think* it happened that way, you have a reasonable doubt. Goes further than that. You don't even have to think it happened that way. All you have to do is think it *could* have happened like that, and you have a reasonable doubt."

Cole paused to give them a chance to absorb his point, then went on. Mr. Blue honked, didn't he? he asked them. Why honk if he wanted to hit her? Think of that a minute. A honk is a warning, would he have warned her if he wanted to hit her? Prosecutor will probably tell you this man was so bad he wanted a moving target! Then Cole fumbled around the surface of the lectern until he found the photographs of Ami O'Rourke taken by the pathologist. Take a look at these pictures, he told them, later on when you're in the jury room, gruesome, awful. See if you don't see what I see. Her left side! These pictures show she got hit on her left side, my friends, coming into the street from over here! He stuck out his hand. Lawyers, people I ask—they all say don't show the jury those pictures. They'll see that tragically torn-up body, they'll convict in a minute. I don't believe that. You are fair-minded, I know a lot of you personally, it's there. I can't explain it, but you look and you'll see it's *there*.

Cole glared at Reddman, who had decided not to draw attention to Cole's comments by objecting. Then Cole leaned forward, as though trying to touch each juror with his soul. "You saw Johnny Blue on the stand. Sure you saw him tell a lie, but then he come clean. You saw a man stripped naked, admitted things to you he'd never admitted to anyone anywhere before, not even himself. And you know what? He isn't that different from any of us, my friends. He's breathed the same air, eaten the same meat, walked and driven the same roads and paths.

"True, he lied—but there are lies, and there are lies. We all know that. There are big ones, and there are little ones, some don't matter, like in a game—but some you can't live with. He admitted lying at that first trial. Told that jury he wasn't drunk with a point-two-seven, didn't work, hell, any lawyer will tell you a man has a constitutional right to that kind of lie!" A few of the jurors smiled. "Then he got trapped. In all innocence, he drove his truck up Mears Street hill, sat up there like he used to do, a kid again. How many of you have some favorite place—what do the Indians call them, a power spot—some place you can go and things are clear? This was Blue's power spot. Except Brenfleck saw him up there, and he couldn't tell Brenfleck he'd been driving, so he lied." Cole shrugged his shoulders. "Said his wife must have driven the truck up there—you know, had to explain, is that really a lie? I mean, that's a kid, telling his mother *I* didn't eat those cookies!" More smiles from the jury. "Except he got caught in it. But not right away.

"When the officers talked to him—Mr. Lopes here and another one—Johnny still buzzed under the awful stress of what he'd just done. That subject never came up. If it had, you can *bet* he'd have told them the truth. Because everything else he said then was true! He told them exactly what happened, how he'd snuck away from Brenfleck and hadn't seen Ami O'Rourke at all, how he'd hit her and got scared and run away. And the officers believed him! These are officers that aren't used to believing stories from defendants, they know how defendants lie, lots of experience at telling the difference. And they believed him! Officer Lopes even *said* so, here, under oath!

"After that, the little story Johnny told Brenfleck came back to haunt him. How? Because then the D.A. filed a murder count!" Cole glared around him, helpless, obviously torn and bothered by the vagaries of fate. "So how did it look then? How did it look *then?*" Cole looked directly at each of the twelve jurors. "Well, Johnny Blue's mother didn't raise no fool. He knew how it looked, like he drove up on that hill, just like the D.A. said, and waited.

"My friends, Johnny Blue loved his lawyer. He'd never say it that way—can't—isn't in him to use words like 'love.' All he can tell you is he admired her, the way she fought, Johnny likes a fighter, he's a fighter himself. Then they charge him with murdering her! Why didn't they leave in that other, vehicular homicide? Maybe they could have proved that one. Maybe that's really what he did.

"But murder? He admitted being drunk, the drunk driving, even admitted the hit-and-run. But, my friends on the jury, he didn't hit her on purpose, couldn't have done that to this woman he loved! And *that's* what they have to show, that he hit her on purpose!"

Cole had drawn them toward him, as a magnet might draw small flecks of metal. "So he lied about his wife—not a big lie in his mind, but one he had to put out there, he thought. Then we get into this trial, he throws it up like a piece of rotten meat in his stomach. Couldn't live with it any longer, and he threw it up. He even admitted to his own cowardice, remember that? Can you see him now on the stand over there, bent over, in pain? He told the prosecutor—excellent job of cross-examination, by the way—he said, 'I didn't mean to run over that woman.' " Again Cole met every juror's eye. " 'But the way it looks, that's the lie.'

"Ladies and gentlemen, I'm begging you. You know this man, you know when he's telling you the truth and when he isn't. There *is* a big lie in this case, charge it as murder. That is a *lie*, my friends. I'm begging you, don't convict Mr. Blue of that terrible lie."

The jury watched Cole walk to his chair, give Blue a reassuring pat on the back, and sit down. Reddman remembered Zack Wolfman's comment: Never bet on a horse race, unless it's fixed.

" 'The way it looks, that's the lie,' " Reddman said a

moment later from the lectern. "You might ask yourself, which way does it look? Remember what the defendant told you when I asked him if his lawyer, Ami O'Rourke, had asked him to lie?" Reddman searched through his legal pad until he found what he was looking for. "He said, and I quote: 'They do it all the time.'

"Now, Mr. Cole has told you there are big lies and little lies. But when you put your hand in the air and swear to tell the truth, are there big ones and little ones?"

Reddman thought for a moment. "I'm not from around here, and Mr. Cole knows you better than I do. So maybe I'm not hearing him right. Does he mean it's okay to lie if your lawyer tells you to? Are all those lies automatically little ones?"

Reddman shifted his weight. "Let me ask you something else. Do lawyers really lie all the time? Are all lawyers crooks? Mr. Cole, me, and the victim in this case, Ami O'Rourke? Do we lie all the time?

"What about the witnesses we call to the stand? If we tell them to lie, does that mean they will? Cindy Strickland, Muriel Doppler, Detective Lopes, Sergeant Donovan, Dr. Wilkerson. Are all of them willing to lie if the lawyers in the case tell them it will help?

"What kind of cynicism is at the bottom of a remark like that? 'They do it all the time.' Mr. Blue's real purpose wasn't humor, either, when he said it. He got a laugh, but that wasn't what he was after. He wanted to divert your attention away from a lie he'd been caught in. Then later on he got caught in another one, a really crucial one—and what did he do? He tried to divert your attention away from that one, too.

"Members of the jury, Johnny Blue lied on the stand. He was under oath, and he lied. And he is so convincing when he lies! So you tell me: How does it look?"

Reddman stopped long enough to look at the backs of his hands. He couldn't tell if they were with him or not. "Try taking his explanation entirely out of this case. You know you can't trust his explanation anyway—'They do it all the time.' So let's move it out of the way"—Reddman pretended to push it away with his hands—"and look at what's left.

"You have this defendant, up on that hill, sitting in his high rider sipping whiskey. His lawyer—and there is evidence to suggest he wants to get even with his lawyer—leaves the courthouse. She starts to cross the street, and at the same time, his truck—that huge high rider—is gliding toward her. She doesn't see it, obviously, or she'd have gotten out of the way. But she's not the only one. Neither did Muriel Doppler or Cindy Strickland or Mr. Goode.

"It *is* possible to do the unexpected. That's how you win wars. No noise, nothing sudden or quick, just a large truck coasting down a hill." Reddman slammed his fist into his palm. "Then the truck hits the woman. Was it a coincidence that he struck his lawyer and then drove off? Or was it the planned, deliberate act of a murderer?

"Look at something else. The defense has painted Ami O'Rourke as a woman in a hurry, a woman with too much to do, a virtual airhead in traffic, right? Well, don't kid yourself. You know a few things about her, too. She was a city girl, brought up in urban areas, and what does that mean? Was she oblivious to traffic, or—as many city people—armed with some kind of sixth sense that told her all she needed to know? Lance Winchester had her dancing out there in the street, doing pirouettes! He implied that if it hadn't been for him, she'd have died a long time ago. Well, do you believe him? Or is it possible he overstated his own heroics? And if she was as careless as he said, how did she stay alive before he came along to protect her?"

I can't read you people, Reddman thought to himself. I can't tell what you're thinking.

"Now look at the evidence—without tainting it with Blue's explanations. There were no skid marks, no swerve marks, nothing to indicate that this truly gifted athlete took any kind of evasive action at all. And there was *time* for evasive action, members of the jury. He had the time.

"He honked his horn and yelled. And then he punched the gas."

Most of the jurors were looking at the floor. Are they avoiding Blue, Reddman wondered, or me?

"Now put his explanation back into the case, remembering that they do it all the time.

"They do it all the time. They tell you to lie when you have a point-twenty-seven and claim you weren't drunk. Do they tell you to lie when you have an eighteen, by claiming you are so drunk you can barely move?"

"Your Honor," Cole roared, obviously wounded. "Improper, highly improper! Move to strike. Mistrial!"

"If it please the court," Reddman responded quickly. "I do not mean to imply or wish in any manner to be understood as accusing Mr. Cole of telling the defendant to lie. I sincerely do not believe Mr. Cole would do that."

"Nor do I, Mr. Reddman. You may proceed."

It took him a moment to get back into it. "They do it all the time," he said, to give himself some time. "Gliding down Mears Street hill—coasting, possibly, so quietly none of the witnesses were even aware of him—becomes him creeping away from Brenfleck, looking over his shoulder, because they do it all the time. Blue telling you he was so drunk he could barely move—so easy for him to say, because they do it all the time. That whole line of questions where he told you his wife left the truck on Mears Street hill and he just happened upon it—so easy for him to put forth those lies, because they do it all the time. And then his absolute and complete flip-flop in the space of fifteen minutes; his recantation; the baring of his soul. How about 'they do it all the time'?

"He told you he didn't see her. This man, this athlete, didn't even see her out of the corner of his eye. He had a whole second there, too, time enough to honk his horn and yell, he said—but no swerving or braking because he 'wasn't thinking right,' I believe he said.

"And the way he looked at me, right in the eye, and

said, 'The way it looks, that's the lie.' Well, why not? 'They do it all the time.' "

There were a thousand other details Reddman wanted to tell them, to remind them of; but he could feel their intensity. Time to quit.

"Members of the jury, it's in your hands."

CHAPTER
TWENTY-ONE

After the jury filed solemnly out of the courtroom, Landry declared that they were in recess. Sharon Sondenburg had already gone. Reddman had watched her leave during final instruction as the bailiff was placed in charge of the jury.

The courtroom emptied slowly. People stood around in knots, discussing the case, speculating on how long it would take the jury to sort it out. Reddman felt empty inside, emotionally drained.

"Wanna beer, kid?" Cole asked.

"Sounds good. Think we'll have time?"

Reddman spoke facetiously, but Cole took him seriously. "Sure, sure, jury'll be out three, four hours anyway. Five, six, if you count lunch. The longer the better for me." He glared at his client. "You wait here," he told Johnny Blue. "They get a verdict, call us at the New York Saloon, gonna take this guy out and buy us two beers apiece, blow off what I made on this case."

Later, after they had settled into a booth at the New York Saloon, Cole said, "You did a good job kid, Jim Trigge should be proud." Cole picked up his beer and offered a salute.

Reddman clinked glasses. "Here's to you, Saul. You came out of left field with some real beauties.

"Think so?" Cole grinned and drained half his mug. "Got to say, my guess is you lost before we even started."

"What?"

"You made a bad mistake, kid, with that jury." Cole shook his head sympathetically. "Not your fault, Randy Turner and Bernie Lopes don't know shit."

"Hey, let's just enjoy the beer, okay?" Reddman asked, nettled. The last thing he wanted was to rehash the trial and all the mistakes he'd made. He couldn't let it lie, though. "Something about the jury?"

"Number ten, front row, third from the end, Gene Parflech?"

"The one you called Swede during voir dire?"

Cole nodded and leered knowingly. "About as Swedish as I am American Indian, looks like one though, giant of a man. He'll be jury foreman, you watch."

"What's wrong with him?" Reddman asked, although he remembered having the uncomfortable feeling in voir dire that the clear-eyed, clean-skinned hulk was too good. He'd given all the right answers. But neither Lopes nor Turner had expressed any misgivings, so Reddman had left him on. "He's the guy who owns the sporting goods store, right? Established businessman, past president Chamber of Commerce, Board of Directors of Crimestoppers. I couldn't understand why *you* didn't kick him off."

"You will." Cole's leer turned into a playful grin. "Man's got a history, you don't know, but Lopes oughta know it, Turner, too. Hard for you—city lawyer came to the country."

"That's TV bullshit, Saul. The law's the law and people are people and most of them have the same sense of justice."

"You really believe that?"

"Yes."

"You're younger'n I thought." Cole sipped his beer. "The Swede's the biggest outlaw in the county, charged

270

with tax evasion ten years ago. Gil Landry represented him before he became a judge, got the case dismissed."

"That son of a bitch!" Reddman exploded. "He answered no when I asked him if he'd ever been a defendant in a criminal case! The judge, too. Why didn't Landry tell me?" It really made him hot. All that work, all that agony, pissed down the tubes before the case got started. And Johnny Good Old Boy Blue would ride off into the sunset.

Cole stuck it in deeper. "What you gonna do, appeal?"

Reddman slumped in his chair. "It hasn't happened yet." Also, he doubted if there was any basis for an appeal—not from his side of the courtroom, at least. "If you knew the jury was packed, why did you try so hard? Who else?"

"Two others I didn't like, left 'em on anyway, too many flakes left in the venire waiting to take their place. So I left on Sherry Houston, CPA, stuck up bitch, too much like Ami, professional woman. She could hang it for you guys. And Martin Swallow. That whole Swallow family's different, fourth generation Sopris County, too, think they'd have better sense, he's a vegetarian! Raises organic, everything organic, on that place of his. He raised hell with the mosquito control people two years ago when they sprayed his farm. Said they killed all his bees."

"He's a veggie?" Reddman asked. "So am I. He can't be all bad."

"I know you are, heard about it, why do you think I ordered hamburgers last night?"

Reddman spluttered his way through a sip of beer and came up laughing.

"Easy, kid." Cole looked at his watch. "Been out half an hour. Don't take country juries long. They know each other, and they get right after it."

"If you knew you couldn't lose, how come you were willing to take a manslaughter?"

"Anything can happen, you know that. Swede might get stampeded into a mistake."

"A mistake! You mean into the truth."

"Come off it, kid. You really think Blue did it, planned it for days, got her schedule down, all that? You think he knew exactly when she'd leave the courthouse, waited, timed it perfectly, ran her down?"

"Not really. I don't think he could plan anything for more than five minutes at a time." Reddman sipped from his mug. "I never did see it as a death penalty case, more of an impulse kill. But I have a vision of him—you know how you get those visions?—sitting in his truck, sucking booze, hurting and hating, and then seeing her in the street. And taking her out."

Cole frowned at his beer. "You know what I just said— plan it for days, get her schedule down, know when she's gonna leave, perfect timing and all? I shoulda made that jury think that's what you had to prove."

Reddman grinned at him. "That would have been a real tough argument. I'm glad you didn't think of it."

"Ain't that the damnedest thing?" Cole's lips tightened, clearly conveying inner anguish. "That's the way I wrote it out last night, my argument, then I stand up there with the jury watching me, the courtroom packed, and I chop it off. Damn." He drank. "Wonder why. I feel things, hit that high point, then quit." Reddman watched him twitch. "Wanna know what Blue told me?"

"Yeah. Wait'll I turn on my tape."

Cole glared at Reddman, then laughed. "Confidence?"

"Right."

"Blue stuck to his story the whole way, just like he told it on the stand. Told me all along his wife put the truck on the hill, too. I believe him when he says he just got caught in that lie."

"You're younger'n I thought," Reddman said, mimicking Cole.

"Yeah. Man's got a mean streak, though. He's the kind who'll run over a porcupine on the highway 'stead of swervin' to miss it. He's in pain all the time, too, you know? A man who hurts like that might have just decided at that last second he couldn't avoid her, could have run her down. Like a second degree. Know what I mean?''

"I'm not sure."

Cole polished off his beer. "You know, most people are on the defensive a little, they'll avoid a collision, get out of the way. But some people are on the offense the whole time. They won't move over on a freeway; they just let the chips fall where they may. I know because I'm kind of offensive myself. The little woman pointed it out to me, and I know the difference now. Made a difference in my life.'' He smiled at Reddman. "I wasn't afraid of manslaughter anyway. I'm not telling you anything you don't know. I'd talked to Gil, he'd have given Blue probation.''

"Shit," Reddman declared. He polished off his beer and motioned the waiter to bring them two more. He raised his empty mug. "Here's to the system.''

The lawyers were waiting in Landry's chambers when Kellerman knocked on the door. "They've got a verdict.''

"Well! It's about time," Landry said. "Five-eighteen. They've been out for more than six hours.''

Reddman had already told himself he didn't have a chance. Still, his palms began to sweat and his breathing quickened. So did Saul Cole's.

The lawyers bumped their way into the courtroom through the attorneys' entrance, took their places, and waited for the judge to appear. All Blue's family—his wife, his children, both sets of parents—were there, as well as many of his friends. Ami O'Rourke's parents were there, too, five or six of her friends, a group of court watchers, and three cops. But Sharon Sondenburg wasn't there. As Reddman looked for her, he saw Zack Wolfman running in through the back door.

"All rise," Kellerman announced as Landry, fully robed, made his appearance. Lopes stood next to Reddman at counsel table, but no one from the D.A.'s office had come over. Reddman wondered if Brin was already trying to distance himself. Blue struggled to his feet, along with

Cole. "District Court of Sopris County, state of Colorado, now in session."

Landry sat down. "Be seated, please." He looked toward Killerman. "Bailiff, has the jury reached a verdict?"

"They have, Your Honor. I've just been so informed by the foreman."

"Very well. Bring in the jury, if you please."

I don't care if I argue before a million juries, Reddman thought to himself. When they bring in a verdict, I will always feel as if I'm frozen on a high wire in a huge wind. His hands were soaked as he stared straight ahead, listening as the jurors filed into the box. When he first started, he used to watch them for signs. If they smiled and looked at the defendant, they would acquit; if they were dead serious, they would convict. But he'd had too many surprises.

"Members of the jury, have you reached a verdict?" Landry asked.

"We have, Judge." Gene Parflech—the Swede—stood while the rest of them sat down. He held the brown envelope that contained the verdict forms in his hand.

"And you are the foreman, Mr. Parflech?"

"Yes, sir."

"You will please hand the verdict to the bailiff."

Kellerman carried the envelope to the bench, and Reddman watched Landry—who appeared merely curious—pull the forms out and inspect them. He frowned. What did that mean?

"I note for the record that the verdict forms appear to be in order in that they have been properly marked and signed. The defendant will please rise."

Blue struggled to his feet and Cole stood beside him. Cole's legs were shaking.

"I will now read the verdicts into the record," Landry said. " 'The people of the state of Colorado versus Johnny Blue, defendant. Jury verdict count number one. We, the jury, find the defendant, Johnny Blue, not guilty of driving while under the influence of alcohol. Signed Gene Parflech, foreman.' "

Reddman's heart dropped. He could feel the cold, hard stare of Bernie Lopes.

" 'The people of the state of Colorado versus Johnny Blue, defendant. Jury verdict count number two. We, the jury, find the defendant, Johnny Blue, guilty of leaving the scene of an accident. Signed Gene Parflech, foreman.' "

Reddman felt as though someone else was breathing for him, forcing air into his lungs. Why do I feel this way? he wondered. What's it to me?

" 'The people of the state of Colorado versus Johnny Blue, defendant. Jury verdict count number three. We, the jury, find the defendant, Johnny Blue, guilty of murder in the first degree. Signed Gene Parflech, foreman.' " Landry raised his eyes. "Is this your verdict, so say you all?"

The jury members looked at one another, nodding. A couple of them said yes.

"Mr. Cole. Do you desire to poll the jury?"

Cole was in shock. He stared straight ahead. "Yes, I do."

I did it, Reddman thought, able to breathe. He could hear commotion behind the rail—expressions of disbelief from the Blues, something like applause from others—and wondered why he didn't feel great.

But all he could manage was relief.

Trigge was on the line. "Congratulations, Davey my boy. Good job!" he shouted exuberantly.

Reddman, in Brim's chair at the district attorney's office, held the telephone a foot away from his ear. He was on his ass. "Thanks. 'Sa great fight. Knew I had him in the seventh." In spite of all the hilarity, Reddman felt alone.

"Hold the phone closer, Davey. I can't hear you!"

"I can hear you, Trigge. Without the telephone."

"Oh." Trigge laughed and lowered his voice. "That better?"

"Yes."

"How do you feel?"

"Like I better not drive. There's a roomful of cops and

one misguided public defender here, tryin' get me drunk."
Someone poured more beer into his coffee cup.

"Zack? Zack Wolfman? You don't say!" Trigge shouted
again, obviously relishing his young soldier's victory.
"You'll be in great shape for that bicycle race. When is
it?"

"Monday. Two days to train."

"Good! Then you'll be back to work Tuesday? There's
a nice neat little double homicide in Iowa City I'd like you
to look at. . . ."

He called Sharon for the umpteenth time that night,
about eleven, his head buzzing and his tongue too big. This
time she was there. "Where've you been?" he asked.
"Been trying to get you."

"Sorry." She sounded far away, on another planet. "I
had a lot of work to catch up on."

"Did you hear about it?"

"Oh, yes. You know something?"

"What?"

"You're as good as you said you were."

She sounded so sad. He wondered if he should ask her
what was wrong. Instead, he told her what the foreman of
the jury had said to Sergeant Donovan: "Hell, I knew he
was guilty or he wouldn't have hired Saul."

She laughed. But her voice had pain. Then: "Why did
they acquit him of drunk driving?"

"Perfeckly consistent," Reddman slurred. "They knew
it took more'n a point-eighteen make him drunk. Can I see
you tonight?"

"No."

"Why? I really need—"

"I'm with someone," she told him. "I'm very sorry."

On Saturday Reddman went for two rides: a twenty-mile
grind in the morning, wearing sweats, where he tried to
wring out all the booze; and a slow thirty-five miler in the

afternoon and evening, with high reps and lots of deep breathing. He tried as hard as he could not to think.

On Sunday the town was filled with cyclists, and Reddman renewed a lot of old friendships. He wanted to get on a team, but no one would take him. He stayed as busy as possible, cleaning his bike, building the right set of gears, putting on his sew-ups, talking strategy with a couple of friends who weren't on teams either, jamming thoughts of Sharon out of his mind, trying not to call her. He knew he wouldn't sleep that night if he couldn't get tired, so he went for a short ten-miler in the late afternoon. He dropped in two hard sprints and almost threw up. He stoked up on carbohydrates that night with Alex Kulpas, a crazy friend who'd moved to Telluride so he could concentrate on racing. He put off going to his hotel room for as long as he could.

He slept okay. On Monday morning, resplendent in blue bicycle tights, he joined the mob of cyclists at the train depot. The sky was blue and clean, with very little wind—a perfect day. When Reddman first started to warm up he could see his breath, but half an hour later, after working up a good sweat and blowing hard, the temperature had jumped to the low sixties. He took off his leg warmers and put them in a duffel bag. Kulpas's wife had agreed to drive the gear to Fools Gold.

He lined up with the mob of Category Three's, alongside Kulpas. He caught himself thinking about Sharon and jammed her face from his vision. Then he saw her, standing on the sidewalk in front of an Arby's half a block away. She was talking to a man in a wheelchair.

The gun went off.

"Hey, man, get it in gear!" someone behind him shouted, and mechanically he started to roll. He was toeing in the cleat on his left shoe when the pack churned past Arby's. He tried to see her, wondering if she saw him, when the clown next to him—not Kulpas—bumped his drop-bars. They almost locked. "Easy, buster!" Reddman shouted, fighting to keep from going down. The race was on.

The first ten miles were easy. The seventy-rider peleton stayed together, some of the teams jockeying their members for position, a lot of joking and camaraderie. Someone on the outside near the rear blew a tire and went down, taking three other riders with him. Reddman worked his way toward the front of the pack—Kulpas stayed back—but when they hit the first real climb, Reddman was not ready. With the suddenness of a gunshot, a breakaway group formed—about ten riders—and he and five or six others surged after them. Too late.

"We can catch them!" Reddman shouted, breathing huge gusts as he stood up and punched forward. "Forty pulls each! Go!"

He was in luck. The others were willing to work. The group formed a line, the riders staying in the same gear, the lead rider dropping to the rear after forty pulls. They towed each other up the hill.

A rider from the peleton bridged up, wearing a Paragon jersey. Then he and two others in Davey's group found they couldn't hold it. They drifted back. Reddman felt tears in his eyes. Why am I crying? he asked himself, straining every muscle in his body with each pull, trying to tear it apart. You know something? he heard her say. You're as good as you said you were.

"Damn right I am!"

At Avalanche—thirty miles in and three thousand feet higher—they caught a group of three who had fallen off from the leaders. The road leveled and then dropped slightly as they sailed across a long mountain bench, heading for the steep, hard seven-mile climb to the top of the first pass.

He reveled in the pain. He wanted to hurt so bad he couldn't feel anything else. Now and then, half a mile in front, his small group of five riders would catch a glimpse of the lead pack. He emptied one water bottle and threw it to the side of the road, then moved his second one into the cage on his forward tube.

Kulpas's wife drove by, along with a long string of support cars and tourists, and he heard her shout encouragement. "Go, Davey!" Then Donald somebody—a nineteen-year-old from Boulder—built up a pile of momentum from the fourth position and jumped ahead. Reddman had to roll around two riders to catch him. When he did, Donald leaned on it harder, and Reddman knew he was dying.

But the funny thing was, he didn't care. Donald didn't know that and thought he could pull away. Somehow Reddman stayed on the kid's wheel, and the two of them widened the gap between themselves and the other three.

They caught two riders from the lead pack. One of them stuck on their wheel for about fifty yards, then dropped off. Donald complained bitterly, accusing Reddman of not working, but Reddman told him to cool it. "You're just pissed because you can't drop me!" The road started to flatten at the top of the pass, and Reddman—ten pounds heavier than Donald—continued to suck on the dude's wheel. It gave him time to get his legs.

The first long descent. Reddman let Donald lead him into the wind, then dropped into his tallest gear. When Donald started to brake at the approach of a corner, Reddman let the vacuum suck him around the Boulderite and flew by. He passed a string of cars, not wanting to know how fast he was going, and got in front of them before the next corner. Donald was blocked. Reddman dropped into a low tuck and blew down the wide highway like a missile.

He gained half a mile on the kid, but got caught toward the top of the final pass. "Hello, Donald." He tried the same tactic—pushed until he died—to get on Donald's wheel, then rested until they started the final descent.

Fool's Gold looked like the London of Peter Pan in a picture book. Little tiny dollhouses spread below him on a carpet of green. He whipped past Donald and let his heavier body do the rest.

He rolled through the finish line, two minutes and four seconds behind the winner. He had come in sixth!

*   *   *

"Hi," a familiar voice said.

Reddman had been sitting on the curb, his legs stretched out in front of him, watching them twitch. He looked up.

"Aren't you about dead?" she said.

He was still too tired to make any sense. His whole body was covered with dried foam; some of it was saliva and sweat, but most of it was the cold beer he had poured over his head. "Oh. Hi." He tried to sound casual, but no way.

She sat down beside him. Then she pulled him toward her and kissed him on the mouth. "You don't smell very good."

"What do you expect?"

"I had no idea a bicycle race could be so fascinating!" she said, her arm still over his shoulder. "Is this all right?"

"Yeah. Feels good."

She got up. In the bright sunlight, she looked great. "I need to tell you a few things about my life," she said. "Can I get you a beer?"